T0368719

DISUNION

A STORY OF LOVE SURMOUNTING THE THREAT

OF AN INEVITABLE CIVIL WAR OVER THE

CONTINUANCE OF SLAVERY IN AMERICA

THE DISCOVERY OF GOLD AND SILVER

AND THE DREAM TO BUILD THE FIRST

TRANSCONTINENTAL RAILWAY FROM

THE PACIFIC TO THE ATLANTIC

A CARROLL FAMILY SAGA

ROYSTON MOORE

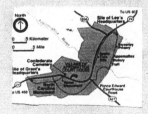

Order this book online at www.trafford.com
or email orders@trafford.com

Most Trafford titles are also available at major online book retailers.

© Copyright 2010 Royston Moore.
All rights reserved. No part of this publication may be reproduced, stored in a retrieval
system, or transmitted, in any form or by any means, electronic, mechanical, photocopying,
recording, or otherwise, without the written prior permission of the author.

Printed in Victoria, BC, Canada.

ISBN: 978-1-4269-1062-3 (sc)

*Our mission is to efficiently provide the world's finest, most comprehensive
book publishing service, enabling every author to experience success.
To find out how to publish your book, your way, and have it available
worldwide, visit us online at www.trafford.com*

Trafford rev. 03/01/2010

 www.trafford.com

North America & international
toll-free: 1 888 232 4444 (USA & Canada)
phone: 250 383 6864 ♦ fax: 812 355 4082

READ OTHER BOOKS BY ROYSTON MOORE

FIVE BOOKS IN THE CARROLL FAMILY SAGA

FICTIONAL LOVE STORIES IN AMERICA FROM 1690 TO 1850

MARYLAND - a Rags to Riches love story around 1690 - Amelia Eliot and David Carroll begin the Carroll Family Saga

OHIO - The love stories of five couples during the "Seven Year War" - really British and French enemies who became friends

LIBERTY - Carroll descendents and other immigrants still survive and discover love during the American Revolution from Britain

GENESIS - The new United States struggles whilst chaos reigns in Europe. New immigrants helped by Carroll's to discover love.

LEBENSTRAUM -*"Living-Dreams"* - Later Carroll descendents also with others continue the expansion west looking for Living Space - Their part in River, Sea and now Railway transport for growing industry

LOVE 3000 YEARS AGO IN ANCIENT EGYPT

MAKERE - THE FEMALE PHAROAH - QUEEN OF SHEBA

Though written as fiction - It describes the actual life of
MAKERE HATSHEPSUT -the only Female Pharaoh of Egypt
- yet proves she was, also the mysterious Queen of Sheba -
Her actual love for lowly web-priest, Senmut and Solomon,
King of All Israel. - Her tempestuous life - so similar to
British Tudor Queen Elizabeth.

PURCHASE ALL AT ANY BOOKSELLER OR ON LINE AT AMAZON.COM OR DIRECT AT TRAFFORD PUBLISHING

FOREWORD

The Missouri Compromise of 1820 and the compromise of 1850 in the United States, merely postponed the inevitable American Civil War which would tear the country into two. These events would fall heavily on all the many descendents of the Carroll Families wherever they may at present reside. However they knew it might equally destroy their ancestral homes particularly in Virginia, for there must be many battles there between the northern states and those to the south. Also it would also effect many other persons coming to, or now living in the country.

However this book is not an account of this Civil War but really a love story, not only concerning the Carroll Family Saga, and those other families when caught up in the terrible conflict. Only when it concerns directly these persons does it involve the conflict. For many each day is a challenge but one which can be overcome if their love is strong enough.

Once again we learn how the many descendents of the two original Carroll families lived, and prepared for the onslaught, very conscious of what they all owe to both Margaret Eliot and Sir David and Amelia Carroll. They knew it was their duty to retain the Union of 1783 and make the country prosperous. However, as in the past it was others, such as Patrick Purcell, a New York Stockbroker, Daniel Mason a banker, Jack and Robert Sinclair prospecting for Gold with Otto Milliken in Colorado, to carry out this task.

We shall see that Charles Doughty and his son Paul, a previous friend of Patrick Purcell, now in Mexico, themselves prospecting for minerals were destined to meet Robert Sinclair and promise even greater riches in future. How the influx of so many Irish Families into New York forced to come because of the potato famine in Ireland, again added to the exploding population of the country.

But it was the vision of men like Kurt Sand who was to overcome the impossible, and drive a railway through the fearsome Rocky mountains to once more bring the country together, as he laid the 'Golden Egg', to built the Central & Union Pacific Railway from Sacramento through the mountains, along the plains, to New York. The first Transcontinental Railway. A railway which would unite the country into one.

See how the love of so many men and women ensured that whatever were the dangers, by living, loving and working together, they could find happiness even as their world disintegrated around them.

So even as you read this book and learn of the terrible consequences of any Civil War, provided their love for each other is strong enough, this love can lead to great happiness. See how this enabled them to overcome the destruction and eventually re-unite a divided country into the present United States of America.

Royston Moore

THE CARROL FAMILIES SAGAS IN AMERICA

MARYLAND – *Is the first of Five books set in America from colonial days in 1688 to 1694, and to the United States in 1850. This book introduces readers first, to the Protestant Carroll family going to America from Somerset to join the Roman Catholic Carroll family living there since they emigrated from Yorkshire. It is a Rags to Riches story of love in the late 17th. Century*

OHIO – *This second book covers the period from 1748 to 1763. the time of the Seven Years War between Britain and France – the first global war. It covers the life of five sets of partners, both British and French who, though should have been enemies, but due to their presence in this new land of Ohio, are drawn together and become friends. Continuing the Carroll Sagas, now with Daniel Carroll, grandson of Amelia and David Carroll.*

LIBERTY – *The period of 1770 to 1789 – The events leading to and the actual War of American Independence from Britain. Many characters from the previous books and the valuable assistance Daniel Carroll and his wife Michelle gave to George Washington during the bleak times of the war. Continuing the sagas of both branches of the Carroll families but introducing many new persons.*

GENESIS – *The New Country. The period from 1793 to 1803 when in a single day the size of the United States doubled with President Jefferson's 'Louisiana Purchase' from Spain. The problems besetting the United States - a country ruled by an elected President and not a king, attempting neutrality, whilst Europe descended into chaos with the French Revolution and the many European wars. Now we meet the numerous off springs of two Carroll families, and their love affairs, again concerning the life of Daniel Carroll, his wife Michelle and their children, and many new emigrants from Europe.*

LEBENSTRAUM– *"Living-Dreams" Covering the period from 1826 to 1850. The expansion Westwards – Texas and Mexico and events in California. The development of an industrial America and the vital part played by both Carroll families in both river and rail transport. Again dealing not only with their love affaires, but those of the many new emigrants coming to America and settling in love there.*

THE ENGLISH & AMERICAN CARROLL FAMILIES TO 1850

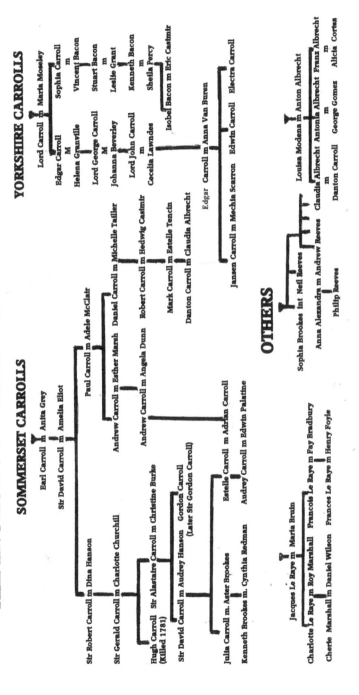

YORKSHIRE CARROLLS

Lord Carroll m Maria Moseley

Sophia Carroll m Vincent Bacon

Edgar Carroll M Helena Granville

Lord George Carroll M Johanna Beverley

Stuart Bacon

Leslie Grant

Kenneth Bacon m Sheila Percy

Lord John Carroll m Cecelia Lawndes

Isobel Bacon m Eric Casimir

Edgar Carroll m Anna Van Buren

Jansen Carroll m Mechia Scarron   Edwin Carroll   Electra Carroll

SOMMERSET CARROLLS

Earl Carroll m Anita Grey

Sir David Carroll m Amelia Eliot

Paul Carroll m Adele McClair

Daniel Carroll m Michelle Tailler

Andrew Carroll m Esther Marsh

Andrew Carroll m Angela Dunn

Robert Carroll m Hedwig Casimir

Mark Carroll m Estelle Tencin

Danton Carroll m Claudia Albrecht

Sir Robert Carroll m Dina Hanson

Sir Gerald Carroll m Charlotte Churchill

Hugh Carroll (Killed 1781)

Sir Alastaire Carroll m Christine Burke

Gordon Carroll (Later Sir Gordon Carroll)

Sir David Carroll m Audrey Hanson

Estelle Carroll m Adrian Carroll

Audrey Carroll m Edwin Palatine

Julia Carroll m. Aster Brookes

Kenneth Brookes m. Cynthia Redman

OTHERS

Sophia Brookes int Neil Reeves

Anna Alexandra m Andrew Reeves

Philip Reeves

Louisa Modena m Anton Albrecht

Claudia Albrecht   Antonia Albrecht   Franz Albrecht m Alicia Cortes

Danton Carroll   George Gomez

Jacques Le Raye m Maria Bruin

Charlotte Le Raye m Roy Marshall   Francois Le Raye m Fay Bradbury   Frances Le Raye m Henry Foyle

Cherie Marshall m Daniel Wilson

DESCENDENTS OF MARGARET ELIOT

John Eliot m Margaret Vine

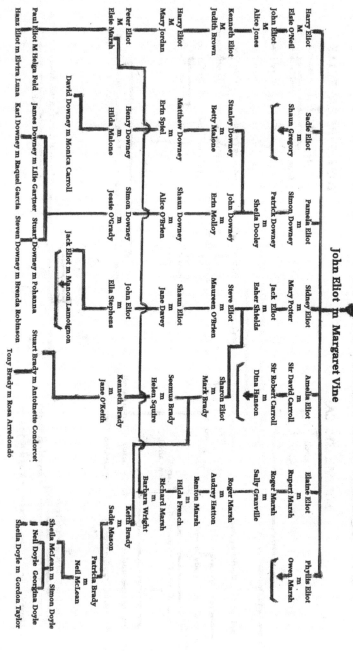

FURTHER CARROLL FAMILY & OTHER DESCENDENTS

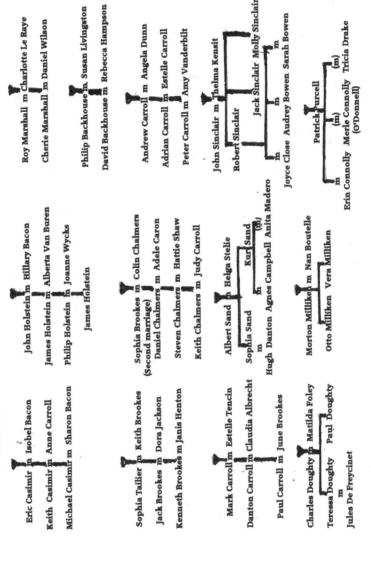

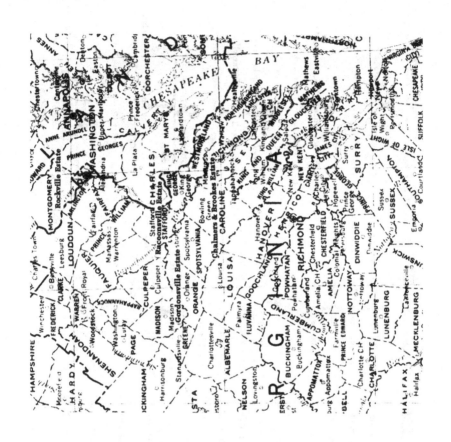

MARYLAND & VIRGINIA DURING THE CIVIL WAR

SHOWING THE MANY CARROLL FAMLY ESTATES

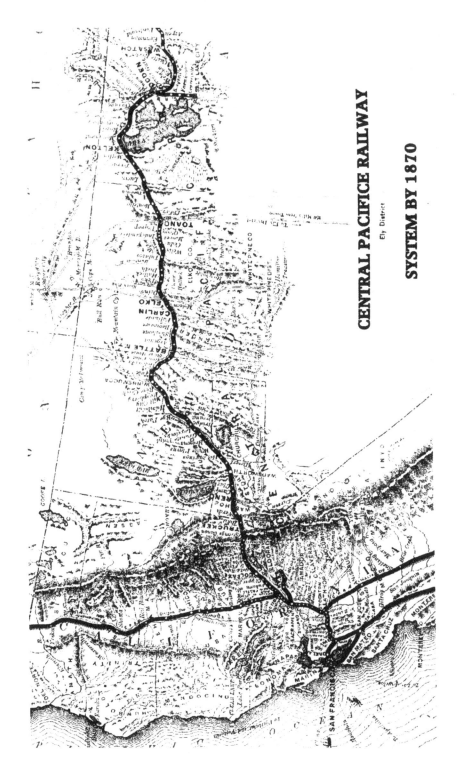

CENTRAL PACIFICE RAILWAY

Ely District

SYSTEM BY 1870

CONTENTS

PART 1

COMPROMISE

DISUNION PART 1
COMPROMISE

COMPROMISE

1.

The Missouri Compromise of 1820 between those in favour of Slavery and those against merely postponed the inevitable split between the Northern and Southern States which would eventually devastate the United States of America. At that time there were eleven states which supported slavery and another eleven which opposed any such restrictions on United States citizenship. For the present it would admit admission of new states to the Federal Constitution in pairs. One in favour of slavery, the other against slavery.

Thus it was agreed that the new state of Missouri could accept slavery south of Latitude 36-30 Degrees North whilst a new state of Maine was admitted to be free from slavery. No further states were admitted until 1836 when Arkansas was admitted as a slave-state and in 1837 Michigan as slave-free state. But feelings were growing in intensity over this issue.

Although it was proclaimed on religious grounds that it was against god to enslave any member of the human race, the real reasons were much more diverse. In truth it was an economic issue. The southern states were mainly involved in agriculture, with cotton, tobacco and sugar growing, their chief sources of wealth. Cheap labour was essential for their prosperity. Even slavery was expensive. Their cost of purchase, feeding, clothing and habitation was not insignificant, although most slaves built their own homes under supervision, but with the need for intensive labour it provided an reasonable profit.

The northern states greatest prosperity came from industry and the workers in these factories were available from the cheap labour provided by the many white settlers coming to those states from Europe, after the years of warfare and chaos, and recently the huge increase from both Ireland and Scotland. The need for slave workers was very much less in the north than in the south. There is no doubt that many of these new comers were often Catholics, Methodists or Quakers with a determination to enforce their strong religious principles.

This new country, only a little over fifty years old, was essentially two different countries attempting to become one. Even President Thomas Jefferson who had fought so hard to found a democratic country, even establishing a political party to ensure freedom for the residents of the new United States, ironically was still in favour and used numerous slaves on his estates. Nor were everyone in North and South in agreement.

There were many pro-slavers in the north and a number of anti-slavers living in the southern states. All the 1820 Missouri Compromise did was to postpone what would inevitably lead to conflict of ideas and beliefs, but at least there was a measure of peace for a time.

By 1845 there were twenty eight states with fifteen slave states but equality in Congress was maintain by admitting Iowa in 1846 and Wisconsin in 1848, as states free from slavery. However with the British Empire abolishing slavery throughout its dominions and using their navies to board and sink slave ships sailing from Africa, the price for new slaves in America increased enormously. The shortage was reduced by slave owners forcing their negresses to conceive and bare more children who could work on their fields.

There was no doubt but the prosperity of Maryland and Virginia from the seventeen century and later, even in what was to be known as West Virginia, was due to the introduction of slave labourers from Africa. They also provided, mainly, for servants on their estates. It is true that in West Virginia their task was mainly in clearing the wooded areas to make it capable of arable farming.

When the protestant branch of the Carroll family arrived in Maryland after their Roman Catholic cousin Edgar Carroll persuaded

David Carroll to come here in 1687, to be given the estate of Rockville – a tobacco plantation – it was extensively staffed by negro slaves. Even David Carroll, before he could bring Amelia Eliot, who he had met and whose body he enjoyed on the ship bringing them here; David Carroll had needed to satisfy the demands of his slave workers to avoid a rebellion. To ensure the slave family still enjoyed the easier task of helping in his mansion and avoid breaking their backs in the tobacco fields, he had been required to take one Negress as his Personal Servant. He had been obliged to use her body and for her to conceive his children.

The fact was that later David acquired a degree of love for his Heide and that when he eventually freed Amelia from her sentence, to bear four children in quick succession, making this lowly Irish peasant girl his wife, it matured and was welcomed by Amelia. Eventually now temporarily Governor of Maryland and commanded to sail to England to become a Knight of the Bath, with his wife becoming Lady Amelia, they brought Heide with them to enjoy this event. This amazing story is told in full in "Maryland" – the first book in this series of the Carroll Family Sagas.

So slavery was the basis of all the Carroll families prosperity, continuing through the many descendents of the original American Carroll's and the other descendents of the amazing Margaret Eliot, who was Amelia's mother.

But then slavery was, equally, the basis for the prosperity of many other emigrants from Europe such as the Casimir's and Holstein's, not mention those Dutch families driven from New York during the American War of Liberation into Pennsylvania and the Potomac valley. Also then slavery there, was a way of life adopted by all who could afford to purchase slaves to make life more easy. All the lives of these many people are completely described in the five earlier books listed for your consideration at the beginning of this book.

However by 1845 even these families and their many descendents now settled in this rapidly expanding country were considering if it was fair to impose such heavy responsibilities on these members of the human race, whose only fault was that they were born as blacks. Surely their god had not intended that anyone should be treated this way.

This change of views did not apply for economic reasons as to others, as cotton and sugar raising developed not only in Virginia but more so in both North and South Carolina and now in Georgia. It seemed to them, to free their slaves must lead to bankruptcy, so must be vigorously apposed.

Yet slavery was not a necessity to those emigrants who had established the Carroll/Marshal Boat and Sailing Companies and was, now, rarely used. Neither was it employed in the building of the new railway lines being laid down from New York to Baltimore and further west – the new revolutionary means of transport. Roads and canals had been laid without slave workers as there was an ever growing influx of new settlers into this rapidly expanding country. So the stage was set for what was to tear this new country of the United States apart. It seemed that the next fifteen years would decide the future of slavery in this land.

2.

Kurt Sand had now completed his education and was a fully qualified engineer, but also was well qualified in geology. So he was now working for his father's company which had made a fortune in first building canals, then roads, and just recently helped in the new construction of railways. His father, Albert Sand, had landed at New York fleeing from probably imprisonment in February 1820, then penniless. Yet had survived to eventually establish his own very successful engineering company.

Kurt remembered almost word for word the tale his father had told him of how he came to live here. It was an exciting story which his father had told him as a young boy. One which made Kurt very proud, and one he was very pleased to tell everyone he knew. The story was as follows.

Albert Sand had stood on the quay on Staten Island, New York, tired distraught and completely exhausted and looked back at the ship from which he had just disembarked Although the name on the bows proclaimed it as the 'Prince of Prussia', it did little to described the horrors he had suffered in the last thirty days since he had boarded it, in a hurry, at Hamburg Docks in Germany. Its cargo was essentially a large group of emigrants, trying to discover a new life in America.

The journey had been, relatively, quite quick. It was a good ship but never built to carry so many people herded together, more like cattle. Endeavouring to stay alive in the storms which swept the Atlantic as water poured down the holds, almost drowning the inhabitants. There had been vomit and all forms of sewerage spreading decease amongst them, but Albert had survived, happy to escape what had waited him in Germany.

Now as he stood holding his few possessions on the dockside he wondered how he might survive in this new land but pleased to have escaped from the horror which had waited him had he not left.

It was February 1820, barely a year since his younger brother, Karl Sand, a student at the University of Jena, on the Elbe, on the boarders of Saxony, had killed the reactionary journalist, August von Kotzebue at Mannheim. This mans death, as the enemy of liberalism, a cause very dear to his radical minded brother, had alarmed Metternich and the King of Prussia and had sanctioned the Carlsbad Decrees. This had lead to repression of liberalism, introducing an inquisition like investigation, into all secret societies.

A pogrom had followed. His family had been imprisoned and he had, barley, escaped with his life. With little money he had made his way, with difficulty, to Hamburg and booked passage on the emigrant ship. Hence his arrival at New York. Though in the final year of his engineering degree at Jena University, it seemed he would never graduate.

For most of his fellow travellers, it was a case of poverty in Germany to an equivalent life in the New World. However able to speak fluently in English and with his knowledge of engineering, this had enabled Albert to, quickly, establish himself in the city. The New York State as well as the city was in an amazing period of development. Whilst the lot of most of the new arrivals was lowly paid labouring jobs, Albert's abilities were, quickly, recognised, resulting him becoming foreman of work on various sights in the city.

He was disappointed in discovering little news about his family and soon had to give up any hope of finding them, since a return to Germany was impossible. His abilities had been recognised by his superiors short of engineers and he was transferred to work on the Erie Canal, which had been started before his arrival. This momentous development which was to make New York City outstrip all its rival seaports, as well as to provide a route for the pioneers attempting to occupy the now open acres of new land to the west, was to provide Albert with adequate resources.

Albert would have admitted that he was a womaniser. His good looks swept many women into his embrace. He never knew how many young women in Germany and later, during his years in America, had suffered by fathering him children, nor did he care. There were many attractive German women amongst the influx of emigrants to fully, satisfy, his amorous desires but when in 1824 he accidentally made Helga Stallo, the daughter of one of the investors in the canal, pregnant, he was trapped. He married Helga and she bore him a daughter, Sophia Sand, the next year.

Setting up home in the town of Batavia, fifty miles from the growing town of Buffalo, now a senior member of the team constructing the canal he had established himself as a prosperous, and much sort after, man of substance. Helga bore him a son, Kurt Sand, in February 1828 when she was nearly twenty two years of age.

Of course Albert was away most of the time and continued with his sexual pleasures. There were many women willing to offer their bodies for his amusement. Helga knew of his constant adultery but accepted it, enjoying a settled life in her large home. Like her husband having strong sexual desires, she was not adverse to taking an occasional lover to satisfy her needs during the long months her husband was away. But she was careful and there were no scandal.

By then the canal had been completed, goods and people were using this route to the Ohio River, down to the Missouri and to the rapidly expanding western states. Though the road west was being developed, leading to the settlement of more western territories. The State of Pennsylvania had realised the potential the new canal had provided and knew it must develop its own communications. They must build new roads and canals for this purpose. This provided an new opportunity for the engineering abilities of Albert Sand, and so was able to establish a business of his own.

He moved his home to the outskirts of Pittsburgh. Although Albert had been denied the chance to become a graduate, he was determined his son, Kurt, should follow in his footsteps, but become fully qualified. So the lives of the Sand's continued and in 1847 Kurt obtained a Bachelor's Degree in both engineering and geology which was to stand him well in his future life.

But both Kurt and his elder sister, Sophia, had inherited the strong sexual desires of their father. After his sister, Sophia, married a foreman in her father's firm, Hugh Danton, having, like her mother conceived by him before she married, she was not adverse to sharing her bed with others when her husband was away. Likewise, when at University, Kurt had enjoyed several young females as his bed companions.

His mother knew of this arrangement. Though she deplored it, after her own, known liaisons, what could she say. She even admitted her own illicit feelings for her handsome son. She knew this did occur amongst some mothers when she lived in Batavia but reluctantly withheld her desires in this more puritan town of Pittsburgh. Though these feelings never deserted her during the rest of her life.

Now Kurt had become an important member of his father's firm of Albert Sand Engineering, both working on canals and road building and now on the new and growing form of transportation which was railway building, acquiring in depth knowledge of all the engineering requirements of all forms of travel.

Though still only seventeen he found it easy, in view of his father's wealth to entertain and enjoy the most intimate pleasures of many of the young women of Pittsburgh. However, though satisfied with the money he obtained by his employment in the firm, he knew he wanted to establish himself, and set up a similar business of his own.

He had become very friendly with a director of the company for which his own family worked, a man called Gordon Taylor, who had many years before been actively engaged in building the first railway in England, the Liverpool to Manchester Railway. Kurt felt he was well qualified to use his knowledge in lands far away from Pittsburgh. The question was where should he go. Gordon Taylor even offered him his help should he establish such a venture, especially if he decided to consider building new railroads there

This decision must await until fate decreed that gold had been discovered at Sutter's Creek, California. Yet this was a little time in the future.

3.

Andrew Campbell with his forty five year old mother, Margaret and eighteen year old sister, Agnes, had just landed on Staten Island, New York, after their very difficult journey across the Atlantic from Glasgow, hoping for a better life than they had recently had to endure in Scotland. They were fortunate as they did have a little money in their pockets, enough to keep them alive until they found a jobs in this new land.

His family and the others before him had worked a small crofters land in the West Highlands. At least it was their own land and since the 1745 rebellion had been profitable to not only feed them but even store, very gradually, a little money. However they had overworked their land and eventually they could no longer grow much oats and, like many others at that time, had to supplement their oat crop with growing potatoes. Still at that time they harvested enough food to feed and rear their family.

Perhaps it was fortunate that his mother Margaret, after sister Agnes was born, was unable to bear her husband more children. Then in the last five years disaster had occurred. First Andrew's father had died, though this meant that with less mouths to feed, they actually acquired just a little more money. However then, like in Ireland and many other parts of Scotland, the potato blight occurred. Soon they were in danger of starving. Worse Margaret Campbell became ill, yet they had not enough money to take her to a hospital for proper attention. The local medicine man feared Margaret had a growth inside her.

Fortunately their croft was on the coast in a beautiful location and their aristocratic landlord wanted to possess it, and develop it to make it part of his estate. He approached them and if they sold the croft at the small price he quoted, he offered to send them on a ship to America to either Canada or the United States. In fact many from Scotland, often in a worse state than the Campbell's, had emigrated to Canada.

However Andrew had learned that there were better opportunities in New York, and from there, should they want it, they could even travel westwards into the new lands being opened up. So for these reasons Andrew persuaded his mother and sister to travel there. With the landlord paying for their journey to Glasgow and then the passage for all of them on a ship going to New York, they had now arrived this day at their destination.

However it had been a very unpleasant journey travelling steerage, the lowest class, often not allowed on deck of the large ship, yet sometimes almost drowned as Atlantic storms battered their ship. There was no doubt that the journey had made his mother's illness far greater. But they had survived and could now walk down the gangway onto dry land once more.

At least after passing through emigration, a long and tiring task, they were directed to a hostel available for all new residents arriving at New York. The price of their accommodation was very small – but then none of them had much money – only the small result of many years of careful saving on their small croft, and the pitiful sum their landlord had given them for the sale of their land.

Obviously their first task was to find work, fortunately it was readily available, though their wages were small. Their mother went to work in a clothing factory and his sister Agnes, mainly because she looked attractive, found employment as a receptionist in the offices of a large trading company.

Only labouring jobs were available to Andrew but fortunately he was very used to heights, even enjoyed rock-climbing in the mountains near his home, when any time was available. So Andrew had little difficulty in finding employment in the building trade, often necessary to climb high laying bricks or stones in the rapidly growing multistory blocks being built to cater for the growing population of this, now, very prosperous city.

He even managed to increase his wages by learning to rivet the many steel girders, which was the framework for these building, requiring many dangerous movements at high levels, as he secured the girders were adequately jointed to accept the great weight of the bricks or stones laid on them as the building progressed. So gradually the whole family were able to settle a little more comfortably, living in rented accommodation, in their new abode.

However Margaret Campbell's illness was not easing, in fact it seemed, it may be getting worse. Yet they still had little money for serious medical treatment, though local doctors were able to help, a little, and at least gave her sedatives to relieve her pain. Andrew knew that somehow very soon the family must save enough of their combined earnings, to enable them to pay for hospital treatment, to remove what seem to be a growth inside her abdomen.

Their was no doubt that Andrew wages were the greatest. He was very generous refraining from the temptation to enjoy life with the many girls who were attracted to his very handsome appearance. However they were told they should, now, apply to become naturalised citizens of the United States. Their rented accommodation being sufficient in New York as registered property dwellers. This they achieved after only a year after they arrived.

However it seemed that sister, Agnes, might have an even happier future. Now just nineteen, she had become a very attractive, a very desirable, young woman. It seemed she caught the eye of a twenty nine year old bachelor, who was a junior director of the company for whom she worked. He was not married and it was rumoured that he had a reputation but it seemed he was attracted to Agnes. Perhaps she was out of her depth for she never had a boy-friend whilst living in Scotland, only meeting them for a short acquaintance at village dances. There was no doubt that she fell completely under his very demonstrative attentions. Invited out to dine at one of the many restaurants, Agnes was completely flattered at his attentions and fell under his spell.

Andrew felt he must warn her, "Agnes, please be careful. You know little about your boy-friend. – He may only want to enjoy you, without any idea of any more permanent relationship."

Perhaps he was even more surprised at her reply, "Andrew, you misjudge him – So far he has never taken any real liberties and he is very kind to me. – The girls in the office have told me how to look after myself." Andrew wondered if Agnes meant she knew, - as now Andrew had learned from remarks by his few girl-friends – of how a girl might limit the dangers of conception.

Andrew was a little suspicious at the mans behaviour but, at that time, it seemed that apart from the expected cuddling as he drove her back to her home later, he still behaved as a gentleman. Over the months it seemed it became a little more serious and sometimes he took the liberty of inviting her to dinner at his sumptuous New York apartments. Andrew, naturally, questioned her on his behaviour, though from what Agnes told him, he still did not appear to go too far, though there was no doubt that, by now, his attentions were far more amorous. Now Agnes was receiving several small but appropriate gifts from this man who it seemed was rapidly becoming her lover

Meantime they were careful with their spending with the one idea of saving enough for Margaret to receive an operation, which the doctors now felt necessary. Andrew now enjoyed the pleasurable attentions of several quite good looking girls. But they were short lived, for it seemed Andrew preferred variety in his love-making. He even confessed to Agnes that he wondered if he could every settle and marry one woman. He felt he need the company of more than a single girl. Perhaps, therefore, he might never marry.

The trouble was that, however careful they were, they did need to acquire articles to make their hard lives a little more pleasurable. So the special savings they were gathering for his mother's operation was still not sufficient for the great expense. Though he did not approve, he still felt he must keep it for his mother's future, when Agnes surprised him bringing home after one of her dinners with her man friend, a reasonable amount of money given to her from him, when he learned of her mother's illness.

In fact Andrew, in spite of his suspicions was beginning to think he had misjudged the man. From what Agnes willingly told him, it seemed her friend may soon, even ask for her hand in marriage. There was no doubt that their relationship had become far more intimate. Yet this was to be expected if it was to eventually become permanent.

It seemed on three or more occasions Agnes was persuade to spend the night at his apartments and did not return home. Andrew did not dare ask but felt sure Agnes had slept with him. This was proven when one day after Agnes returning from working at the office she collapsed on her bed sobbing in desperation. It seemed her man-friend had found another woman working in the same office and heard him invite her out to dinner.

It seemed her happy times with him were over, for he completely ignored her whenever he was near at work and all her invitations ceased. Andrew realised his first impressions had been right. The man had now used her then discarded her. Worse he now, at last, was able to persuade Agnes to confess her behaviour with him. It seemed she had finally overcome her reluctance and had accepted full intercourse several times. However from other girls in her office she had found ways of limiting her chances of conceiving. She was not pregnant – but Agnes, who like the whole family - had been brought-up as religious persons, knew the worse.

As she sobbed with Andrew's arms around her trying to comfort her she alarmed him by what she said, "Andrew, I've slept with him – let him do those things to me.- What can I do. I can no longer come to any man as pure as I ought to be. – What reason have I for going on living?"

She may not be pregnant but Agnes now believed she was a 'fallen woman' – no longer a virgin – now she feared no man would ever want her as a wife. In fact Andrew feared for her life as he realised she even contemplated suicide. He knew the whole family must get away from New York, or it would happen. But what of the need for his mother's operation.

A short headline on the pages of the newspaper gave Andrew hope. First he knew, even if they stayed, it would be at least three more years before they would have acquired sufficient money for the operation. The newspaper might give them the answer. They must move westwards very quickly. Perhaps cross the continent, for in the west was a possible quick way of obtaining this for their mother.

They left New York only three days later. At least they had sufficient funds for their travel. Their journey might even bring them a fortune.

4.

Patrick Purcell was born in Tipperary which was a, predominately, Roman Catholic area, but like his father, Joseph Purcell, was a staunch Protestant. However neither of them could appreciate the entrenched protestant dislike of their Roman Catholic neighbours but they did believe in a free Ireland, separate from Britain, ruling itself as a sovereign country.

His father a very successful stockbroker with its main offices in Dublin but with its original offices in Waterford. Patrick was very intelligent young man and happily served his apprenticeship in his father's business, obtaining full qualifications before he was twenty. Patrick was so imbued with his desire for a free Ireland that he respected the orations of Daniel O'Connell, the Irish leader for reform of the restrictions then imposed on Catholics. With his efforts, having persuaded the British Prime Minister to pass the Emancipation Act, so O'Connell took his seat at Westminster.

Though only fourteen Patrick, had listened to O'Connell's orations advocating dissolving, the Anglo-Irish legislative union advocating Home Rule for Ireland and Patrick joined the Young Ireland movement Here he met a young protestant radical. Charles Doughty, a qualified geological and surveying engineer. Charles was employed by the government in surveying in the southern mountains for materials, readily, available for road construction and minerals. Many years later he was to become very friendly with his son, Paul, in America.

However he was even more influenced by another protestant British Member of Parliament, William O'Brien.. O'Brien had supported the union until O'Connell was arrested for 'seditious conspiracy' and joined the anti-union association, serving as deputy leader, whilst O'Connell was in jail. Patrick enthusiasm for freedom was greatly effected by O'Brien, though he supported O'Connell in resisting the use of force

Patrick was handsome, and he attracted girls to him like flies, even at school and later at college. He enjoyed 'petting' and soon knew the intimate parts of several girls, but he never went too far. Sometimes he felt to their disappointment. However he started 'gong steady' with Erin Connolly, a Roman Catholic girl, then sixteen, who he met in the Young Ireland movement. This was much to the displeasure of his men friends who disliked liaison between a protestant and a Catholic – but this did not disturb him. Eventually they got engaged and were to be married the next year. His family approved of his choice. By now Patrick had taken charge of his father's offices in Waterford, to which he travelled each day from his home in Tipperary, close to where Erin lived. Patrick was by now a well established young stockbroker and wealthy.

Then to his horror O'Brien became militant and on July 29th. 1848 he led a futile rising in Ballingarry, easily dispatched by the police. Now the Young Ireland movement were outlawed, O'Brien was arrested, and all members, including Patrick, were likely to be imprisoned. Worse still, militant gangs of protestants became a mob attacking Catholic homes in Tipperary, burning and killing.

Patrick was at work in Waterford when Erin's home was attacked. Her mother, father and brothers were all killed and poor Erin, and her fourteen year old sister Merle were raped by six different men. Patrick arrived home to find the two girls in great distress, having taken refuge with his mother. There was every chance that they had both conceived. He learned that a warrant was to be made against Patrick for his membership of the movement, and in a few days he would be in jail. That night when his father returned, it was obvious he must leave Ireland, immediately. Erin and Merle had no future and no home. If they had conceived they would be outcasts.

Patrick took a sobbing Erin in his arms and loved her, "Erin dear, I must go away today or I will be arrested and thrown in jail – You must come with me – we must marry as soon as possible." Then turning to Merle he continued, "Merle you must come with us – get away from here – and any shame you might feel if you stay. – I promise to look after you, just as much as I will do for Erin."

Patrick was rewarded by a lovely smile which lit up her tear stained face. All she said was, "Thank you, Patrick, I will come with you – you are so kind to me." What Patrick did not know that at that moment suddenly Merle had discovered that her true feelings for Patrick were very different from what they had been until today.

Patrick loved Erin and would not leave without her. His father had the resources and contacts. Before the warrant could be delivered they drove to Waterford and paid a fishing boat to take them to Bristol where he could take a ship to New York, for it would be just as unsafe to stay in England. Erin and Merle were very happy to emigrate with him.

After their hasty and difficult journey to Bristol, Patrick had sufficient wealth to purchase comfortable cabins for their journey across the Atlantic. Also he carried a letter addressed to, the West Street brokerage firm of Drew, Robinson and Company of New York given him by his father, who had many times done business with them. His father would, also, be writing direct to them. This would ensure employment in their firm when they arrived.

It was evident both girls feared they were pregnant, expecting a bleak future. Patrick told Erin he still loved her and still wished to marry her, even more after what she had just suffered. Her reply was desperate. "But Patrick I may be carrying another man's child. You know as a Catholic I would never agree to an abortion. I must release you from your promise to marry. I cannot believe you would want to marry me, after what has happened."

Patrick took her in his arms and kissed her, there, in front of Merle. "Don't talk nonsense. I love you. Of course I want to marry you – yes and I promise to look after Merle – I promise we will be one large family – I will see to her child if she has conceived. The ship's captain can marry us today. Only the honeymoon will be delayed. That can come later."

That was not the end of the matter. Although she was desperately in love with him, she considered herself 'damaged goods'. She pleaded with him to wait and see what happened being willing, only, if she was not pregnant, even if dishonoured. She could not come to him as a virgin. They argued but Patrick was adamant. Eventually he persuaded her he was not offering this as a sense of duty. He truly wanted her as his wife.

He also hugged Merle to him "I want you with us for as long as you want to remain – and until you are old enough to find a man of your own." Merle came and kissed him on the lips, "Patrick, you are so kind to me. If Erin does not mind, I would love to come and live with you, but like Erin I will not abort my child. Then what will everyone think of me." Patrick tried hard to console her saying America was a different country where her shame would be much less. What he did not know was that far more than the shame of being and unmarried woman, with a child, her real shame was far worse. She now knew she should not have those feelings for him, yet she could not help herself.

So three days into the voyage Erin Connolly married Patrick on the boat. That night Erin left her joint cabin with Merle and slept with Patrick. She already knew he was an accomplished lover. Even his manual explorations of her body in the past had enabled her to reach some satisfaction. That night was the happiest night of her life. Her ordeal had at least removed the one thing she had feared – the pain of her first deflowering, of which her mother had warned her. Erin knew she had a husband she would love to the end of her days, no matter what he did in the future.

5.

It seemed Patrick Purcell's friend, Charles Doughty, had like Patrick needed to escape from Ireland to avoid arrest. Charles took his wife Matilda and their children, Teressa and Paul on a boat from Dublin to France, where he knew with his qualifications, the French Government would be pleased to employ him as the British Government had done in Ireland. He bought a house and settled in the Loire Valley at Vendome.

Likewise, it was fortunate that the entire Purcell family gained their wealth from stock brokering and so did not suffer as did the Irish peasants on their small arable holdings, living in poverty as they did not own but had to pay rent to their Irish landowners. However in 1846 Ireland was struck, far more severely by the potato plague than even Andrew Campbell and his family had to suffer in Scotland. Though it was certainly one of main reasons for them immigrating to America, it was not the only one.

The blight hit Ireland far more severely, and as potato growing was virtually the only source of their food, soon very many families, already desperately poor, were starving. Worse, as now they could not raise any crops they had not the means to pay their rent and soon were turned off their land, becoming destitute. Many died of starvation. The Whig or Liberal government at Westminster did little to help. The small amount of food given to them was too little for the many homeless and distress people.

Then the taxation Laws passed on the landlords based on the number of dwellings on the land they owned, accentuated the situation, for now these landlords evicted the peasants for not paying rent and demolished their small habitations, simply to avoid taxation. So unless they were going to die from starvation, their only chance of escape was to follow many others immigrating to either Canada or the United States. This was the situation of the Nolan family who had rented a farm in King's County. Their landlord was only too pleased to persuade them to leave, even giving them just enough money to buy a passage on a small boat from Dublin to Liverpool.

There they had been told the government, only too anxious to rid this multitude of deposed people from Britain would supply the means for them to go to any part of America. they chose. So Case Nolan and his wife, Delma, took their two daughters, Camay just eighteen years of age and her sister, Maeve, and walked to Dublin, not too great a distance from where they had lived in the centre of Ireland. It was fortunate that all being Roman Catholics, Delma had been unable to conceive any more children after Maeve was born.

Then they paid and boarded a very small ship, and very overcrowded with others immigrating the same as they, to land at the rapidly expanding port of Liverpool which, with the access of the railways was now becoming the more important port for people going to America. Sheltered temporarily in a workhouse they were very anxious to leave and sail from this hell hole. It was there that they meet several other families also immigrating and came to know several in the short time they resided in Liverpool. They had decided that they should try to sail to New York and not either Boston nor Canada, for they had heard of the great difficulties encountered in these other places, being Roman Catholics.

They particularly set up a friendship with a family, immigrating like them, who had lived for centuries in Wicklow County in Ireland. They, also, had decided to make New York the place they wished to go. However it seemed the father of the family had already died of disease, no doubt due to lack of food. So Devin Regan, twenty years of age, had like the Nolan family walked to Dublin taking his mother, Arin, and his sister, Ellis, and come to Liverpool as they had done. Again apart from there other members of the family who had succumbed and died like their father, this was the extent of the Regan family.

Forced to live in close proximity due to the masses waiting for a ship, it was only natural that Devin tried to monopolise the very pretty, Camay Nolan. Of course Camay, never having any real opportunity of finding a boy-friend in the last precarious two years, was very flattered by Devin's attentions, and hoped it might continue. Though very severe as were the confines of the workhouse, it ensured it was entirely a platonic friendship, Camay, never-the-less, hoped it might develop more, for she took an immediate liking to Devin, and hope it may extend to further pleasures.

At last the two families were ordered to board a ship waiting for these refugees, one which was sailing to New York. Only too pleased to leave this terrible building, even though they knew once the boarded the ship, it would be in steerage, well below decks, with little sanitation, an almost without light. For they had been told they would never be allowed on deck. In fact they could see this would be virtually impossible. So cramped was the area allotted to them.

They knew these had been christened 'Coffin Ships', for many were so heavily overloaded, they had founded and sunk before they could reach America. They all knew this but just had to get to there. Still both Regan's and the Nolan's were successful in finding places close to each other. At least it did mean that both Camay and Devin also lived close to each other.

In spite of the overloading, there was two very small areas reserved for them to entertain themselves during the long journey across the Atlantic. On the few occasions when they were not battered by storms and even were almost becalmed, all the immigrants below decks would come together and dance to the music of the pipes, which had always been an Irish way of enjoying themselves, before the potato famine occurred.

Now at last Devin could take a willing Camay in his arms direct her into a free space on the floor and dance a jig with her, even daring to steal a quick kiss, without Camay showing any disapproval, and even showing she liked it. In fact she would whisper in Devin's ear, "You really are a naughty boy, but, please, I don't mind if you do it again, anytime." Devin felt he had made some progress.

After a few occasions like that they made sure they both detached themselves from their families. Although it was impossible to be alone, like several other couples of the same age, they could speak to each other as lovers do, not caring that other couples were near them. For in fact this was just what those around them were doing. Devin asked Camay, "What do you intend to do when we all reach New York?" Poor Camay shook her head, "I do not know. In fact father is worried what may await us there. None of us know anything but cultivating our land. He believes we shall be one of the many non-skilled workers he has heard about working hard for little money. – But none of us mind. – It will be better than starving to death, which would have occurred if we had stayed in Ireland."

Devin smiled and replied, "It's just the same for us – though my father is dead – so I must now look after family including my sister, Ellis and baby Brogan. – Camay, you must know by now, I've come to think a lot about you. I do hope we will still be able to see each other, when we get to New York – Would you be willing to continue to be my friend."

Now it was Camay's turn to kiss Devin and she did so quite passionately and unashamedly. When there lips broke apart she added, "I hope that proves I would love it if you could still call on me – perhaps take me out to see the sights – You see I want that just as much as it seems you want it too." After that occasion when the weather allowed them to steal way and meet this way, there love making became more intimate, but Camay did not mind – She knew she wanted it –Then she thought, perhaps America may be a much happier place to live than was Ireland.

Though the crossing was very rough and several people were injured due to falling as mountainous waved battered their ship. In fact seven people died on the journey but this was because they were already very ill, or starving, when they came on board. At last the ship slowed and they were told they were approaching the quay alongside New York's large harbour. Eventually they stopped and tied up. Then in turn they were ushered up above onto the deck. At last they walked down the gangway and both families placed their feet on dry land. It was almost a miracle that in spite of the dangers, they had arrived in America. Now what did the future hold for everyone landing there that day.

6.

Estelle Carroll stood looking out of that very large window, made up of countless small frames of glass, in their equally large bedroom, looking across the river with the state of Virginia on the opposite bank, but with a glimpse of mountains behind. Estelle wondered how many times dear Amelia had looked this way, wondering what lay behind those hills.

Estelle was very happy, and as she only looked, spoke aloud her feelings "Dearest Amelia, I only wish I could speak to you, for I feel, now, you are close by watching me. –It was you, not Sir David who made this wonderful house of Rockville such a happy place to live. – I only hope neither I, not any of my family, ever disgrace Rockville. I do hope Peter will come to live here after I've gone. – Yes! And all his descendents for many years to come."

Estelle knew by heart, almost the whole history of that amazing woman, who was her beloved ancester. She knew that but for Amelia, she would not be standing here admiring the view. Estelle thought of that first day when the then David Carroll had at last managed to free Amelia from the purgatory as an indentured servant, sentenced to bare three more children in quick succession, besides the one inside her. The one the evil Edward Calvert had given her when he had seized and raped her, when as a servant in Ireland, as she was tidying a bed.

Her beloved David, who she had met on that terrible ship sailing to Annapolis, had managed to get her paroled to him, though she was still under sentence to conceive three more children by men chosen for her. Estelle knew how soon after, to Amelia's amazement, David had told her he had fallen in love with her. Though she had willing yielded her pregnant body to him on that ship after he had saved her life, and knew only two days after this, she had fallen desperately in love with David, Amelia never dreamed this could happen.

She was a low born peasant from Ireland. Now a dishonoured and pregnant woman, through no fault of her own. Few men would even consider her as a temporary mistress, yet this David born into high aristocracy had now told her he loved her. It could not be true It was impossible. Yet he had just confessed this to her.

However Estelle knew only too well the fairy story which became fact. This man, not only married his Amelia against his father's wishes. Then when he became Governor of Maryland and even risked imprisonment by King William III, to beg and receive the right for all in Maryland to have Freedom to Worship as they chose. Finally he became a Knight of the Bath and making her Lady Amelia. Then for both to live so long in happiness. A fairy tale that never ended. All this is told in the first book "Maryland".

Estelle was extremely proud of Amelia as her many times 'great grandmother'. Even more proud that her adored husband, Adrian, was equally, a direct descendent of Sir David and Amelia Carroll, but by a different son of Amelia. Equally proud to stand looking through this wonderful window in this magnificent mansion of Rockville, on the estate given to Sir David to work and then to acquire, by his Roman Catholic cousin, Edgar Carroll.

Her marriage to Adrian in 1803, when both could then, separately, claim to be the owners of Rockville, but their happy marriage had ensured this when her mother-in-law and father-in-law died. Now Adrian and Estelle Carroll were Master and Mistress of this legacy given to Sir David in 1687. There claims were a complicated story, yet in the end, it had been settled amicably.

Estelle had celebrated her sixty first birthday two days before. It had been a magnificent day with so many parts of the convoluted descendents of Sir David and Amelia, coming together to celebrate – and yet love again – this mansion of Rockville, which was the reason they were all alive, here, today.

Besides the six children of her marriage to Adrian, they had all brought their many offspring. How she had been delighted that her eldest son. Peter, married now to Amy Vanderbilt for twenty years, and although living in wealth and comfort in New York, had told Estelle now when both Adrian and Estelle died they would leave New York and take-up residence in Rockville, if only to ensure it was occupied by the direct line of descent from Sir David. Also that their eldest son Andrew, now twenty, named after his grandfather, also promised, in due course to finally settle here.

To Estelle this was possibly the best gift she received that day for she was sure Sir David and Amelia would want it that way. Of course Estelle hoped it would still be many years before Peter and Amy came to stay permanently, for she still felt quite well though her bones at time gave her a little pain due to arthritis. Estelle had no wish to die for she was so very happy with the man she loved so deeply and who had befriended her the first day she arrived at Rockville, rescued from a sinking ship as she had sailed from England, so long ago, when attacked by a French privateer during the French Revolutionary Wars.

Estelle was equally pleased that Danton Carroll and his wife, Claudia, could be present on her birthday. Danton had been part of the Diplomatic Contingent in Mexico for many years, well before Texas rebelled, and defeated Santa Anna, and declared Texas Independent. Though President Van Buren refused Samuel Houston' request to give Texas Statehood and part of the United States, President Polk had no reservations in accepting a later request, which precipitated war with Mexico.

Danton had been present when the United States representative, John Slidell, appeared to negotiate a peaceful transfer of Texas from Mexico and also land to the west, including California, which had become known as the 'Magnificent Obsession'. The extension of the boundaries of the United States from the Atlantic to the Pacific ocean. However the Mexican Government fell and war was declared in May 1846. Then Danton along with all other members of the United States Delegation were forced to leave and so Danton and Claudia had returned to their home at Racoonsville in Virginia.

Since then many battles had been fought though most were eventually won by the United States. At the same time as these troops invaded Mexico itself, other United States forces, aided by the numerous Missouri volunteers, invaded New Mexico and eventually, sparsely populated California. Now in 1847, it seemed that as General Scott pressed home his own attack towards Mexico City, from Vera Cruz, against a determined Santa Anna The end to the war was in sight, and victory was assured. Danton brought the news and this was well celebrated on Estelle's Birthday.

But far more serious discussions had occurred that same day which might, in fact, seriously disturb the peace of both Maryland and Virginia. Only time would tell. The main opposition to the war was President Polk's determination to admit Texas to the Union. For if so Texas would become a slave owning state, which would destroy the delicate balance of entry of one slave state, and one opposed to slavery. Again what would be the fate if California and other territories were later accepted.

After the end of the American War of Independence in 1783 the owners of Rockville, Racoonsville and Gordonville being extremely rich, had rewarded many who had fought so hard in the militia by settling them on parts of their estates, giving them ownership of their land, sometimes as large as fifty acres, some smaller. In doing so they instituted a fief on their holdings of ten percent of their profits each year if successful. This gave each of these families a chance to gradually earn wealth, and yet it also ensured, good dividends to the owners of the original estates.

Although, should it be their wish, these now independent owners could still continue to employ slaves, it was no longer a necessity for those occupying Rockville, Racoonsville or Gordonsville. In fact due first to Robert Carroll, then his son, Mark Carroll, becoming Senators for Virginia, influence by the views of the northern members of Congress, they had felt that slavery was basically wrong.

Consequently by 1820, though still retaining their services they had freed all slave workers on their own estates, and instead began paying them small wages. This did nothing more than ensure, even further, the loyalty of these people, for they had always been treated kindly, ensuring their marriages were what they wanted. In fact the sons and daughters of the previous slaves, usually begged to continue to work on their estates.

However the Mexican War had strained their loyalty to the Whig Party in Congress instituted by Henry Clay in opposition to the corruption introduced once Democrat President Andrew Jackson had been elected. For they had respected Senator Henry Clay of Kentucky and so it had been natural that when the Whig Party opposed slavery, they had taken the action they had done with their own slaves.

However they had for a long time believed that the whole of Mexico should have chosen to become part of the United States after Mexico broke its ownership by Spain. They especially believed, that Texas and California should become part of their country. Supporting a relative, Donald Reid, who had so vigorously worked for California to become part of the United States, and had now settled in California. Because of the slavery issue, the Whig Party had strongly opposed Democrat President Polk's, acceptance Texas as a new state of the Union, and the declaration of War in 1846.

Accordingly, though members of the Whig Party they had supported President Polk voting with Democrats and so had supported the war. Now those many branches who in some way or other were either descendents of Margaret Eliot, her daughter Amelia, or the original David Carroll, had met together as they celebrated Estelle's birthday, realising the coming difficulties when Mexico was defeated.

Then not only would Texas, a slave state, become part of Congress, their was the question of all the other lands such as California and the great area between it and Texas. In time these areas must give rise to a number of new states. If these followed the example of Texas and voted for slavery, there was a great danger of civil war for the northern states would never contemplate allowing the southern slave states to have a majority of votes in Congress.

At the moment Maryland was mainly, but not entirely, against slavery. Yet Virginia was predominately a slave state, essential for its economic prosperity. If such a civil war was to occur these two states must be the centre of any warfare. What then would happen to their estates, and worse which side should they support.

Unfortunately after much discussion no answer could be found. Again that day was to celebrate beloved Estelle's birthday. However they knew, in the future they must, all, meet again, so as to be prepared should such circumstances occur.

7.

In San Francisco Donald and Rachael Reid lay resting on their patio on their beautiful estate in San Leandro, Oakland, looking down at the sea below them and across the bay to their previous home in Yerba Buena. They were two very happy people. Now having established themselves as one of the richest people in this rapidly growing township, which they knew would now grow even larger.

Rachael was so happy admiring the magnificent vista and turned to Donald, "Donald dear I love you so much. Thank you for bringing me here. When I agreed on that boat to leave my cruel husband and come with you. – I really feared you only wanted to use me – enjoy me – yet, even then I did not care – you were so handsome – so even that type of life with you must be far better than the life I was living at that moment. –Then amazingly you accepted me and made me your wife. Now you have brought me here, given me eleven years of happiness. How can I ever thank you enough?"

Donald laughed, "Don't be silly. It was you when we stayed at San Diego who persuaded me to travel and come here. Even then, your only wish was for me to achieve my desire to see California and agreed to settle here. You never cared of the dangers. Since then you have given me these wonderful years of happiness and the wonderful family you have given us."

For only a week before Donald had achieved his ambition which had burnt inside him as he had listened near the Great Salt Lake to the tales of Jedediah Smith, Mountain Man, in 1827. From that very moment Donald had decided to spend his life to try to make this wonderful country called California, part of the United States. Knowing if so the United States would extend from the Atlantic to the Pacific Ocean. Donald had tried so hard without success, even though he had, eventually settled in San Francisco, then part of Mexico. But this was after marrying his beloved Rachael, after probably saving her life when she miscarried the baby of the Mormon husband she had been forced to marry.

Encouraged by his wife, who did not mind the dangers so long as she was able to be with the man she loved, they have come to visit California. First buying a small house in San Diego, then travelled again northwards buying another small house on Grant Avenue in Yerba Buena, and settled there in 1836.

After setting up a prosperous shipping business, buying two ships from Cornelius Vanderbilt, trading not only along the Pacific coast, but also with China and the Far East, sending their goods via Panama, across the isthmus, and up to the United States and North America. It had become a very successful business and grown rapidly in size, making them very prosperous.

Soon they had met and employed David Backhouse, a Canadian, as their much needed accountant, only then to find they were related as it seemed David was a descendent of Blanche Carroll, the first child of the then Amelia Eliot, born, the result of her raping in Ireland by evil Edward Calvert. However Donald knew of his own relationship with Amelia's mother, Margaret Eliot. So, though the land then belonged to Mexico, and though David believed San Francisco, should be part of Canada whilst Donald was sure it belonged to the United States, they had become great friends.

Only a week ago the United States military had landed and taken possession of the town. Now their was no doubt but the peace treaty with Mexico would ensure it became part of that country. So Donald, with only a little of his help, had at last achieved his long ambition.

Although his wife, when forced to marry, with her sister, Constance, an older Mormon, Sidney Gilbert, conceived his child, ran away with Donald and dangerously miscarried her child, her life, no doubt saved by Donald rescuing her from that boat on which they both sailed. In time this had turned to love and they had married. Then a happy Rachael had been delighted to accompany her new husband and travel with him to his much desired California, so to settle there and establish his rich business.

Since then Rachael had delightedly born him four children, the last Adrian, only less than two years before. Rachael knew these would never be enough for her. But besides the happiness Donald had given her, he had managed to bring her elder sister, Constance, who she loved, with her second husband, to come and stay with them, employing her new husband to take charge of his extensive storehouses.

This had not been easy for Constance thought her younger sister had performed blasphemy, when Rachael ran away from her lawful husband, and then marry again to Donald. The truth was that their Mormon husband, was a very evil man, who preyed on women. After marrying his first wife, Nancy, then had intercourse with Constance who conceived. Their father forced Constance to marry Sidney, but at the same time forced Rachael to become his third wife.

Sidney frightened his women with his religious views and completely dominated them. It was a miracle that Donald discovered Rachael's terrible plight on that boat sailing to the promised land of Zion, at Independence, persuaded her to leave with him, but with Rachael, having to accept blind trust of Donald. A decision which saved her life. However Constance, at that time, could not forgive her sister, and feared for her eternal life.

Even when the gentiles, with help from the militia removed all Mormons from Independence, killing many. Even after Constance and his other wives, later discovered that Sidney, anxious to escape alive, had deserted them, fleeing without them. However his evil deeds caught up with him. The mob found him and painfully battered him to death, making his wives widows. Still they considered he was a good man.

It took years of patience of Donald's elder sister, Sharon, and then the love of this new man, who she fell in love with, which eventually was to change her mind. At last she came to accept that her sister had not done anything wrong. Donald realised how valuable would be Constance's new husband to his own business as a skilled storehouse manager. He paid for them both to come as their honeymoon to San

Francisco. Then offered him the position which he gladly accepted and so stayed.

Now Constance and her husband, Jack, lived in Rachael and Donald's old house on Grant Avenue. So at last the two sisters were united and had settled together in this new town. All now part of Donald Reid's vast shipping business. They had moved to this new estate having purchased enormous stretches of land in Oakland. Built their own mansion with its own private estate around it. Now they could sit in the sun enjoying their prosperity and enjoying the view.

Donald asked Rachael, "Are you happy?". Rachael turned smiling at him, "Of course darling. Why should I not be. I'm with the man I love more than life who has given me such a wonderful family. But Donald, it's nearly two years since I bore Adrian, - please soon – let us add to our family. You know I did wait a long time after we married before I conceived Conrad. I know it was necessary, for if not I would have stopped you achieving your ambition to see California. Still we have still only four children and it is eleven years since we married. Really, I do want another baby."

Donald got up and came behind where Rachael was sitting putting his arms around the chair and about her. Then bent over and kissed her." Then he smiled, "Of course, my dear. If that is what you want – For I, too, would love another child. After what happened last week I think, if it were possible, I would give you the world."

Continuing Donald said, "You know I was very pleased to receive that letter from Cherie and her husband, Daniel Wilson, telling us how pleased her father Roy Marshal was that we established this RMCV Company, now so profitable. It was Roy who persuaded both the Vanderbilt's and the Carroll's to invest with us in it. It seems Daniel is very much involved in the eastern part of our business. Roy has encouraged him in this and likes his son-in-law so has ensured both he and Roy's daughter, Cherie, are financially secure."

Rachael laughed, "Oh! Yes! In it Cherie even stated she would like to come with Daniel to live in California now they have learned of the large tracts of land available here. If so, I think I must be very careful. You once told me she was one of your earlier girl friends."

Donald gave her bottom a cautionary slap. "Don't talk nonsense – I never had the chance – as soon as Gordon Taylor arrived – her eyes were on him and with her friend tried hard to entice him. – Do you know. It was her rejection of me which made me go on that boat and where I first met you. - You have reason to thank her for it was my disappointment which made me sail to St. Louis."

Now rapidly changing the subject. "Rachael dear," he continued, "I never thought it would happen. I never thought we could win California for the United States. I tried so hard to get this to happen, even trying to find routes for persons to come and live here. – Yet I failed – but because you trusted me and became my wife, agreeing to travel with me and come her, at least we achieved wealth. – Then last week it happened. Soon California will become a state on it's own. I may stand for election to the State Legislate. – I shall see?"

Rachael laughed, "Why not, you are already one of the most important men in this growing town. – However I think soon we might have an invasion of people – and not all will be the ones we want. – Did you see that article in the News last week?"

Donald assented, "Yes, it made me very worried. When we arrived here we had heard the rumours of gold being seen in some streams in the hinterland. Fortunately it was unconfirmed. However now it seems gold has been discovered floating in a stream at Sutter's Fort, nearer the mountains and that new village of Sacramento."

Now he became serious. "You know gold makes men mad. If confirmed, thousand will arrive, caring little for the dangers. Not all will be good men. – It will encourage the worse elements of mankind – desperadoes caring little for life and property. If it becomes a gold rush, we shall have to employ many men to guard all our possessions. – Rachael, it is not this type of Americans I wanted to come to occupy California. – But we shall have no choice."

They became silent thinking that their wonderful world might soon be torn apart. Nor were they wrong, - very soon multitudes of men and women would descend on this place – desperate to find gold and a possible rich future.

8.

What Andrew Campbell had seen in the newspaper was that gold had been discovered floating in the stream at Sutter's Fort in California. This might be the answer to his prayer. If they could all go there, find gold, there would be enough money to pay for any operation his mother Margaret might require. True, it was a gamble, but Andrew knew, without this, his dear mother would never be alive in three years time, even if by then, they had raised enough money.

The other reason was he was afraid of his sister's mental state. Agnes had told him she knew she was a dishonoured woman, she felt god must punish her. Yet she was already enduring punishment every day when she saw her ex-lover. Andrew knew if she stayed in New York, even if she left her present job, every part of this city reminded her of the wonderful hours she had spent with him.

For both reasons Andrew knew they must leave. He even smiled to himself and thought, 'If we did find gold, we might all become rich. Then we could all enjoy a life so much better than any we have had before'. When he proposed that they should go to California, and the reason, he was delighted that they all agreed, and wanted to go there as quickly as possible, before many others arrived. So three days later they set out.

They knew the route they must take. It was the one they had found so many others who landed at New York had taken, if only to find and settle in the rich farmland out west. It had been pioneered now for many years. More important they all had enough money to pay for the journey.

They must sail up the Hudson to Albany. Change and sail along the new Eire Canal. Then from Buffalo they must join the River Ohio, then sail along it until it joined the River Mississippi. Finally sail northward until they reached the twin towns of Kansas City and Independence. From there the journey west could begin by buying a wagon, join a wagon train, and then, as many before them, travel across the plains, somehow take their wagon over the mountains until they could at last reach Sutter's Fort and begin prospecting for gold.

This they did as quickly as possible and found an inn in which to sleep. Meanwhile Andrew went out to buy the wagon, find and sign up to a wagon train, buying all the essentials, including food and water which the wagon master would suggest they obtain. So leaving them at the inn, Andrew went to perform this task.

*   *   *   *   *   *   *   *   *   *   *   *   *   *   *

Almost at the same time Kurt Sand was thinking the same way. He also had read of the finding of gold in California. Was this not the place he should go and set up his own business, in conjunction with his father's firm. It was certain that they would need roads, perhaps canals, or later, even railways. Since the Mexican War had released so much land to the west and the attractiveness of the growing vast spaces of California on the west pacific coast, was beckoning many pioneers to go west, Kurt knew he must see this paradise.

Perhaps he would have decided to take the opportunity of travelling the long journey from New York around Cape Horn to the seaport of San Francisco and see if he could use his considerable skills in developing engineering projects so needed in California but the newspapers in early 1848 reporting of gold being discovered at Sutter's Fort in California, he knew this called for speed and the need to arrive there quickly.

This provided the catalyst, and with his father's blessing but with the disapproval of both his mother and sister, carrying both a considerable quantity of money and several bills of credit he set off to join the growing numbers of gold prospectors. He knew, even if he failed to find gold, he would have sufficient resources to set up a profitable business of his own in California.

It was his desire for adventure, more than the discovery of gold which appealed to him. The die was cast. The journey for Kurt Sand was easier than the one the Campbell family had been forced to choose. He lived near Pittsburgh. The journey to the river was much shorter and he knew well the steamboats which sailed to Independence. As speed was essential he acted immediately on his idea. If gold was there, Kurt knew many more than him would be making that same journey, as quickly as possible.

Once he arrived like Andrew Campbell he went to the inn and took a room then went to buy a wagon – the best available at that time, for he was not short of money. In fact he met Andrew just as he was, also, trying to purchase one. He even told Andrew, because the journey would be difficult, especially as he found he would be accompanied by two women, although they were expensive, he must buy, like him, a Conestoga wagon, which he did.

Then they both went to discover a wagon train and in fact saw one just leaving as they arrived at the sight. But they were fortunate as they found attempts were on offer to join another wagon train and the wagon master was like Andrew, a Scotsman, Alastaire MacLean. There were several other persons all arriving there with their wagons so they were all called together so MacLean could address them.

Alastaire MacLean, was a seasoned traveller who had travelled the route many times. Now, though he would ensure the people reached Sacramento who wanted to reach the town, he, with most of the wagons would not go further then Sutter's Fort, his son would complete the journey.

MacLean, asking them to form a circle, which included Kurt Sand and Andrew Campbell, soon to become great friends. MacLean, told them he knew that most wanted to arrive at the diggings as soon as possible, so he suggested an alternative route, which he had explored six years before, and one the last wagon train was travelling.

Instead of taking the Santa Fe Trail they should travel north west along the Republican River heading into Cheyenne country and Colorado, To cross the range of mountains known as the Medicine Row

Range and on to Salt Lake City where the Mormons had established themselves. The route, sometimes called the Oregon Trail, was hard but he had successfully driven three heavy wagons through the passes. It was, already, late April and by the time they reached the mountains the snow would have gone.

His friend was the wagon master in the train which had just left. They might even catch up with it. In any case the appearance of so many wagons would lessen indian attacks, though not eliminate them. The prize for taking this route was that it would reduce, by at least, a month, the journey, if they got through. As the aim of most of them were to arrive at he gold fields as soon as possible, everyone agreed to take the risk.

The decision taken Kurt walked with Andrew back to their inn and was introduced to his mother, forty six year old Margaret Campbell and to his nineteen year old sister, Agnes. Although Kurt had met Andrew the previous day he had not met his family before. Kurt at once realised how lovely was Andrew's sister and made a mental note to use his charms on her during the journey.

They were surprised he was travelling alone but he told them of his plans, even if not successful at the diggings, to set up a business in California, hinting he had sufficient resources. It seemed the Campbell's were gambling on striking it lucky as this was the only reason for embarking on this perilous journey. Leaving the women they went into Independence for a night of drinking realising it would be sometime before they entered a saloon again. Andrew then told him their own story. Their life as a crofter in the Western Isles, their coming to and working in New York. About the illness of his mother and whilst he hoped they would find gold, enough to pay for her operation.

This was all Andrew told him, not mentioning anything about his sister's troubles. Still, that night a firm friendship was established between Kurt and Andrew, promising to help each other on the long journey which now lay before them.

9.

Gordon Taylor had long conversations with Kurt Sand when he learned of his desire to go west and set up an engineering business of his own there constructing roads, possibly canals, and even railways . Gordon had liked Kurt since he first met him, whilst Kurt had been surprised at Gordon's interest, since he knew Gordon was a Junior Director of the large company.

"Kurt," he said, "If ever you indulge in railway construction remember how essential it is first survey, very carefully, the best route. You must be very careful that the gradients are not too great, steam locomotives cannot climb steep hills. You may have to consider dynamiting and even boring tunnels. From your survey you must convert this information into graphs by draftsmanship. That is why Charlotte Marshall is so valuable to our firm."

Of course Kurt Sand knew of Charlotte Marshall and had met her, the wife of the managing director of the firm. This amazing woman, already over sixty years of age, was even a fully qualified engineer, as well as an accomplished draughtswoman. Remarkable as she was a woman and in many ways was responsible for the financial success of their firm. The rumour was that she had qualified as an engineer in France, as demanded by her father along with her brother, Francois, before the French Revolution, In fact it was a miracle she had escaped from France during the 1793 Terror in that country.

As they parted Gordon added, "Remember you can always call on me to advise you if you had to make a serious decision I would be glad to help. Yes! If you would allow me, even come to watch as you constructed, yet another, railroad."

Kurt thanked Gordon for his generosity but also gained the name and address of a Donald Reid, who was in someway related to the Marshall Family and had established his own shipping line in San Francisco. Gordon assured him of a warm welcome there if his journey west was as far as California. All this occurred before Kurt began his adventurous journey west.

Gordon Taylor smiled to himself as he promised Kurt Sand help, now he was going west. For he was presently to surprise his wife Sheila. It was the idea of taking their whole family on a similar long journey. But if so, it would be in the opposite direction to the one Kurt Sand would take. However it was one he felt he must take as it was now twenty years since he had come from England. He came to his home and found Sheila was expecting him.

Sheila had just received a letter from her mother, Patricia. Her family now lived in Kentucky on land purchased by Gordon Taylor for them, near Camargo. It had been essential after Sheila's previous husband, Simon Doyle's death. Simon Doyle had been responsible for Sheila's terrible years as his wife The memories of both the Doyle and McLean families were too recent. Gordon and Sheila persuaded them to sell their Missouri farm, move to Kentucky where Neil could raise both cattle and horses, ensured of easy sales to the families at Camargo. Though not rich, they were now quite prosperous. Both could not fail to see the irony, that it was Gordon Taylor, now married to their daughter, the man they had felt unfitted for her to marry, who now had provided this happy new life for them.

Gordon had kept in touch with his family in Manchester, ever since he arrived at Pittsburgh. It seemed they too had progressed and acquired some wealth, due to their involvement in the many railway lines being driven through the country. So much so, that the entire family had moved into the rapidly growing and very upmarket area of Moss Side, with its many green fields and large houses. For in the mid nineteen century, this was a very desirable area in which to live. Each family including, Gordon's, were pleased that they could write frequently to each other.

Sheila was telling Gordon how happy were her family and once again thanked their wonderful son-in-law for his kindness. Naturally he was pleased, however he replied, "You know my position in the firm now gives me an opportunity to take a rest. All my foremen are capable of seeing to our railway development for many months without my supervision. Really I now only act as overseer, and I know Charlotte would enjoy substituting for me whilst I am away."

He placed his arm around a very willing Sheila. "Sheila, though I know all your family, - you have never met mine. It pleases me that you have established a regular communication with both James' wife and sister Elizabeth. It's high time you met them. Sally is two years old and able to travel, as is all our family. We must all go to New York in the New Year, and take a ship to Liverpool. My family can meet us there and take us on the railway to Manchester."

Sheila turned and kissed the side of Gordon's face, "Dearest, I'd love that, and so would the children. I can never forget that it was on board a ship I discovered this wonderful Prince Charming who has given me already nearly thirteen years of paradise. Perhaps if we stayed there you could take me to London on the railway they have built. It's a place I always wanted to see, but never thought it would be possible."

Gordon pulled her close to him and smoothed her lips in a profusion of kisses. "Yes! We will do that. We can show our children, Buckingham Palace, the Tower of London, and of course, the Houses of Parliament, and we can go there on the railway. You know it is these wonderful railways, that has ensured all our fortunes, both in America and in Britain. Yet, it was my families growing so rapidly, with so many children, that I had to come to Uncle Silas. You know I worked by hand, my truck on the railway line to get to Liverpool to come here. Then I met you on that ship. So even then a railway played its part."

As so often happened when either of them relived in the minds the happy moments of the past, for ever excluding that terrible period they lived separate lives, it was the beginning of yet another period of intimate love making. To Sheila's delight, with the children playing outside or away from the house, she was thrilled, for she knew what was to happen.

Now Gordon picked up her tiny body in his arms and carried her upstairs to their bedroom, just as on that wonderful day, after their marriage and honeymoon, he had done as he made her mistress of this palace. Like then, Sheila now believed he had turned her, his Cinderella, into a princess. But unlike those lovely stories, her story never ended

However as he laid beside her on the bed wanting much, what she knew was about to happen, and which she so desperately desired, she said, "Much as I want you, you must wait a minute. If we are soon to got to England, you will have to forego – at least for a few months, - before letting me add to our family."

But it was only a temporary pause, and soon Gordon was ensuring once again, that her desires, rose into the paradise of their intimate embrace as her Prince Charming made his Princess a very happy woman. Afterwards as they lay, a little exhausted, Sheila, again remembered how Gordon, on that ship coming to America had placed his arm around her waist, scaring her, yet, even then, wanting it to go further. Now they could enjoy this until the end of their lives.

Yes! She knew she would enjoy repeating this on a new ship going to England, - repeating those wonderful moments – only this time – there would be no reason for stopping them achieving, what at that time she dare not do. She thought, 'Perhaps in England I may add to our family. I could conceive a baby there. It would be both English as well as American, but I know it is America where I will always want to live'.

10.

Patrick Purcell had ample resources once they had passed customs and he took all of them and registered in an hotel in New York recommended by his father. Only after resting and ensuring the two girls were as comfortable as possible, did he call of the Company of Drew, Robinson on Wall Street. He was, immediately shown into the office of the major partner, Daniel Drew, an imposing man of about fifty, giving him his father's letter.

Daniel was expecting him as his father had sent another letter by special courier, employed in the banking community. Reading his qualifications and experience, Daniel, immediately offered, a junior position in the firm. He also set in motion, with Patrick's approval, the means to eventually obtain United States Citizenship.

As Daniel had been informed of the reason for his quick escape from Ireland, he told him it was essential that he should do this. With his contacts, and a liberal investment of money, he promised it would be expedited within a month. This was the first occasion on which he learned that in this country bribes were essential for any progress.

Daniel told him he had met his father in London some time before and was happy to perform this service. Not only did he have a job but Daniel, quickly, rented a reasonably sized house, in the Bronx, until he could find a permanent habitation. Patrick spent a week before he stared work transferring all of them into this house and furnishing it, using his father's letters of credit.

Both women were still traumatised by their terrible experience and still lived in fear of the consequences. Erin, at least knew she could rely on her husband's generous promise to register her child, if it occurred, as his own but it seemed if Merle had conceived, her child would be illegitimate and she would be an unmarried mother, whilst still, almost a child, carrying with it the terrible stigma, through no fault of her own.

Patrick, though he admitted to himself, he had no real plans, promised he would, somehow, see she did not suffer this embarrassment. He was becoming to admire the courageous way Merle was accepting her position, conscious of the complete trust she had in him Yet he could not see how he could help her except to ensure she had a loving home in which to be cherished.

Having started to work he found the way brokers operated in America was very different from the staid way things occurred in both London and Dublin. The Drew company, like so many others in New York, sailed very close to the legal limits in their dealings, with phoney stocks, bribery and corruption of officials to obtain their success. This, particularly, applied to railway stocks, as so many companies tried to profit in this new form of locomotion. Lines were being laid through north eastern United States.

Of course Patrick was, quickly, introduced into New York social life and all three were invited to enjoy the pleasures of dinners and soirees. Again how different this was to Ireland and how hypocritical. Although they drove the Mormons, further and further west, deploring their polygamous marriages, most men, though married, enjoyed one or more mistresses, often with the blessing of their own wives. It was their way of life in both New York and Washington.

Further more the original Dutch settlers who had created New Amsterdam, now renamed New York, evidently were not adverted to nudity in their own large estates and even more unusual practices.

Patrick was not sure if these liaisons might help poor Merle but had decided to explore its possibilities. He wondered if Erin might consent to Merle becoming his mistress, if Merle was, also, agreeable. He had taken the, instinctive, precaution, to Erin and Merle's consternation, of registering Merle as Merle O'Donnell, Erin's grandmother's maiden name. This was to further confuse any investigation into his own position.

By October is was certain both Erin and Merle had conceived. At present there was nothing they could do but accept their condition. Patrick immersed himself in learning the intricacies of the New York Stock Exchange including the use of political contacts to further the profitability of Daniel Drew's company. Even this resulted in him receiving a portion of the proceeds. He was becoming richer.

Their condition meant a quiet Christmas and New Year and the two girls wanted to stay close to the house and not celebrate with his colleagues. More for appearance Patrick went alone to one party. It was a riotous affair, almost a drunken orgy where the wives were happy to swap partners and retired, upstairs, to a vacant bedroom for sexual pleasures.

As Patrick had always been a womaniser, he found the advances, of a still attractive woman of fifty, too much to ignore. Knowing there was little chance of scandal, he enjoyed her voluptuous body which she willing offered him. She told afterwards he was a very capable bed companion. He did not tell any of the girls of this encounter. Life here was very different to Ireland.

Then in January Erin went into labour when five months pregnant and miscarried. Erin had a bad time and it was a week before she was out of danger. When she had recovered she told Patrick she was pleased it had happened and swore she had not done anything to cause it. Poor Merle told Patrick she wished it had happened to her and broke down in tears. "I am a burden to you and soon I will cause you embarrassment with your New York friends. I wish I could die. Only my religion stops me ending it. I know I should leave you before it happens – but where could I go,"

Patrick hugged her to him. "Dear Merle do not think of these things. We all love you and want you to stay. I've become very fond of you. Erin knows. If we were not married – if I had come to New York, alone, with you. I would have asked you to marry me – no – not for pity – but because you are a girl I could love. – In fact Erin knows – I do love you – very much – you are so like Erin. Please believe me I want you to live – and for you to be near me. Would you consider aborting your child. You know it is possible here. Some wives do this, particularly after they have laid with other men, and conceived."

Merle smiled through her tears "You truly are a wonderful man After what you have just said, I will not be foolish – I promise – but dear Patrick I could never agree to an abortion. That would be a terrible sin – besides, I don't hate this child inside me – I want it – Can you understand.?"

Patrick hugged her closely to him and then kissed her on the lips, not passionately, but lovingly and she understood and was happy. It was obvious to Patrick that Merle's feelings for him were no longer those of a sister-in-law. They were much deeper – more than for gratitude or looking after her. He thought about it for two days. Then, almost in fear, he approached Erin as they lay in bed, though neither considered intimacy, as she was still weak

"Please Erin, don't be angry at what I'm about to say. There is a solution for Merle if you and she could agree to a great sacrifice. None of our friends know you have miscarried. - Merle's baby will be born at the time your child should have been born. If we kept it a secret – Could you both possibly agree to Merle bearing her child in secrecy. It can be done. Then I would register her baby as our own, and we could continue to live together so she could grow up with her child –even if it did not bear her name.".

Erin was astonished at the idea. It would be stealing her own sister's child. Yet it would absolve Merle from any shame. They talked about it throughout the night. In the morning they both agreed to approach Merle and see if she could agree – more important, that she wanted this.

11.

It was a very happy day at Racoonsville as Mark and Estelle Carroll's twenty two year old daughter, Judy Carroll, married Keith Chalmers bringing together the large estates of Racoonsville and Chalmers. Estelle had the same name as the owner of Rockville, being a distant relative. Judy was Mark and Estelle's sixth child born in 1826. Keith Chalmers, on the other hand was the son of Steve and Hattie Chalmers. However Keith was also the great grandson of Sophia and Colon Chalmers who had married at the end of the War of Independence combining their two large estates they each owned, making it one as large as Racoonsville.

Though a very happy day, poor Estelle, now sixty three, was exhausted, for she had been involved now for over two months in ensuing her daughter's wedding was as wonderful as all her other daughters. Further more she knew as now Mistress of Racoonsville she must ensure the occasion was just as great as those other wonderful weddings of the now long since deceased, Michelle Carroll, who had supervised them on their estate. Once again the church at Racoons Ferry was where the couple plighted their troth.

Michelle Carroll was Mark's wonderful grandmother, who after an adventurous life, living with but not married to Donald Wilson, an ex-smuggler who rescued her from the custom men in France and brought her to America, acting as his wife for ten years but not conceiving any of his children. Then she had been courted by the famous Daniel Carroll, frustrating and refusing him until at last they married and came to live in Racoonsville after Daniel's grandfather, Sir Robert Carroll, gave them the estate on their marriage.

Both Mark and Estelle, herself the granddaughter of Anton Tencin, who it seemed was an illegitimate son of King Louis XIV of France, were exceedingly proud of both Daniel and Michelle. These two people had done much to establish this countries prosperity. It was Daniel, as described in the third book in this series, 'Liberty', greatly assisting George Washington in eventually freeing the United States from Britain.

In the wonderfully happy years Michelle had lived with Daniel she had taken responsibility for overseeing and arranging so many weddings at that church in which the marriage had occurred today. Estelle had needed to exhaust herself in its planning for she knew, if not the ghost of Michelle would haunt her. Now Estelle, though tired was very happy it had proved so successful.

Now after her daughter and her husband had left on their honeymoon, and as the several of the guests had accepted Estelle's invitation to stay the night at Racoonsville, she had accepted for her son, Danton and his wife Claudia, to take over the proceedings, which would last long into the night. So at last with Mark, Estelle had been able to leave her guests and come her bedroom to rest.

They had undressed and now lay besides each other on their bed, but Estelle was delighted that her kind husband was rewarding her knowing the strain his wife had endured that day. As so many times in the past, Mark was gently stroking her naked body, and his ministrations were quite intimate, but both knew they were too tired for it to go much further. Neither did they want it too. However it would have been very different even twenty years before.

Estelle enjoying her husband's gentle intimacy could not help herself and she turned over and firmly kissed him on the lips. This was the signal for Mark, also to turn, then pull her lovely soft body against his hard one. For a moment she broke away and said, "Oh! Mark! I do so love you. I love you just as much as when we too stole away for our honeymoon. "

He kissed her again before replying, "Dearest Estelle, I love you just as much as I did then. I was so proud of you today. You know both father and mother adored you, so pleased you could accept me as your husband." Now even as they were clasped to each other, Estelle gave a little laugh, "Mark, that day I not only married the man I loved but as your mother, Hedwig spoke to me as we left to go. I shall always remember her kind words 'Remember Estelle, someday this lovely estate will become yours. It is what we both want. But please remember we all owe so much the Daniel and Michelle' ".

Mark kissed her again then added, "Today you were as wonderful as both Michelle and Hedwig in ensuring the success of Judy's wedding. However I wonder how much longer we can all enjoy occasions such as today. As I told you Senator Abraham Lincoln is enticing all members of the Whig party to use force if necessary, to make all states free from slavery. Southern Carolina last week in Congress, demanded Lincoln was restrained or open rebellion would occur."

Now poor Estelle forgot this lovely day, forgot the nice way her kind husband was trying to ease her tired body. "Mark, we must consider what we should do if conflict should occur. We must heed to its possibilities. None of us could find an answer at Rockville on Estelle Carroll's birthday. Now Mexico has signed the peace treaty giving us not only Texas and California but so much other land which in time must become new states."

Mark had to agree, "Yes, and now Texas will be admitted as a slave state. – Then possibly California will follow suit. I know the northern states will never consider allowing there to be a majority of slave demanding states. Soon Lincoln will get his way and bloodshed will occur – It will become a civil war. You know if so the battle ground will be on our own, and Gordonville and Rockville. All our estates will be ravaged and destroyed. Surely there is no need for this. Estelle all the Carroll families, not just here but in West Virginia must try to maintain peace. Estelle, somehow we must find a compromise."

They said no more that night and once again tried to forget these problems and remembered again the wonderful happiness they had enjoyed that day. However if Senator Abraham Lincoln inspired others to follow his lead, they knew that such a compromise would be very difficult to achieve.

But it was not just these estates which were in danger if conflict occurred, they knew it could lead to a complete disintegration of the Federal United States. It could break into two separate countries – one in favour and one opposed to slavery. Surely they must stop this happening – try to continue in future, as had happened since the Missouri Compromise had been agreed.

Even during the American War of Independence, it had been not just a war against Britain, but it was both a civil and indian war, which had torn whole families apart some as loyalists – some as rebels. However then there had been a much greater number who were against Britain than in favour. If a compromise was not found it would be very different for both sides might also have nearly equal numbers. How great then would be the bloodshed and fighting. Somehow this must not happen.

Peace was just as important to the industrial north with the cotton mills, steel works and mining. It was even more vital for the Carroll/Marshall Boat Company and its auxiliary shipping and now railway building companies. There were many descendents of Margaret Eliot and Amelia Carroll who would suffer it were to happen. What of the Eliot, Downey, and Brady families now firmly settled in Texas.

Did Donald and Rachael sitting on their patio observing the view – did Hanz and Elvira Eliot in Texas – did Gordon Taylor sailing to England or did Kurt Sand and Andrew Campbell realise that they might all become involved in the maelstrom? Even if they did, could they in any way avoid it happening?

It seemed such a civil war would tear apart so many branches of their families. They might even fight and kill each other. Like Mark and Estelle, the descendent families must, somehow work together. They must find a compromise and stop this happening. But how could they bring together so many persons separated by so many miles.

It seemed 1848 was a very dangerous year, even though the war had been won. The victory might have been disastrous for the United States. Even the discovery of gold in California, which would bring hordes of people, some very undesirable ones, into this new region. Instead of a blessing for many poor people, it might start the conflagration. Only time would tell.

PART 2

ATONEMENT

DISUNION PART 2
ATONEMENT

ATONEMENT

1.

The discovery of gold at Sutter's Fort, California in 1848 attracted first a swarm, then enormous multitude of persons from many countries, but particularly those already living in America. Many on the United States eastern seaboard took their lives in the hands by sailing on unsuitable, overloaded ships down South America, surviving Cape Horn, then back northwards to land at San Francisco.

However Donald Reid's shipping company, on the Pacific side along with the shipping company of Cornelius Vanderbilt on the Atlantic side, derived a fortune taking would be prospectors much quicker ways to the Gold Fields. Firstly on the route already established for goods and passengers, down to Panama, across the isthmus, then on Donald's ships to San Francisco. Then, an even shorter route pioneered by Vanderbilt, crossing the lakes of Nicaragua to the Pacific, to join Donald's ships again.

But even more took the now, well established route west via the Hudson, Erie canal, to the Ohio River and so to Independence, Missouri. Then to join the wagon trains, first travelling the well used routes west via Santa Fe – but now with extensions of the Oregon trail, to join the new Californian trail over the Rockie Mountains, to their goal.

Not only had they to withstand the terrible demands and hard labour of those trails, but had to survive the very real danger of indian attacks who considered these people as invaders of their land. This was the route which both Kurt Sand and the Campbell family decided to take, well aware of all its dangers, and one they wanted to begin as soon as possible, for speed was essential.

The wagon train left the next day. The beginning of their trek was easy along the valley of the Republican River and was well used so progress was good. There was no fear of Indians in this region. There only difficulties were the terrain which gradually became more warn and strewn with boulders.

When they reached the town of Republican, by a small lake, they rested long enough to replenish their supplies and enjoyed a wagon party to raise their spirits for they knew this would be the real start of their problems. Kurt had used this time from Independence and used his charms to try to captivate Agnes' attentions, with some success though he found her a more difficult conquest than usual. No doubt her recent unhappy experience contributed. He did eventually manage to persuade her to talk of the episode. Then she started to cry. "No man will ever want me. I am a dishonoured woman. You know what that means. I trusted him. I loved him. Then he rejected me. I believe you should know this for I admit I am pleased you seem to think I am worth your attention."

Kurt immediately felt sorry for her. "Don't talk silly. In Pittsburgh, the girls believe it important to sample these delights before they marry. You will find a man who cares little about these things." She looked at him. "And are you one of these men who would dishonour a girl for your pleasure?"

Kurt was surprised at her blunt approach. He was not sure how he should reply. Realising the truth was necessary he replied. "Yes. I admit I have enjoyed pleasurable relations with a few girls. I would never force them. It has always been their choice. It seems your strict upbringing tells you this is wrong. Someday you will find this is not the case."

After that night by the lake their relationship became more restrained. At times she avoided him, as much as possible in such a company. She even persuaded her brother to take a position far way from his wagon So Kurt considered he must accept defeat. Unfortunately he could not feel interested in any of the other women in the train. As he was an experienced horse rider, whenever he had the opportunity he would leave the train when it stopped to rest, to explore the surrounding plains.

His engineering experience helping his father, with the planning of roads and canals and recently the beginning of railway construction, instinctively caused him to consider possible routes for any form of communication in future. Kurt was to remember this in future years.

The wagon master, Alastaire MacLean, had warned everyone that as they were now travelling along the Platte River, they were entering the territory where both Cheyenne and Pawnee but even the Kiowa Indians roamed. A rider from the wagon train in front of them had called to warn them many Indians had been sited on each side of the trail, though none had attacked

MacLean felt they might not have sufficient strength for an all out attack. However as the Indians main prize was their horses and cattle it might involved 'cutting out' raids, aimed at the rear of the train, which was the weakest part to defend. In future the wagons would be rotated so each in turn would take up the rear position. They could only spare three outriders to defend their rear, though others could come to their assistance. In his excursions into the countryside Kurt did see several lone Indians who he thought were roaming from an encampment to the north east, but he could not see any camp. He reported his find to MacLean.

They travelled unmolested for nearly fifty miles. Then suddenly at dawn a party of twenty Pawnee's made a lightening attack on the last two wagons of the train. The three outriders were slain as was the single old man driving the rear wagon. Worse the penultimate wagon belonged to the Campbell's. Andrew was killed. instantly, by an arrow and before any one could come to their aid, the party mounted these two wagons and drove them off at speed.

It happened so quickly that there was little they could do so stop them and they quickly vanished over the horizon. Kurt's wagon, due to his estrangement with Agnes was in the centre of the train and had been powerless to intervene. To his horror he had seen Agnes and her mother attempting to fight the robbers as they drove her wagon away. He knew they had failed to prevent this, but could see they were still alive.

Kurt now blamed himself for what had happened. Perhaps if he had been in his usual position immediately behind the Campbell's, being an excellent shot he might have saved them. Now he was too late.

2.

What could they do. If they sent men to pursue them, it would leave the remainder under staffed to defend the train if attacked, but Kurt demanded they must try. He persuaded MacLean to let him lead a small party of experienced riffle men, to try to follow in a general direction, of what he thought might be the Pawnee encampment. There was no shortage of volunteers for they knew just what indian's did to white women they captured. The train would wait for them to return for two whole days before resuming their journey. MacLean remained in case they were attacked.

The tracks of the wagon made it easy to follow but they had not found them as night fell. Reluctant to waste time they proceed in the dark still following the wagon tracks. In the morning, at least they discovered the war party had camped overnight. The disturbing fact was they found pieces of women's clothes, including under garments around the burnt out fire. They could guess what this meant.

Then just after noon they saw the two wagons being driven erratically. They knew the old man had hoarded whisky in his wagon and was an inveterate drinker, twice being warned for appearing in the morning worse for wear. It seemed the war party had enjoyed themselves as they camped during the night. Kurt led the attack. The Indians were unprepared and Kurt and his men easily dispatched the twenty hostiles, killing everyone. Only then did they find the true horror of what had happened.

They found a nearly naked Agnes in her wagon holding her, equally, naked mother in her arms, sobbing violently as she cradled her body to her chest. For Margaret Campbell was dead. As they had feared both women had been repeatedly raped by the Pawnee's in an orgy of drunkenness and licentious revelry. Poor Margaret, already weak, had succumbed and Agnes was little better after her ordeal.

Although traumatised after her experience, Agnes was, desperately, trying to conceal her own and her mother's nakedness. Kurt quickly took off his long coat and wrapped it round her body as another man did the same for her mother. Kurt was rewarded by a grateful look from Agnes but felt conscience stricken as he knew he had enjoyed the sight of her barely concealed nakedness. Agnes had a truly magnificent, and desirable body.

The two Conestoga wagons, true 'prairie schooners', were still in good condition, too valuable to be discarded. So Agnes was installed, in as much comfort as possible, in her own wagon, which Kurt offered to drive whilst her mother was laid in the other. They still had enough time to drive back to the train arriving just before dawn

They were made very welcome and MacLean, who had decided to leave without them in the morning, but now agreed to wait another day. The women in the train quickly saw to Agnes' needs, bathing, soothing and attempting to ease her suffering but they could not heal her wounded mind. Margaret was buried, as Andrew, the old man and the three outriders had been buried the day before, there, on the plain with a full funeral service. This proved even more painful to Agnes.

Suddenly Kurt was caught in emotion. He had never felt like this about any woman before. They were mere recipients of his and their pleasure, except for some desire for his sister, but never fulfilled, and the girls around Pittsburgh, they had been the means be which he had enjoyed his carnal desires. Now for the first time in his life he realised Agnes meant more to him than the others. What, previously, had been a flirtation with an attractive girl – who had, virtually, rejected him – now meant much more to him.

So he put his arms around this lovely girl sobbing out her heart at the loss of her dear mother and brother. Poor Agnes was distraught and tried to divest herself of his kind embrace, turning angrily on him. "It is not fitted for you to touch me. I have been defiled by a savage, used and raped repeatedly by several of them. I may well be carrying their child. There is no future for me. I have no wish to go on living. My mother is fortunate to has not lived to learn her dishonour. I am not worthy of any persons attention. I wish I could die." Her sobbing became intense.

Kurt could not control himself. He grasped her fiercely, as she fought him, and buried his lips of her tear stained face. "Never say that. You are a wonderful girl. What has happened makes no difference to me. I want you to live – I know now that I need you – just as much as you need me. I promise I shall ensure you have every reason to live. I know you mean more to me than anyone, except my own family. Please let me help you – I want to." Agnes was still sobbing but now looked into his face. "Tell me truthfully - could any man want me - even desire me – now I have been so misused. Please do not lie to me – I am unclean – I must know?"

Kurt now kissed on the lips, kindly without passion. "All I know is that you are very desirable to me. I cannot answer for others. Please let me try to convince you. It may take time. Because of what has happened – you may reject me – I've heard this does happen to girls who have suffered as you have. I want to get to know you – properly. Before, I know I was, merely, enjoying flirting with a beautiful girl – as I confess I have done so many times before. But after yesterday – when I saw what you had been through – it was different."

He paused "After your experience it may take some time. I believe I have fallen in love with you – I want to try to make you feel you could love me the same way. We must come to know each other – see if you could accept me, as I am. For I shall never change. I told you truthfully of that many weeks ago. I know if you could accept me – I want you for my own."

Even after this she broke away from him. She turned cynically on him. "And if I've conceived that savages child – would you still want me?" Kurt refused her rejection and hugged her to him again. "I assure you that it would make no difference. I intend to prove this to you. Please give me the chance."

Agnes broke away but still held his hand. "Let us see what happens. I believe, in spite of what you told me before, you are a kind man – but at the moment – I really believe you are, merely, sorry for me. – Even this is helpful – only time will tell."

There were no more Indian attacks and they reached the fork of the Platte River and took the northern fork to Fort Laramie proceeding ever upwards often with great difficulty. The old man's wagon had been sold but Agnes agreed to keep her own wagon. Kurt paid one of the young sons of a large family on the train to drive it. Promising a substantial reward at their journey's end.

At Kurt's request Agnes travelled, side by side, in his wagon though she always went to sleep each night in her own. It did give both of them a chance to become to know each other better and soon there was genuine friendship between them. However Agnes did not tell Kurt of the nightmares she often experienced as see slept and she still could not believe he really wanted her – and that he could really love her. She must seem desirable to him. At least this was something for she feared no man would feel little about her. Then just before they arrived at the fort Agnes started getting morning sickness. The other woman confirmed her fears. She had conceived.

The day before they arrived at the fort, Agnes came to Kurt and abruptly informed him. "I'm pregnant! Afterwards I've decided, that if you still want me and are willing to provide for me – I am willing to become your mistress - I shall be prepared to conceive your children - I do not expect marriage – only a home to live in, and to keep if you find another woman" Then just as abruptly she left him amazed and confused but refused any further conversation

3.

The plan was for the train to rest there for two days to recover themselves before the hazardous climb over the mountain summit. Agnes still avoided him. At last Kurt cornered her behind the only store by which she was trying to escape from him. She even fought him as he caught hold of her and hugged her to him. "Agnes dear. For God's sake listen to me. I thought you trusted me. Weeks ago I told you I thought I loved you. Now I know I do. I don't want you as my mistress – I want you as my wife – I want this even if you cannot love me – but I hope, that given the chance, you might find you too could love me -----"

Agnes was going to interrupt and he shouted at her "Listen to me – please listen. I want to marry you and accept your baby as my own – that is if you want to keep it. ------" Now she did interrupt. "Kurt I will have to keep it. I'm not leaving the train. I cannot abort on the journey – it would cost me my life – it will be too late when we arrive – even if I went on the Sacramento – that's why if you still want me I can not make any demands on you – but I can repay you by becoming your mistress. I became a dishonoured woman in the east. Now am defiled and carry an savage's child. I shall be content if you will accept me in this way and not discard me------"

He stopped her there and buried his lips on hers. "Discard you. Darling I love you. I want you as my wife. I want you to love me. – but I warned you I can never change. If you marry me – there will be others – mistresses – but those will never replace my love for you. I cannot help it. If you are willing to accept me. You must first learn my own past – and those of my family – Please listen and be patient. I could never marry you without you knowing the type of man I am."

Behind that store still hugging her close to him he told her of both his father's and mother's adulteries. Then he shocked her further by telling her of his intimacies with the other girls with whom he had slept saying, "But I swear it was what they wanted, not expecting any permanent relationship."

He continued, "So you see the sort of man I am. I'm not ashamed – I believe I did not love these girls and neither did they love me – so I see nothing wrong in what we did. I know there may be others in the future. If so I want you to believe that my love for you – which has grown daily since the terrible days with the savages – is much greater. – and will last for ever. Darling I know I love you – and always will – but I have inherited my father's faults – and I will not change. After what I have told you could you still accept me as your husband – Dearest

Agnes, I do not lust for you. That is why I could never accept you as my mistress."

He paused again. "Before you answer I want you to know if you cannot accept me as I am. I will still not be willing to make you my mistress. Though I would not make any sexual demands on you – but I promise when we get to California – after prospecting in the diggings, I will establish you with sufficient money to see to you and your baby. I would hope we could still be friends."

Agnes was silent. She was sobbing and tears were rolling down her face. Kurt felt sure he had lost her. She had never hinted that she loved him. He admired her for this and could understand her attitude after his confession – and expecting her to accept – in advance – his future indiscretions. He knew, now, how badly he wanted her as his wife – but if so there must never be secrets between them. She must know that she would not be expected to marry him because of her plight. Still no answer came and he did not know what to say but simply continued to kiss away the tears in her eyes. At last the spell was broken.

Agnes raised her face and pressed her lips to his. "Oh! Darling! Kurt I love you – I have done so since we first met in Independence. But I knew I could never expect it from you after I told you I was dishonoured. Then my body was defiled. I could not believe you could really love me after that, though I was grateful that you did not discard me and did your best to comfort me. "

Now she smiled at him. "Dearest these last few weeks have been hell for me – though it's not your fault. You were so kind to me. I was sure you were simply sorry for me. It was wonderful but I knew it could not last. If I showed my love you would soon learn to despise me. Then I knew I was pregnant I could not expect more. However I still wanted you – That's why I offered to become your mistress – at least I would have you for a while."

She kissed him again. "Now you have confessed your faults – though you know little of mine – and I am ashamed of what I did. I do not understand your intimacies with your other girls – but you have not kept them secret from me. Andrew told me long ago that marriage for him would be difficult – he told me he could never promise to only love one woman. It seems you feel the same – darling if you will accept me – as I am – I shall love to accept you as you are. Just promise we shall never have secrets. If you find another woman – please tell me – never let me discover it by accident. I shall love you till I die – my body is yours."

There was nothing more to say. They went immediately to the captain of the fort who was empowered to marry them. His chaplain carried out the ceremony, neither had difficulty in finding a best man or bridesmaids. Before they recommenced their journey they left as Mr. and Mrs. Kurt Sand, leaving without the chance of a honeymoon – as they said – this would come later.

The rest of the journey, though very hard, was completed without further mishaps. The climb up to the south pass in the Colorado mountains was difficult. MacLean had decided to by-pass Salt Lake City to save time. Proceeding northwards to where the Oregon Trail went northwards via the Snake River. Instead they followed the new Californian Trail to the south west. It was high sierra, strewn with boulders but the gradients were reasonable, and after their climb to the pass it was much easier. They made good progress.

Kurt did not know then but this track through the Sierra Nevada mountains was one he would remember years later leading to great wealth. His training as an engineer never left him. In his mind he saw this as a possible route for roads – perhaps railways, if they were to become accepted – but not for any future canals.

Both Agnes and Kurt were deliriously happy. Her pregnancy was advancing and no longer did she suffer 'morning sickness'. Now they slept together in his wagon. Agnes discovered he was an accomplished lover, gained no doubt in his days in Pittsburgh. This did not trouble her. She was delighted to experience sexual pleasure she had never before enjoyed, certainly not with her lover in the east. He did not mind her swelling stomach and enjoyed placing his hands on it saying. "Remember this is <u>our</u> child." She knew he had accepted this. It made her happy.

Agnes also discovered the strange way men could enjoy a woman's breasts – and even before the birth they were quite firm an large. It was a rather painful squeeze of both of them but it also excited her, which more than repaid her for her suffering. For Kurt gave her the satisfaction she had never properly enjoyed with her lover in New York Agnes never complained. She considered it worthwhile. Perhaps this is what women were expected to endure if they really loved a man and wanted to enjoy full their pleasure.

By the time they reached Sutter's Fort they were both experienced lovers. But both now knew it was time to terminate their strange honeymoon. There was the business of trying to discover a gold mine of their own and a very prosperous future. But they soon found they had many competitors and more were arriving each day. It was August 1848. At least they were well ahead of the multitude that would descend on them in the coming months.

Their route was well chosen. They arrived at the site before another wagon train, that had left Independence nearly a month before them arrived, having taken the Santa Fe Trail. They all owed much to the decision made by Alastaire MacLean. He too had alighted at the fort whilst his son took the three wagons, who wanted to arrive at Sacramento, into the town, before returning to the diggings.

4.

The war with Mexico was over and the Treaty of Guadalupe had been signed in February 1948. Texas had been accepted as a new state of the United States, with the Democrat majority insisting it was admitted as a slave state, in spite of the many protestations of men like Senator Abraham Lincoln and many others in the Whig party. However it placed a number of residents of the new state in some difficulties.

These were some families which had fought in 1836 to make and establish an independent Texas from Mexico. They included the Luna, Garcia, Downey, Brady and Eliot families. All were delighted at Texas been admitted as a new state, but were not so sure if they really supported slavery. Certainly the new families, the Eliot's, Downey's and

Brady's, did not need many slaves. Their ranches were involved in horse breeding which, whilst they employed slaves both in the work and in their homes, as the numbers were small, did not need slaves and, also like the Luna's and Garcia's, they were exceedingly rich and could easily pay them for their work.

However on the cattle ranches now covering large areas of Texas, as many were of American and not Mexican extraction, wanted to retain their slaves being used to this when they lived, originally, in the United States. They often were newcomers with little wealth, coming to Texas to obtain virtually free land. This also applied to those growing cotton near the gulf. There was a good economic need for slaves if they were eventually to become rich.

Hanz Eliot and Karl Downey, were not opposed to slavery but could manage, like many of the other families, and reap rich dividends without them. In fact their consciences troubled them. At heart, they believed all people should be free. This was why they had risked their own lives to free Texas from Mexico which had been controlled by dictators. Never-the-less they were now Texans, and since the majority believed in slavery they would not oppose it. However they were well aware of the fighting in Congress about this question, particularly the orations of Senator Abraham Lincoln.

As they sat one Sunday afternoon drinking after lunch, Hanz' beloved wife Elvira said, "You know if this matter in what you call Congress, is not solved, we may all be involved in yet another war. It seems we are surrounded by so many of your southern states who would fight if attempts were made to stop slavery in their lands. – I do wish we had not joined and remained an independent country. – Surely our men must not take up arms and fight again, after what we have been through?"

Hanz smiled, "You may be right my dear, but remember Mexico still refused to accept out independence. I'm certain, in time, they would have attacked us and taken this land back as part of Mexico. Now, after the peace treaty we are safe from this." Elvira was not satisfied, "But what if war does break out. The United States army will be much stronger than even that of Santa Anna." Hanz smiled, "Yes but if so, all the southern states would stand with us and we would have to fight them together. – Still, I agree with you. – We do not want any more wars."

Now Hanz changed the subject. "Please, after the letter you received the other day from Lilie, would you like us to accept their invitation and go again to spend a month with them at Camargo?" Elvira was pleased to think about more pleasant things and laughed, "I've already spoken to Raquel and together we have spoken to Rosa and the others, if you husbands will agree with us, we would like to go, we were making arrangements to travel to Kentucky next week. – We now have plenty of trained people who can see to all our ranches for that time without any loss of earnings. You know I would like to meet Gordon and Sheila Taylor and her mother, who it seems is someway related to you."

Now it was Hanz time to laugh, "Well you really are scheming women. It seems we men will have no option but to agree that we must go there. – I suppose Karl, Tony and the others will have to obey their wife's demands, just as it seems I must do. – But I suppose after the fears we all had during the war, wondering if we would be victorious, we all deserve a little holiday. – If the others agree, I to will capitulate." So in a short time it was accepted by all, with them all taking their many children with them. So it would be a large party which descended on Kentucky.

How Hanz Eliot came to first know then fall in love and eventually persuade Elvira to marry him, is a very long story, as with similar marriage of Karl Downey to Raquel. Both men coming from their home on the cattle ranch, Camargo, in Kentucky, just seeking adventure and nothing more. How when arriving at San Marcos they discovered land very suitable for horse rearing was available at a pittance, they decided to stay.

Then each were to meet and learn to love their future Mexican wives, becoming involved in trying to curb the dictatorial dictates from the men in Mexico City, even eventually have to pit their puny forces against the Mexican General Santa Anna. Almost by luck, but possibly because of the way that evil man had seize, raped and defiled her so that she conceived his child, her daughter Adela This happened to Elvira, months before Hanz came to know her. Wanting her revenge and to kill this man, willing to sacrifice her life, if she could free her land from this monster, but she failed.

Yet perhaps the result was better than she could have imagined. For the poison did not kill him but so incapacitated him, that he and, therefore his large army were unable to plan their own defence. So a much smaller Texan army at San Jacinto, had penetrated their defences, and in only a few minutes won this great battle which they should never have won. They had captured Santa Anna and that day established Texas as an independent country.

Only years later, and not until after this last Mexican War, had they at last become a new state of the United States. Now with other relatives coming to make their life with them from their original home in Kentucky, also marrying and staying here, they now lived in some wealth on four separate ranches near to each other, all breading horses being in huge demand for them, on the many and growing cattle ranches flourishing since independence from Mexico was achieved.

So it was no surprise that all these four families and their many children wanted to return to the place of their husbands' birth on that large horse breading estates of Camargo, in Kentucky. It would not be the first time by any means that they had visited their birthplace. In fact until the last war had occurred it had happened several times in the past. However it was a little different as it seemed all four families would be travelling together, with their children,. Of course it was a long journey, and with so many children, it would need good planning. However all knew the wonderful welcome they would all receive when they arrived in Kentucky.

It seemed the men had very little to do in planning their journey. Their wives had, unknown to them, had been planning it ever since Elvira received her letter. A series of coaches would take them to Galveston, then board a ship and sail to New Orleans. There they would stay for a few nights and see the wonders of this magical city with its combined influences of French, Spanish and now American predecessors. Listen to the Soul Music of the Negroes and enjoy mid-tulips by the score.

Then boarded a Carroll/ Marshall steam boat, and sailed up the River Mississippi noticing the high levies on either side, which tried in vain to stop the river flooding, as the river flowed higher than the surrounding land, between the levies. After reaching Cairo the ship would sail up the River Ohio, which had joined it at this town. Then land at the newer city of Cincinnati, built around the old Fort Washington, a relic of the many indian wars in the past. Here an equally large bevy of coaches sent for them from Camargo, would take all of them to the estate. None of them doubted the wonderful welcome they would all receive when they arrived there.

So just one week after Elvira had dropped the bombshell on an unsuspecting husband they all left on their journey. It was as pleasant as had been planned. Few difficulties were encounted, though the length of the journey tired many of their children. Eventually they were all drawing up at the mansion of James and Lilie Downey both nearly seventy years of age. But the welcome they received from all the families at Camargo made their journey well worth while.

5.

Slavery was not the only thing that was tearing the nation apart. It seemed that religion was another reason, for many persons in the United States differed very strongly as how they should behave. The midwest, as settlers poured into the new lands opened for exploitation, were adopting a very strong evangelical form of the protestant religion. Possibly because of the great dangers they encounted every day, they believed every word that the bible told them, and lived strictly to its demands.

This was why they felt so strongly at the invasion of people of the Mormon faith into their lands, and these evangelical families became known as gentiles. As Mormons appeared to believe it was right to accept polygamous marriages, the gentiles believed these men and women were heathens. That was why they attacked them in Missouri, first at the place they call Zion, then further north, at Far West, driving them out of the state. After that the Mormons now settled at Commerce, renaming it Nauvoo, and after one of their leaders, Brigham Young, went to Britain, made over eight thousand converts and brought them by ship to live at Nauvoo, the place became virtually a city.

Yet still the gentiles were not willing to accept them, imprisoning their President Joseph Smith, only for him to be executed by a mob which descended on the jail, so Brigham Young became their leader. Realising these gentiles would never tolerate them, he was responsible for the Mormons making their amazing several thousand mile trek to establish a permanent home creating Salt Lake City in Utah.

So it seemed the gentiles had won and multiple marriages would never be accepted in the mid-west, and possibly anywhere in the east of the United States. However what they failed to understand was the religious behaviour there, particularly amongst the upper and rich classes of New York and Washington, who were now involved in another form of polygamy – though it did not actually involve multiple marriages, only the acquiescence of the men's wives to accept that their husbands would take other women, besides themselves, as mistresses.

Unlike the vast population of these cities, who were often surviving in poverty or at the best a poor level of living, as it was their lack of wealth, which prevented most from indulging in these amorous pleasures. The Campbell family, the Nolan and Ragan families had little opportunity to live that way. Only those sufficiently high in society and rich enough to indulge in these pleasures were able to follow the Mormon example, up to a point.

There was no doubt but that the wives of these important men, knew only too well the infidelities of their husbands. Even that their mistresses conceived, sometimes aborted but often bore babies to their husbands. In fact in many cases, their wives entertained their rivals to social functions, being satisfied with straying themselves and happy to find a bed companion from one of the other husbands, or other unattached men. Again if so they knew they could very easily avoid a scandal as abortion was readily available.

In quite a numbers of cases, except for the absence of a marriage ring, some families virtually copied the Mormon way of living, which at the same time they so strongly deprecated. For often their wives, either to avoid the pain and inconvenience of labour as it reduced the number of pregnancies, now expected by their husbands. So these wives were happy for their husbands to let his mistresses come and live with them – yes, often conceive his children, sparing their wives this travail.

By 1848 it was not uncommon for high society to know all about these liaisons. Of course not all of these mistresses could rely that they would be granted any permanency in their liaisons. It was really a business arrangement, profitable financially to these women. Soon they may be discarded, and supplemented by another woman though in that case any children they had born were well provided for their future after the association cease.

However in a minority of cases, the desire of these men for their extra women, and in a few cases, the actual love which was engendered between, not just the man and his mistress, but even the true love of the wives for their husband's other women. It was as near to multiple marriage as was possible but missing only the legal document which pronounced them as another wife.

In fact Patrick Purcell had learned all about these arrangements very soon after he came to live in New York and was why, unknown to either Eric or Merle, he had indulged in enjoyable intercourse with a few women at these parties, for they dare not attend because of their obvious pregnancies, which would have disgraced poor Merle

However Patrick was very concerned about Merle. He already knew she meant far more to him than just his sister-in-law. Also he had promised her he would somehow finding a way of avoiding her suffering any disgrace. An idea entered his head – but dare he even suggest this answer. He would never hurt Erin who he loved now even more than when they courted in Ireland.

Really, it was insane to think of raising the matter with Erin, particularly after she had lost her baby. A baby she knew Erin had wanted, in spite of the way in which it had been conceived. No he must not think anymore about this, but somehow persuade Merle to let Erin and he adopt her baby when it was born. Patrick knew even this would be difficult. Like Erin, Merle wanted this child. Was there any chance whatever of persuading her to give up this baby as Erin and he had proposed. Yet he knew he must confront Merle at the earliest opportunity.

6.

"You want me to give my baby to Erin", Merle replied as Patrick told her what he and Erin had planned. "I can't do that. It will be mine. I want to keep my baby. Now, I do not mind how it happened. I want it with me for ever." Patrick had expected this. "No! Dear Merle we do not want you to give up your baby. This is only a way that we can protect you from the shame of being a young girl, with a baby, but unmarried. You will continue to live with us and enjoy watching your baby grow up. You will always be here – and with us – until you find a man who you want – and is willing to accept your baby."

She was going to interrupt. "Please listen – let me explain. It will simply bear my surname – not yours. If you meet a man who you can marry, I swear, Erin and I will let you adopt it and take it with you when you leave us." He took her in his arms. "Merle dear, you are a very beautiful girl. I know you will find this man. I confessed to you the other day. If I had not found Erin – and was free – I swear I would have proposed marriage to you – even knowing what had happened. It would not have mattered – It would not have been pity. I know I love you just as much as Erin – But I cannot do this."

At last Merle was silent. She seemed to be struggling with her emotions. There was fear in her eyes. At last she sighed. "Oh! – It is terrible – You are both so kind to me. I will never want to hurt either of you – But after baby is born – I cannot stay here – somehow I must get away – and take baby with me – there must be a way."

Neither Patrick nor Erin could understand her. It was Patrick who replied. "Leave us – why – we both want you to remain with us and cherish you.. We could not bear for you to leave us until you find a man – and I swear, again, whatever you may think – There will be such a man. A man who will love you just as much as I. One free to marry you and give you a home."

This did not help and he could see she was struggling how she could reply. Eventually with tears running down her face she placed her hands on her sister's. "Erin dear, I love you terribly. I cannot hurt you – you mean so much to me. – but you must know – I have fallen, hopelessly, in love with Patrick – that is why I must leave as soon as I find a way – If I stay here I will hurt you and I will not do this." Erin was amazed at her admission that Merle was in love with her husband but, she still wanted to help her. and told her so by placing her hands on her lips. kissing them..

Merle though still sobbing, smiled at her, before, like Erin she kissed her hands. "Erin Dearest. We both suffered together on that terrible day when they dishonoured us. The pain was terrible as they ravaged our bodies, then we conceived. I knew that in spite of this, like me, you wanted your baby, and found Patrick wanted it too. I know what you suffered when you lost it."

She paused then kissed their hands again. "But dearest, you have told me, that with Patrick's help you learned to enjoy intimacy – just as we had been told. I was so glad this was possible. - But now I'm six months pregnant – yet have never known these things. Like you, I long to give myself to a man - a man who wants me to enjoy him as much as he wants me. – Erin. It is terrible, I love Patrick – I want him to do those things to me which he does to you. When you are well enough I'm certain you will want him to give you another child."

Now she really broke down sobbing violently, they could hardly hear her words. "I want to keep my child – I want to learn to enjoy intimacy – before and after it happens – but I know there is only one man with whom I want this to happen – I know there is only one man – and he is Patrick. So can you understand why I must leave for I could never steal him from you."

Patrick had remained silence listening to Merle's confessions. He knew she was offering herself to him. He also knew that one woman would never be enough for him. He had, already, been unfaithful to

Erin, without her knowing. It would occur again. But with Merle, as much as he desired her, it was different. He did love her – yes, as much as he loved Erin. If Merle stayed he knew what would happen, and it would break Erin's heart. He loved her too much for this to happen.

They looked at each other not knowing what to say. Finally Erin hugged Merle to her. "Merle, I want you to stay, in spite of what you have said. Please go an rest. Patrick and I must find a solution – there must be a way – please let us see if we can find it."

Still without hope and very sad, Merle thanked them. Before she left she only said. "I feel so ashamed. I hope I may die when I give birth. It will be a blessing." After she left they both knew they must find a solution, They knew her religion would stop her committing suicide but they both feared what her state of mind would be as she went into labour. In any case, Merle had not agreed to registering her baby as theirs.

Merle stayed in her room for the remainder of the day and refused the food they sent to her. In her absence they talked together trying to find a solution but could not find one. In bed that night, although Erin was still a little weak for intercourse, she did enjoy, Patrick's loving exploration of her body, even without passion. Erin thought. 'Poor Merle, how much she wants this, yet it is denied to her.'

Suddenly Erin sat up, surprising Patrick, thinking she was unwell. "Patrick, tell me truthfully, would you like to do these things to Merle." Patrick hugged her to him. He knew just how much he loved her, and could not cause Erin pain. But he had to reply.. "Yes dear. Though I'm ashamed, I confess I would like it – but I love you too much to hurt you – or Merle. You see though she is a very desirable girl – well – no - it is not that – You see she is right – I do love her – I could never hurt or despoil her it would be too cruel – not after what she has already – and is still – suffering."

Erin sighed, unsure of herself. "If you wanted – I – I - would be willing to share you with her." – Then after an even longer sigh – "Yes! Even let you give her babies – It would be a solution – If she agreed, – she could be your mistress. Your men friends do this with their wives knowledge – I love Merle so much. I want her to be happy – I want her to stay with us. I want her to go on living. Please let us try and see if she would be willing."

The next morning when Merle still failed to appear for breakfast Erin placed a note under her bedroom door, begging her to come downstairs. Still desperately ashamed Merle dressed and came down to face them, relieved to find they were both smiling. Erin ran to welcome her. Patrick left her to explain. "There may be a way, though it may make you, even more ashamed. I've told Patrick I love him and I love you just as much. I've told him I am willing to share him with you – in every way – Yes, even him giving you babies – If that is what you want – But he can never marry you so long as I'm alive. You would have to be willing to become his mistress – just as other wives now accept this. I would be glad to do this."

Now Patrick went on to explain. "Erin knows – for I've told her – I love you both. I don't want you just because you are so desirable – You may not understand – I love you just as much – in the same way – as I love Erin. You know the Mormons believe this is possible. Though you would be known as my mistress – You have a different name to Erin – so it is possible. – However I should always regard you as my second wife – I would treat you, equally. Could you accept this?"

Merle's face lit up. She turned to Erin. "Could you really accept me in this way. I could never be jealous of you – Could you not be jealous of me." Erin hugged her more closely. "Yes dearest. I can. Listen. If you agree, you must first discover if you really want Patrick – you must sleep with him. I cannot do my duty as a wife, at present. You must see if you wanted to live with him, just as a wife, and for as long as you live. After what you have suffered you may find you hate intimacy – with any man. You must know how you, really, feel – before you bare your child."

Merle had no doubt. She wanted to go on living with the man she loved, and always, would. Merle did not mind becoming Patrick's mistress. The stigma meant nothing to her – not even the fact she would be sinning. Her only question was to Erin. "Could you agree to me giving him babies – the babies I long for, after this child is born?"

When Erin assured her she would not only accept, but expect it, if she was to become a second wife.

The same night Merle gladly entered his bed. In spite of her terrible experience she found she could submit to his embrace, not even drawing back as he entered her pregnant body. His skill ensured she achieved satisfaction for the first time in her life – so much better than those she had known to please herself. In the morning both Patrick and Erin knew they had solved the problem. Now Patrick had two sisters to love and be intimate with him. He knew he would never know which one he loved the most.

7.

"You know Michael when we freed our slaves in our combined Annapolis house, most of them are quite old, I think we should consider letting them retire with a little money. They and the forebears have served us well for very many years." Sharon Casimir was speaking to her forty three year old husband Michael Casimir, great, great grandson of the famous Michael Casimir and now bore his name.

The Casimir's from Poland and the Holstein's from Sweden, had landed together from the same ship which had brought all their rich families from Europe, coming not from persecution, but from the fear of war between Russia and Prussia. With their wealth the two families had established themselves in mansions in the upper Potomac valley, as well as purchasing several other estates in West Virginia.

The families had all prospered, and were pleased to help many families in the past. In fact the elder Michael Casimir was really responsible for enabling a prostitute from Bristol, who Michael felt was the reincarnation of his original girl friend Clara, who had killed herself after Michael's family had refused their sons permission to marry her. Even if this was not the case, he managed to provide a settled and prosperous life for Clare Collins ensuring her eventual marriage to a rich widower, Philip Wycks.

His eldest son, Eric Casimir, who like his father, besides becoming a Senator in Congress, though a protestant, had married Roman Catholic Isabel Bacon. Then with his father had established the Casimir/Holstein Bank and associated this bank with the Bank of Manhattan. Neither changed their faith, marrying in each of their churches and brought up their children to understand each of their religions, leaving them to chose later how they should worship.

This practice had been one of the benefits of the constitution of the United States, allowing complete freedom of worship. It had continued in the marriage twenty years before as the present Michael Casimir, also a protestant, when he married the Roman Catholic Sharon Bacon great, great granddaughter of Sheila and Kenneth Bacon, who had been staunch Catholics. In fact this was behind Sharon's reason for speaking to her husband today.

"I'm sure the Holstein's will agree to this, I had a word with Joanne last week. She very much approves of my suggestion, even though Philip and Joanne are strong protestants." Sharon had continued to interest her husband in her plans. For like them the Holstein's were continuing the friendship which the original Holstein's had with the original Casimir's.

Seeing her husband was interested she went on, "I've told you many times how sorry I am for those many Irish Roman Catholic's fleeing from impoverishment in Ireland with the potato famine, many starving to death, only to receive barbaric treatment when they arrive in Boston or other American ports. – If you will agree I believe we should try to take a family just landing in New York and persuade them to replace our slaves in our town house."

Michael smiled for he still could not understand his wife's strong Catholic's beliefs. He said, "And just what Philip and Joanne think of the idea – you know it is a joint holding, given to both our families by Eric and John when they died? It was a place very dear to them for it enabled them to live intimate lives with Isabel and Hillary when both their parents disapproved of their conduct, simply because of their different religions."

71

Now it was time for Sharon to smile. "Joanne fully approves – you know she was a Wicks before she married Philip – and like us believe in freedom of worship. Joanne feels the same as me that those devils in Boston are persecuting the arrivals simply because they are Catholics."

Michael laughed, "You know I can still not understand your entrenched belief in Catholicism - but I know you will always love me and I was even astonished when you accepted my proposal – but as we agreed then, you have kept your promise, all our children have chosen what to believe. Just as Isobel and Hilary did so long ago."

Now he took Sharon into his arms, hugged her to him and kissed her passionately. "If that is what you want then I most certainly will agree. In any case I feel as strongly as you and deplore the entrenched protestant beliefs of those living in our New England states. – They are still mainly puritans. They have little to be proud of – their ancestors even burned women alive, claiming they were witches. You noticed it was women they mainly burnt. – Sharon, if it is what you want – go to New York and see what you can do, I will make sure Philip will approved as well as Joanne."

There was no need for haste and Sharon was delighted that Michael had accepted. Taking the man she loved to her, threw her arms around him, pressing her still attractive forty year old body strongly against his then whispered in his ear, "Come darling –You always seem to pander to my whims – I think it is high time I rewarded you for your patience with me. – Please take me upstairs now – I want you ---Though I'm sorry to say I do not today want to add to our family – perhaps another day."

After that, there was only one answer. Just as he had done after they had returned from their honeymoon in the Caribbean, so long go, he picked her delightful body in his strong arms and carried her slowly up those large circular stairs and into their bedroom, locked the door and, then laid on her on the bed. Then he showed her just how much he loved her.

Almost in a dream she surrendered her body to him, thinking again of the many hours she had enjoyed in his embrace. However she knew it was not just her love for him but his patience and his understanding of her religious preferences. Again today, she knew he only wanted to please her but, also, had admitted his own dislike of what was happening to these Irish immigrants landing in a new country with little resources, and many ill and starving. It seemed their religious differences even brought them closer together, for they both had ensured it would in no way alter their happy lives, or the way they lived.

Though a strong Catholic she still felt disgust at the way her predecessors had behaved. For Sheila and Kenneth Bacon as well as the Mowbray's, had for so long refused to sanction the marriages of Eric to Isabel and John to Hilary. Sharon knew their histories. It was only because of the threats from this man Daniel Carroll, who so many persons talked about, threats to withhold their wealth after the war with Britain, that forced them to let the marriages take place. Their women were already very pregnant by them and had refused to consider aborting their children.

Much as she was a catholic she could never understand why two persons who worshipped differently should not be allow to marry. If this foolishness had continued Sharon would not now be enjoying these wonderful intimacies with the man she loved so passionately, and who once again had acceded to her requests. This man who made life worth living and who had given her so many lovely children.

The next day she left in their coaches and were driven to New York. Sharon needed to be prepared to transport any number of persons she might hire to become the staff for their Annapolis household. She knew her particular requirement were female servants though she would gladly appoint on trial, a man and his wife to act as housekeepers. She had no need to employ coachmen or grooms as their freed negro slaves who at present did this task, were still young enough and asked to stay in these positions.

Arriving at the city she alighted from her coach, and leaving the others under one coachman to guard them, sailed with two others to Staten Island, then to the immigration buildings. Sharon then watched just as a new ship from Liverpool drew up alongside the large quay, between the many other ships off loading at the same quay, in this large port. Sharon watched as the almost countless queues of humanity,

73

obviously in a bad state after their long and perilous sail, staggered drunkenly down that gangway, glad to once again stand on firm dry land.

Sharon felt amongst this multitude there must be at least one family who would be delighted to come and work for her and staff their Annapolis home so that their present freed slave staff could enjoy, at last, a well earned retirement.

8.

The Nolan and Ragan families felt relieved they had survived that terrible journey. Not caring that they were treated almost like cattle as they were led into the immigration buildings. The females were separated from the men and had to form a very long queue. For evidently their first task was a quick medical assessment to discover if they were ill and carried any diseases which may be contingence. In fact several were found to be this way and unceremoniously were quickly removed to be sent to the quarantine buildings set aside for this reason.

This took a long time but at last they all reappeared and were united as a family once again. However this was only the start of their ordeal. Now, in turn, they were led to another section and as a family, they were sternly interrogated by port officials. It took a long time and again they had to form queues before being led to the interrogating officer.

They were all treated, almost as criminals, questioned about everything in their past lives. They had to swear on the bible that they had not left Ireland because of a crime and fear of discovery. This same question was raised again many times during their interview. Their place of birth and age were recorded, as well as their religion, though, as expected, they like the others arriving, most were all Roman Catholics.

As they each waited for this treatment, at least tables had been set aside against the wall of the building with food, of a kind, and drinks were available free of charge. Half starving as they had been the whole time on the ship, it mattered little to them that the food was not of a very high quality. In fact to both the Nolan's and the Regan's, it tasted like a feast.

At last their first questioning was over. Then the two families, desperate not to be separated, were led to another room where more persons, but later they found these were volunteers, who genuinely were concerned for their well being. These kind people tried hard to tell them of the opportunities in New York, admitting there were not many, but where they may find temporary habitation, however of a very basic nature and a very overcrowded kind. Finally they were warned of the unscrupulous people who would promise them many things but were only wanting to use them and steal whatever they had from them. They were called 'runners' and once they had conned them and got their trust could lead the female members into a life of prostitution in the many brothels in the city.

These kind people now gave each of them a very small amount of American money to help tidy them over the first two days of their stay. Later they found it was from the subscription funds they had accumulated for this purpose from the various religious and civic societies, for distribution to needy people, arriving from Ireland. Still they all knew, at least they would have enough to live on for the first two days, during which time they all knew they must not only find where to live, but also see what work was available.

There is no doubt that both families were disappointed. As they talked together on the ship coming over they had hoped that in the United States, they might have found people more ready to help their plight than what they had received in both Ireland and Britain. It now seemed from their reception and their coming was not what the people of New York wanted. They were outcasts. Only the few who had been so kind to them today had given them any charity.

Very sadly they now followed the hundreds into the large reception hall where they could see what was on offer and where they might, at least, find a place to sleep. There were several well dressed persons circulating through the crowd holding placards offering one thing or another. After their warning they wondered how many of these were the 'runners' about which the dear voluntary ladies had told them. They were perplexed, wondering just what they should do.

At this moment as Devin was leading them, he was almost accosted by two young men, reasonably dressed, one of whom was holding a placate which read in large letters 'IDLE' – then below 'Irish Democratic League Executive'. It seems to all of them that these two men might in fact be persons wanting to help them simply because they were Irish. So when they spoke kindly to Devin with a proposal the two families were very willing to listen.

They offered to take them all on behalf of the Manhattan Lodge of the Democratic Party of the United States into Manhattan to accommodate them, temporary, and then tell them where they might look for employment to keep themselves in this large city. Of course they were interested and all might, at that time have accepted their offer, except for at that very moment a negro in the uniform of a coachmen. came up to them from behind, bringing with her a very well dressed lady.

This man assisted by the lady spoke to both Arin and Delma telling them that his mistress wished to speak with them. As Devin listened to what the two men were offering the lady spoke most kindly to the two women, first introducing herself. "Dear ladies, I am Sharon Casimir and I am at the moment trying to find persons who might wish to enter my employ and staff the large mansion we hold in the City of Annapolis, a little distance from where you are. Frankly I'm only really interested in female staff, to replaced the slaves we have freed from their servitude and now I wish to give them a happy retirement. – They disserved this as they have catered so well for us for many years."

Now she asked, "Are you one large family?" It was Delma who replied, "No, my husband and my two daughters, Camay and Maeve, make up our family and we are called Nolan's. Arin, here, is a widow, and hers include Devin, who is speaking to the two men at the moment. This is her daughter Ellis, and they are called Regan's. – But I can speak for all of us, neither of our two families would wish to be separated, as we have established a firm friendship on the ship."

Sharon smiled, "Then this is a great difficulty, for as I said, the vacancies in the household are for female staff." – She paused for a moment then continued, "Mrs. Nolan, since you are obviously the right age I want, I believe I would be willing to accept you and your husband, as a team. To both act as housekeepers and your husband to be the doorman and possibly the butler for the house. But I, definitely, have no vacancy for your friend Arin's son, Devin."

As expected his created a serious problem and both Delma and Arin were in considerable difficulties as to what they should do. The offer this woman was making them seemed like a gift from heaven. At least they would have a roof over their head, and would be fed and receive wages sufficient for them to survive. However, naturally, they could not leave poor Devin, alone and uncared for. They interrupted his long conversations with his two men, telling him the position.

They were surprised for it seemed this might solve his own problem, for he had learned that it was he who these two men wanted to recruit, though they would take the others with them and leave them to find work for themselves. Of course Devin, though he liked what they had offered him, would never have left the others to an unknown fate. Now it seemed this lady might solve his problem.

Devin laughed, then said, "Mother and Mrs. Nolan, you must all accept this wonderful offer and accept employment in Annapolis. I will gladly, stay here in New York and go with these two men. But before we part I must ask this lady for the address in Annapolis, for once I'm settled I know I shall want to come to you there, and meet again my dear, Camay."

Camay who had been listening throughout to the various conversations was appalled at the thought of being separated from her new boy-friend. Yet she knew her mother must accept for the benefit of both families. To Sharon's pleasure, an agreement was accepted, and five women, with Case Nolan, left with Sharon and her coachman to cross to Manhattan and then board the waiting coaches to take them all to Annapolis. Whilst Devin left with the two Irish men, also to sail to Manhattan, but then to be separated.

However before they arrived at Manhattan, Devin had taken Camay in his arms and kissed her passionately, "Camay dear, I will come to you. I promise. Soon I may have found a good job and have enough money to come to see you regularly. – You know I do want this." Camay responded just as lovingly, "Oh! Please Devin – Do come – I do want to be with you – and perhaps we may find we might want to spend even more time together – Please do not forget me."

So they parted. It seemed that they all, at least for a time, had found a way to stay alive in this new country. The situation was very different from what it had seemed only two hours before. But Camay wondered if Devin would keep his promise. She knew there must be many other girls of his age in Manhattan. Worse they would live there but she would be many miles away, - she did not know how many, – but they must be quite a distance. She thought, 'Devin will you really come and call on me?'

9.

Meanwhile Kurt Sand and Agnes had arrived at the diggings near Sutter's Fort, realising they must now begin a very hard life, worse than on the past journey. As Kurt had expected from the news which had reached them, most prospectors were 'panning' the river, in which the original gold had been discovered. He choose an unoccupied spot, which seemed promising and registered a claim. Agnes, in spite of her pregnancy, was anxious to assist. More to arrest suspicion he showed her what to do and left her knee deep in water searching in the running waters.

Kurt had other ideas. With his excellent knowledge of geology he had studied the few maps showing some of the outcrops in the area. These maps had shown, though they were few and not necessary accurate, but were sufficient to give him an idea. He knew the whole Sierra Nevada mountains had resulted from the massive mountain building epoch of what geologists called the Tertiary Period. The gold in the river must be coming from hidden veins in the surrounding hills. His task was to find these mother veins.

He guessed they would occur in outcrops probably where violent movements in the past had excreted molten granite rocks between the limestone and sandstone of which the hills were made. Leaving Agnes at her task he set our alone into the hills, returning from time to time to see Agnes. It was a laborious task. Then at the end of October he struck lucky. He knew it was not a rich vein but its potential was superior to the results of panning.

Fortunately as his father's apprentice, he understood explosives, and had brought them with him on his wagon. Ensuring no one was in the vicinity he exposed the cleft. The broken rocks contained veins of gold. It would take hard work to separate this from the rock as he did not have the chemicals, nor the plant, to dissolve away the metal. He needed Agnes to help, and at least prepare his food, so he returned to the river.

He had become very friendly with the Stewart family, whose young son had driven Agnes wagon over the mountains. Agnes had been more successful in the sight his experience had chosen, rather than the area they had registered. They had four sons and were barely panning enough gold to keep them alive. He came to an agreement with them, to give them a half share in his river claim, to pan there along with their own site. He even gave them a little money to prevent them starving. This removed any suspicions when he took Agnes into the hills managing to drive his wagon near to the foot of his new find.

They both worked through the winter, without stopping, to separate the broken rocks which he had dynamited. He even widened a cave to live in during the worse weather, but by February Agnes was well advance in her pregnancy. They had, already, collected enough gold to see to their own needs for several years. Now they had wealth if not excessively rich.

Having opened the area and found further veins proving the potential of his find, he took Agnes in his wagon into Sacramento, deposited his gold in the bank, registered his claim and bought a small house in which Agnes could deliver her child. Now the gold rush was in earnest and thousands were arriving each day. Knowing he could not hope to keep his find secret much longer, and might be stolen, he looked for other ways of disposing it.

With his new found wealth and the letters of credit from his father he approached a small mining firm which had been established to capitalise on the miner's finds. Taking them to his own site he went into partnership with them. In future they would develop the find, for several years. Together they set up a store and warehouse selling mining implements and machinery as well as enlarging his original finds. By the following spring Kurt Sand was a rich and prosperous business man in the Sacramento fraternity

Before Mexico had succeeded their territory to the United States, giving away California, New Mexico and the other territories, the Mexican families on the haciendas were rich and prosperous farmers. Now there were no one to defend them. The lawless gangs were pillaging and burning many homes of, previously, prosperous Mexicans, even occupying their land.

In the summer a group of these renegades invaded Sacramento and took over a section of the town close to their warehouses. They had plundered a nearby rich hacienda, looting it, and killing most of its inhabitants. Now they were enjoying their new acquired wealth in the town. As Kurt's warehouse was near and in danger, he sent his bodyguards, assisted by those of his colleagues into town. After a fierce street battle the entire gang was destroyed.

They liberated a number of girls who had been their prisoners, and who they had viscously misused. Most were local saloon girls but they discovered the daughter of the hacienda, Anita Madero, a well bred girl of nineteen and her maid Ella Motiva, in a serious conditions. Both had been severely beaten and raped many times. They were, barely, alive. They were brought to Kurt's house for medical attention.

Agnes, having suffered viscous rape, was only too pleased to help them. She and her servants saw to their wounds, bathed and dressed them. After a doctor's attention, they were allowed to rest and recover. Both girls were in a critical state for several days but with care they eventually recovered. Kurt and Agnes knew they must learn more of their predicament and what had happened, for them to result in their terrible ordeal.

Before then, in late March, Agnes had safely delivered her child. It was a daughter, who to her delight, Kurt registered as Fiona Sand. Fortunately she showed little of her indian parentage, with a light skin and black hair. Only her beautiful brown eyes showed any of her possible lineage. The love Kurt bore to her daughter, treating her as much as if it was his, ensured Agnes would love her husband to the end of her life, no matter might be his future infidelities.

By the next spring, Kurt had written to his father and given him a minor share in their new company, Sacramento Mining. He had sold his first house and moved to a new mansion on the edge of town, as the town had become lawless. California was not, yet, a state There was no real legal authority. Worse the gold rush had brought with it the dregs of humanity where no one was safe. That was why it had been necessary for Kurt to employ several men, as did his colleagues, to defend his new home and the warehouses in the town.

Kurt felt that Agnes, as a woman was the person to make these inquires. So it must be Agnes who must be able to persuade them to confess their ordeal. She quickly persuaded Anita to tell her about herself. Anita was the only daughter of her father, Adolfo Madero, but her mother had born four sons. It seemed the gang when they descended on the hacienda, virtually undefended, had murdered all her family – her mother, father and her four brothers having already killed all the servants in the house.

Because of their wish to enjoy Anita's body, she had been spared death but she was taken with her maid, Ella, into the town, to suffer an even worse fate. Anita told Agnes she had no wish to live. Only her religion prevented her from committing suicide. She had been defiled and raped so frequently by numerous men that she felt certain she had conceived, now she was sorry that the effects of her misuse had not killed her.

Ella had suffered similarly to her mistress but she had known men in the past and even the thought she may have conceived, it did not drive her to despair. She had miscarried two years ago and felt sure some man would want her. She was, however, completely loyal to her mistress and wished to stay with her.

Agnes and Kurt promised they would look after them and that they could stay with them for as long as they liked, but Anita, though grateful had no wish to live. Agnes, though she knew Anita would never kill herself, was afraid her mental condition would ensure she gradually lost interest and would die simply by neglect. When in fact it was certain that Anita, unlike Ella, was pregnant, she now refused to eat, hoping she would die.

Up to now Agnes had never told anyone about her defilement by the Pawnee's. Unable to convince Anita that she was still a desirable woman, decided to confide in her, realising it was the only way, if only to prove she could have a happy future, in spite of what has happened. So she brought baby, Fiona, into Anita's bedroom as an excuse for visiting her.

10.

The Texan families had enjoyed a rapturous reception after they arrival at Camargo. Used to riding around their Texas ranch they enjoyed to the full the vast and beautiful landscapes of Kentucky with its luxurious acres of green grass. Of course the originators of the Camargo estate were now well advanced in age, but, in the main were healthy and still quite active. However by now the running of the combined establishment had long since been given to their many sons and daughters, each with their many homes erected on the spacious land of their estate.

How this land became to be occupied was in itself a very long story. How it was discovered by James and Stuart Downey along with Paul Eliot after they had managed to find and rescue two girls Lilie Garner and Helga Feld from an indian encampment to which they had been taken by these Miami Indians. This was after they had ravaged their small township of Anderson, where most of the inhabitants had been murdered.

For over two years these poor girls had to suffer rape and conceived by their indian captors living as their white squaws each bearing daughters to their captors. The reason for their eventual deliverance was firstly when the United States army with an even larger numbers of militia had defeated the indians after the 'Battle of the Fallen Timbers'. James, Stuart and Paul were the part of that militia which had ensured the victory.

Yet the very reason why these men were there to achieve this success was simply because some years earlier they had discovered, when part of an earlier militia, Lilie and Helga, living in the community of Anderson. Unknowingly at that time it seemed that James and Paul had committed a discretion – one which they had unknowingly transgressed. It seemed they had been forced to leave as it was felt they had made unacceptable attacks on these girls, though they felt they had not done anything wrong, but only what they had been used to doing with their previous girl friends in the Potomac valley.

The damage done they had left realising their inability to speak German prevented them explaining their behaviour. In spite of this, as time past the two men had known that their feelings for both Lilia and Helga was far greater that just a desire for a flirtation, Hoping in future to return again to Anderson and then be able to explain their conduct they had used this time to learn German.

To their horror they had learned of the indians destruction of the community. Yet, somehow they could not believe these two girls would be killed as they knew of the indians practice of seizing women and using them for their pleasure. Perhaps it was a forlorn hope but it was one they believed possible. So after the army, which they had not joined, had suffered another severe defeat by the indians and then an officer from their first militia wrote requesting them to join yet another militia. As the intention this time was to destroy all indian power in the region, perhaps, without hope they agreed to join.

This was why they had been able to acquit themselves so well and ensure victory. Afterwards with the officers blessing, were given the opportunity of searching the indian villages for the women they had come to like, still believing they might be alive. It was a miracle they achieved their mission and were then able to persuade very willing Lilie and Helga, along with their indian girl, Pohanna, and to bring them to a new life in their home near Fort Cumberland. On that way home they had discovered this lovely acres of green grass near Winchester.

Later they had returned now married to Lilia and Helga with Stuart also married to Pohanna, along with two other recently married couples of David and Monica Downey, with Stuart and Antoinette Brady. In fact Antoinette was a French high born émigré whilst Monica was the daughter of the very famous Daniel Carroll It was these five couples who were responsible for establishing this, now, extremely wealthy horse breading ranch of Camargo so many years before.

In fact those many Texans who had come to visit them included the sons of these original five families. In the past they had gone to Texas originally for adventure, settled there and married, becoming involved in establishing Texas and freeing it from Mexico. It was only natural these men had wanted to return to visit their families, but they were even more pleased that their Mexican wives were, equally, anxious for this visit.

However another reason for their visit was that now Texas was a slave state and knew that Kentucky, in the main opposed slavery, they wondered what would be their position if the war Elvira Eliot had feared might happen. As expected the residents of Camargo where completely opposed to slavery. So if a war did occur it seemed their large family may well be fighting on opposite sides., for they felt they must support Texas, even though they had no strong desire to retain slavery.

This was the main reason why they all had felt they should come together and see if there was a solution to the problem, apart from the joy of spending a wonderful holiday together. However, first, they would enjoy their reunion before they indulged in their other discussions.

Of course they were pleased to learn that Louisa and Anton Albrecht were still alive, though now over seventy years of age, and were still living in Tennessee but even happier to meet again Neil and Patricia McLean. Again Patricia, a Brady before she married, was a distant relative having a common ancestor in Margaret Eliot born in Ireland in the seventeenth century.

Neil and Patricia were now living on a much smaller horse breading ranch near to Camargo, settling there after their daughter, Sheila had married her second husband Gordon Taylor. However they learned they would not have a chance of meeting again Gordon and Sheila, as it seemed they had gone to England for Sheila to be introduced to his parents in Manchester. Now soon they must sit together and see if they could decide what they should do if the war they hoped would not occur became a reality.

11.

Gordon Taylor and his family had set sail from New York and arrived in Britain at Liverpool, in early 1848. They were met on the quay by Gordon's elder brother James Taylor and his wife. Maureen as well as his sister Elizabeth and her husband Stewart Mosley. Then they boarded the train to Manchester, Gordon reminding Sheila this was the railway line he had helped to build, over twenty years before. Then coaches were there to take them to the Taylor residence in upper class Moss Side. This would be their base whilst they stayed in England.

It was a very happy reunion for Gordon to be once again with his English family in which he had been raised. Like him they had become quite prosperous, helping in the construction of many more railways but more in fabricating locomotives for many lines. Their business was now wealthy enough to provide a reasonably comfortable life for all their families, each now with a house to themselves but near to where James and Maureen lived.

Of course they made Sheila extremely welcome, even commiserating on her terrible life whilst married to Simon Doyle. For their children it seemed they had entered another world for in Manchester, and what they saw on their journey here, was very different from around Pittsburgh. Gordon took all of them around this rapidly growing city, even showing them the place where Roy Marshall had burnt down that cotton mill.

However much had changed since he had left Manchester. Near to where they were staying they saw Owens's College now becoming the Victoria University of Manchester. But there were many other places. The Rochdale Canal which pierced Manchester, the Mechanics Institute where Gordon had qualified, and of course the magnificent Cathedral by the River Irwell. It was time of re-discovery for Gordon as much as his family.

Open country was still very near and they took coach rides southwards through the small villages of Fallowfield, and Didsbury. Travelling even as far as the tiny town of Wilmslow, near the border with Cheshire. Yes! In spite of the growing cities of Liverpool, Manchester and Salford, there was still much lovely countryside to enjoy by the River Mersey,

One evening after they had dined James had asked, "Do you ever intend to come back and live here?" Gordon shook his head, "No! Never, we all love where we live. Life in the United States is very different from life here. In fact I think it would shock everyone of you being so strong Methodists, if you were to realise the number of men and women who may live together for many years, but never marry. In no way are they castigated for their behaviour. My wonderful Charlotte Marshall, who though a woman, is a fully trained engineer and with her husband own the many businesses of which I am a minor director, admits she lived with Roy for many years before they married even baring his child."

There was no doubt by that both James and Maureen were very shocked but Gordon laughed adding, "Believe me it happens many times – the country is so vast – life there is totally different than in Britain. In fact in New York and Washington most of the prosperous men take several mistresses some even living in the same house as their wives. I believe this is not unknown, here, in London."

But his family were anxious to see as much of England as they could, especially to go to London. With the new railway, this was very easy and through James and others business friends who had informed them of the importance of Gordon Taylor, who was building new railways in the United States. So they travelled first class in a special carriage attached to the train with areas to rest and even sleep. So they arrived in London in style.

They spent nearly a fortnight in London, staying at the new railway hotel of Charring Cross, near to the London station. From there Gordon ensured his whole family saw all there was to see, such as the Tower of London, the many large markets, the Houses of Parliament and of course both Saint James and Buckingham Palace.

They were all enchanted by the River Thames and enjoyed sailing on its winding river. On a lovely day they sat in the sun in Hyde Park and fed the swans. However the places Gordon was, particularly, anxious to see were the now, many London Railway Stations, including Euston, Kings Cross and Paddington.

The latter was the beginning of the new Great Western Railway finally constructed only seven years before, as far as Bristol in the west. The handiwork of the amazing Isambard Brunel. What fascinated Gordon was that this line had a very different and very large gauge, the distance the two lines were apart. This was seven feet whereas all the other lines, and even those Gordon constructed, were of the standard gauge of four feet eight and a half inches.

In fact it had recently caused great difficulties, because whenever this railway met another line in any town there could be no transfer of locomotives between these lines. An act of Parliament had forbidden any further lines to be built unless it was of the standard gauge to ensure compatibility. Though Brunel had opposed this, he had to concede and at present was installing and extra line at the correct gauge in between his other lines.

To test this unusual line Gordon took his family on a return journey to Bristol and back. Afterwards even Gordon had to admit that the journey was far more comfortable than on the other railways and felt sorry they were not to be the one accepted. However in America he knew he must conform to the standard gauge, simply because this was what was expected.

At last they all returned to Manchester to complete their holiday, enjoying a reunion of the families and even going short journeys on the other railways being constructed now so rapidly. It seemed their holiday had been one of sampling what England had to offer in way of railway transport. Of course whatever the railway on which they travelled, they always received first class accommodation.

It was whilst they stayed in London they heard of the discovery of gold in California. Also it seemed that many persons, who had enough money for the journey were leaving Britain to travel to America with the one idea of finding a route to the gold fields. But this was happening all over Europe, and not everyone travelling west were of the best behaviour. Gold attracted the dregs of society as Kurt Sand had discovered when Anita and Ella had been kidnapped and raped.

Though at that time Gordon did not know it, he did wonder if Kurt had arrived at the gold fields and if he might have been successful, for he liked Kurt Sand and wished him well. Then Gordon realised that if he was successful Kurt might one day carry out his promise to build a railway, right across the United States. Gordon knew if so like Kurt, he must involve himself in this project.

However it was now time to leave and return to America and earn his salary there. So after a very large final dinner with all the families eating together, it was time for them to be escorted to Liverpool and board another ship to return to America. Everyone were present as they went on board and there were many tears from everyone.

However they had promised to return again one day, and their English families had, also, promised, one day to cross the Atlantic and visit them. However, sad as she felt in leaving Britain Sheila whispered in Gordon's ear. "You are soon to become a father again." Sheila had got her wish she had conceived by Gordon during their stay. So the child when born but be a little British, as well as an American. It was now late 1848.

Yet Gordon and Sheila were not alone on that ship for they had persuaded a twenty one year old son of his sister, Elizabeth, and her husband Stuart, a young man called Alan Mosley, to return with them. Alan was a very well qualified engineer and worked on several of the new railways being constructed in England. Gordon knew he would be a great asset to him, and be capable of taking charge of the new lines in which Gordon was engaged. He had promised him a good salary and would be given site management when he arrived. Alan was delighted to come as he had no girl friend of a permanent nature and Gordon had assured him there were many unattached women in America.

It had been a very important year in the history of the United States. However so many problems still awaited all of them, slavery, religious bigotry which was tearing the whole country apart, just as quickly as it was expanding in size. It seemed that so many families, including the many descendents of the Carroll's but many more not related to them had, perhaps unknowingly, been trying to accommodate to the changing conditions. Yet it had also been a time of atonement where everyone feared for their future and the threat of conflict. Yet perhaps if they atoned for their many sins, peace might still be maintained.

PART 3

COMMUNION

DISUNION PART 3
COMMUNION

COMMUNION

1.

It seemed that they had solved the problem of preventing Merle's disgrace by apparently bearing a child when so young and not married, though Merle was astonished that his sister could share Patrick with her, even Patrick giving her babies. She still wanted to be sure that this was really her sister's wish, and not just to save her from shame.

Merle kissed Erin. "Erin dear, will you not feel some jealousy of me when I sleep with Patrick? You know I could never hurt you. But dear, I promise I will never be jealous of you, whatever happens in the future. – You see I really do love Patrick, though I know it is wrong – as he belongs to you – from today I know the only thing I will ever want for the rest of my life is to make both you and Patrick happy – please tell me if – in future – you want this to stop – I promise I will understand and cease being with Patrick." Now tears came into Merle's eyes.

Erin came smiling to her and hugged Merle to her. "Merle, I could never be jealous of you, - you never need fear I shall ever want you to leave us." She kissed her on the lips, before adding, "You see we both know we only want to make Patrick happy. – actually, now, I'm glad it has happened this way. – Darling, almost since we left Ireland, I saw Patrick's great interest in you. Then I knew he had fallen in love with you – but he would not admit it. – I know he does love you – yes – just as much I know he still loves me. – It was tearing him apart."

Now Erin laughed, "Long ago in Ireland as we courted he confessed to me of the many girl friends he had when at college and before he found he could love me. – Even at that time he told me, even as he kissed and loved me, that I would not be the only woman in his life. – He said this to me before he proposed . –Yet when he did so he promised it would not make his love for me any less – but there would be other women."

She even sighed, "Even as he begged me to marry him, he said I must not accept him if I could not allow him to stray that way. For he knew it would happen. You do not know but at that moment I was so shocked, I told him I must refuse his offer – Very kindly, he told me he understood – but he also told me he would always love me, even though I had not accepted him as my husband. I was disappointed and went away and thought about what he had said. I knew I was desperately in love with him. – I thought – he need not have told me these things. He really must love me if he was willing to jeopardise a life with me simply because he must tell me he would be unfaithful in future. – He could have done what other men have done, proposed marry me, only afterwards taking other women. - So I went back to him asking him to explain."

Erin gripped Merle's hand. "Then he said he did not want mistresses. He never wanted to hurt a woman. He would have to believe he loved the woman, if he was to stray that way. What he wanted, was more than one wife, but only women he could truly love."

Erin shook her head, "I thought was this not what these terrible Mormons we castigate claimed – and did not these women gladly accept a man as their husband, even though they knew he would marry other women. Yet there are many women willing to accept the Mormon faith, and accept multiple marriages. Surely this is better for the wife than for her husband to go elsewhere and enjoy the body of his mistress. – I knew then Patrick was sincere – I went back and accepted his offer of marriage."

Again she kissed Merle, "Patrick proved his sincerity by still wanting me to marry him after our raping. He pleaded with me swearing he loved me and that was why he wanted to marry him. – That day I decided I would never blame him no matter how many other women he chose, so long as he told me about them and never let me discovery them by accident. – Dear Merle, I'm delighted that it is you he had chosen as his 'second wife'. At least he has fallen in love with another woman I love just as much as him – Dearest, I'm so pleased it has happened this way – Now please let us both make him happy."

After that Merle, felt completely relieved and she gladly agreed to their plan to let her baby be registered as theirs, though she insisted that all future babies Patrick gave her would bear her new surname as O'Donnell. After all to his friends she would be simply known as his mistress, approved by his wife. However she knew she meant far more to him than that. Merle was so grateful to Erin that throughout the rest of her life Merle did everything possible to ensure she did not hurt her.

They could share his bed, sometimes, together on each side of him, without any jealousy. They would talk together, when he was at work, happily discussing their intimacies with him. Both had agreed that as Merle was so young, after she bore her child she must wait, and in New York they had discovered ways of avoiding this. Patrick must first give Erin a child, one to replace that which she had lost. Only then would Merle try to conceive his child. Afterwards they would probably alternate their pregnancies.

They both knew what a demanding man he was, it was as well he had two 'wives' otherwise he would. seriously, task their lives – for they knew they would never refuse him when he wanted it to happen. They also knew, even two women would not be enough for Patrick. Erin had confessed to Merle, one the reasons she had been willing to accept her, was her fear he would soon find another woman – another mistress. Erin had laughed and told Merle she preferred that mistress to live in their house, and not to fear he had enjoyed another woman without her knowledge.

In May 1850 Merle bore a son, Matthew, registered as Matthew Purcell. Though only fifteen Merle had a, surprisingly, easy birth, though it took over eight hours. Merle had rarely gone out of the house, so there could be no danger of the deception being discovered. During her future pregnancies by Patrick, there would be no need to hide her state, as she would simply be known in New York circles as Patrick's 'honourable and accepted' mistress.

By then Patrick had been established as a very competent New York Stockbroker in his firm. Soon he might be admitted as a junior member of the New York Stock Exchange. This was the way he came into contact with the various branches of the Carroll Family. And those in the Potomac valley. As the Marshall's, with Gordon Taylor, were so greatly involved in railway construction, it was natural that Patrick was involved in their investment in shares in their firms, as well as river transport and shipping. In fact his company were immersed in railway share dealings, and Patrick admitted, at times they were not necessary legal exploits. Yet this was the way things then operated in the United States.

Through Cornelius Vanderbilt and his shipping company he met first Peter Carroll and also the Fallon's and the Ibsen's. It was not long before Patrick, Erin and Merle were entertained by Adrian and Estelle Carroll at Rockville, becoming part of the social life of the area.

Naturally Patrick's work brought him constantly, in touch with both the Manhattan as well as the Casimir/Holstein Banks. Simply because of a social evening at Rockville he was introduced to the Chalmer family living on their estate near Richmond. It seemed, for convenience this family used a smaller but growing Mason Bank of Petersburg, Virginia. Patrick could well remember a director of that bank, Daniel Mason. Admiring Daniel's ability in investments even scoring over the larger banks. Patrick made a mental note to get to know this man better.

So the whole Purcell family were now very happily settled and were becoming very wealthy and prosperous. However, though it was a necessity, Patrick disapproved of illegal ways the Drew Company were often involved, even though, at the same time, he benefited financially from its operations. By now he accepted bribery was essential if only to obtain political support in their investments – but Patrick knew his father would never approve of the way he was forced to act.

2.

The end of the Mexican War created a very dangerous situation in the United States, threatening the destruction of the entire Union. Texans wished to be admitted as a slave state which would alter the balance in Congress giving slave owning states a majority. The northern states could not allow this. Mark Carroll, Francois Tencin and the Virginian, Maryland and other Congress members, long associated by family relationships, created great demands on their time as they tried to find a solution.

They gladly supported the Whig Leader, Henry Clay, with others, even Democrat Senator Stephen Douglas. The situation was in the balance until the sudden death of President Zachary Taylor, who was demanding the end of slavery throughout the United States. A solution was possible when Vice-President Millard Fillmore took the oath and a very difficult new compromise was voted through in January 1850.

It was only achieved by hard bargaining to get the northern and southern states to agree. The problem of the excessive size demanded by Texas was solved by paying off their enormous debts, when they relinquished large areas to the west. Now Texas was admitted as a slave state whilst California, with its influx of so many searching for gold, was admitted as a slave-free state.

This still left for solution the new land taken from Texas, called the territories of New Mexico and Utah. Again a compromise was agreed which only postponed the eventual difficult decision They would be organised by 'popular sovereignty' leaving the question open as whether they would be slave or anti-slave areas. Finally the southern states demanded and won, against much disquiet, the Fugitive Slave Act which placed on all northern states the responsibility of returning any escaping slaves entering northern states to be returned to their southern masters. Perhaps this act, so violently opposed in the north, was one of the chief causes of the civil war ten years later.

The compromise of 1850 would never solve the problem of future slavery. By now the situation was far worse than thirty years earlier. All it did was to provide a period of uneasy peace and delay the inevitable conflict which would tear the United States asunder. This compromise was known to the large populations in most of the settled states. However it did not provide a solution to these Texan visitors enjoying a long vacation of some six weeks with their relations at Camargo.

Hanz Eliot said, "It seems Congresses decisions do little to help us. Though we all now agree that none of us need – nay - even want slavery, – But we are now all true Texans. – and we all believe we should abide by the democratically decided decisions by others where we live. – It seems if a conflict occurs we may fight on opposite sides." Karl Downey confirmed this. "We cannot accept that these northern states have the right to override ones the people of Texas have voted, and accepted. I thought our constitution gave us, all, the right to make these decisions."

It was Karl's elderly seventy-eight mother Helga Eliot who pulled her son Hanz down and kissed him before saying, "Oh! Dear! Dear! Hanz! I could not bear to think of us hurting each other – None of us must let this happen. – There must be a way." They all agreed. Then Hanz added, "Look it may not come to this. – At least it has postponed any possible trouble. – The reason we came here was so we could all enjoy our stay – Please let us forget this – for now – let us enjoy, as we have so far, this wonderful holiday with you all. – You've made us so very happy."

And they did enjoy their visit. Unfortunately Karl Downey's mother and father had died, as had Hanz' father, Paul. Stuart Downey had died but his wonderful indian wife, Pohanna , Steven Downey's mother, was still alive, as was Stuart and Antoinette Brady, and Tony Brady's mother and father. All these parents had been the ones who in 1795 had come from West Virginia and together, had established this vast ranch of Camargo in Kentucky.

The wives were fortunate to be alive to be able to come to live there at that time. Lilie, Karl's mother, with her friend Helga had been captured and raped by Miami indians, conceiving and bearing daughters before they were rescued by James and Stuart Downey along with Paul Eliot, saving them, falling in love, and marrying them. Antoinette Condorcet, as she was called before her marriage, was a French aristocrat who was rescued during the Terror in France in 1793. There were reasons why they all came to marry their husbands and come together, virtually, to form one large extended family.

Of course the party from Texas were equally delighted to meet again their brothers and sisters and the many children they had born. They were happy to journey to La Falette, in Tennessee, to call again on seventy seven year old Louisa Albrecht, though by now she was very infirm and knew her life would soon come to an end. Neither did she mind for her beloved husband Anton had died recently. This couple were born as Prince and Princess of Austria, but had needed to flee to save their own lives and that of their unborn child. All the events of all these people, are told in full in the book named "Genesis'.

Louisa had thanked them for coming, "Please tell me how is Sam Houston doing since Texas became free from Mexico? Anton and I loved that man and helped in a way for him to leave here and go to Texas." Hanz was able to tell her of Huston's periods as President of Independent Texas and then becoming now Governor of the new state. He added, "You know we did not like and opposed him for a long time, But we know we now owe so much to him, in winning an impossible battle and setting us all free."

Their second son, Charles and his wife, Phyllis made them very welcome. They soon would inherit the estate as well as the town house in Nashville. The party returned just in time to meet again Gordon Taylor and his wife Sheila, newly return from their happy visit to England. Now come to meet Sheila's mother and father Neil and Patricia McLean who lived on a smaller ranch next to Camargo. Ironically this was provided for them by Gordon, after the long time they had opposed his marriage to their daughter.

Those unpleasant events in the past had long since been forgotten and they knew just how fortunate was the fact, that Gordon had persisted and eventually married Sheila after her disastrous first marriage. Gordon and Sheila had arrived only a few days before they all had to return to Texas. At last after six weeks of holiday it was time to part again. As they parted they hoped the day would never come when their two families supported different sides in a civil war.

*　*　*　*　*　*　*　*　*　*　*　*　*　*　*

Far away in California, Donald and Rachael Reid were too wondering if the compromise signed in Washington might prolong peace. California was now admitted as a free state and there would be no slavery in these lands. They were fortunate that as California was so far from where the main places of conflict would occur, they might not even notice it would be a civil war.

However they knew their very prosperous shipping company might soon be under attack from others far nearer to where they lived. The 1849 Gold Rush had brought to this land the very dregs of society. Though now a new state, California, still did not have the means to completely control society. Donald was now, more than ever, determined to stand for the State Legatetor. He felt it was time all men of property should ruthlessly remove this lawlessness. He felt sure, because of his known importance in the town he would be elected.

Taking hold of Rachael's hands he said. "It seems that Cherie and Daniel Wilson, have left Pittsburgh and intend to travel on one of our ships down to Central America and then sail up to San Francisco. You know Cherie has wanted for a long time to come and settle here. Well now she's got her chance. Roy Marshall feels we should become far more involved in trading with the Far East than we are at present doing. Roy knows the strain on me at present and believes I need some help from a person like Daniel who has been so much involved in furthering Vanderbilt's shipping empire. Frankly I shall welcome any help he can give me."

Now he smiled at Rachael, "Also you should know Gordon Taylor has written to me just before he returned to visit his family in England. He wished to inform me of a man whose firm helps him construct these new railways in the east. Evidently a man called Kurt Sand, who intended to come here perhaps to establish a company here building railways."

Rachael bent and kissed him. "Well we could do with them. The roads here are hopeless. It's only are own ships which enable us to visit other places on the coast. Now after the influx of so many coming for gold, all we are left with are ruts. – Yes, I hope he does come and builds railways. – I wonder what they are like. – You know we must try to discover him if he does set up a business here."

Donald agreed but added, "We may not need to look, Gordon gave this man Kurt our address – he may call on us if he arrives and decides to live here." Little did they know he had arrived and the exciting life he had experienced before and after settling in California.

3.

Agnes had come to Anita and into the room where she sat. After asking her if she felt if she was recovering from her ordeal, she sat down besides her, still holding her baby in her arms. Then she gently kissed the side of Anita's wet face, for Agnes could see she had been crying, feeling completely hopeless, and now knowing her own condition.

Agnes bared her breasts and proceeded to let her baby feed. She then turned to Anita. "Dearest. In spite of how it happened, in a few months you will be able to hold your own baby to your breasts. Remember this is denied to many women. If you look after yourself there is no reason whilst you will not be able to do this." Anita started sobbing. "Please do not torment me. I have no right to do this. I shall bare a bastard. It is a sin and god will punish me. It is better for both of us that it does not happen."

Agnes put her baby down and hugged Anita to her naked bust. "If your religion teaches you that, through no fault of your own, it is a sin to have conceived a child. Then your teaching is not only wrong, but evil. I believe god is a just and understanding person. Remember he made us all this way so we could continue our race."

It did little to comfort Anita. "You are kind, but my baby will not be like yours. You are fortunate, you have a loving husband. I have, already seen, what a wonderful kind man he is. No man, now, could ever accept me as his wife."

Her sobbing became more intense. Agnes hugged her more closely. "Yes! I agree with you that I have been fortunate to find a man like Kurt. But you don't know, just, how fortunate. Darling, baby Fiona, is not Kurt's child. You see I have suffered just as much as you. Kurt will confirm this, if you ask him. Fiona is by a Pawnee brave. On the journey to California I was taken by several Indians and raped many times. My mother died after so many attacks. You see I have suffered the same defilement as you." Anita could not believe her ears. "Fiona is not Kurt's child. Yet she is called Fiona Sand."

Now Agnes kissed her wet face. "Yes! For he was near when the Indians kidnapped me. Like you I believe I had no future. Kurt consoled me. He told me he loved me and wanted to marry me – but I did not believe him – You see he warned me if so – I would never be the only women in his life. Realising his offer meant I could continue to live, I told him I would not marry him, but would become his mistress, and share him with others, provided he would look after me and the child I bore."

A little understanding was dawning on Anita. "So – You are - not – married – to Kurt." Agnes smiled and kissed her again. "No dear, you are wrong. Kurt insisted I married him. He would not take me as his mistress. Since then he has given me so much happiness, even registering Fiona as his own child. No matter how many other women he enjoys in future, I shall love him till I die." To her surprise Anita started subbing again. "You have, merely, confirmed, what I already knew. Kurt is a truly wonderful man – a man I admire and like one I would have longed to marry – but where could I find one. Before my child was born."

Agnes hugged her again. "There is a chance. Kurt could not marry you but we must both talk with him, – if you can agree. I've told him I want to wait two years before I give him a child of my own. I have not spoken to him but, I know how worried he is, of your wanting to die. He's told me how wonderful you are. I know he desperately wants to help. He wants you to stay with us for as long you wish and is willing to look after you. If he agreed – and I have not enquired of him – would you let Kurt adopt and register your child as his – as if he had conceived it."

There was no doubt Anita was shocked at the idea of giving up her child. Yet if so she knew it would be cared for and brought up in the right way. Perhaps Kurt would let her stay with her child until it was old enough. It would give her a reason to live, at least for a time. Almost reluctantly she agreed to go to him with Agnes to see if it was possible.

They decided to do this that same evening after he returned from work. Agnes had prepared the way but she was surprised for he, immediately, told Anita what Agnes had asked of him. "Dear Anita. If it is your wish I will, willingly, accept your child as mine. We both want you to live. I am rich enough, now, to look after both of you. But I don't want you to give up your child. That is why I was delighted to accept Fiona, as my own. I've always wanted to raise a family. Now it seems two women can do this for without any effort of my own."

Even Anita smiled at his words. Then he went on. "As I said, I don't want you to give up your child. I want you to continue to live here, with all of us, to see your child grow up, knowing it is yours. Further more, should you find a man who could love you, and marry you, and accept this child, I promise I will let him adopt it."

The only doubt in her mind had been removed. She could continue to live in this family and bring her child up as she wanted. Only when it was old enough would it be told the truth. Without any hesitation, Anita, gladly accepted his offer, unable to stop herself she threw her arms around Kurt smoothing him in kisses and thanking him. "I shall never forget what you have offered me today. Now I want to continue living. You have both given me a future."

As the weeks went on Anita felt ashamed for she new the impossible had happened. She had fallen in love with Kurt but never mentioned it for she would never hurt, either him, nor Agnes. In March 1850 Anita gave birth to a beautiful daughter, she christened Conchita, though it's surname was Sand. Knowing Kurt admired her body she rewarded him by baring her breasts to him as she suckled her child. By then Agnes was trying to conceive by Kurt. The first child he could claim his own.

They had been very happy months for Anita. Kurt had been, especially, attentive to her needs. Although his growing business occupied so much of his time he tried to spent as much time with her and Conchita, as he did with Agnes and Fiona, not neglecting her, now Agnes wanted to be pregnant again.

But Anita found it difficult to conciliate her strong religious beliefs, with her emotions. Though she knew it was a sin she also knew she was jealous that Agnes would soon be pregnant by Kurt. She had no doubt that she was wildly in love with him. Now it was even worse, because she badly wanted to give him a child. A child of love. But her love for Agnes, who had made her new life possible was tearing her apart. If it had been for this she knew she would have seduced Kurt – gladly becoming his mistress – and condemning her soul to perdition.

It was not long before Agnes recognised her torment. "You're in love with Kurt – aren't you – tell me the truth?" Anita sighed. "Is it so obvious – but after what you have done for me, I swear I will never hurt you. If only I could get away – but I have no means to support Conchita and myself. It is so impossible. I will not disgrace you. I promise." Agnes by now two months pregnant took hold of Anita's hands in hers. "Is it so impossible. Although marriage is impossible. Could you live with Kurt as his mistress. – If so – you would have my blessing."

Anita was astounded. "You mean you would be willing to share Kurt with me?" Agnes squeezed her hands. "Yes! And gladly. I told you Kurt told me before we married – there would be other women. I've seen it in him for several months. I know he does not want to hurt me, but I also know his eyes are on several of the wives of our friends who find him attractive. I do not mind, but I fear the scandal would ruin us. Now listen."

Agnes put her arm around Anita. "I would be blind if I had failed to notice the way he looks at you – But he would never make advances to you – not after what you have, already, suffered – he knows you are grateful – for that reason you might submit to him as a reward – even if you hated it. If Kurt needs another woman – I would be glad if it was you."

"It is wonderful for you to take this view, "Anita replied. "But you do not understand. I'm a very passionate woman in love with your own husband – It's not a reward – but I could not resist – however much I tried - I would want to bare him children." Agnes smiled and kissed her. "I know. – but if you could be patient and wait – so any children you bore, like Conchita, could be registered as mine. If you could make this terrible sacrifice – it would be possible – You know we should both, always consider them as yours – just like Conchita."

They talked for hours exchanging views, almost like sisters the outcome was they both approached a bemused Kurt, together. Eventually before Agnes bore Kurt his first son, Andrew Sand, named after her dead brother, by then a very happy Anita had slept with Kurt in his bed, many times, with Agnes' blessing. Kurt now had a very willing mistress to share with Agnes. They were not to know that in New York another man, named Patrick Purcell, had copied their life style and was now enjoying the complete love of two women who were, actually sisters.

Now, at last Kurt believed he should try to make the acquaintance of this Donald Reid, whose address, Gordon Taylor had given him sometime in the past. Of course he knew of the large shipping company in San Francisco, which bore his name. He also knew he was standing for office in the new State Government. He had even received pamphlets requesting his vote. Kurt decided he would like to meet him and must try to do so in the near future. However Kurt felt he must first discuss his ideas with his business associates in Sacramento.

4.

Devin Regan, with regret, was parted from his beloved Camay and went with the Irish men into Manhattan. They took him first, to a large apartment block. It was already over populated with many having to share a room. Devin had to share with another man, recently arrived from Ireland, a man name Shamus O'Brien, two years his senior. Like Devin, Shamus had been brought here by the Irish Democratic League, a few days previous. Seeing the conditions and the way so many Irish families had to live so closely together, Devin was pleased that his family and the Nolan's had been given the opportunity of much better accommodation.

Devin was used to depravity but was soon to learn it went much further than that. Yet it seemed he must learn to live with this. The Irish Democratic League was a front for recruiting, particularly men, to come and work for the Democratic Party which controlled New York and were determined to continue to do so. For it seemed the caucus which controlled the city had found means to capitalise from its control, even using violence to control the polls.

It seemed all this was controlled from Tammany Hall on 14th. Street and the head of the organisation was William Tweed – though due to his autocratic manner was referred to as 'Boss' Tweed. He was an Scottish-Irish American born on Lower East side but prosperous in trading, he eventually set up the Americus Fire Company, so vital with the crowded buildings of Upper West Side, New York. Soon Tweed had control of the voting in Upper West Side and which had helped him establish himself in control of Tammany Hall.

Tammany Hall after 1840 was essentially an Irish community and helped so many impoverish Irish often providing them with food, coal and even rent money. However, and most important, it provided new immigrants with naturalisation making them United States citizens very quickly, though the methods were somewhat illegal. Still it did much good work for all newcomers and particularly Irish men and women who had lived there for sometime. It provided a type of Social service.

This was what was expected of Devin and he gladly immersed himself in working, diligently, with the Irish Democratic League. He received sufficient in wages to not only feed and house himself, but even giving him sufficient to enjoy more manly pleasures. However he was pleased that none of the others in the families which had come with him on the boat, had needed to live as he had to live.

Shamus and he had become good friends, as they now both worked and lived together. In spite of his romantic feelings for Camay, now such a long distance away, he was still a young man with all its desires.

Now both with a little money to spend, both Devin and Shamus looked around for possible feminine company, as well as partaking of the cheap beer on offer.

Though still somewhat reserved, Devin found the local girls were willing to submit to more amorous behaviour than would have been possible in Ireland. Of course one of the reasons for their popularity was that they both had a little money to spend, unlike many other men in the community. Devin found a very willing, Kasey, whilst Shamus found a similarly responsive, Aeryn, to join them in the locals for drinking, conversation, but more important to the two men, more amorous amusement, allowing them more intimate pleasures of fondling their clothed bodies.

Yet Devin could not forget Camay and though he enjoyed his escapades, he did not feel strongly attracted to Kasey, though thoroughly enjoyed her company. So the weeks past and Devin was fully occupied in his work for the League. However, gradually, he was to discover a more distasteful side of the Tammany Hall organisation.

This was some of the ways the organisation obtained their resources to finance their social front. They virtually controlled the local police by corruption. In fact they were mainly responsible for many recruits being admitted to the force, with the understanding that their first duty was not to the people – but to Tammany Hall. Worse, Devin was completely shocked to find one of the chief sources of their revenue was by establishing brothels in East side which were frequently by many rich New York men from the New York Upper classes.

With Irish immigration exploding, many families found it difficult to obtain employment, never having, in the past, any knowledge but of farming. Soon many were driven to starvation and needed to resort to desperate means to stay alive. Under these conditions many quite young, but pretty girls, decided a life of prostitution was better than starving to death.

In fact these brothels were well run, each with a number of control boss men. Some were of a more high class variety, well furnished with private rooms where these poor girls 'entertained' rich men. It mattered little if the poor girls conceived from their occupation as, a somewhat painful abortion, was readily available to remove their problem. The girls were very poorly paid for their sexual service but all food and lodgings were provided free, so if they were careful, the unfortunate girls could in a few years, uncommitted with any living child, could retire. Their past meant little in the lascivious living of that city, sometimes even finding a man to marry and raise a family of their own.

To these women whilst working in the brothel, their bodies would prove attractive to their rich lovers. So, even for a short time, on a stipulated sum of money, deposited in their account, accepted the position as their possessions. This was overseen by the boss man, even with provision for them, if they were to conceive children. They then retired to their rich owners separate apartments to live as their mistresses and even conceive their children.

Though Devin was appalled at what was happening, he had to admit that these poor girls had found a way of staying alive and might someday have a better life. He did not feel any aversion to these girls, realising why they had needed to submit. Devin had heard of prostitution in Ireland now realised these girls, perhaps sometimes, were able to achieve a better life than the poor girls in Ireland. But he was disgusted that Tammany Hall, whilst doing so much for the Irish community were using these methods to obtain some of their finances.

However Devin, in spite of the pleasures Kasey was willing to give him, felt no strong affection for her. She, merely, was the recipient of his desires and felt sure he would not want her as a more permanent partner, even sampling the offers of several other willing and attractive Irish girls. Devin knew his feeling for Camay were far stronger than what he had found in his own amorous associations.

But Camay now lived so far away from him, Though he now had a little money, his work kept him completely occupied and he could not find an opportunity to leave New York and visit her. The League demanded so much from him, and in many ways, he realised he was helping many poor Irish families to live a little better life. So such a journey to Annapolis must wait.

Meantime Sharon Casimir had taken Camay, her family, and the Regan's to her house in Annapolis in her many coaches. Once there she had told everyone their duties. She explained this mansion belonged and was used, from time to time, by two families who were friends and usually lived elsewhere. They were the Casimir's and the Holsteins and were part of a large banking family owning the Casimir/Holstein Banks. They would often be left alone and may at other times, be occupied by either family. An agent in Annapolis would call regularly to ensure they had the finances to look after their holdings but he would pay and purchase all their requirements, Their task was to see to the smooth running of the house and provide services under the supervision of Casa and Delma Nolan.

Though unused to such duties they had many times acted temporary in the big houses in Ireland and knew what they must do. Soon all were quickly involved in their new life. It seemed like paradise after what they had previously endured. Now safe, with a place to live, and with food to eat. However small was their wages, it was many times more than they could have hoped to earn in Ireland. Soon, even before Sharon Casimir left they were now fully ensconced in their new life.

But though she was happy to still be with her family and was well used to hard work, working now as a maid of all duties, but often without any guests to serve. However poor Camay knew her life, though a happy one, was missing the one thing she desired. Her so many happy hours with Devin she had enjoyed, even on that terrible ship. Yet so far she had not heard from him, and worse he had not appeared as he had promised.

5.

"It seems David is now settled and happily married to Rebecca, living in San Francisco, working for Donald Reid's shipping company." Amy Carroll was enjoying her stay with Danton and Susan Backhouse in Montreal. With her husband, Peter, so involved in his attempts along with Amy's brother, Cornelius, to introduce propeller propulsion into ocean going steam ships, Amy had been delighted to come to Montreal to stay with the Backhouse's.

Susan had laughed, "Yes! Even though he has now accepted United States citizenship, David is still true to his Canadian roots. Why he still enjoys berating his employer, Donald Reid, telling him the United States had no right to own California. But then he knows how much Donald relies on him for ensuring his financial success. David is not only Donald's chief accountant, he is overall manager and now a junior director of his firm. "

Susan smiled, "You know Donald was desperately trying to run his business, as well as see to its financial success when David called on him wanting employment. It seemed Donald could not obtained men trained sufficiently to do this work and it was David's coming which freed him to run the business side. Though Donald had been desperate, and knew he must employ David, even though actually on that day David told him how strong were his views that San Francisco should be part of Canada, it seems Donald liked David's forthright statements. In fact they immediately became friends and invited David home to met his wife, Rachel, that very evening."

Amy asked, "Did either of them know at that time that they were distant relatives?" Susan replied, "Oh! Yes! For it seems his wife Rachael, had learned of our own convoluted history, and the descendents of Blanche Carroll when she conceived and ran away with Felix Backhouse to New York after they married." At this point Diana Livingston intervened. "You should know Amy, I would not be sitting her now but for the fact that Blanche's younger sister, Anita Carroll, followed Blanche to New York a few years later, against her mother and father's wishes and married into the Livingston family. You know my husband, Philip, is a direct descendent of Anita Carroll's marriage to Robert Livingston, through six generations."

Diana Livingston had come today to visit both Susan and Amy, thrilled that Amy was still trying to complete the life lines of the many descendents of Sir David and Amelia Carroll's daughter's, both Blanche and Anita, who fled from their home at Rockville to go many miles away to New York at the start of the 18th. Century. Amy was anxious to complement the work her mother-in-law, Estelle Carroll had begun when she decided to add to the excellent work Manon Eliot had done, so many years before in tracing the histories of the two Carroll families who in the 17th. Century had come from Yorkshire and Somerset to settle in Maryland.

Amy was a proud as Estelle of her relationship with the famous Sir David and Amelia Carroll. Though Amy could only claim that right by her happy marriage to Peter Carroll. She was, never-the-less, a true Carroll now, in spite of being born a Vanderbilt.

These conversations only once again resulted in them comparing the very different loyalties of those descended from either Blanche or Anita, compared with those other children of Sir David and Amelia, all very staunch Americans and now of the United States. For after the United States won its independence from Britain as Blanche and Anita's descendents, living in New York had been equally staunch Royalists, so after they lost they had to leave New York very quickly and seek sanctuary in Montreal in Canada.

As they concluded their excursions into their past, it was left to Amy to now voice her own fears. "You know Estelle, and so many of us living in Virginia and Maryland, are now desperately worried that soon the whole of the United States will be torn apart in Civil War. The South fighting to retain slavery and we refusing this to be allowed. Yet Virginia, even more than Maryland which is equally split, many in Virginia will fight to the death to retain slavery, claiming it is necessary for them to be economically viable. If so those battlefield will be on or around are own vast estates."

Now Susan asked, "And which side will you take?" Amy smiled, "We have no choice. Though we are not strongly anti-slavery but have, already, set all our own servants free, with our relatives elected to Congress, they have aligned themselves to the wishes of the Northern states. Yet, though the majority of us will take this view, some of our relatives now live in Texas. It is certain they will support the Southern states. – You know Susan and Diana, some of us might have to repeat what you had to do, we may come begging to you for you to give us sanctuary."

Now Susan irrupted into uncontrollable laughter and took some time to regain her composer at last able to say, "If – that should happen – I'm sure David will write to us – demanding you all became – Canadians. Then what would you do?"

Amy was a little taken aback "Well – I hold nothing against you foreigners in Canada – but I would never relinquish my citizenship of the United States." Then herself irrupted in laughing, "Perhaps you might allow me to become a Canadian as well at belonging to my own country. Really I still believe we should all be one large country – I'm not saying it should be called the United States – but we might find another new name to cover both countries." On the offer of an olive-branch, none of them pursued this subject any further.

*   *   *   *   *   *   *   *   *   *   *   *   *   *   *

It had been a very busy weekend at the Reid family mansion. The day before they had been entertaining Cherie and Daniel Wilson. It was really a welcoming party as Cherie and Daniel had only arrived in San Francisco three months ago. Donald and Rachel had met them when their ship had arrived and for a time took them to their home whilst they looked for a suitable place to establish their new home.

The Wilson's had arrived with some wealth and wanted an estate like theirs to live in. Actually this was easy as Donald some years before had purchased several tracts of land going at a pittance, intending to sell this at an inflated price to new comers with wealth who came to settle here.

Both Cherie and Daniel were delighted at what Donald had to offer and purchased from him a delightful and picturesque tract only seven miles from where they lived in Oakland. Like their home it looked across the whole of the San Francisco bay. This done the two of them had stayed with them until a suitable mansion was built on their land. So ten days before the couple had moved into their new abode. So yesterday's party was to welcome them properly to the growing community of Oakland.

Donald had been glad to do this for now he had someone, well versed in shipping matters, to help him develop the much needed trade with the Far east, as well as bringing many Chinese workers for his shipyards. Persons very willing to do menial tasks and at an extremely low wage. Now today Donald and Rachael were entertaining David and Rebecca Backhouse to dinner.

David and Rebecca Backhouse were enjoying their after meal drinks in Donald and Rachael's mansion in Oakland after consuming a wonderful dinner. He was telling them that he had just received a letter from his mother, Susan. To say Amy Carroll was visiting his mother in Montreal, as she tried desperately to compile the life lines of his family at the request of Estelle Carroll of Rockville.

Donald had smiled, "You know you should thank Rachael for informing me that we were possibly related to each other in someway, otherwise after your confrontation with me earlier on that day – I might never have agreed to employ you." David corrected him, "You know you had to employ me or you might have become bankrupt – It was foolish the way you tried to cover so many tasks."

Donald laughed, "Of course you are right. I dare not have allowed you to get away. – In any case your outright statements only made me admire you even more. I knew how much you needed that job – Yet you still were determined to tell me we were stealing this city from its rightful owners in Canada. " Now David turned and kissed his wife. "Rebecca, in those few moments, irrespective of how much I needed employment, Donald's cheerful response convince me that I would like him to become my friend – The countries of our origin no longer mattered. You should know Rachael told me as much that very evening after Donald brought me to visit her." He turned to Rachael, "Rebecca and I are extremely grateful for your kindness to all of us. Donald and you have made us rich. We only hope we can always be your friends."

Now Donald changed the subject "I would like both of you to come here again next weekend to meet a man I've never met before. A Kurt Sand, who it seems has come west from Pittsburgh and recently established his own business in Sacramento. Naturally it is connected with the Gold Rush but it seems he is anxious to interest many of we rich persons in California in establishing another company to start building railways."

He smiled, "My good friend Gordon Taylor has written to me recommended this man, as evidently Kurt Sand and his father have been considerably involved in building some of these new railways in the East. Rachael and I believe there may be a profitable business in constructed these railways in California. I would hope you might be willing to listen to his proposals and see if we such invest in them." Though he was dubious of the idea, David admitted he felt they should listen to what Kurt Sand had to say. So all four would meet again when Kurt Sand and his wife came to dinner the following week before they then listened to what he had to offer.

Some miles away Kurt Sand had just received Donald Reid's invitation and intended to take, not just Agnes, but Anita with him to enjoy a dinner date.

6.

After having established his successful business with his partners Kurt Sand had made friends with many other men who had come to Sacramento during the early Gold Rush but after attempting to mine for a time had, themselves, established similar businesses in the town.

It had been the many lawless attacks such as Anita had suffered, for all of them to need to employ bodyguards for protection, which brought them together, ensuring if their stores were attacked they had mutual co-operation if required. Kurt was particularly attracted to four men whose stores had been at one time attacked. These were Charles Crocker, Collis Huntington, Mark Hopkins and Leland Stanford. All men about his own age, though Leland was a little older, and though a trained lawyer, was also the owner of a very successful store.

It was not long before they established many enjoyable social occasions, dinning together or separately, at each of their homes. Of course Kurt would always be accompanied with both Agnes and Anita, and it was not long before they all knew Kurt enjoyed his relationships with two women who were virtually his wives, and that Anita was not merely his mistress. It took a little time for his colleagues wives to accept this fact, though all knew that many men in the town had mistresses.

Often whilst their wives amused themselves in feminine small talk, the men would adjourn to smoke and drink and tell each other their earlier lives. It seemed all had recently come west from several towns in the east, just as Kurt had done. However they were all fascinated when they learned of Kurt and his father's business in Pittsburgh. Their building of roads and more recently even railways. Of course whilst living in the east they had known of the gradual extension of railway tracks there, though they had never before met anyone who was involved in their construction.

"Do you think anyone will ever build railways in California?", Charles Crocker had asked. Kurt had smiled, "Oh Yes! Do you know the real reason I came to California was for that purpose. I had intended to start a business here. Instead I met my wonderful wife on our journey to the Gold fields – then discovered the rich seam which is the basis of my wealth. This has distracted me from my ambition, as my increasing wealth has been due to our mining business."

Collis Huntington asked, "Do you ever intend to return to your idea and start building railways in California? Heaven knows we badly need both good roads and railways here, if California is to prosper as a state."

Again Kurt smiled, "Yes! I have often thought about this. However it would need a far greater influx of capital if it was to become a success. We shall need to build steel works to construct the railway lines. Though we might import them from the east – but think of the expense in transporting heavy metal let alone the locomotives – the steam engines – which pull the trucks and carriages along these lines.- Remember, we could not acquire any return from our investments until the railways were completed. Just think of our expenditure before we were able to profit from our endevours."

Now Leland Stanford intervened, "But there are many successful business men in San Francisco and Sacramento with sufficient wealth to invest in such projects, even be willing to lose that stake on the knowledge of the riches they would acquire once built."

"Yes! I agree with you," Collis Huntington exclaimed, "You know I came here by ship to Panama, crossed the isthmus, sailed on a ship owned by a Donald Reid, a very respected business man in Oakland, San Francisco, who is now standing for the state legislature. I'm certain we could interest him in such a scheme."

Kurt Sand burst into uncontrollable laughing, "Of course. I know of him. I've even been given an introduction to him from Gordon Taylor, for whose firm my father and I worked for in the east, as we helped him construct railways there. If you are all interested I will use this and see if I could get him to join us in such an enterprise."

They all affirmed their own interest telling Kurt they would invest in such a project as they were all rich enough to invest in such a gamble. Then Kurt dropped his bombshell. The idea by which he has amused his two wives now for several years. What he called the 'Golden Egg' – but something he thought few men would dare to conceive.

Very dramatically he added, "How besides building a few railroads around this large state. What do you think of doing something far bigger. Something unthinkable unless we could interest many to invest much greater amounts of money – but with far greater danger of losses. – However if successful it would provide the 'Golden Egg' and give us all riches we could never contemplate. ---- Why should we not build a railway all the way from Sacramento to New York and anywhere in the east. --- The very first transcontinental railway from the Pacific to the Atlantic. – Gentlemen – What do you think of such an idea?"

For a moment the was complete silence. It seemed they could not even imagine such a proposal. Then almost as one the attacked him with the salient question. "Was it possible?"

Kurt had smiled, "Oh! Yes! Very possible. I well remember my own journey here from the east. Our great difficulty is the enormous mountains behind us. But I remember the gradients. We should need to plan the line gaining height gradually by extending its length so that it circled as it tried to gain height. Of course we should have to tunnel through the rock faces, many times, adding still more to the expense. It would be hellishly expensive. I think I know a man who could help us in surveying the possibility of such a route, and I'm trained to help him. His name is Theodore Judah. – But gentlemen, such an idea is well beyond the resources any of us have at this time. – even possibly beyond any in California, who might have such wealth. It simple means we must interest the United States Government in investing heavily. They already do this in road building where the returns are not sufficient for private investment to precipitate. Why not in a railway which would unite the union even more than any political statements."

His proposal had shocked them. Yet, even then they thought of its value in trading the many farm products of California and sending them quickly, before they could deteriorate to the very willing markets in the heavily populated east. It would establish California as the food producer, particularly for fruit, for the east But they all knew even to prospect a possible route, let alone build the railway, they would need many more people to invest in the idea before it could progress.

Though shocked. They all agreed they would join with others in just seeing if such a route was possible. Even if they could not raise the funds to build such a line. If they, already, had working plans of how it might be achieved, they might sell these to a far greater consortium – or even to the government itself, if it ever contemplated the idea.

At least Kurt knew the name and had an introduction to one man in San Francisco who might invest and they begged him to visit him and see if he could interest him in doing so. So it was a very excited group of men who rejoined their ladies to enjoy the social occasion they had come to enjoy.

7.

Devin Regan inevitably became more involved, than he would have wished, in Tammany Hall's despicable ways of raising money for other more social requirements, by their growing involvement in prostitution. Almost without him knowing it, Devin found as he worked for them, and attempted to settle new Irish immigrants in places to live when they landed at Ellis Island, he was unknowingly helping Tammany Hall obtain young girls for their distasteful life of shame.

It seemed he was providing a source of poor young particularly beautiful Irish girls, whose parents were destitute and starving, for a life in their brothels. There was no way he could avoid this and realised that some young girls arriving with their families, suddenly disappeared, presuming this was their fate.

Of course his friend Shamus O'Brien often had the same unpleasant task as Devin. However whilst Devin had not established any lasting friendship with Kasey, Shamus had begun a more lasting relationship with Aeryn, and it might become more permanent. Devin's heart was still very much the possession of Camay and was beginning to think she might eventually become his partner for life.

Actually, it gave Devin another chance to meet again several of those kind ladies who had spoken and advised their families when they, also, had landed from the ship. He was most impressed with the way these dear ladies volunteered their time in trying to help so many Irish men and women. He had been forthright in telling them what he had discovered, though not surprised when they replied that they knew of this but had failed to stop this trade in girlish flesh.

Two people he met quite frequently were a Mrs. Erin Purcell and her friend, Merle O'Donnell, and was impressed at their devotion to this task. They were able to tell him a little of why they did this task. Evidently Mrs. Purcell was married to a rich Stockbroker, who was a junior Partner in the firm Drew Robinson Company. Their greatest wish was to help older women who arrived without a husband but with daughters, and had been able to place a few of such families, denied the support of a man, to find employment as domestic servants in the many estates around New York.

They even gave him a telephone number to call if Devin should find any young girl in very desperate needs, as they were impressed by Devin's great concern at the way parts of Tammany Hall operated. They also told him that as Tammany Hall virtually controlled the police force, and with their political control of New York City, there was no way they could bring these evil men to justice. In fact they knew that some very distinguished rich business men living on Long Island used Tammany Hall to provide them with young beautiful mistresses.

Though Devin had neither the wish nor the resources to avail himself of the sexual pleasures offered in these brothels, he had no option but to become a frequent visitor to them, as he worked for the Irish League. Though it excited him, he felt pity for a number of girls offering themselves to male visitors, often seeing them semi naked, exposing themselves to ensure their male clients knew what they had to offer. In fact Devin became well known to a number of them and when he had the opportunity, would involve them in conversation. They all knew he was in someway involved in the trade, yet, unlike their boss men never made any unwanted demands on them.

The high class brothels located nearer to the affluent Long Island with its many rich estates were quite different from those in the centre of the city. In fact it consisted of a number of tiny estates of their own. Often with a large house where clients assembled, with a reception area, and lifts to the many private suites of rooms, where rich men could choose a girl to please him intimately for as long as he wished to stay. Sometimes paying for more than one girl at a time. However inside the grounds were smaller but fully equipped chalets which the richest men would hire privately for some months and where he could 'entertain' any one or more girls for several days on end, as they lived as his temporary mistresses.

Devin had been appalled when he found these men could use their influence to even force these unfortunate girls to conceive their child, then using them, keeping them virtually as prisoners in these chalets until they bore his child. Though these girls were better paid for their sexual servitude they had no claim on their babies when born. The fate of many were unknown, though some, it seems, were adopted by infertile rich women unable to provide an issue for their husband.

For some girls it was even worse for their possessors were often sadists, who would from time to time use a whip and other methods on their unprotected bodies. In these cases these men would pay to keep them until they were about six months pregnant and then, to Devin's horror, he found these men forced them to have a painful and dangerous abortion of their child as they enjoyed watching their pain. Devin wondered just how low some men could descend and it seemed their were quite a few men who had sunk to such depravity.

One evening Devin had needed to bring to one of these high class estates packets of food and clothing and many necessities required by the establishment to help these poor girls from conceiving when it was not demanded of them. Their were several half dressed girls sitting waiting for the clients who had reserved them and Devin felt very sorry for them as they were quite attractive women. He left feeling very sad for them and wished there was some way he could help them. As a man he had to admitted their half naked bodies attracted him but he knew, whatever money he had, he could never use a woman that way.

His sadness increased as he left the brilliantly lit house and entered the gardens heading for the gate to walk down the road to where a number of local boats operated which would take him and others back into New York. He passed close to several of the smaller chalets. Suddenly the darkness was lit up as the door of won of the chalets flew open and he could see a young half naked girl rush out screaming in fear. She suddenly saw him – stopped for a moment in fear – then hoping she might get help rushed up to him.

"Please whoever you are – help me – don't send me back – I'll kill myself rather than go back into that house. I beg you to help me – If you can save me – I'll be willing to let you use me – as other men do – but please if so – do not make me give you a baby. I'll do anything for you, other than that, if you can save me from that horrible man."

Devin was perplexed, surprised and unable to think sensibly. Possibly her lovely Irish voice awoke him. He realised why this girl had run out of that chalet, for the man who had purchased her must have told her he was going to make her conceive his child. He realised she thought he was just another of those men who had used her now for three months, but she just hoped he would be satisfied with her giving him pleasure and not demand more.

Realising she was half undressed to her surprise he took off the large coat he was wearing and placed it over her vulnerable body. As he did this he spoke as he could see she was confused by his action. "Dear girl, I'm not one of those evil men. I did not come here for intimate pleasures of a woman. You asked me for help – I'm not rich but I do want to help you. Come you must trust me. We must leave here immediately. I'll take you back with me on the boat I was to catch. Then we can talk and can decided what is best for you.

Now the girl was perplexed and surprised. She had thought this man would have accepted her offer of sexual pleasures and possibly save her from what her evil client had demanded. Instead it seemed he was just a poor man who must have come here for other reasons, possibly worked for the brothel owners. Yet by putting his coat around her had shown her he was not another man wanting to use her. Whenever was his motives he seemed much kinder than any man she had known since she had arrived to start her life of sin, which as a devoted Roman Catholic she feared for what she had done now for three terrible months.

Now he even put his arm around her and hurried her shoeless down that drive on the road and boat stage. However it was a loving embrace dissipating her fears as he spoke quietly to her. "My name is Devin Regan –please tell me your name. I don't know how – but I know I want to help you – I promise you can trust me?"

Now a warm feeling passed through her recently misused body. This man seemed to be a kind man, she even turned towards him in the small light. Devin could see she was smiling and very pretty. Again in that same lyrical Irish voice she replied, "I'm called Morna Lynch and I do trust you – please soon let us talk and see if there is some way you could save me from the fate that man demanded of me" Devin smiled back and said, "Somehow, I'll find a way."

8.

Erin Purcell, now twenty two and her eighteen year old sister, Merle, arrived back from their mornings work on Ellis Island where they had tried to help the most recent arrivals from Ireland, warning them of their dangers and giving them a little money to help them for a short time. Both dashed to hold and hug their two children. Matthew Purcell was Merle's baby the result of her viscous raping in Ireland. He was now two years old and was rapidly growing into a very determined young boy.

Erin took her one year old son, Arnold Purcell, in her arms, as he was glad to see his mother had returned. Erin had born Arnold to her beloved husband over a year ago, and knew she must wait sometime before she conceived again by Patrick as he had promised Merle to start her first pregnancy by him on her nineteenth birthday and this time it would bear her assumed name of O'Donnell, though she knew all of them felt Matthew was hers in spite of his assumed surname.

They both enjoyed a wonderful life free from any jealousy as they knew Patrick regarded both of them as his wives. Many were the times when they would both join him in bed, none of them feeling any shame as they gladly responded to his loving and very passionate embraces. It was this love he gave them which determined both of them to do everything in their power to help those people coming from Ireland to start a new life in the United States, just as they had done today.

As they held their children close to them giving them the love they needed Erin commented. "You know I did like that man Devin Regan we talked with today. He is a good man and hates the way we know these evil men use these young girls and force them into prostitution admitting he has to accept that, in a small way, he too is involved, but dare not interfere in any way. Perhaps like Devin there are some good men in the Irish League who in the same way help our countrymen, like us, to find a happy life here."

Merle smiled, "Erin I agree with you. I too liked Devin Regan. I felt sorry when he told us about that girl Camay he met on the ship coming here but is now living many miles way in Annapolis. – I too was convinced of his sincerity. – I believe if he was able he would like to help some of these poor women forced into brothels for the enjoyment of men. – I was pleased you gave him our phone number. – If he should call asking us to help we must persuade Patrick to assist him."

Erin sighed, "Merle it seems we shall be without Patrick to please us this evening. – I don't feel like sleeping alone, will you sleep with me tonight." Merle laughed, "I should love that," – then laughed louder before continuing, "I think we now know the ways we can enjoy our night together, even without Patrick's ministrations." Now Erin responding laughingly, "Yes! That is just another blessing we both can enjoy by being two women in love with the same man. – You know that may be the reason why Mormon women are quite pleased to marry a man already with one wife!"

The reason why the two of them were denied Patrick Purcell's ardent love making was because he had gone to Petersburg to the Mason Bank there, to discuss matters with the junior director of that bank. It had been necessary for Patrick to do this to discuss with him investments for the rich Chalmer family of Virginia. Also Patrick had great confidence in Daniel Mason, having seen how he bettered the much larger Manhattan and Casmir/Holstein Banks in the past. Patrick knew Daniel would challenge his proposals until he was convinced they were what was best for that family, and Patrick admired him for his attitude, protecting the best interests of his clients.

Their business finished successively to both their satisfaction, Daniel Mason had invited Patrick out for a late lunch, and now had the opportunity to talk of more personal matters. It was Daniel who opened the conversation. "You know Patrick the reason why I was so hard on you today, is because I admired that Chalmer family very much. Of course they have a large and very prosperous plantation but they especially please me for they have freed all the slaves on their land and now employ them to work for them. So unlike that plantation of Henry Byrd which is just to the north of Petersburg. That man not only cruelly uses these slaves, he delights in making many young negresses pregnant even though barely twelve years of age to produce offspring who in time will work his fields."

For a moment Patrick was taken aback. "Then Daniel you do not approve of slavery yet you are a Virginian?" Daniel responded with some vigour, "Indeed I do not. You see I am a Quaker and we believe that no man should enslave another for any reason. I'm so delighted the British have outlawed slavery and use their large navies to stop slave ships bring slaves from Africa to America – that's why Henry Byrd behaves as he does for the price of slaves has rising greatly, so he sires more to eventually work for him. – Tell me truthfully, what is your view of slavery?"

Patrick smiled, "Daniel I'm an Irishman. I have no need to employ any slaves. Most of my servants are Irishmen men and women who my wife rescues as they land here giving them a better life than if they still lived in Ireland. – Though I have no strong views, I suppose I support the northern states in trying to make this country free from slavery. – Yet it surprises me you take this view because you live here amongst it all."

Daniel seemed pleased at his reply and added, "No my father freed all our slaves some years before and we employ them now just as the Chalmers do. – That man Byrd maintains slavery is essential to ensure his financial success. That is not true. It is his lavish life style way of living which is his undoing. His land is overworked and his yields are getting less. If he spent some money on fertilising the worked out soil he would not need slaves. Henry Byrd is still living as a spendthrift – just as his famous predecessor William Byrd did in the past. But William Byrd, even though he used slaves denoted large sums of money to the community, helping those living in poverty. My father tells me Henry is nearly bankrupt and that is why he acts as he does."

Now Patrick asked, "Are you married?" Daniel smiled, "No! Not yet. Though I'm trying to court Henry Byrd's eldest daughter, Sally Byrd, but I doubt if I've any chance, for her father would ensure we never had a life together." With this information they turned to discuss many other matters and particularly the present economic situation, not forgetting how near to civil war it had come in 1850.

That night as he slept in his hotel wondering if his two wives were missing him he also pondered again at what Daniel Mason had spoken that day. Patrick could not but admire this man. The way he had challenged him on the investments Patrick had suggested for the Chalmer families. There was no doubt in Patrick's mind that Daniel Mason's strong beliefs and in his honesty. Of course Daniel was right as Drew and Robison Company were known for dealing with stocks not of the most honest kind.

Again Patrick knew of this and did his best to avoid becoming involved in such matters though he was not opposed to using bribery to obtain senatorial support when it was required, but then this was then the custom in the United States. Patrick, would never, unknowingly recommend any stock which he thought might be dubious, even though he lost rich rewards by doing so.

However what had amazed Patrick most was not just Daniel Mason's honest approach to investments but Daniel being a man living in an area of Virginia with strong support for slavery, yet both him, his father and their bank was doing everything possible, speaking out so strongly against slavery, yet their bank depended on the local planters using its services. What Patrick did not know was these planters had little option as their land was mortgaged to the hilt, even depending on it to obtain credit from the Mason bank for they could never hope to get it elsewhere.

As he lay back deciding he must now relax he realised just how much he would that night miss the loving embraces of the two women he now loved so deeply.

9

Donald, Rachael, Rebecca and David were standing in Donald's hallway, just one week later, as their butler opened the magnificent front door to usher Kurt Sands in to the house. Of course they had invited both Kurt and his wife, Agnes, to come from Sacramento, as their guests for the weekend. However they had not expected them to be accompanied with another lady, elegantly dressed. For Kurt had never given them any intimation he would be doing so.

They tried not to show their surprise as Kurt Sand introduced the lady as Anita Madero, so the introductions finished they led them all into the large withdrawing room to sit as the servants poured them drinks. Only then did the conversations begin.

Donald began, "I believe you struck a rich gold vein in 1849. Is this then now your business?" Kurt smiled, "Well yes, that is the source of our wealth, though I am now increasing my wealth in providing everything necessary for the mining companies now part of the Sacramento fraternity. – Yet! This has been forced on me due to circumstances. You see I am a fully trained engineer and geologist. My father in Pittsburgh owns a large engineering firm. He came from Germany in 1820 and helped to build the Eire Canal before setting up his own business. Once I graduated I formed part of the firm."

Donald a little surprised asked, "Was it a fortune in gold which made you come here? Again Kurt laughed, "Yes! Though my real reason was to set up a similar business to my father's here, in California. – Perhaps to build roads – which you know we badly need – But - You see in the east, I was very involved in building these new railways there. – However finding that gold has altered my choices."

Donald was satisfied, "So, now, do you intend building these roads. – Is it this which caused you to approach me to see if I might invest?" Very determinedly Kurt replied, "Oh! No! Something far more ambitious. I want to build railways here in California to help develop trade in the large state."

Naturally Donald inquired if this was possible and what could he expect in profits if he invested and Kurt explained the urgent need for better communications if only to bring the arable products of the state to market, let alone to give much easier transport of people.

"Let me make it clear," Kurt continued, "no dividends could accrue until the lines are completed It is then that our investments will multiply many times. – Of course, as always, it is a gamble. I have discussed this with many business men here and several are willing to invest. – Though we would accept anything you might like to offer, we have already decided to start doing this on a small scale. --- However I and my friends have a far greater – yes, and far more risky idea – what we have christened the 'Golden Egg'."

Now he laughed openly, "Would you like to be involved in building one gigantic railway form Sacramento or San Francisco to New York. A line joining the Pacific to the Atlantic?" There was no doubt they were all astounded at such an idea, and David Backhouse asked, "And is this possible – What about the mountains – Surely, as I understand these trains cannot manage large hills – it would be impossible."

Very quickly, as he had done some days before to others, Kurt explain how this could be overcome by circling the lines and driving tunnels through the rocks. Then completed by saying as an engineer he knew it was not only possible but very necessary if the present fragile Union could be maintained – A Transcontinental Railway joining east and west. – However he stated very determinedly just how expensive would be such a massive project.

Before they could interrupt he rapidly continued saying, it was unlikely that private investors would be willing to risk such large sums unless the government would be willing to heavily subsidise the project, just as they did at present with road building. It was therefore imperative that a person was sent and supported financially. to go to live in Washington to sell this idea, to lobby Congress –simply on the urgent need to unify the Union which now was in great danger.

Finally he concluded, "Besides this I believe we all should be willing to invest in researching a possible route through the mountains. A very detailed and properly costed project. This, though the investment would be very much less, might again not produce dividends until it was subsided and more money raised to build such a railway. – However if this was available and in our possession, we could sell this at a very great profit - it is with this project I have come to you today, to see if it may interest you."

Nothing more could be said as it was time for lunch. During this Donald and David told their guests a little of their own earlier life, amazing them by saying they were very distant relatives whose predecessors came to America in 1687. Even more when Donald told them how he met Rachael on a boat coming to St, Louis but did not fully inform them of the details.

Only after they had finished were they introduced to The Reid's children who had been taken for a treat over the bay into China Town. Only then did their host request Kurt to tell them of his earlier life. Now it was their turn to be shocked when Rachael asked Agnes if she had any children. Agnes opening phrase was enough, "O! Yes! You see I was captured and raped pregnant by Pawnee braves. Kurt rescued me, then married me and adopted my daughter, Fiona, just as he has done for poor Anita here who was seized by bad men during 1849 and conceived their child. Again Kurt has adopted Anita's daughter, Conchita, for Anita is Mexican born."

Both Rachael and Rebecca responded warmly saying how kind it was for Kurt to adopt two children. However the were all shocked when Agnes continued. In fact they had decided to acquaint them of their unusual relations as soon as possible. "I think you should know that besides dear Kurt not only rescuing me, then almost forcing me to marry him, refusing my offer to become his mistress. – Well it seemed Kurt's rescuing of Anita and adopting her child, made Anita to confess she had fallen in love with Kurt. - I knew Kurt liked her – and after what he had done for me, I agreed that Anita should continue to live with us, and now we share him in a loving way."

Rachael almost shouted, "You mean the three of you live together and Anita is Kurt's mistress. Now Kurt who had been silent intervened, "Oh! No! Anita is not my mistress – although we can never legally marry – Anita, - and Agnes knows, is not my mistress, I really have two wonderful wives. – Agnes has just given me a son and soon Anita has told me she wants my child. – You must know it is customary for the rich men in the east to take mistresses – well, I don't believe that is fair – As Agnes so kindly has agreed – We shall always believe I have two lovely ladies who want to be my wives.

After such an admission it was obvious that their hosts and hostesses were completely embarrassed and for a moment remained very silent – Then Donald recovered himself. There was little he could say, so instead he took the easy course. "Please may I offer all of you another drink." It broke the spell, they all roared and began immersed in continuing laugher. It would be much later before they were to talk of more serious matters.

Though everyone was surprised at Kurt's confessions, he had done nothing more than so many persons had done this last three years. He had communicated his position freely to everyone. Just like the many families in the east had done. These years had been years of communion. Communion with themselves but with others who had decidedly different views. At least it had enabled them, for a time to find a compromise, and avoid using violence to assert their views. But for how much longer would there be communion, between the northern and southern states.

10.

Devin took a frightened Morna Lynch down to the landing stage and they purchased passage back to New York. He kept trying to comfort her, telling her he would take care of her, yet he really had no idea what he should do. He felt he should not take her back to his lodgings, firstly because Shamus might be there and disapprove of what he had done, even fearing repercussions. In any case Tammany Hall might easy trace Morna there and force her back into prostitution again, which if possible, he wanted to avoid.

Then he remembered the phone number those kind ladies had given him. So as soon as they landed, though it was very late evening he called the number. After some delay he spoke to someone who seemed to be a servant. Devin told him it was an emergency and the lady of the house had asked him to ring her if this was the case. Again some delay, then a lovely ladies voice came on the phone though, obviously, had already retired to bed, as it seemed she was still only half awake.

Briefly he told her about Morna and how she had come running to him after being misused in the chalet in the brothel. Then he begged her to help the poor girl. He had to be brief as the call might be disconnected any minute. It seemed her mind worked quickly. She told him to take her to Times Square and wait there. She would send her coach to collect both of them and bring them to her home. She told him the coachman's name was Shaun. Devin must give this man his and Morna name and he would then bring them to her house on Long Island. Devin was delighted to accept her offer and told her so.

Then slowly Devin lead poor frightened Morna along the many passageways towards Times Square and as he did so tried to tell her what he had tried to do.

He held her hand, "Morna I know these ladies, I've met them many times, they spend a lot of time trying to help Irish immigrants when they first land in America. I know they will help you, but you must trust them and do everything they say. However first you must tell me how you came to be in that terrible place."

Now for the first time she wondered who he was. It seemed he was in someway connected with the brothel – and yet he did not seem to take their side. So she asked this and very briefly he told her just why he had been there that night. So she knew he still must be connected to Tammany Hall – yet still seemed to want to help her. Now she told him her story.

"Mother and I were starving in Ireland we got help to go to Liverpool and then came on one of those ships. But when we arrived here there were few people to help us, mother collapsed for we had got little to eat on that journey. Then some men came and took her away, saying they would take her where she could rest and recover. They were so nice I trusted them. After my mother was taken away, they came to me again and said they would look after me and I must go with them. I did so willingly, for they had been so kind to mother."

Now Morna broke down and began sobbing. It was obvious to Devin that Morna was ashamed and was not sure how she should continue her story. So Devin kindly took her hand and kissed them.

"Please tell me – do not be afraid – I know what these evil men do – It was not your fault – but please tell me."

Though still sobbing a small smile of thankfulness lit up her face, and now Devin realised what a very pretty girl she was. Finally she continued, "Then you can guess what happened. They took me in a coach telling me they would see I had a place to live and I felt very relieved. – Well you can guess the rest – as you must know what happens at that terrible place. – It seemed I had been taken to a large house – I was not sure but thought they knew the owners of the house needed servants. – I had worked in Ireland as a servant. – I would be glad to work here like this in New York."

Now her sobbing became more intense and for a time she could not continue. Devin comforted her and she pressed her face into his chest. Then, eventually, she broke apart, "Well – almost immediately I entered that house it happened – I was seized and two old women took me upstairs and forced me to undress and bathe. – Then once dry I was taken to another room virtually thrown inside and the door locked behind me. On the windows I saw were iron bars so I was a prisoner.- Even then I began to realise why I had been brought there.------"

Though sobbing she raised her head and looked straight into Devin's face and said, "Need I say more – You must have guessed, what was my fate – The next day I was told I was there to give men pleasure – I would be fed – I would be given a small some of money every time I successfully entertained a man - I must wear the clothes they gave me – and there were many garments – but as you see me now – only what a girl is supposed to wear under her top dress – but I was never given one of the dresses."

Now with some shame she continued, "Then very day I was forced into a bedroom and a client had chosen me as I had stood with other girls in a line – Oh! God – He took me with force for I fought him and he bruised my face with slaps of his hand – Then pushed me onto the bed – yes! And ravished me – I still remember the agony – You see I was still a virgin."

Again she paused and Devin knew she was reliving those terrible moments again. Eventually she continued, "Well its been like that for the last three months – but lately, as it seems I am attractive to some more wealth men – I was 'promoted' three weeks ago to the 'Chalet department' – dressed (or undressed) more appropriately. A few days ago one particular man chose me – The one I was with last night – Then just before I rushed out and met you – he told me that now I must conceive his child but I and the child I bore would be 'looked after' – I could guess what that meant – Then he took me forced me flat and –er - I just panicked - Though I believed I had no escape – I just screamed –ran out ---and met you. Now you've brought me here."

Her tale finished Devin looked kindly at her, again took hold of her hands and kissed them saying, "Morna, It's over – You are not going back there – I don't know how – but I'm certain those kind ladies will look after you. " There was no time for her to answer as a coach entered the square and stopped and the coachman descended and was obviously looking at the crowded thoroughfare for someone . Devin took Morna with him to the man introducing himself and the girl and asking if he was called Shaun. The man's face literally beamed telling him he was that man and asked them to climb into the coach, which they gladly did.

Very little was said on that long journey to Long Island and they now felt very tired. At last they entered the long drive, drew up a the front door, alighted and went inside. They found two quite young women waiting to welcome them, but even in their nightwear Devin recognised the two kind ladies. They came and took Morna by the hand.

She said to her, "You can stay here till we see what we can do for you. You will be safe here. My husband will be back tomorrow. He then will be willing to help you." It was the lady he heard being called Erin. But the other lady also told Morna she would be safe. Now though he was very tired decided he must leave and said so.

However the two ladies would not hear of it. The one called Erin said, "Merle take him upstairs to the upper bedroom. He can sleep there and spend the night. I'm sure he will want to know what we are going to do with Morna." Devin did not deter. He was delighted to think he did not have that long journey back and let the lady called Merle lead him upstairs and left him.

Very quickly Devin undressed but retained his underclothes. At least he now knew both the names of the two ladies who had helped him. Tired as he was he could not get the picture of Morna from his mind. He knew she was a very attractive girl, enough to excite any warm blooded male. – But could he even try to make progress with her. Then did he want to do so, however much he knew Morna pleased him. – But what of Camay – 'Oh! Dear! Until today I knew it was with Camay I hoped to develop our past friendship. – But she is miles away and it seems Morna will be living much closer.' Devin said to himself then added 'I might have two girls to give me pleasure – and today has made this possible'

Once again two people had come together, almost by accident, he had established the basis for a relationship. Once again there had been communion between them – on the boat – and in Times Square. Once again it had created problems – yet what happened in the future would decide if they could be solved

PART 4

SOBRIETY

DISUNION PART 4 SOBRIETY

SOBRIETY

1.

The years from 1850 to 1854 in the United Sates were a time of apparent calm after the convulsions during the debates in Congress leading to the Second Missouri Compromise. Yet they did little to hide the underlying dissentions concerning slavery. The two years as Whig President, Millard Fillmore following the quick death of President Zachary Taylor in 1850, were uneventful but he failed to be re-nominated. This led to Democratic Franklin Pierce being elected for four years by a landslide. Yet it seemed he was to be known as the worst President in its history, for though a Democrat he was considered a 'doughface' for he firmly believed in slavery., and failed to be nominated again four years later.

There were two important events in that period. Firstly the Gadsden Purchase in 1853 of essential land from Mexico in southern Arizona and New Mexico which might allow in future a southern railway route west, should finances be acquired to build it. Secondly, an event which greatly affected the United States future world position, when Commodore Perry using the might of the United States Navy forced Japan, to at last, open its doors for trade. These years did allow the various branches of the Carroll families to prosper and extend their fortunes both in California, the east coast, Texas and other areas won from Mexico.

Yet those families in Texas who feared what would happen if a Civil War occurred little knew of two families living in these new southern areas which in time would greatly affect their lives. These were the Sinclair family of western Texas and the Mormon Milliken family living in Salt Lake City. .

John and Thelma Sinclair had emigrated to western Texas soon after their marriage in 1836 and bore a son, Jack Sinclair a year later and another son, Robert Sinclair in 1844. Though poor, Thelma conceived but miscarried several times due to the very hard life they all lived. It was not the luxurious life of those living near San Marcos. The Sinclair's tended a small impoverished cattle ranch near Cagtry on the River Pecos.

John's younger sister, Dora Sinclair who had come with her brother when they settled there and hoped to relieve their poverty. Then she fell in love and married Wendle Jackson, whose family worked the local Cagtry store in 1853, bearing a son, Eric two years later. This was a year before Thelma bore her last child Molly Sinclair. However exhausted by their labours both John and Thelma died two years later leaving Jack, Robert and baby, Molly parentless. This event, we shall see, trigged the decision for both Jack and Robert to leave the ranch and try to derive a fortune elsewhere.

At the same time the Mormon Milliken family at Salt lake City were bringing up their children in a plural marriage. Morton Milliken had married both Nan Boutelle and two sisters, Joan and Elias Penny, before the migration west of the Mormons under Brigham Young in 1847. Nan as a dutiful Mormon wife, who loved her husband, had born him five children in rotation as Joan and Elias bore their own family.

Meanwhile Nan's brother, Adam Boutelle, had married three wives, Morton's sister, Edna Milliken and two sisters, Nancy and Jean Dover. They like Nan, had given their husband a growing family. By 1855 Nan had born Morton, a daughter Alice, a son Otto, another two daughters, Cathleen and Vera and just born a baby when Morton died. As was the Mormon custom Nan's eldest son Otto now had the responsibilities to see to 'all his mother needs' – which was interpretive in the Mormon way quite literally. Otto had now the complete responsibility of his mothers future life in every way.

Nan was young enough to marry again and she knew she would be welcomed as a new plural wife of the many men in Salt Lake City. However her last birth had been dangerous and she did not want to conceive again too quickly. Also she had dearly loved her husband who had been a dear man and good father, and did not want to give herself to another – at least – not for some time.

So like Jack and Robert Sinclair, when Otto told his mother he wanted to leave Salt Lake City to win a fortune for himself, Nan gladly agreed to accompany him and see to his comforts, washing his clothes and preparing his meals. Nan's older children had married, or old enough to look after themselves, except for Vera and her new baby, who Alice agreed to accept into her married family.

However its seemed five year old Vera had no wish to stay with Alice, for her brother was the most wonderful man she could ever meet. Almost reluctantly Nan and Otto, though they knew the future might be difficult, accepted Vera should join them. But all these arrangements only occurred after Morton's death, and were not apparent even by 1854.

These two families – the Sinclair's and the Milliken's were not then to know it, but they were destined to meet and live together. It was this meeting, along with another family, that of Charles Doherty, who were to establish their own future in both minerals and oil. By doing so they were, in due course, to alter the future of the United States and several of the Carroll families decedents, which sometime in the future we shall understand. Their lives would also involve the Purcell's and the Sand's emphasising how by its vastness the United States gave opportunities for everyone to prosper, provided they were willing to accept the risks

For the present we leave the Sinclair's in western Texas and the Milliken's in Salt Lake City and return to the results of those meetings between the David Reid and their guests, Kurt, Agnes and Anita Sand, in San Francisco and David's possible investment to research a possible route for a Transcontinental Railway. However several developments had occurred within the Purcell family during those years.

Erin had born a son, Arnold, to her beloved husband over a year ago, and knew she must wait sometime before she conceived again by Patrick as he had promised Merle to start her first pregnancy by him on her nineteenth birthday and this time it would bear her assumed name of O'Donnell, though she knew all of them felt Matthew was hers in spite of his different surname.

They both knew what a demanding man he was, it was as well he had two 'wives' otherwise he would. seriously, task their lives – for they knew they would never refuse him when he wanted it to happen. They also knew, even two women would not be enough for Patrick. Erin had confessed to Merle, one of the reasons she had been willing to accept her, was her fear he would soon find another woman – another mistress. Erin had laughed and told Merle she preferred that mistress to live in their house, and not to fear he had enjoyed another woman without her knowledge.

Now it was Merle's turn, begun, at her request on her nineteenth birthday, leading to a daughter, Marina O'Donnell the next year. By then Patrick had established himself as a successful New York Stockbroker in the company. He was admitted as a junior member of the New York Stock Exchange a few months after Erin bore his second child, a daughter, Alexis Purcell in early 1856.

They were now quite wealthy. They had moved to a small estate on Long Island and entertained quite frequently. Patrick had been in constant communication with his family, learning he had been pardoned, and if he wanted he could move back to Ireland, but neither he, nor his two 'wives', desired this. They were now American citizens. He did consider his father's suggestion to soon leave the Drew's company and start one on his own, even an American offshoot of his father's company. Though he considered it too early, there were good reasons for leaving.

Firstly, though reaping the benefits of is work – now quite used to bribing and accepting valuable retainers to ensure the success of his own and the firm's investment, still a large proportion of the profits went to the company.

But there were other reasons. Though now, not adverse to use methods which his father would consider, deplorable, he was not pleased with the business associations Daniel Drew was making. It seemed to him many of these investments were illegal. If discovered it could ruin the company. He knew, however, that many other New York

Stockbrokers were dealing with worthless shares for a quick profit. As far possible Patrick kept apart from these stocks. He was making friends with many bankers both in New York and Washington.

Though not the only stocks he dealt with, gradually, Patrick became more involved in Railway stocks, as various companies were reaping the benefit of the public's demands for easy travel. Every town in the north eastern United States were clamouring for railway transport, and having to pay a high price for the privilege

Nor was his love life less exciting. As they had expected, in the free sexual abandonment of the city, Patrick was delighted to enjoy the bodies of several of his New York contacts. He always told his two wives of his encounters, and they did not discourage him. They were too happy in their own satisfying pleasures with him. Neither were adverse to, occasionally, straying themselves with his business colleagues. It was the normal way of life in the city.

2.

Charles Doughty and his family after their escape from imprisonment in Ireland had sailed to France. There, with his resources he had bought a delightful house in the Loire valley at Vendome. Charles, a qualified survey engineer, had no difficulty in finding employment with the French Government surveying for minerals for road building as he had previously done in Ireland. He often wondered whether his good friend Patrick Purcell had survived imprisonment like him. For Charles, like Patrick. believed in a free Ireland and was why they had both joined the Free Ireland movement.

Many were the times they had been present in demonstrations and listened to the orations of Daniel O'Connell, as he espoused his beliefs that the British Government were subjugating the people of Ireland – both Roman Catholics and Protestants – delighted that, at last O'Connell was elected as a Member of Parliament and allowed to take his place at Westminster. They were both appalled when he was arrested and William O'Brien carried on his work.

But like Patrick, Charles believed in peaceful demonstrations within the law, and was disgusted when O'Brien had become militant resulting in the necessity of leaving the country he loved and escaping to France. He knew this was the end of the movement for a Free Ireland, and it would be years before the British Government considered their case again. However Charles was a pragmatic man and quickly forget the past enjoying once again his intimate associations with women in their vicinity, just as he had done in Ireland.

Of course his wife, Matilda, knew her husband was a 'womaniser' but had no option be to accept his infidelities as she did truly love her husband, in spite of his faults. Perhaps what caused her the greatest pain was when Charles started an association with the wife of one of their neighbours, Marie de Freycinet.

The Freycinet's were very prosperous Roman Catholics and were related to the famous Charles de Freycinet, who many times had served as a Minister for France. In fact the family were very strong and god fearing Roman Catholics quite different from the protestant Doughty's.

Even Charles could see the dichotomy in their strong religious views, whilst they attended mass and appeared to considered the Doughty's as virtually heathens with their own heretical protestant views. In spite of this it seemed that Marie de Freycinet failed to see she was not abiding by the teachings of her church. It even amused Charles when as they lay together in complete intimacy, she calmly told him she absolved her sins every week in her confessional and paid the fee stipulated to free her from perdition.

This intimate association did little to lessen the growing relationships between the two families they spent many days in each others company. Both were now quite rich and could further their friendships as, together, they enjoyed the delightful countryside and the pleasant views by the river in the Loire. Neither took a great interest in politics and though they supported their new Emperor Napoleon III, now king of France, but they did not always approve his obvious military ambitions. Both strongly believed in peace and was the reason why Charles had so strongly disapproved of William O'Brien's actions.

By now the French Government had realised the great abilities Charles had to offer them, and sent him to their Colonises in North Africa looking for mineral wealth in those countries. This necessitated Charles being absent from his growing family for long periods. More important he was successful finding many noble metal deposits as well as iron and copper ore which could so easily be developed. This in turn increased Charles wealth as it did the same for the government.

However, now absent from either Matilda or Marie for long periods, Charles was not without intimate feminine company, availing himself of the generous offers of the wives of French business men and officials of the resident French empire. These poor women living in what they considered a foreign country, with few male suitors other than their husbands, were delighted to bestow their favours on this amorous Irishman, so different for the men in their own society. Again Charles was a very handsome man – the reason for his success in illicit love affairs.

Charles enjoyed his stay in North Africa. Not only was it adding to his wealth but it seemed the country could provide him with pleasures more difficult to obtain in Vendome. Charles never knew if he fathered any off strings from these affairs, and never cared. He knew that abortions, though strictly illegal in France, were available if it was necessary to avoid a scandal.

Of course Charles often returned home for a vacation and resumed his liaison with both Matilda and Marie before once again returning to North Africa. His daughter Teressa was now twelve years old, rapidly becoming a beautiful young woman. So strong were Charles' sexual desires that to her consternation he would embarrass her by suddenly entering the bathroom as she bathed even using a sponge to help her clean her naked body.

At first this act terrified Teressa but she was proud of her body and was quickly developing the urges of a girl entering puberty, so she did not stop him nor report these happenings to her mother. Now proud of the effect she seemed to have on her father, and knew of his relations with Marie, which so hurt the mother she loved, she even tried to see if she caused similar reactions with her three year younger brother.

She deliberately ensured that Paul accidentally saw her nearly nude or half dressed body, disappointed when he showed only surprise but never attempted to touch her. Teressa knew that even though Paul was her brother she had expected a different result. What she did not know, and what was to later lead to greater intimacy, was that Paul, though still a young boy, this had awakened in his adolescent mind a liking for intimacy. It seemed that Paul was to follow his fathers faults in sexual matters though at this stage they were virtually undeveloped.

Of course as she grew older Teressa was to desire the friendship of young men and with her good looks quickly ensured that Jules de Freycinet, the son of Marie, became one of her string of growing boyfriends. Not adverse to coltishly entice her father, when on leave, to take her in his arms and love her, but allowing him to accidentally place his hands on her covered breasts. At present this was as far as it developed.

Charles had imbued in his son the same desire for a life as a mineral surveyor as he was. Charles told him he would send him to college to study engineering and geology. Paul responded willing, now of a sufficient age, knowing there would be opportunities there for more amorous association than was possible in the tight community in which he, at present lived.

Neither Charles nor Paul knew then that years later this decision was to take them very far from France to Mexico and then for Paul to travel to the United States. There to meet both the Sinclair's and the Milliken's and eventually to acquire a fortune in minerals and oil. But this would not occurred for many years.

Likewise, what Teressa did not know was that her earlier, and apparently unresponsive, attempts to interest her brother in her charms, had awakened in Paul desires for his sister which he knew were very improper. At present he had no opportunity to make many girlish conquests – and Teressa – sister or not – was a very pretty girl who had seemed to arise those wicked desires within him.

3..

Far away in Annapolis The Nolan and Ragan families were quite happy in the household duties to there benefactors. Though there were periods when the house was unoccupied but for themselves, they gratefully ensured it was ready for occupation by any of the Casimir or Holstein families or their guests. However Camay was now twenty six and as a woman was longing to find a man with whom she could settle and start the family she longed for.

But Devin was still in New York and not yet kept his promise to come and visit her, though she did receive quite loving letters from him from time to time. Neither did she have many opportunities of finding a possible alternate boy-friend as she was kept so busy and the house was on the northern approaches to the large city of Annapolis.

Once again the Holstein family arrived to spend a time in the city. Philip Holstein was furthering his son, James Holstein, financial education in the large Casimir/Holstein Bank in the city. This branch was very involved in Shipping interest in this large port with its many trading outlets along the Atlantic coast, but also with ports in both Central and South America and the Caribbean.

To his fathers displeasure James now thirty had never settled with one woman but enjoyed the many offered opportunities with society ladies. Though quite intimate they were only casual affairs offered but not meant for any permanent attachments by either party. He was very handsome and found very attractive, so had not any desire for it to progress. But this was now the normal way of life in the eastern states, particularly Annapolis and New York.

It was, therefore, not surprising that he found his maid servant, Camay, a possible conquest, as he had enjoyed liaisons with other servant girls in their mansion in Pittsburgh. He freely flirted with Camay who was glad to respond. missing the ardent attention Devin had given her, now so long ago. Accidentally he discovered Camay bending over mending the bed in his room, and came behind her to place a quick kiss on the nape of her neck.

Camay surprised turn round to finding him smiling at her and blushed. "Camay, don't be astonished, you know you are a very attractive young lady. I'm sure your many boy friends think the same as me. Don't be shy, tell me who is the one which particularly pleases you?"

Still blushing Camay replied, "Sir, I have no men friends of my own. You see we live a very isolated life here." Still flirting James continued, "You mean you don't go out with anyone – not see the wonderful things this city of Annapolis have to offer. – My dear Camay, that is a crime. Would you allow me to increase your education. Would you like me to act as your guide. If you would allow me, I will speak to your parents to see if I might do this, if only to show you that my offer is only because I feel it is wrong that a pretty girl like you have not had this opportunity until now."

Still bewildered at his sudden interest in her she almost gasped out her thanks and he left her completely perplexed at this morning encounter. Naturally she ran immediately to her mother, Delma, telling her what had happened. Of course her mother was equally surprised but when James later that day called on her asking her permission for her daughter to accompany her for an evening in the city, Delma thought perhaps his approach was an honourable one. Also she knew how desperately lonely was her daughter, despairing at Devin's failure to come to visit her.

Naturally she warned Camay very seriously of the possible pitfalls and of James's attentions, and not to succumb if he should make less desirable approaches during that evening. However, if only so that Camay could at least enjoy a single night of happiness, somewhat reluctantly she agreed. It was a wonderful occasion for Camay. By now she had seen at table how the rich ladies dinned, so when James took her in his carriage to a fine restaurant giving her a meal, which in the past she had been forced to serve for their guests, she knew how to behave. Then taken to a theatre for the first time in her life, Camay returned believing she had spent a full evening in paradise.

James had behaved very correctly. To begin with his only familiarity was to take hold of her hand and gently kiss it. Throughout the evening he behaved as a perfect gentleman never taking nor expecting any liberties. Only after they drove home and before she alighted from the coach did he bend over and briefly kiss her on the lips, immediately thanking her for a delightful evening before helping her to alight. Leading her on his arm into the house and finally offering her a drink.

After that he behaved impeccably by ringing for their maid, Maeve, then asking her to summon their mother. Finally, thanking Delma for so kindly loaning her beautiful daughter who had given him such an enjoyable evening. After that both Delma and Camay felt James was indeed an honourable man whose intentions were essentially sincere. So in the coming weeks James asked, and was granted three more enjoyable evenings whilst Camay now felt completely at ease and found little difficulty in more serious and even more intimate conversations. Even Delma now believed that there was a possible, even if remote chance, that James might come to think of giving Camay as a possible happy future.

By now they dinning in greater privacy, eating in the side saloons with curtains to ensure they were not disturbed. Of course James frequently used this occasions for holding her lovingly in his arms and sometimes kissing her as they sat afterwards. He would tell her how beautiful she was then leading to greater intimacy as they talked, once or twice his hands straying to her covered breasts. When she reacted showing her disapproval James did not apologise.

"Camay dear," he said. "You must know by now that I find you very attractive. Of course you must have guessed that at my age I have flirted with girls before. It seems since you were raised in Ireland you thought it wrong what I just did. Camay that's not so. In America all girls of your age enjoy these little attentions. Does it not thrill you just as it does me. Please let me show you how wonderful it is to let a man court you in the usual intimate way we all behave here."

She did not reply, unsure what she should say and he took no further liberties that evening. However when an a subsequent date he came behind her after they stood up to leave and now placed both his hands firmly on her bust. Gently squeezed them and kiss her neck, she knew she liked it and let it continue. Gradually on further occasions his hands strayed further and Camay felt her emotions rise, so when those hands pulled up her dress as he held her tightly from behind they now rested close and pressed to that secret area below her abdomen Camay gasped but found a growing feeling of excitement and did not rebuff him. Almost to her disappointment it went no further

A week later James came to tell her the family were returning to Pittsburgh and begged her to have one final special evening together. This time he took her where he had never taken her before. It was a dinning establishment specially suited for lovers assignations consisting in a small suite of rooms. A dinning area and a place for 'retiring'. Camay mind was in a whirl. She knew this would be the last meeting with him for some time and by now she wanted it to continue, hoping he would return soon, and possibly to offer her even more.

She was excited and it increased as he seduced her with his delightful manipulations of her body. She gladly accepted the large quantities of wine he gave her. Though not really drunk she felt her inhibitions go. She now felt she loved James. She seemed incapable of controlling her self. Suddenly though still conscious she let him lead her to the day-bed and fell back on it. completely under his control. She probably drifted into unconsciousness. Suddenly she was awoken crying out her the pain in her abdomen. She awoke to find James was half undressed, as was she, but he was virtually raping her and then he collapsed exhausted on top of her.

Suddenly she realised what had happened. She was no longer a virgin – that had been the cause of her pain – but she now knew he had used her in the way she had been taught must never happen until she married. Camay that night became a 'fallen women'. James had enjoyed her body to the full. Quickly she arose and tried to dress properly again, demanding James took her home.

He said nothing on that journey. Did not explain or apologise for what he had done. When she arrived back at the house she ran in fear to her mother. But it was too late. Delma now knew James had used her daughter, seduced her and been fully intimate with her. Delma did her best to prevent any further damage and gave her a sleeping pill before putting her to bed.

The next morning when they arose they found James and the entire Holstein family had left early before taking any food. James was gone. He had once again enjoyed the body of one of their maids. He had timed his seduction to perfection. Now the house was empty once again and for three weeks the whole family feared for Camay. They had reason to be afraid for there was no visible sign that she was safe. Six weeks later poor Camay started 'morning sickness'. She now knew she carried inside her James' unborn child.

4..

When Gordon Taylor brought his twenty seven year old nephew, Alan Mosley, to America to act as one of his site managers, Alan discovered quickly that there were many more opportunities of illicit intimacy than he had been allowed to enjoy in Britain. However, in spite of this, Alan, having never married, had enjoyed many less intimate but enjoyable relationships with quite a number of women in Manchester.

Now he was quickly introduced to the Marshall, Le Raye, Wilson and many other well established families in Pittsburgh. He had the opportunity at many social occasions to opportune several very willing married ladies and received several invitations for assignations with these ladies whenever their husbands were not available. Even spending several nights of sexual enjoyment in their beds. It was the way most rich families behaved in the city.

Inevitably his work brought him in contact with Albert Sands and his company helping to build these new railways. So was invited to dinner several times and it was there he was to meet Albert and Helga Sand's daughter, Sophia, only two years younger than him, now married to one of the company foreman, Hugh Danton. However it had been a marriage forced on Sophia as she conceived by Hugh before they married. It is doubtful if Sophia really loved her husband, who was far less intelligent that she was.

Like her entire family she was very promiscuous, which had led to her downfall. In fact she felt far stronger illegal sexual feelings for her brother Kurt. True intimacy had never occurred with him, though she

149

had tried very hard to entice him into her bed after she married Hugh. As a woman she wanted children but probably due to her opinion of her husband she ensured she only conceived when her desire for a baby became too intense to resist. So, although now married seven years, Sophia had only borne Hugh two children. A son, Keith Danton and a recent daughter, Susan.

Sophia quickly found herself attracted to this handsome man her own age who flattered her with his complements. They very quickly realised that they both wanted to develop their relationships more than this As she, like Alan, had indulged in intimacy with others before, it was natural that it would be reciprocated. Since his work took Hugh away for many weeks, they both had the opportunity to enjoy assignations. Very quickly they became lovers and spent several nights together in either of their homes..

As they lay together on one of these occasions, exhausted by their exertions but too tired to go to sleep they had a chance to converse together. It was Sophia who opened, "Alan have you ever had a real girl friend of your own when you lived in Britain? I'm not a fool – I know you only use me simply for your pleasure."

Alan laughed, "Of course I do Why not! I know you like it. – Go on admit it." Sophia felt annoyed at his directness. "But I have responsibilities which evidently you do not! Have you never even considered settling down with just one woman?"

Quickly he replied, "Of course not with so many women willing to please me as I know I please you – why should I tie myself to just one woman. – It is obvious – you do not love your husband – yet like me – you use him – get him to give you those babies you want. Are you not simply using him in the same way?"

Sophia had to admit he was right. "Yes! Marriage to Hugh was a mistake – It was my fault I was not careful enough and conceived. I had loved intimacy since I was very young. You see my mother and father – though I know they still love each other – have never been faithful to each other. – It's in our blood. – Do you know my younger brother Kurt, virtually has two wives, Agnes and Anita, but he swears in his letters to me that Anita is not his mistress and he regards her as his second wife."

Alan was intrigued, "You must tell me more. I think that is what I would want. Two women living with me giving me children when I wanted it – just like the Mormons – but I would not want to marry either of them. – Why I might want to replace one or other of them after a time."

Now Sophia was very annoyed, "You brute you would use them. Not mind the pain it caused them when they bore your children – and then discard them afterwards. Kurt tells me both his women have born him children but he sincerely believes he is completely married to both of them and would never think of discarding Anita although she is not his legal wife. – It seems you are a very evil man. – If you should want to behave like that – why should not a woman choose two men."

Alan retaliated, "Isn't that just what you do. You use both me and Hugh." Sophia had to laugh, "I suppose you are right. – But then I would never think of giving you children. If I ever wished to give a baby to any man who was not my husband, I would want to ensure we both had strong feelings for each other – not the causal intercourse you offer me. – Alan I doubt if you would fit that bill. – I'm content for Hugh to provide for me whilst I take my pleasures elsewhere. – I'm not complaining about our relationship. I hope it continues. It's just I think we should both know where we stand."

That was the end of their conversation. At last they found they needed to rest and they lay together, their naked bodies pressed closely to each other, contented in what they had done. But then Sophia was not the only married woman with whom he spent many hours of intimacy. He often had the pleasure of Paula Carroll. daughter of Fay and Francois Le Raye, long time married to Edwin and Linda Carroll's son, Frank. But then Paula knew that her husband, Frank, still enjoyed his relationship with Joanne Brakel, one of the Dutch families who settled in Pittsburgh during the American war of independence. Joanne had been Frank's intimate girl friends before they married, so Paula saw nothing wrong in relieving her loneliness whilst her husband was away.

No Alan was adamant that he would remain a single man, enjoy liaison with as many willing women as possible. Yet he had to admit that he felt far stronger feelings for Sophia than the other women he amused. Perhaps if she was free he might have considered her as a more permanent partner, even if not his wife. He knew in spite of what he had told Sophia, he did want a family of his own. However Sophia was not free and so not available to him.

5..

Devin Ragan had been very tired and it was late when he awoke and now remembered what had happened the previous night. He washed, dressed and came downstairs a little self-conscious appearing so late in the morning and was pleased that the two ladies were already downstairs as was Morna Lynch, to whom they were talking.

It was Erin who addressed him, "It seemed you were very tired. Please sit down whilst I order breakfast for you. Then after I have finished telling Morna what we intend to do I know you must want to talk with her." Devin smiled, relieved she was not castigating him for rising so late, sat down as requested and enjoyed a large breakfast served to him.

As he ate he heard Erin tell Morna she must stay with them for a time until her husband arrived home and she knew he would know how to help her. Devin could see Morna was very relieved as he feared she would be traumatised after the events the previous night. Once finished he explained he must return to see to his work, though fortunately no tasks had been given to him but must return to Tammany Hall for instructions.

Erin understood but felt he would like to talk to Morna in private after what he had done for her, and after finding he was free at the weekend told him he must come and call on them again and then he would learn about Morna's future. The dear lady smiled and left them alone, yet Devin now felt very self-conscious and unsure of himself. However Morna quickly put him at his ease.

"Dear Devin", she said. "I just don't know how to thank you for bringing me here to these kind ladies. When I dashed out and almost collided with you – well – I just thought you were another of those horrible men who wanted to use us – as so many have done to me these last three months. Even then I knew I would rather give myself to you than that horrible man. – Then you pitied me – you were so kind to me - and brought me here. – Please do come back here next weekend. – I do want you to – it would be wonderful if you could possibly become my friend – for until today – I have had none."

Of course Devin was pleased and told her so. Then she continued. "You know – I might have escaped too late. – That evil man had seized, and raped me before I could stop him – I was not prepared – Do you understand – I may be carrying his child. – I've told the dear lady and she seems to understand telling me her husband will know what to do if so. ----- I just thought you should know. – If so – well – er – you may not believe I am a fit person for you to befriend me."

Devin's heart went out to the poor girl. Instinctively he seized hold of her hands, placed them to lips, and kissed them saying, "Oh! No! That would not make any difference. – It was not your fault – You see I know how they tricked you into coming to that horrible place. ---- I know I would love to come to know you properly. Perhaps you might let me call on you – whatever the good ladies do for you. - In any case I shall return this weekend and then we can talk about it "

A delightful smile spread across Morna's face, "Oh! Devin that would be wonderful." He smiled back apologised for leaving so quickly but made it clear he did want to see her again. Then after saying a quick farewell to both ladies, as the other lady called Merle had now joined them.

The remaining days to the weekend seemed endless but he was delighted when Saturday arrived to take the train to the railway station only two miles from the estate and to call on them. Receiving a rapturous reception from Morna and an equal welcome from Erin who now introduced herself as Erin Purcell and the other lady as Merle O'Donnell. However Erin told him he must first meet her husband who would tell him of what was planned for Morna's future, then lead Devin to his study where he was working on some important papers.

He stood before his desk but the kind man immediately stood up and came to him asking him to sit in a chair whilst he sat opposite him. Now the man smiled, "I am Patrick Purcell. Those papers on my desk should tell you I am a very busy business man. I'm a city stockbroker, but I can tell you I'm delighted to meet you after what my wife has told me how you removed Morna from those evil men. It was very courageous of you. – Yet it seems you work for them and Tammany Hall. I know they do some good for Irish emigrants but I do not approve of their corruption and misuse of so many women. Please tell me truthfully - in what way you are involved."

Devin was at pains to tell him everything and how he worked for the Democratic league but had little to do with their evil side, though like the other night, was forced to act as a courier to take goods, and messages from time to time, to these brothels. "Mr. Purcell, I cannot avoid doing that – but ask you to believe me that I have never been involved in any of their illicit plans – nor have I ever used any of those girls when I was forced to visit those brothels.

Now to his relief this man smiled and told him he believed him if only because of his kind consideration for Morna and kindly bringing Morna here. "Now you must want to know of our plans for poor Morna. Well we have a wonderful Irish housekeeper, who we saved from a life like Morna, as we have for her daughter and another young maid my two ladies saved some time ago. Morna has agreed to stay with us and become another maid to help us.."

Again he smiled, "Morna has already told us she told you of her fears and she says that does not discourage you for wanting to know her better. – We shall have to wait and see if her fears are justified – if it happens I know what we can do. That is our and Morna's problem. – However I'm sure you want to stay and speak with Morna again. Please do so. – I will add – if it is your wish – we should be glad if you could call on us again regularly – and so help Morna to feel she has someone she can trust."

Immediately Devin made sure he knew that this would be what he would like, they shook hands and then led him to another room where Morna was, already dusting the furniture. As soon as she saw him she came and threw her arms around him, unabashed as he pressed his lips to hers. After that they sat together on one of the chairs and Morna told him how kind everyone had been to her and now she could stay here and work without any fears for her future.

The household were very understanding and they let Morna leave her duties and for Devin to take her into the large garden of the estate where they could talk at length – each telling the other of their previous lives – though Devin did not tell her everything about Camay and his affection for her. She took him to the kitchen and the cook kindly gave both of them some food before once again retiring outside until it was time for him to leave.

As she showed him to the door Erin came to them smiling "Mr. Ragan, my husband is very pleased with you and understands the work you have to do. We all want Morna to be happy here so please call on us again, whenever you can, and particularly at the weekends – I know Morna would like that very much.. – You see all of us here come from Ireland – just as you do - and want to help as many Irish people as we can. "

Devin was a very happy man as he walked slowly back to the station to return to his home. However he could not quite satisfy his conscience. He thought, 'What would Camay think of me – and how do I really feel about Morna. – Surely I cannot come to think of Morna as my girlfriend – Yet Camay is so far away – and now I shall see Morna very regularly. – But I am a man – and want a girlfriend who I can see regularly. – I never promised Camay anything more than I would call upon her – Yes! I suppose I am in the wrong – I have not done so – I must try – to – er – at least do this soon."

He felt a little more relieved. After all he had saved Morna from that evil man and helped to give her a future. He would let things take their course. However he remembered that his duties to Tammany Hall would inevitably bring him again many times to have to play a part in their wicked use of poor young girls. Could he continue doing this. At present there was no way he could avoid it. Again he needed this job and in many ways he was doing good things and helping many Irish people. In any case he doubted if he could find any other employment.

6..

However both Erin and Merle knew by now they had a problem of their own and one they could do little to avoid. It seemed that Patrick had discovered another woman who interested him. They knew her name, for he had told them. It was Tricia Drake, a woman with some wealth, the widow of a man much older than herself who had left her a reasonably large mansion and a small estate. It seemed that Patrick managed her investments and was how he came to know her. Never-the-less he had confessed to both of them that it was now more than just a business acquaintance.

Patrick had told Erin when he proposed to her, that she would never be the only woman in his life if she married him. She had accepted this for he had promised his infidelities would never be a secret and that he would always love her. Then both she and Merle were raped pregnant and yet, not only had he demanded she still married him, but also provided a loving solution for the sister she loved. It was one reason why Erin had accepted Merle's position in the family. Now he had confessed his infidelity, though he told them little about Tricia, only that that their relationship had become intimate and they knew he now sometimes stayed a night at her home and then slept with her.

Both Erin and Merle had expected this for sometime but it seemed his affection for both of them was if anything even stronger than in the past. It was simply that they knew Patrick needed more than one woman to gratify his lust, and as this regularly occurred in the New York society, so they accepted this as quite normal. A least Patrick had told them that after she bore a daughter she was now infertile, so at least it seemed Patrick could not add to their own family.

Tricia Drake had first employed Patrick as her stockbroker to ensure her investments were in order. However from the start he had been surprised at her knowledge of the stock market, particularly as she had never received any training in these matters. It seemed she had acquired a knowledge from her husband, for though he was a very cruel man and for over five years had treated her abominately, blaming her for something for which she was innocent, it had given Tricia a training she might never otherwise have acquired..

It took a long time before he was to learn the facts and not before they had started an association. Tricia was the daughter of Stephen Hawthorne, a successful writer who had married Emily Backhouse. But Emily had died in childbirth as she delivered Tricia, so Tricia had never known her mother. Only later, as she grew up did Tricia learn that Emily was a beautiful black girl. Her father fell in love with her and never really recovered from her early death when only nineteen years old. Stephen was a disciple for women's education. He had encouraged Tricia to study and paid for her education in the Western Reserve College. But he died as she finished her education.

Tricia had graduated in 1848 and soon afterwards her father died leaving her few resources. Thomas Drake, a rich stockbroker, and governor of the college, had fallen for her during the degree ceremony. Though he was sixty three years of age, knowing Thomas had married twice before, with little money she accepted his proposal of marriage the same year, and bore Ranee ten months later and her husband could see Ranee was a black child.

Tricia had never told Thomas of her ancestry so when after a horrendous birth, during which she almost died. Believing Ranee was not his child and convinced Tricia had conceived by his black servant, he had beaten her, unmercifully, a few days later. Future intercourse with Thomas, and later with other men, proved she was no longer capable of pregnancy.

Poor Tricia then endured five years of hell, frequently beaten by her husband who refused to accept that her baby may have been black because of her ancestry. With her father dead, she had no means of proving it. As they lay together, naked, Patrick could still see some of the scars from her mistreatment. As his hands traced this evidence over her lovely body. Tricia had added that after her birth he had merely abused her for his own pleasure, not even surprised that she could not give him more children.

Although there was no longer any love between her and Thomas, he had found that her intelligent mind and training, could help him, being a stockbroker like Patrick. Very quickly she became proficient in her work. Tricia then explained when her husband died and left her a small endowment, with her acquired knowledge of the stock market, she had invested wisely, and was now a wealthy woman. Patrick was intrigued by her knowledge and was soon involving her in his own transactions. It was, mutually, rewarding

Both Erin and Merle knew they had no option but to accept it. It did not, in any way, affect his love for them, and still enjoyed fully satisfying intercourse. Eventually he brought Tricia to meet them, He left them together, expressing the hope that they might, all, come to an understanding. Both Erin and Merle were pleased at her frank admission. She told them she was not sure if she was in love with Patrick though she felt sure their relationship was not a causal one. Tricia spoke kindly to them.

"I think you should know. Patrick told me some time ago. His love for both of you was far greater than his feelings for me. In fact this has made me admire him. I promise I have no wish to take your place and content to enjoy his kindness to me, after suffering so badly, during my marriage. I confess I am very sorry I cannot bear him children. If I could I would, already, have conceived. He is such a wonderful man."

Gradually their initial feeling of jealousy, evaporated. She was not a threat to them. They had known for years something like this would happen. It seemed she could, even, help him in his work. Before Erin conceived again by Patrick, the following year, Tricia had become part of an enlarged family. What pleased Tricia the most, was their acceptance and love they bestowed on her now, eight year old black daughter, Ranee Drake. They treated her the same as they treated their own children. It seemed Patrick now had two mistresses but he, always, treated, all of them, as if they were his legally married wives.

* * * * * * * * * * * * * * *

Daniel Mason had told Patrick of his love for Sally Byrd, the daughter of the cruel Plantation owner, Henry Byrd, who firmly believed in slavery and that all black persons were born to serve their white masters. Henry believe this very strongly but also that it was economically essential for the prosperity of his plantation. There was no doubt which side Henry would support if a civil war occurred. He would support very firmly the southern states.

This seriously effected Daniel's progress in trying to win Sally as his wife. Perhaps he even annoyed Henry even more as he persuaded Sally that any form of slavery was wicked, even converting her to his own beliefs. There was no doubt that Sally had fallen in love with Daniel just as strongly as was his love for her.

However though eventually Daniel proposed marriage to Sally he received an immediate rebuff form her father, who violently refused permission for their marriage, even forbidding any further liaison with his daughter. In spite of this they both found ways of meeting in secret. Yet it seemed they would never have the chance of marrying and enjoying a life together.

Then in 1853 happenings occurred which were to alter this but events of a terrible nature – events none of them would have wanted to happen.

7.

After Kurt's shocking disclosures that day at the Reid mansion their was little time before they retired to dress for dinner to discuss further Kurt's proposition about future railways. Instead Donald took everyone outside to see the extent of his huge estate. Their visitors marvelled at the wonderful vista of the San Francisco bay which was possible from their vantage point. Then they returned dressed for dinner and enjoyed a evening telling each about their previous lives.

When it was time to retire Kurt again surprised them by saying that though they had allocated a room for Anita, as their unexpected guest, he told them Agnes would be sleeping there tonight as Anita wished to sleep with him as she had just conceived his first child. Though surprised their hosts gladly assented. The next morning each arose at different times and breakfasted. Then it was time for the men to adjourn to the large withdrawing room to discuss Kurt's plans for railways, whilst their hostesses took Agnes and Anita on a coach drive around their estate and to call on Cherie and Daniel Wilson's estate nearby.

Now it was left to Kurt to explain what he and his partners were considering doing in establishing a small company called Pacific Railways, to see if they might interest others in planning and building railways in California and to research a possible route through the mountains to eventually break out onto the plains. Then, possibly joining other companies who might drive west from New York, or more probably from existing lines in the east, to join their own lines, thereby constructing a Transcontinental Railway.

He surprised them even more by explaining why this Transcontinental line might need to be the one first to be built. There were few steel mills of any size and industrial undertakings were at present very small in the state. To build railways here they would have to import the steel and ready built locomotives to drive the trains which might prove far too expensive. However this could be avoided if these articles could be carried on their trains directly from the east.. He believed that there would not be people in the whole of California with assets great enough to invest in such a project.

His plan was to carefully research and cost a line from San Francisco or Sacramento though the mountains to give access, at least to the new middle west states being populated by many immigrants. This would cost a lot of money with no dividends apparent at present. However these would be available for sale at a good price should money be raised to build the actual line. He admitted it was a gamble with no immediate results but it would put them well ahead of any competitors if it became a fact. Finally admitting he knew a man, Theodore Judah, capable of doing this and he was himself, a trained engineer and geologist, who could help him.

"Gentlemen," he said, "I believe this line will only be built if the U.S. Government heavily invests in it, as they do at present in road building, simply because it might still unify this union which is at present in peril. So we must be able to send to Washington, and finance a man to live there, to persuade officials that of its necessity. Also to see if he can find any possible investors who, provided that Government invest, would wish to become part of a consortium."

He paused, "I have already acquainted Gordon Taylor, a friend of mine, - and I believe a friend of yours - a director of the large firms actively building railways in the east, of my ideas. He entirely approves of my idea and will start to see if he could start a similar project as ours to build the other part of the railway coming from the east. In his case he has the added advantage of knowing several members of Congress to help in lobbing others there for this purpose."

Now Kurt played his trump card. "My colleagues, good and well established business men intend to do this in any case. Collis Huntington has agreed to go east for this purpose and we shall finance him for his work. Donald Raid, in view of your own family relationships with many in the east, we felt we should offer you a chance to join our own consortium and invest in this project. – That is the reason for my visit. – We intend to do this in any case - but, with you now a well established business man here – and with your own acquaintances, it might persuade other to join us."

It was clear that David Backhouse was not so sure they should be involved and petitioned Donald not to do so. However it seemed the idea had intrigued Donald. For most of his life he had tried so hard to persuade the government to take California from Mexico, by force if necessary. Though he had not been successful, others had performed the task even going to war with Mexico. Building such a Transcontinental Railway would be furthering his desire for the United States to really become one gigantic country stretching from the Atlantic to the Pacific.

Donald laughed, "Kurt Sands, it seems you are a very unorthodox man, even in the way you live. It is not surprising that you now so fervently press this project on us. I fear, as it seems you do – this fragile union of states are in danger of disintegrating - building such a line might well still keep us together. I will, willing, invest in Pacific Railways, at least to determine the feasibility of building this railways across California and the mountains. – I also accept we need someone like your, Collis Huntington, to go east to bring some much needed sense into our government. – David here will draw up the papers and I will come to Sacramento to meet your colleagues and sign these in your presence. – Now let us enjoy what is left of this beautiful day and go to join the ladies when they return from their journey."

They adjourned for drinks as they waited their ladies return. Kurt asked permission to leave them and sat down to write a very long letter to send to Gordon Taylor, telling him of the days success, as he had previously told him his intentions, particularly because of Donald Reid's obvious relationship with the powerful Carroll/Marshall company and its other companies building railways in the east. He knew Gordon would be delighted at the news and no doubt would quickly meet and liaise with Collis Huntington when he arrived. Also Gordon would now see the importance of trying to bring together others in the east and interest them in building the other part of the railway, so necessary if it was to be a success.

Having finished and sealed the letter for sending he could not avoid contemplating on how he even came to be in California. His success to date was not why he came here. His wealth at present came from mining and its accessories, not why he had made that long and dangerous journey. Yet if he had not the idea of establishing a business for road building – yes and railways. – just like his fathers business – then he would never have arrived.

Then he again thought of the happiness that journey had given him. If not he would never have met Agnes – nor later – Anita, and never enjoyed the five years of happiness they had bestowed on him. Yielding their bodies and conceiving his children, providing him with a family, which he loved. That journey had been worthwhile just for this .

Now today, it seemed he might soon be returning to complete the original reason for his coming. He knew what he had proposed was really a dream. – The 'Golden Egg' may never be possible. – Yet, if it happened he knew his wealth from mining would be insignificant with the wealth he would gain from this railway. Further more it was the life he really wanted. He had enjoyed his short time in railway construction in the east. He also realised that through Huntington they must find others in the east – successful and wealthy business men, stockbrokers and bankers willing to risk their money for the benefits which would accrue if they were successful.

He knew this must also be own task. Suppose bedsides this railway he could interest others all over the United States in forming another consortium quite separate from Pacific Railways – one only interested in investing in railways. If this happened – if he was part of that consortium – he could achieve riches greater than he could visualise. That night he retired to bed with an equally happy, and pregnant Anita, who listened, though she really did not understand, his ideas for a very successful future.

8.

Once the Nolan family knew Camay had conceived they were very concerned for her future. Of course it was worse for poor Camay, not only would she soon become an unmarried mother, but she now knew that she could never expect any future with Devin. Camay even felt this was her punishment for even accepting her enjoyable days with James Holstein. She knew she had been unfaithful to Devin. Then again, she knew, if Devin had kept his promise and even come occasionally to see her, she knew she would never had allowed any association with James to develop. What now did the future hold for her.

All felt as if their wonderful life since they had come to live in Annapolis must soon come to an end. They knew the Mistress of the House, Sharon Carroll, being a strong Roman Catholic, like themselves, would never countenance Camay having an abortion. Further more would Camay's behaviour seem to Mistress Sharon, that they were not truly fitted persons to act as housekeepers and servants of her house. It was in trepidation they awaited her arrival

In fact both Sharon and Michael Casimir arrived shortly after they were all sure poor Camay was pregnant. Believing they should immediately be informed of the situation it was left for Delma Nolan at speak to Sharon in private. She did so in some trepidation but swore the man responsible for Camay's condition was none other than James Holstein, the son of their two great friends, Philip and Joanne Holstein.. Of course Sharon was appalled, especially as it was James Holstein who was responsible. As expected Sharon told them Camay must keep her child and somehow they would find a way for looking after Camay and her baby after it happened. She could never agree to an abortion.

Naturally, later, in private Sharon told her husband all about Camay's plight. Now Michael was far more practical and, as a protestant, had never deplored abortion as was his wife's belief. Also he not only felt very sorry for Camay and yet, also, felt a little responsible. Philip Holstein had told Michael a long time before about his sons deplorable life style. Already he had sired two children by their maids in Pittsburgh. However as James was now nearly as rich as himself and had then been in his late twenties, there was no way Philip could prevent it happening. However he had insisted, at James expense, that these poor girls achieved an abortion paid for by James.

Michael now felt responsible for not having warned the Nolan family of James Holstein's sexual behaviour. If he had warned, particularly, Delma Nolan, she might have preventing Camay forming an association with James. In spite of his knowledge of his wife's intense horror of abortion, believing it was murder, even believing the woman must pay for her sin, by baring a child, Michael did not agree. Somehow he must persuade both his wife and the Nolan family, that for Camay's sake she should abort her unborn child.

Though Case and Delma Nolan had never before agreed with abortion accepting the strict teachings of their church. Now it was their own daughter who was in trouble they no longer felt so strongly against the idea. Further more during their stay in Annapolis they had known many women in the city resorted to this when necessary. They did not want Camay to be known as an unmarried mother. Also, even though Sharon Casimir had assured them she or her husband would see to the financial future of Camay's child, hinting they might arrange for it to be adopted, they felt sure their daughter would never agree to this if she bore her child.

So when Michael Casimir approached them they had agreed they would try to persuade Camay she should abort her child. He had requested they sort Camay's views and Camay, though believing it was a sin, also wished to still have a better future accepted and Michael was informed.

Michael received a very different reception when he confronted his wife. On no account could she agree to this thing. Once again, it seemed their two religious views were in conflict, but in spite of this, Michael felt he must pursue the idea. Fortunately a few days after their arrival Michael receive an urgent need to return to Pittsburgh concerning their own investments. This provided the excuse to return there and then confront if necessary both Philip and James Holstein.

Naturally as soon as Michael told him of his sons behaviour, he was furious, and together confronted James. Again James showed his independence, simply telling them, if an abortion could be arranged he would foot the bill, even adding, if not he would settle a little money on his child after it was borne. It seemed James cared little for poor Camay's travail in bearing his unwanted child, nor the future life she must still endure as an unmarried mother.

So it seemed that both Philip and Michael must discover a better solution. Though Michael admitted he did not want this to damage his relationship with his wife. It seemed that Joanne Holstein would find a solution. She was probably more astonished and disgusted with Sharon's religious stand on this subject. Joanne born a Wycks, and a very strong protestant of Dutch ancestry, had many times taken Sharon to task for her religious views. She had told her that whatever she believed she had no right to interfere in other persons beliefs. Joanne now felt Sharon was doing this and condemning Camay to a very unhappy life.

She quite understood Michael's reluctance and wish to avoid unpleasant relations with his wife but also felt as James was her son, she must ensure Camay did not suffer for James' behaviour. Joanne simply told both of them she would return with Michael and ensure the damage was limited, and she did. Of course they thought she was going to get Sharon to change her views. In fact Joanne had decided to take matters into her own hands.

Once she arrived at Annapolis she abraded Sharon telling her how unjust she was on Camay. As she expected Sharon showed no remorse believing she could never go against the beliefs of her church. Then Joanne spoke privately with Camay, ensuring she was agreeable to the abortion. Then she explained her plan and got Camay to agree. Having found that poor Camay had not yet received a doctors attention she again spoke crossly to Sharon for not discovering whether she was strong enough to bear a child. Indignantly she told Sharon she was taking Camay into Annapolis to see a specialist and would stay with her until she knew the doctor was satisfied after a thorough examination.

She did this and she and Camay were away two full days but when she returned Camay was no longer pregnant. Joanne had instructed the specialist to abort Camay's two month old foetus and paid for the operation. Only then did she confront an astonished and disgusted Sharon.

Joanne's answer was very direct. "Sharon, Camay is your servant, not your daughter. It was my son who was responsible. Though he never even asked her to marry him, I consider she is far more my own daughter-in-law, than any relationship you have with her. I acted as her future mother-in-law and ensured I freed this poor young woman from the life my own son had condemned her. You have every right to hold your own views on abortion, - but you employ – not own – Camay. That baby would have been my grandchild even though James did not marry Camay. Once I got Camay to agree it was my duty to put matters right."

Though Sharon was still very annoyed she had to accept that Joanne had far more right than she to see to Camay's future. But Sharon was still angry, abortion appalled her. Though it took a little time for good relations to be once again established between them. They had been friends since childhood and she knew Joanne's strong protestant views. She would never change Joanne's views and would never accept Joanne's beliefs., but was not that the real test of religious toleration. Eventually good relationships were established again between the two families. Though Joanne knew she still had a problem with her own son which might never be settled as she desired.

As a result Camay was given a better future than she had believed two months before. Now if it happened, perhaps she might still have a future with Devin, knowing now she wanted this above everything. However Camay did not know of the relationship Devin had already formed with Morna Lynch. Camay may never gain the happiness she sort.

9.

In Petersburg, Virginia a terrible set of events occurred but one that completely altered the lives of both Daniel Mason and Sally Byrd. Henry Byrd considered the Masons as dangerous people as they frequently bought slaves from other plantations and set them free. It was not surprising when his daughter Sally fell in love with Daniel that he refused her plea to let her marry Daniel, when he proposed to her. Even more so for Sally had been convinced by Daniel's beliefs to free all slaves and then employ them giving them wages to work for them. This Henry Byrd considered would have led to bankruptcy.

It seemed that the two of them had no chance of marrying. Henry was jealous of the wealth the Mason's were acquiring, as he said, due their mortgaging of many plantations, blaming their bank for their parlous situation. However even more than this was his strong belief that all black persons had been created to work for white men. As a worshipping Anglican he believed that Quakers, with their entrenched religious views were evil people. Historically, slavery had been a corner stone of all past civilizations – people they considered inferior were born to serve them. How could anyone think these inferior blacks were an equal of their masters.

It seemed a freed slave by the name of Nat Torman, had set up his own store and married. His wife, also a freed slave, bore him two daughters, Harriet and Janet Torman but then miscarried and was barren. This was not surprising for his wife had born four children and suffered three miscarriages for which she was, severely whipped, starting from the age of twelve, before she married Nat when only twenty. This had resulted in Nat hating all white men and even helped some slaves to escape on the 'underground railway'. This was the means many northerners arranged for slaves to escape from their slavery and flee to the northern states, a major cause of trouble between the north and south.

It angered Henry Byrd, although none of his slaves had been freed in this way. He knew Nat Torman was behind this traffic but failed to prove it. It angered him even more that Nat was becoming prosperous living in a comfortable style, here in the centre of slavery. His desperate financial position had driven him to drink. To prove to his daughter that Negro women were not fit to be free and teach Nat Torman a lesson, knowing that no court in Virginia at that time, would commit him for trial, when drunk, he took matters into his own hands.

With the help of some of his overseers he kidnapped both Harriet and Janet, took them home and forced Sally to watch as he first deflowered each virgin girl and raped them. Poor Sally had to be restrained as she tried to protect them.

In a drunken rage he shouted at her and she always remembered his words. "This is what all black women were born to endure. It is men like your Daniel Mason who try to brainwash you into supporting anti-slavery. A white woman should approve of this as it saves you from too many pregnancies." Poor Sally was terrified. He left her sobbing taking away the two girls and spent the next month enjoying their poor bodies.

Once he was sure they had conceived he set them down opposite their father's store. Harriet was just sixteen and Janet then, was even three years younger. Their father, Nat Torman, knowing that there was no way of bringing a man as important as Henry Byrd to justice decided he must take matters into his own hands even though it would mean his own death. Leaving his wife to see to his distressed daughters he devised a plan.

Braking into Henry Byrd's large mansion at night, finding Henry and Sally sitting together after their evening meal, with no servants around, he thrust a revolver at Henry's head and he ordered Sally to undress and then lie of the floor, completely naked. She had no choice, though she feared what she must accept. Her father could not protect her for Nat had reversed the revolver in his hands and used it to smash his skull. Henry died immediately without emitting a sound.

Then he leaped on the helpless Sally, deflowered her agonisingly, covering her mouth with his hands so she could not scream. Then he raped her several times. Nat was a very virile man and he ejaculated inside her sore vagina each time saying, "This is what your father did to my daughters – now you know how it feels. I hope you bear a black child."

It was during his fifth raping of her now inert body, that servants broke into the room which he had locked. Content on his revenge he stood up turned the revolver on himself and killed himself. Although everyone rushed to help Sally, once she had recovered some sense of what had happened, she felt certain Nat Torman had completed his revenge, and that she had conceived his child.

Daniel Mason came to Sally as soon as he heard and insisted she came to his house, trying to console her. He told her they must get married at once as there was nothing now to prevent her marrying him. However Sally felt he was sorry for her and told him it was impossible as she thought she had conceived and, if so, she might bear a coloured child. Daniel had asked her, "If so will you keep this child?' Sally had always been against abortion so she told him she had no option but to keep it and become the unmarried mother of a black child.

To Sally's surprise Daniel took here in his arms and pressed her to him, smiling and kissing her passionately and simply said, "Then you must marry me. You are the woman I love. I've loved you for so long. If it occurs I want this baby to be mine as well as yours. It matters not whether it is black or white. It has come from your body which I adore."

Although she still objected still believing he was sorry for her – but also she was afraid – She could not see how she could live, in desperation she agreed –feeling certain he would regret this later.

It took some time for Daniel to convince her that it was not for pity he wanted her as his wife but because he had for so long loved her, telling her he did not care if her child was black or white. It would be her child and it mattered little to him that Nat Torman would be its father.

Daniel now informed her of the degree of her father's debts. She was penniless. The Bank owned her plantation. If she married him his father would sell her property but place the proceeds in trust for her to use as she wanted and not become his property. Daniel then asked her a favour – he never demanded it – he merely felt he must right a wrong. He wanted to take both Harriet and Janet Torman into their home – not his father's but his own home, which he would purchase for all of them. He would help to right the terrible thing her father had done to them and what had resulted in her own desperate position. If so Sally must be willing to bring up their children as part of their family, and not as servants, accepting their children as if they were his.

Sally had been delighted to accept, especially has he had not made any attempt to force her into agreeing. It was the least she could do after what her father had done. Now both Daniel and his father were realistic. By then they knew Sally was pregnant. There was no way she could live here in Virginia after what everyone knew had happened, as the sympathy of the local owners was for her father and they considered Sally should have aborted her child.

His family were rich. The bank was prosperous but there was a growing hatred against them and their ideals. They were Quakers not god loving Anglicans. The growing tensions between north and south must soon reach a climax. If secession from the Union occurred, they could not stay there in Petersburg with their anti-slavery views, with Virginia fighting to maintain slavery.

Daniel would take his new wife and the two pregnant Negress to Washington and open a bank there using their expertise and their support against slavery to attract customers from the rich industrial northern states. It worked and before any babies were born the Washington branch of the Mason Bank had been successfully established. It quickly grew in size. By then Sally, Harriet and Janet had become close friends, each pregnant by a man they disliked but united in their grief.

His willingness to marry him after what had happened, not only proved how sincere his beliefs were but showed just how much he loved her. She knew then she would love him for the rest of his life – no matter how many other women he might find. Harriet was the first and bore a nearly white son she called Desmond Torman and the next week Janet bore a coloured daughter she called Natalie Torman after her father. Then just two weeks later Sally bore a completely black daughter, Sharon, which Daniel demanded was registered as his child. This action, as well as by then, she knew that Daniel was not looking on either Harriet and Janet as servants, made her love Daniel even more.

Now with the Mason Bank of Washington firmly established in the capitol meant that Patrick Purcell met Daniel Mason many times and Patrick used his banking faculties for more than other banks. For by then Patrick, was a free agent, having severed his employment with the Daniel Drew and, following his fathers advice. had set up his own business as a Stockbroker in New York, naming it as 'Purcell Enterprises'.

10.

Immediately Kurt returned to Sacramento and had written to Gordon Taylor of his success and that he had formed a consortium to survey a possible railway line from San Francisco to the east. He hoped that now Gordon would do what he had considered so long ago as Kurt had worked so closely with him. He pressed on Gordon the need to start exploring the possibility of other persons being willing to begin a similar survey starting from the end of one of their existing lines, then drive west. Hoping eventually this might meet their own line driving east.

Then he told Gordon of their decision to send Collis Huntington to Washington to try to persuade the government to invest in the project, as they did in roads. He emphasised that a fully constructed

Transcontinental Line would help unify the United States more than any speeches in Congress. He begged Gordon to go and meet him once he arrived.

Finally he explained how fortunate they were to persuade Donald Reid to join them, knowing he too would do his best to interest his many relatives in the east to support his action. After all they had already invested and enabled a number of lines to be constructed in the east. Again Kurt knew how strong was Gordon's relationship with both Charlotte and Roy Marshall. They too were in a good position to petition the government to act.

Collis Huntington had left soon after Donald agreed to join. He would stay some time in Washington, his expenses paid by the consortium but he would also return from time to time using the Reid shipping facilities. It was after Gordon had called on Collis after he had settled in Washington that Gordon introduced him to both Patrick Purcell and Daniel Mason as Gordon, naturally had used their services many times. Collis was delighted that it seemed both Patrick and Daniel were interested in the project. Patrick, being already, so heavily engaged in railway investments, quickly convinced Daniel they should work together to try to encourage others in the project.

It was Tricia Drake who convinced Patrick that as in California they had already done far more than in the east by investing money – money which might be lost – in researching a possible route. If the idea got government approval then they would have a head start on anyone else, and could sell their ideas, if necessary to a third party. You see by now Tricia had become a junior director in 'Purcell Enterprises' investing some of her own money when Patrick began his new business in which several of his business colleagues had invested, becoming directors, knowing Patrick's business acumen.

Since Patrick had started his intimate association with Tricia, he had many times called on her own expertise to help him as he worked for the Drew company. Eventually it had become a daily event. There was no doubt that professionally Tricia was a great asset to Patrick. It seemed she had a very inquiring mind able to restrain at times, though often suggesting a different approach, to his own ideas. There was no doubt that Tricia greatly added to Patrick's own abilities. Also she was a woman where professionally there were few. Neither was she adverse to use her feminine wiles to obtain secret information which Patrick would never have obtained.

Perhaps this was one the reasons why both Erin and Merle had accepted her into their family. They knew now how much Patrick depended on Tricia's advice and forward thinking, and why they fully approved of Patrick making her a junior director of his new company. In fact, though at first his fellow directors did not fully approve of her appointment, they quickly realised how wrong they had been. Even how much importance was her presence when tricky investments were discussed. It seemed she had been befriended by Cornelius Vanderbilt as well as other male investors.

Tricia and Patrick met with both Daniel and Collis Huntington in Washington as he was trying to persuade Daniel that the Californian project, being at present being surveyed should be where they might make initial investments, if only to protect their position if it were to become a reality. Collis quickly informed the Californian consortium of his success in obtain at least some financial support from both 'Purcell Enterprises' and the 'Mason Bank'.

Back in Sacramento Kurt at once realised how important was this acquisition and wrote personally to both Patrick and Daniel, thanking them for their interest and clearly explained his own proven expertise in railway construction when he lived in the east and as well as his qualifications in both engineering and geology. Then he went on to explain the presence of Donald Reid and his great shipping company in their consortium explaining of Donald's close relationship to both the Carroll/Marshall companies as well as with the Vanderbilt family.

Kurt felt rewarded when both Patrick Purcell and Daniel Mason separately replied to him, thanking him, telling him they would try to get others to invest at least in their survey. Perhaps Daniel's greater interest in the west was because he knew that Gordon Taylor was trying to assemble a group of investors to start a similar project in the east. However they knew Gordon Taylor was working far more closely with the Casimir/ Holstein and Manhattan Banks then his own, and those banks were Daniel's rivals.

Now both Patrick and Tricia met Daniel frequently but except for one or two social occasions when Daniel invited both of them to dinner with his wife Sally, though they knew he owned a large estate, neither were invited to his home. Although they knew he was a Quaker, they were surprised at his opposition to slavery. Since they knew he was born a Virginian and his father still owned a bank in Petersburg, though that branch might soon close, they could discover little about his private life. It seemed to Tricia and Patrick that Daniel might have a secret and might be why as a Virginian was so against slavery. Perhaps this was the reason he had come to establish his bank in Washington.

Hard as they tried they failed to discover more but both knew they admired Daniel for his strict business ethics, never being associated with anything which might be illegal in anyway. In any case both he and Sally seemed to be exceptionally nice people and would like them all to become friends. Of course Tricia and Patrick, though had no strong feelings against slavery having lived so long in the northern states and they now feared a civil war was inevitable. If so, this might totally destroy their own business as well as the Union they strongly supported, for economic reasons. They were not to know that this question was not just a political one, but could personally effect the lives of ordinary people, causing severe disruption in their lives, as it had done to the Masons, and this before there was any military hostilities.

Could not every person in the United States see how important it was ensure Sobriety and Temperance should prevail. Surely none had the right to force others to agree to their views, whether it was in religion, business nor private beliefs. At least the Missouri Comprises had engendered a period of peace. There was still a degree of Moderation prevailing. Would it still be possible to avoid the Armageddon and the chaos of civil war. At least there was still a chance to avoid this castrophy.

PART 5

DISCOVERY

DISUNION PART 5 DISCOVERY

DISCOVERY

1.

Although in the main the period from 1850 to 1856 in the United States, after the 1850 Missouri Compromise, was in fact a largely peaceful period, although the northern and southern states often clashed in Congress. However there was not always moderation either there or elsewhere. It is true that the many descendents of the Carroll family supported Henry Clay and the Whig Party, but they had never liked Abraham Lincoln, even though he professed to be a Whig supporter.

They agreed with him on his stand against slavery but as he was no doubt both a brilliant lawyer and an even greater orator. It seemed to them that most of his speeches inflamed the people and feared he might incite the people to take action and destroy their period of peace At this stage they were not sure of his sincerity, fearing he mainly wanted political power for himself.

Abraham Lincoln was very much a self made man. Born into relative poverty, though his family prospered, he virtually taught himself to become a successful lawyer. Eventually entering the House of Representatives as a Whig candidate in 1846. It was here he took issue against the Democrats vigorously opposing the Mexican War and incensed their dislike by opposing the introduction of Texas as a new state, citing his objection to their support for slavery. They were pleased when he did not stand for re-election the next time, devoting himself to his work as a lawyer.

But even after that he continued his strong verbal attacks on slavery, so it was natural that when the Kansas/Nebraska Act of 1854 reached Congress with Kansas demanding to be admitted as a slave-state, this representative too would give a majority in Congress to those supporting slavery. Of course by then he had found a good platform against this proposal which had caused terrible civil disobedience, resulting in what became known as 'Bloody Kansas'.

Congress had sort a solution by giving the people of Kansas the right to vote for their own preference. However the result was obviously illegal. With only a population of two thousand over six thousand votes had been counted in favour of slavery, resulting in the state control demanding slavery. Thousands of slave demanding people from Missouri had 'invaded' Kansas enabling the illegal result. It was to lead to open warfare and deaths.

Those believing it should be a free state, set up in opposition their own state government in Topeka. Worse, so called religious bigots from New England now invaded the state attacking all pro-slavers. It was then that a man called John Brown and his followers attacked them at Pottawatomic Creek burning many pro-slavers houses and butchering and killing five men with broadswords. At last the government had to act.

This gave Abraham Lincoln a chance to make his famous Peoria Speech demanding the eventual ending of slavery. For the first time he made clear his own intentions in case the southern states decided, at last, they must secede from the Union and form a new country. Lincoln said the Declaration signed in Philadelphia could never be dissolved and all states must always be part of one United States. This statement was the basis for creating the civil war, which occurred when the south tried to secede seven years later.

It was just what the Carroll family feared, and from that day they did everything to oppose Lincoln. Even more so when in 1856 he, with others wishing to breakaway from the Whig Party, believing they were not strongly opposing slavery, created a new Republican Party. Though they put forward a candidate for President in 1856, Buchanan, a Democrat, was elected. He was able to bring together a number of pro and anti-slavers and declared the election in Kansas void. This resulted in Kansas entering as a free state.

For a moment Lincoln's ambitions were curtailed but by now his brilliant oratory ensured he was now the foremost politician against slavery. He, evidently, in spite of his past speech, advocated a peaceful solution of sane men and women realising that though Blacks and Whites were not equals, the blacks had rights the same as whites decreed in the constitution, but they were not the equal of whites. So again a measure of peace descended on the land.

But black oil seeping from the ground in Pennsylvania had been known for many years. People had found it was inflammable and could be used to produce both heat and light. Then several people drilling for water to help remove the thirst of their cattle found it was often contaminated by the black liquid. Though this was not what they wanted, other persons began to think if it could be obtained in quantity, it would provide a solution better than candles for lighting. Many persons became interested in the idea.

It would be left for John Rockefeller and others to see a commercial advantage so see if this substance could be obtained in quantity. It might have other uses, and as gas often came with the oil, this would provide an even better means of lighting towns and even houses. Why this might become 'black gold'.

Again a number of prospectors who had travelled late to the California Gold Rush and failed to find sufficient amounts in the streams, for the best sights had long since been obtained. Really to stay alive, they had explored many other streams in the neighbouring Rocky Mountains, some even trying their luck in the central eastern parts, and not always disappointed. Though it did not make them rich it gave them plenty of money to live on. So soon the news became known that there were other places than California were gold might exist.

It seemed the best area for prospecting was to the far western part of the Kansas territory which carried a local name of Colorado. Eventually some very resolute miners achieved some real success for it seemed that the area, known locally as Pikes' Peak appeared to offer the best prospects. With the Californian Gold Rush virtually over, several failed prospectors gravitated to Pike's Peak and what they found made them very happy. Unfortunately this news very quickly became public knowledge and like in the past, many persons, attracted to the possibility of riches began pouring into this area of the Rockies quickly to become known as Colorado. A new Gold Rush had started virtually ten years after the previous one.

It now seemed that minerals such as gold, copper and oil might become a vital part of the United States economy. Those seeking these minerals never thought they were possibly adding to the general wealth of the country, they were only interested in their own good fortune, willing to endure great hardships so long as they eventually became rich

2.

Kurt Sand had met the manger and owner of the Anderson Bank, Harrison Anderson, in Sacramento as early as 1849 and liked the man. Harrison had confessed to him he was a Mormon. This bank was a branch of the larger bank he owned in Salt Lake City, but had come, temporarily, to Sacramento to ensure the success of this branch. Harrison had brought with him his two eldest sons, Nathan and Edward Anderson, who were to follow him in the Banking fraternity. Kurt had heard so many different tales about the Mormons, as many believed they were heathens indulging in multiple marriages. However Kurt had an open mind on this matter.

As the Anderson Bank invested heavily in their original project of developing the gold strike he had discovered, Kurt was delighted when Harrison agreed to tell him of his life in Salt Lake and his past history. Harrison admitted he had married three women who had born him children. Two were sons by his wife Elizabeth, two daughters by Hilda and another daughter by a younger wife Martha.. All had come with him and a Morton Milliken, a cousin of his wife, Elizabeth., to Salt Lake when Brigham Young had made his historic journey there and Harrison established his major bank there, having studied finance in New York many years before.

Of course Kurt had confessed to Harrison that in fact he really had two wives. Harrison had laughed, "I congratulate you. You see you are following the practice we have discovered believing in multiple marriages. – One woman can never be enough for any man, Yet as you have discovered it does not mean we consider our women inferior to us in any way. In fact they are very willing to join us that way. – You know it does spare them from enduring too many dangerous quick pregnancies, yet they can still enjoy the pleasures all women have, and which we men to enjoy," Kurt knew that this applied equally to Agnes and Anita.

Kurt found he liked Harrison Anderson. – He was completely open about his past and felt no shame in his behaviour. Little did he know then, that in some fifteen years later he was to come to know and meet Otto Milliken – the son of Morton Milliken – who was the cousin of Harrison's wife, Elizabeth. Nor was Kurt to know that this meeting was to bring him riches by mineral wealth, not from gold but from oil.

It was Harrison Anderson who gave Elizabeth and Otto Milliken the money for them to take Vera and themselves from Salt Lake City when Otto wanted to discover a fortune in gold in Colorado, now it was rumoured that it had been found there. His father Morton had died but left very little money for his wives and children. As previously explained, his mother, Nan, wished to accompany and look after her two children.

It was along and tiring journey to the gold fields and it took some time in the wagon to travel those many miles, but eventually they arrived there. To Otto's dismay it seemed most persons were panning the river for gold dust in its waters, just as it had been the way it had originally been worked at Sutter's Fort, in California.

Otto was disappointed as he had dreamed of prospecting the local mountains looking for outcrops, just as the old miners, who had passed through Salt Lake on their way to the Californian gold fields. As a young man he had been intrigued with their tales. They had even shown and demonstrated how to lay and fire dynamite to separate the rocks. Otto considered he now would be able to use this knowledge, instead most people where simply panning the river in which gold had been discovered.

At this time he had no option but to select a portion and register a claim and then both he and his mother, helped as far as possible by nearly six year old Vera. It was pain staking work with very poor results barely panning enough gold to keep them alive. Then two other young men appeared and registered a claim next to theirs.

*   *   *   *   *   *   *   *   *   *   *   *   *   *   *

The Sinclair family on their poor impoverished ranch at Cagtry on the River Pecos had suffered two quick tragedies Thelma Sinclair had died in 1856, killed by overwork and with her emancipated body. Then their father John, disillusioned and despairing any future had succumbed and died of a broken heart only six months later. Their aunt Dora married to Wendle Jackson had long since left Cagtry to set up their own store at Clifton near Waco in east Texas. So now Jack Sinclair, aged nineteen, his brother Robert, only thirteen, with baby Molly barely two years old were left as orphans.

They too had heard the news of gold being discovered in Colorado. Jack knew if they stayed and continued to work the ranch, the position was unlikely to improve. It seemed there was no real future for them there. With both parents dead they now owned the ranch but Jack did not want to spend a life in poverty as they had endured, almost since he was born. He discussed an idea with Robert.

They would leave the ranch drive their few cattle some seventy miles to the north to Sheffield, take Molly with them and call on the few friends they had made, going to the MacDonald family who worked a similar impoverished ranch there. Robert was glad to agree wanting to begin a new life, caring little for its dangers. So they did this and begged the MacDonald's to look after Molly, telling them what they intended to do, giving them the small number of cattle they had brought to help pay for Molly's upkeep, but promising if they were successful when they returned they were amply recompense them for doing this.

Flora MacDonald had just miscarried her child and was delighted to easy her pain by mothering a young daughter like Molly. So it was agreed and the two of them left Molly at Sheffield and in their wagon made the long and tiring journey of some six hundred miles, to the gold fields of Colorado. It took them many weeks but they eventually arrived at Central City

The name, Central City, was a joke. It consisted of several log cabins and shacks. The Sinclair's discovered a little gold had been found in the nearby stream. This small find was, already, attracting a number of prospectors like them. At first they tried their hands at panning the stream in which the gold had been found. Although they discovered enough gold dust to barely keep them alive, but they quickly made friends with a young man, a woman and a young girl, panning next to them.

They introduced themselves and found the man was Otto Milliken, the same age as Jack and the woman was his forty five year old mother, Nan. Their new friends admitted they were Mormons who had come to Colorado from Salt Lake City after his father, who had married three woman, died the year before. Nan was quite attractive and no doubt could have become another pluralist wife of other men in Salt Lake. However when Otto decided to try his luck in Colorado Nan had decided to accompany him. She had born her husband, Morton Milliken five children since their marriage in 1829 and was not anxious to get pregnant again

So this was how the two families of the Milliken's and the Sinclair's were to meet and come to know each other. Again, at that time, neither knew that this chance meeting would eventually make both families virtually one. Together they would prosper and gain much wealth both in gold, copper and later oil.

Nan had told them her eldest daughter Alice, had married another Mormon, a cousin, for before she married Morton she was a Boutelle and with several brothers, who had come to Utah with Brigham Young, settled there and married. Alice, with her husbands approval had been willing to take care of her other four children if she went with Otto to Colorado. However her second youngest daughter, Vera, then only five years of age, was determined to accompany her brother Otto, who she adored, so all three of them came here.

Otto explained that the Mormons believed that a son, after his father's death, was responsible for her and his sister's, '*for all their needs*'.

Neither the Sinclair's nor Milliken's came from mining families but Otto had told them he had learned a lot from the miners who traveled through Salt Lake City on their way to California. The Old Timers had told him. 'Stop panning, follow the river carefully upstream and look carefully. The dust in the stream must come from a lode in the mountains – find it – It will take a long time – it will be tiring but if you're patient you will get your reward.'

Of greater importance they had shown Otto how to use dynamite, something of which Jack, had only a little knowledge. They were making so little progress in the stream they are discussed a plan to go upstream and see what they could find. The trouble was they all had to live, meantime. Eventually it was agreed they would pool their resources. Robert, Nan and Vera would continue panning, endeavoring to obtain enough dust to keep them all alive. Meanwhile Jack and Otto would go upstream.

It seemed that this decision was to prove a very wise one, but its success would only be achieved by risking great dangers and almost dying of starvation. However it was these dangers of death which were to cement their loyalties to each other far more than the riches they were eventually to enjoy.

3.

Before Harrison Anderson returned to Salt lake City, Kurt had spent many hours talking to both him and his two sons, Nathan and Edward. Kurt was very impressed with their financial expertise and was able to convince his friends of their abilities. Since Harrison had told him he hoped, in due course, to open an even bigger financial institution in Washington, but more particularly to gain access to political sources, Kurt realised if so this would greatly help Collis Huntington in his own attempts to help get government support for the Transcontinental railway.

He got the support of Charles Crocker, Collis Huntington and particular, their lawyer, Leland Stanford. As both Nathan and Edward had stayed for a time in Sacramento after their father had returned, as they had told Kurt it would be their responsibility to establish what they would call the 'House of Anderson' in Washington, Kurt brought all three of them to meet them.

It was agreed that whilst Huntington was in Washington they would liaise with each other agreeing terms for any profits from their encounters. As it seemed that Huntington, having already started this work, and would be staying in Washington, he would have established himself there before the Anderson's arrived. So they would contribute to some of his expenses during their absence. By the time they followed their father back to Utah a business relationship had been established.

In 1854 Anita happily presented Kurt with a daughter of his own, Alvira Sand then Agnes bore him a daughter, Margaret Sand, named after her mother following her previous daughter, Lisa Sand. However Kurt knew that Anita in spite of the love he gave her as well as the home he had provided for her, felt she should have been able to bring to him some of the wealth her family had enjoyed before those evil men ransacked her hacienda. Kurt had been determined to rid her mind of this. So Kurt had fought hard to get Modero's Mexican lands resorted to her, as the only surviving member of her family. Once this had been established, after a long fight, it made Anita a wealthy woman in her own right. Once completed he spoke to her.

"Dearest Anita, you must know by now my love for you is just as great as it is for Agnes. We both love you. I cannot make you my wife – though I would love to do so. All I can offer you is the same love I give Agnes. Your children, though registered as Agnes children, will always be known as both of ours. There will never be any difference from an inheritance point of view."

Anita kissed him "Dear Kurt I know that. I feel I am your wife and I love you as much as I could ever love a husband – more now after what you have done for me in restoring my birthright. Only my religion makes me realise I have sinned – and I will gladly continue to sin – so long as you want me."

185

Kurt felt he must now remove her feeling of guilt "Now Anita you are a women of wealth. Though it will break my heart – for I will always love you, the same, until I die – remember what I said when you agreed to live with me. It was impossible for you then, as you had no means to provide for your children. Now you have those resources. If you should ever meet another man – one you would want to marry – I shall never stand in your way. You see I realise you might want to find a man who could legally marry you"

Anita hugged him to her. "I shall never leave you – for as long as you want me. I want more children by you – even though I perjure my soul - It is wonderful that Agnes can share you with me. Please keep your love for both of us-----for we both know – even if you deny it – you will want other women – We both know this – we both understand."

Kurt held her close and kissed the side of her face. He knew he was a fortunate man. He also knew Anita was right, though he would not admit it to her. He still remembered the loving embraces of his sister Sophia. He saw again her beautiful nearly naked body as she smiled at him, enjoying trying to entice him to be intimate with her.

As an engineer his mind still regressed and remembered his difficult journey over the Oregon Trail. His mind reprised on the possible route. Across the plains, it would be possible but the gradients over the Sierra Nevada mountains and then those still higher near the summit were preventative. Fortunately his company had already acquired the services of the brilliant survey engineer, Theodore Judah, who had once worked on railways in the east.

Kurt was determined to utilise this man's expertise to survey a possible route through the mountains, offering for him to become part of a company, now with sufficient money to finance such a survey. Of course it did not mean they could bring it into fruition but should resources become available, at least they would be ahead of any competitors. Even knowing this might mean the loss of the initial investment, they were all rich enough to lose it. If not the information might be profitable in the future.

Theodore Judah was given the task, and when possible Kurt would visit him in his task and by 1857 he had soon proved it was possible but extremely expensive. Judah believed he would have finished a complete survey in a further two years. One sufficient to build such a railway. On the strength of this Huntington again travelled east, representing the company, now called the Central Pacific Railway Company acting as a political lobbyist and soon would have the assistance of the 'House of Anderson' after it was established in Washington. In any case, nothing was possible unless resources were available, far greater than any they could inject, so much depended on Huntington's success in obtaining investors in the east, particularly on persuading Congress to vote government money for the project of a East-West continental railway.

Kurt had been intrigued by Collis Huntington's discovery of a possible banker and stockbroker. Even more so by the fact that though, probably willing to invest in Central Pacific, they were not willing to become part of its company. Looking to the future, he knew new railways must be built throughout the United States.

After those first letters he had received from them Kurt began to think of far greater propositions than even Central Pacific. In any case his own investment was smaller than either Donald Read or Charles Crocker. He was really a junior director in the company. Realising the standing of these men in the east, if they could form a partnership – a consortium – Patrick Purcell as the stockbroker, Daniel Mason as the banker and he supplying the essential engineering expertise, deciding the costs involved in building any railway to ascertain if any investment was worthwhile.

On these lines he wrote to both of them suggesting that some time in the future they should meet to consider such possibilities emphasizing their own important, but different, abilities. He was rewarded with encouraging replies, each stating their interest, even that after his letters they had discussed them together. However, as he had expected, they stated any such project would have to wait until the three of them could meet together. As Kurt now lived thousands of miles from them and with his other business commitments which, at present was the only source of any wealth, Kurt could not consider making that long journey.

He smiled, if it were to be built, perhaps this new Transcontinental railway might be the answer.

4.

Of course as Devin had ceased writing to Camay long before he met Morna Leach so he did not know about poor Camay's problems and that she had needed an abortion. Actually Devin felt conscience stricken for he now knew he had developed strong feelings for Morna – yet in spite of this – he still remember those wonderful days with Camay on the ship. Again now he felt disgust at having to work for Tammany Hall. Although his work for them did help a number of impoverished Irish families, he now knew first hand the terrible fate they inflicted on so many innocent young girls. Even if Tammany Hall used these brothels to obtain funds to help many families, he realised that most of these illicit takings went into the pockets of their leaders. Morna's plight had confirmed his suspicions.

Devin had been delighted to return to Long Island to meet Morna again the following weekend, and was welcomed by everyone, especially by Morna. The family were very understanding and always ensured Devin had the opportunity of being with and talking to Morna each time, releasing her from some of her duties soon after he arrived. By now Morna let Devin enjoy more intimate pleasures when they were alone, pleased that she found this did not make Devin feel any ill of her.

Morna had been a completely innocent young girl until her body was defiled in the brothel, but even this had awakened her feminine desires and knowing she owed so much to Devin for taking her out of that hell hole, she wanted to reward him in some way for his kindness. Then on the third weekend when he came to visit her she had to inform him of what had happened.

In great trepidation Morna began, "Devin dear, I wanted to be the person to tell you of my condition. It seemed I left the brothel too late. It has been confirmed that I carry one of those evil men's child. – You have been so kind to me since I arrived here and I shall never forget that it was you who freed me from that hell. --- However – well –er

– I want you to know I will understand if now you no longer want to come and visit me as you have made me so happy each weekend." Poor Morna now broke down tears running down her face and she turned away from him.

To her surprise – but more to her delight – Devin gripped her, pull her round then buried his lips on hers. After a moment he pulled back his head and said, "Morna don't talk nonsense. – Why should I behave that way. – It's not your fault – you could not avoid it. – I still want to get to know you - But – what is important – have you told the two ladies and if so what is their reactions."

"Mistress Erin and Merle are wonderful," Morna replied. "You know we are all strong Roman Catholics but Master Patrick is a very strong protestant. They have all kept their beliefs. However it seems long ago he persuaded them – although they would never have an abortion – they should let each person decide for themselves what they wished to do. Master Patrick has asked me to tell him if I would like him to pay for me to have an abortion. – Devin – I'm not sure. – I think I would want this but it is against God. – Please tell me – truthfully what I should do?"

Again Morna broke down now sobbing quite violently and once again Devin seized her and pressed her tiny body to his. Then he said, "Forget what our church has told you. – Although I know you girls want babies. – forget whether it is right or wrong. – Do you really want to bare a baby forced on you by a man you must hate. - Think too of your future. – I know the kind ladies would see to you. – but you are young and have a life to live. – Though I assure you if you keep your baby, it will not affect the way I look at you. – Whatever you do I could not say, honestly, that I could promise to ask you to spend your life with me. – But I do want to help you, and do want to get to know you better. – I would strongly advise you to accept Patrick Purcell's kind offer and abort your child."

He could see Morna was pleased though she was still suffering. Then she said, "You do not think it would be a terrible sin. Surely God would punish me. – Oh! Dear Devin – I don't know – but I know I don't want this baby." Once again Devin took Morna in his arms trying to reassure her. Finally he said, "Morna – I beg you – let me go now to Master Patrick and tell him you have accepted his kind offer. – At present I cannot, honestly, say I love you – The reason is that on the ship coming here to America I met another girl, who I did, then, think I loved. – Unfortunately as soon as we arrived she had to go with her family to live miles away in Annapolis. – Since then I have not seen her – yet I still have strong feelings for her."

Now he hugged her again and kissed her, "Morna dear, I'm not sure of my true feelings – for I've found out what a wonderful girl you are. – Certainly I want to help to make you happy – Your baby would not affect me in any way. – But suppose after you kindly let me to continue seeing you, I then decided I could not marry you as I was still in love with this other girl. – Really – it would be much better for you if you let me go to Master Patrick and tell him I've persuaded you to have an abortion."

At last Morna managed a little smile before kissing him again. "Devin – you've just proved what a wonderful man you are. – You had no need to tell me this – yet you did – I would truly like to continue to come to know you. – See if I might supplant this other girl in your mind. – In spite of your assurance it would make no difference – I really feel I would have a better chance if I did not have a baby you would have to support."

Now at last she broke free but still held his hands, "Please Devin go to Master Patrick and tell him I want that abortion. – Strangely – I no longer feel I am such a wicked girl." Devin still pulled her to him again, hugged and thanked her. Then he left her and went to see if he could find, and be allowed to speak to Patrick Purcell. At that time he did not know it but that meeting was to open a new way of life for him in the future.

5.

The families had returned to Texas, happy to be once again be living on their prosperous estates. But for how much longer would they be able to live this way. Soon their happy life may be torn asunder as once again they may be involved, in yet another, bloody conflict to decide their right to make their own decisions. However this time it would be a civil war with the northern states fighting the southern states on the vexed question of slavery.

As at Camargo they had continued to debate what they must do if it occurred. None of their families, Texan or Mexican needed slaves but they had already freed the ones they used, now paying them a wage, a wage they could easily afford. Yet around them many ranches continued to use slaves and was one of the many reasons why they had fought Mexico to gain their independence. Worse their menfolk would then have to decide which side they should support and if possibly fight. It seemed because of their family connections with those at Camargo, they might leave Texas and go and fight up north.

Similarly all those rich families, the descendents of the Carroll family, and those descended in any way from Margaret Eliot in Maryland and Virginia, were faced with the same problem. Even worse, they knew most of the original battles which must occur if the civil war happened, would be fought on their own estates, even destroying them and their wealth. As they had already freed their slaves, everyone would believe they supported the north. Again which side would they join. A civil war was the worse form of conflict for it tore apart individual members of a family as they knew, only too well, occurred during the American War for Independence. At least they could still wait to make that decision, but they must now begin to make plans should it happen.

*   *   *   *   *   *   *   *   *   *   *   *   *   *   *

Many miles away in Colorado, near the town of Central City, Jack Sinclair and Otto Milliken had left Robert, Nan and young Vera still panning the river, gaining just enough gold dust to keep them alive. Jack and Otto had followed the old miners advice – follow the stream towards its source look carefully for then you may become rich. As they rose they looked carefully at the mountains on either side of the valley. The miners had said somewhere their would be lodes of metal, difficult to see, as it would probably be in intrusions of rock which had occurred millions of years before.

The prospecting took months, they worked throughout the summer and autumn. Their only success was some gold dust floating in the already shallow river rapidly decreasing even more. They returned to the others from time to time and with their meager horde and those found by the others, they were able to exist. In spite of the snow and cold they returned upstream to their task. By February, the conditions were so bad they could not even go down for new stores. When the weather eased they had planed to abandon their search.

However, the Old Timers words were correct. 'Have patience'. The skies cleared at last. For the end of February the weather, suddenly, turned warm. Though nearly starving, living on roots and a few snared rabbits they decided to remain for one more week, deciding to explore an area which had looked promising before the snow came.

The miracle happened. Exploring an outcrop, Jack went on one side and Otto to the other. They knew there were several clefts on each side. When they returned that night they both felt they might become lucky. The nest day, quite independently, the both, literally struck gold in fissures on either side of the outcrop. There was no doubt that Otto's find was the most valuable, though Jack's was a good find. Now it was necessary to return quickly to Central City to register their claims before others found them.

Jack said, "We'll register them as separate claims – yours is much better than mine." Otto said "After what we've been through – there will be no divisions. We'll register joint claims and share the hardships and the loot. We Mormons may have progressive views on sex but have been taught to be honest from being young. We'll mine them together."

Prizing out a few pieces of virtually metallic gold from each of their finds they returned to their families and registered their claims. They used the gold nuggets and the small dust found in the river to purchase supplies for four months, two tents, a pack horse and most important dynamite. Of course their find caused too much local interest so they quietly stole away under darkness, ensuring no one was following, arriving back at their findings two days later. It was early March.

Otto showed Jack and Robert how to lay charges and the mining of their gold was started. The life was hard but rewarding. What surprised both Jack and Robert was that Otto, his mother and sister seemed happy to live together in one tent which denied them any privacy, but they did not comment.

An incident occurred in May which ensured Otto's permanent friendship. Dynamiting was a dangerous business and they had a few narrow escapes, Then one day Nan appeared at their own cleft telling them Otto had been involved in an accident and was trapped. It seems the explosion had been successful but a hour after he went in to work the mine and remove the rubble, some rocks from the ceiling, loosened by the blast had fallen on Otto, imprisoning him.

Everyone rushed to the site, they eventually freed him and apart from severe bruising and a bad leg for several weeks, Otto had escaped serious injury. However he knew that neither, he nor his mother, could have removed the heavy stones from him, he would have been trapped and certainly starved to death. Otto showed he was grateful. "We registered these claims in both our names. We all know that my find is better than yours. This will never, make us separate. We are one firm for life, to share equally our gains, no matter that we may go our different ways in future."

By June they had uncovered a small fortune in gold but they all realized that to excavate the working more efficiently they must risk others thieving their gains.. Their finds were at what is now called Cripple Creek, which was much nearer the growing town of Colorado Springs than it was to Central City, so they took their treasure there.

When they deposited their gold and received considerable cash credit they spent the rest of June in buying a small shack with two rooms on a hill two miles from the town. They left Nan and Vera to set up a home for them whilst the others were able to hire several able men who were, already in desperate circumstances, having failed to achieve personal success. A large and well build man, called Jacob, and his two thirty year sons, appeared very reliable and they hired them mainly as security men. They were from Kansas and were god fearing, even religious, people and very trustworthy. Otto made them overseers of the other six men who would provide the hard labour.

Having recruited them Otto, Jack and Robert, leaving the women at the shack to look after their personnel needs, they purchased large quantities of supplies, loaded onto to two wagons and horses and took them to the mines. Once there, they started their men on recovering, and separating the ore. By the end of July they had enough gold to fill a wagon and the three of them returned to Colorado Springs to deposit it, in what was becoming a small bank.

Having replenished their supplies they returned to the shack for a short rest before returning to the mines. Otto and Jack went back in the town at night but left fourteen year old Robert, to his annoyance, at home. After they had left Robert had asked Nan why had they gone and left him. She merely smiled and replied, "They are men and they must do what men must do. Soon you will learn."

6.

Poor Camay Nolan was very sad. In spite of how it happened and the cruel way James Holstein had treated her, she was a woman and had wanted that baby she had aborted. Worse the few letters and his words of love from Devin Ragan had ceased. It was now months since she received the last letter from him which she held close to her breast to remind her of those heavenly days even on that terrible ship.

Camay began to feel, either he had lost interest in her as they now lived so far apart. Or she feared Devin may have found another girl near where he now lived in New York. He may have, even have found he loved her. She felt her life had ended. She had little chance of finding another man who might find her interesting. Every day was the same. She had to work the moment she arose in the morning, and had to help in the house whether they had visitors or not.

In the few times she had to rest she reprised those wonderful days when James had taken her into Annapolis and entertained her. She so vividly remembered those lovely restaurants where they had eaten. She craved to be loved and was why she had so easily fallen under his evil spell. For the first time in her life Camay had been shown the joys of city living. Born into poverty and before she came to America, she had only known a simple life in the country. Just for a short time she had lived in a very different world. In spite of what he had done to her, now at least she knew it did exist.

* * * * * * * * * * * * * * *

Meanwhile Devin Ragan had gone in search of Patrick Purcell, eventually finding him drinking with the two ladies. A servant in the household went to Patrick telling him that Devin Reagan would like to speak with Patrick, so he excused himself, found a waiting Devin and took him to his study where they could talk. Telling him to sit opposite him as he sat behind his desk.

"Mister Patrick," Devin began. "I've spoken at length with Morna and she has now accepted she would be very agreeable if you could arrange for her to abort her child. Although, like I believe do your good ladies, she thinks it is a sin, but I have convinced her it is the right thing to do."

Patrick smiled kindly, then asked, "May I be as bold as to ask you about your own feelings for Morna for it seems you have, undoubtly, an influence over her. She had almost refused my offer and I know my ladies felt it was wrong. Now it seems she has changed her mind – and I can tell you I am pleased that you have been able to do this. I shall see Morna is given the best treatment for she is a very kind girl who has been so badly treated. I know she feels very strongly about you and blesses you for saving her from that hell. Have you developed any similar feelings towards her, for I want her to have a happy life?"

Not expecting this question, Devin was not sure how he should reply. Then smilingly he decided he should tell him the truth. "Sir. Like you I feel privileged to bring Morna here and I thank you profusely for giving her a home in which to live. – It is difficult for me to answer your question."

Again smiling he continued, "I do like Morna and it is not because she has had to submit herself to these evil men. However I cannot, honestly, say I love her. I've already told Morna this. Until now I have believed I was in love with another girl, Camay Nolan, who I met on the ship coming to America. But she now lives miles away working as a servant in a mansion near Annapolis. I've written to her but never had the time to go and visit her. Meeting Morna has made me think again, though as I told Morna, I still feel very strongly attracted to Camay. However I do like Morna and would never want to hurt her."

Now it was time for Patrick to smile, "I will not press you further on that point, but you know you are always welcome to come here and meet Morna, Please let me change the subject."

Still smiling he continued, "I remember what you told me about your work and it seems, at present, you do not need to take any active part of their evil traffic in women. Would you consider leaving your employment with Tammany Hall?" Devin was shaken, "Sir. I could not. I must work for them if I am to live – but yes, I now fear I might be forced to become involved in their horrible trade. The man I live with, Shamus O'Brien, has already become involved. I realise I too may be forced into this."

Patrick seemed pleased at his reply "Suppose I offered to employ you. I warn you it may be dangerous. --- Several good friends of mine want to try to stop – or at least curb – these things in the city. Three of them – you my even know of them for they are quite famous, would like to join me in providing an alternative for these Irish folks landing here and help them to never have to live in the city. Instead we want to meet them when they arrive and persuade and help them to move west to new lands there. Would you consider working for us to achieve this."

Smiling he continued, "I fully approve of the magnificent work my ladies do to avoid this but we believe we must do more. I would like you to work with them, perhaps ask Morna to join them, so together with you, you could warn them of the dangers of staying here in New

York. Of course there is a danger that Tammany Hall might be greatly annoyed at us doing this and know only too well and you know their intent and you are able to accurately describe the dangers. It is unlikely they would do anything at Ellis Island with ladies present. But they have the power to remove you permanently from the scene."

Smiling even more he concluded, "Of course at times you would be working alongside both my ladies and Morna, and would have many more opportunities of meeting her."

Now it was time for Devin to smile, "Sir! How soon can I begin this work. The dangers mean little to me. I now hate these men and what they do and did to poor Morna. I am willing to start as soon as you can arrange it. The only difficulty is where I could live as I dare not stay in my present flat."

Patrick had the answer. "Besides your time spent at Ellis Island, most of your work would be concerned in arranging for the transport west of these emigrants – sometimes even accompanying them on their journey. We have already bought a large building in the better part of New York. You would work, with others in charge there and have to help run the operation. We shall be employing others to help, again this may be a task for Morna which I'm sure she would like. I shall ensure that you could live on the premises when necessary. If you agree – and I warn you again of the dangers – you could begin your work next week after you have told Tammany Hall you have found other employment. – Then, with others, I would tell you what we want you to do"

In a few minutes Devin had accept his new employment and raced to tell Morna what was to happen and more that they would even work closely together. "Morna," he said, "We shall often be near to each other. I'm sure we shall both quickly get to know each other better." Morna smiled, "Oh! Devin. I would like that. – Fancy working with you at my side. That would be wonderful." It was two very happy persons who now spent more time together that afternoon and early evening.

7.

There were many reasons why Patrick Purcell had with others, prepared a means of helping these Irish immigrants who landed at New York and preventing them being misused by Tammany Hall quite apart from, also, the genuine help the Hall gave them. Firstly, he fully approved of the help both Erin and Merle gave, along with other good women, to these poor Irish families when they first landed. However he knew now, and now Morna Lynch's misuse, had confirmed what he had already believed of the Tammany Hall trafficking in young women. They had to do more to help these poor people.

He disliked Henton Whitney, another stockbroker, and a very good friend of Daniel Drew for whom he worked, still he was forced to meet Henton, even accompanied with both Erin and Merle at social evenings, where along with others Henton, was present. Henton Whitney was married to Judith Platt, daughter of a very famous family. However poor Judith found pregnancy a very dangerous thing. Then soon after Judith bore her first child a son in 1855, it seemed Henton had taken a mistress.

Her name was Winifred Collins, who was then only eighteen years old. As was not uncommon on these evenings. Winifred, like most women on those evenings, even including both Erin and Merle, were not adverse to rather intimate affairs with other men present, and Winifred had allowed Patrick these pleasures. As they enjoyed, rather intimately, each others company, Winifred was to tell him her sad life since she arrived in America.

Almost as soon as she landed coming from Dublin, Winifred's mother and father already very emancipated, had died leaving her alone Poor Winifred was starving but at least she had retained her good looks and for her there was no option but to become a prostitute. Perhaps she was fortunate for though she was forced to join a Tammany Hall brothel, it was of the same high class type in which Morna Lynch had suffered. However like Morna she had conceived very quickly – she did not know the father – though it could well have been Henton Whitney, for she had frequently been his bed companion.

In any case she considered herself lucky for once Henton discovered her condition he offered to take her into his house for her to act as his mistress, to save Judith, his wife, from further quick and dangerous pregnancies. It was there that her daughter, Phillis Collins was born. Now poor Winifred had to submit to Henton whenever he required her.

Winifred told Patrick, Henton was a very cruel man and was also a sadist. He would often beat her naked body for any small indiscretion, including when she failed to satisfy him during intercourse. But she had no recourse but to endure it, now with a very young baby. Of course Patrick felt very sorry for her, for Winifred seemed to be a very kind and pretty women. This confirmed his opinion of Henton who he had disliked long before this.

However this was confirmed, even before Morna came to live with them, that Tammany Hall had established this special brothels to obtain even greater wealth from men of high station to use to satisfy their sexual perversions, including making their women pregnant. In fact it seemed to Patrick that these places were virtually becoming 'Baby Farms'.

After this, again before Morna had been brought to his home, he had decided he must try to do more for these Irish immigrants, than what his wives and their good ladies were doing. So he had approached many of his wealthy male friends of good standing to join together to provide this alternative for them once they landed. A chance to find a new life in the west, helping to build this new country, instead of remaining in poverty in New York.

Patrick had never felt strongly about politics, having suffered because of this in Ireland. However as it was the Democrats who really controlled New York City, it was natural that these estates on Long Island favored the Republican Party. So it was to known Republicans he went to see if they would join him in helping these poor Irish families.

Edwin Morgan was a state Senator, firstly supporting the Whig Party, then changed to the Republican Party once it was formed. William Henry Steward, also a Republican, was rising rapidly to senior positions in the Republican Party. Finally he went to his very good friend Franklin Tracy, a very successful New York Lawyer. They were willing to support him for they also knew of this trafficking in women, but more because they hated the Democrat control of the city, knowing Tammany Hall were its strongest supporters.

They had pooled their resources and often it was their own wives who often helped Erin and Merle in their work. They bought this large block in a good area of New York and altered it to serve their purpose. Each delegated one or two members of their staff to serve as administers and accountants. However they knew they needed several other men like Devin Regan to do the actual work. Here Patrick realised that Devin was especially placed to help them if only for his actual experience working for Tammany Hall. It would be left for Devin to take charge of the others they must employ in first persuading and then supporting these families so as they could successfully make the long journey to the free land in the west which would be given to them to work. As most had been farmers in Ireland, they could easily settle on that land and derive an income from it to keep their families in a better state than they had suffered in Ireland. Patrick ensured these other appointments were men of Irish descent.

The following weekend Devin came again to Long Island. He had severed his employment with Tammany Hall, said goodbye to Shamus O'Brien soon to marry Aeryn Magee, took all his belongs, for he had been told he was to stay with the Purcell's until he would move into the living accommodation which was a part of the new buildings in New York..

By then Morna had aborted her unwanted child and was convalescing under the supervision of both Erin and Merle . Though still not recovered, he was allowed to speak with her for a short time. Now able to confirm she would work beside him and others at Ellis Island, trying to persuade the new immigrants to accept their offer of a new life in the west, rather than the dangers if they stay in New York, still in poverty. Both Devin and Morna would tell them first hand of why they should not stay, Morna even unashamedly telling them of her own experience.

Of course Morna for at least a time would still live at the Purcell's, coming with Erin or Merle or both to meet the Irish families. However she was more pleased when Devin told him Patrick Purcell had told him that day. Later, part of her work would be to come to New York to help with the families, temporary housing them in small accommodation areas in that large building. Then Morna would sleep many times in a little area near Devin, although she would often return to Long Island to perform her other tasks, still helping as a servant when required.

This thrilled Morna for she knew now the many hours she would spend close to Devin, even sleeping sometimes not far from the area given to him. Whatever was Devin's feelings for his lost Camay, Morna knew she hoped she could encourage him to have far stronger feelings for her. Morna now even fantasised she might have a more permanent place in his heart. Whatever happened she was determined to do all she could to achieve that goal. Morna was now glad she had accepted his advice and aborted her baby, for in spite of the way it had occurred, Morna knew how great was her desire for a baby of her own.

8.

Kurt Sand had continued to correspond with Harrison Anderson in Salt Lake City. He liked Harrison and had developed a strong attachment with his sons Nathan and Edward. Once again he heard of the Milliken families. Harrison had told him that he had given money to Nan Milliken, as her now deceased husband, Morton, was his cousin, to go with her son, Otto and young daughter, Vera, to go prospecting for gold in the new finds in Colorado.

Harrison had said, 'I doubt if they will be successful – but young Otto wants to establish himself, try to become rich. At least he has strong beliefs in himself, which I approve, and has promised to look after his family. I believe in him, though I know he is like me a womaniser. It would not surprise me – if he fails – he might well set up a prosperous brothel in Colorado. I'm sure there will be need for this with so many men now streaming there to gain their fortune.'

Kurt smiled to himself. He had never had the need to frequent such places, being handsome he had enjoyed bedding many willing young ladies in Pittsburgh before he came west and met his Agnes, and he had told her about this before he married her. However it intrigued him that this Otto Milliken was following his idea when he went west, met Agnes and together had found a gold mine. Though he occasionally received letters from both his father and sister, Sophia, they were not very frequent. Even smiling remembering the way that Sophia had tried to encourage him to enjoy more intimate pleasures forgetting they were brother and sister. Perhaps it was fortunate he had found both Agnes and Anita.

However Kurt now had far more important desires. However prosperous was his business in Sacramento, he was still a railway man. He truly believed he could lay the 'Golden Egg'. So he now, with the agreement of his partners, promising them a good stake in the railway if it was ever built, left them as well as both Agnes and Anita, and joined Theodore Judah helping to research the best possible route the railway should take were it to become a possibility. So he left them alone for long periods.

By now Agnes had presented him with another daughter Margaret Sand, named after her dead mother, whilst Anita had gladly given him too more daughters, Alvira Sands and more recently, Edwina Sands. So the Sand family was expanding quite rapidly. Also this greatly increased their expenditure. At present his only wealth came from the gold deposit and his original business in Sacramento. It was essential that this was successful, for any proceeds from the possible railway were still simply a dream.

Consequently both Agnes and Anita did their best to take his place in the firm, now he was working so far away in the mountains. They even surprised his business partners with their capability, and played a important part in ensuring its profitability. Agnes was surprised that none of their wives seem to dislike her for she knew Kurt had enjoyed several amorous affairs with them before they discovered Anita. This had been one of the reasons why Agnes had approved Kurt taking Anita as a second wife, fearing the scandal should it be discovered.

Even by 1858 both Kurt and Theodore Judah felt they had arrived at the best route but both were astonished after Kurt used his expertise, gained so well when he worked in the east, and began to estimate the colossal expenditure which would have to be raised for the railway to become a reality. There we no men in California who had sufficient wealth, even jointly, to build the railway. Now it was even more important for Colin Huntington to lobby government to invest heavily in its construction – and more important get other men like Patrick Purcell and Daniel Mason to invest.

When he returned Kurt was a very saddened man. He began to doubt it would ever be built. The risk was too great and any dividends would be long delayed. Worse Huntington had already informed them that with the possibility of a civil war looming, he was not receiving very encouraging response from government circles. If war were to occur then both sides would forget about any railways and would have to concentrate their wealth on building up the strengths of their opposing armies.

At least Kurt found a letter waiting for him from his sister, Sophia.

*   *   *   *   *   *   *   *   *   *   *   *   *   *   *

Sophia Danton had born her third child to her husband Hugh. A son, John Danton, in 1856. Her pregnancy had enabled Sophia to enjoy many short but pleasurable intimate affairs with other men in Pittsburgh as her husband was often absent for many weeks. It had, also been a time when she could developed further her previous affair with Alan Mosley. Of course Sophia was no fool. She knew he was really only interested in the sexual pleasures she offered him.

By now she was convinced he was a confirmed bachelor who might never marry, as being handsome he could attract many women to him for amorous pleasures. Still, at present, this did not present a problem to Sophia. She lived in a comfortable home, an apparently happily married woman. Though by now she had lost all her original feelings for Hugh, though he did, up to a point satisfy her immediate desires, and more important gave her the babies she adored. Now she also had the time to enjoy her illicit affairs with others, without arousing any notoriety, and she knew she enjoyed her intimacy with Alan far more than with any other man.

However there was no doubt but that she felt very strong, and she knew, very wrong, desires for her younger brother. So all her letters to Kurt were of a quite intimate nature. Sophia briefly described to Kurt her enjoyable affairs with her men friends, and he knew they were quite intimate. She did this deliberately as she tried to revive his interest in her.

Alan Mosley was now very involved in their railway acquisitions, helping to build and extend the lines, just as he had done in England. He was away from Pittsburgh for many weeks but still managed to enjoy himself with local women near where he worked. Yet in spite of this he had to admit that his continuing affair with Sophia was more pleasurable than with others. Further more it was safe as Sophia was a long married woman with children, and he knew she knew how to look after herself. Still, Alan was sure that his bachelor life was preferable than tying himself to one woman.

He often met Gordon Taylor, very grateful to him from bringing him to America, for he found the pleasures of the flesh were far superior than the offers he would have received in England. Alan knew Gordon wrote frequently to Kurt in California and, already, was involved with others, in the possibility of an East-West railway to join one Kurt might be able to construct to drive west and meet their own line.

Gordon had told him that he was in contact with many possible investors such as Daniel Drew, Jay Gould and others and too, was lobbying for Federal Government support. Gordon had met Colin Huntington attempting similar investments. A little disappointed that Patrick Purcell and Daniel Mason were far more interested in what was happening in California than his own project. .

Alan Mosley knew for certain he would enjoy the challenge of helping to build this east-west railway, but he very much doubted if it would ever become a reality. Not now with the danger of civil war looming. Government investment appeared to be very remote under these circumstances.

9.

Nan Milliken's remark had puzzled Robert. What did she mean when she said 'To do what men must do.' Do what, he thought?

However when he asked his brother, Jack had said, "Just to enjoy ourselves." Although it was supposed to be prohibited to Mormons, Robert knew Otto both drank and smoked. He assumed that was the reason – but if so – why not take him. He had long since started drinking now they could afford it.

The Sinclair's lived in one room in the shack, whilst Otto, and the two women slept in the other. It seemed unusual for a son to sleep in the same room as his mother and sister. There was room even in their small shack for Otto to sleep there, surely neither of them could have any privacy when they undressed. Though Jack thought he knew, he refused to explain it to Robert.

Another event occurred which increased Robert's education. In late August Robert was detailed to return to the shack for some implements and a cache of tobacco. He arrived at midday and found the shack empty. Since he was not sure where the tools were kept he went looking for the women. He knew they usually went to the nearby creek to wash their clothes. When he got there he found both Nan and Vera bathing. As soon as they saw him they waved and came out of the water but to Robert's surprise they were both entirely naked yet they made no attempt to hide their nudity.

It was the first time Robert had seen a naked women. He had never encountered his mother nor Dora in this condition, he could not take his eyes off either of them, devouring the young slim body of Vera, now over six years old. But he also realized that Nan, now forty six, and showing the strains of the hard life she had lead, with strain marks on her abdomen due to her previous pregnancies. However she was, still, to Robert, a very pretty woman, who stirred his adolescent mind.

Nan noticed this and laughed. "It seems nudity is a new thing to you, you are surprised that we do not attempt to cover ourselves. But all our bodies are the creation of God, who made in two different forms. There can be no sin in exposing them to view. If God created us this way we should never be ashamed of them. Our clothes are only to keep us warm and not to hide our form." Then they both dressed and clothed themselves before returning to the shack. Robert would never forget that moment

As winter approached the three men now, often, retired to the shack leaving Jacob to carryon their work in their absence. Otto had allowed his men time off in rotation, to return to Colorado Springs, with their wages paid in gold, but they always returned anxious to replenish their income. Two more men with some mining experience had been recruited by Jacob on his own visits to town and even in the wintry conditions progress was still being made and more gold extracted.

During one of their visits to the shack, Jack had gone to town for their own supplies and stayed overnight. It was Sunday and Nan came out of their room. Robert saw her face was stern but when she saw Robert, it softened. "You will not understand but I have sinned. There is none of our preachers here but all Mormon men, are introduced into low priesthood, so I am going out with Otto to pray with him and he will help me to absolve my sin."

She left, followed by Otto but Robert noticed when she returned her eyes were wet with tears and to him she was in some pain, as her hands were held tightly to her body.. But she smiled at Robert saying, happily, "I am free from sin." It was months later before Robert found what had happened.

Otto and Jack still continued to go into town, often staying away until dawn. They still refused to take him. Left with Nan, he was able to question her about her past life. It seemed that Nan, and her Boutelle brother, had joined the Mormon sect when Joseph Smith had come, with his followers to Kirkland, in Ohio, to avoid persecution. He made many converts and as their parents had just died, they knew their faith enabled Adam Boutelle to legally marry, under the Mormon faith, the three women he claimed to love and who were willing to share him.

They were Edna Milliken and the two sisters, Nancy and Jean Dover. There, Nan met and married Edna's younger brother, Morton Milliken, knowing he was also taking two other wives, again sisters, Joan and Elias Penny. She was then twenty three and Morton was twenty eight. Nan realized that Robert was astonished at their willingness to share a single husband but Nan had explained

"Both my own and Edna's mother had died in childbirth after enduring almost permanent pregnancy and suckling. Yet, you may not know this, we women have urges difficult to control. It was part of the Mormon faith that not only would our husband share his favors with us and see to our needs, but we should be allowed to take turns in conceiving his children. You must learn, we women have found ways of regulating this."

Robert was puzzled. "Why should a man need more than one woman?"

Nan laughed, "You have yet to learn that *every* man wants *more than* one woman. Remember there are times when a woman cannot properly respond to her husbands urges. It is better for all of them to have another woman at these times. You must now know that Otto and your brother, Jack, have such needs at times. That is why they go into town, and spend the night with women – though they may have to pay for their services."

Robert was shocked. He knew she meant they frequented prostitutes. However, she was continuing her account, and he had no time to digest her information. "My eldest daughter, Alice, was born in 1836 and Otto was born three years later after Joan and Eliza had born him children. We were all very happy but the local people disliked us. To avoid further persecution Smith decide we must move again and we traveled to Nauvoo in Illinois. That was 1839".

"Four years later as anger against Mormons increased, Joseph Smith was murdered., I had just born my second daughter, Cathleen. The Council of the twelve Apostles appointed their senior member, Brigham Young, to be our new president. Matters became serious and other members were killed. It was then that Young gathered us, all together, telling us we must go with him and find, a new world to live in, far away from other people. Other Mormons followed Joseph Smith's dictate to go to Missouri to found a new Zion there .- So began our famous thousand mile quest, eventually establishing a new town near a salt lake in Utah. We named it Salt Lake City. In spite of the inhospitable land, we quickly received new converts and the town grew in size, but it was hard work.

I bore Vera in 1852 and another baby in 1855, all, except Vera, and the others not married, are now being looked after by my eldest daughter, Alice. Then two years ago Morton died. It was Otto's duty to provide for our needs so after leaving the other children, except Vera, we came here last year."

Robert was intrigued and wanted to ask her more but Vera had caught a chill. She had awakened and was crying so Nan had to go to attend to her..

10.

Back in Pittsburgh Joanne still felt appalled at the cruel way her son had treated poor Camay. When Michael and Sharon returned to Pittsburgh, Joanne found an opportunity to speak in private with Michael. He told her that they had found Camay was terribly unhappy when they last visited Annapolis. He also felt a responsibility to Camay for he should have warned her mother that James Holstein was not a reliable man where women were concerned.

Now Joanne felt compelled to act. It seemed to her, even if she had aborted her unwanted child, she had a responsibility to improve poor Camay's life. Her own religious beliefs, which were in their way, as strong as those Sharon held, made her believe that Camay had virtually become her own daughter-in-law, though not married in church. Somehow she must ensure a better life for Camay.

Michael felt sure one of Camay's despair was her isolation in their Annapolis house. Camay, for a short time had been taken into the city and now knew how other people lived. He had found her crying one day and spoke kindly to her discovering this to be a fact. Now Joanne had an idea of how she could help Camay. She must go to Annapolis and speak to her mother, persuade her to let her take Camay away from the house and bring her to live in Pittsburgh. Still to act as a servant but ensure she had the opportunity, have some resources, and from time to time, able to go into that city and once again enjoy some life there with others.

Joanne knew she dare not bring her to live with them as her son, James, though living separately, often called on them. It would be too cruel for poor Camay to, so easily, meet again the man who had disgraced her. But that would be unlikely the case if she came to work in her mother and father's household. Of course Michael might take her to his mother and father's house, though she feared Sharon might not like that.

In any case Joanne's parents, both over seventy, and long since retired, lived within the city, but in a very prosperous part of it. If so Camay would live and work truly within city life and could herself, in her spare time go out and see what city life was really like. Again as her parents were somewhat infirm. They would welcome the attention of a young servant girl like Camay. She spoke to them and her mother, Alberta, was delighted as she needed a new personal maid for herself, as her previous maid had married and left them. .

Now Joanne specially went to Annapolis and spoke to Delma Nolan, Camay's mother, explaining how she felt responsible for Camay, so ashamed of her own son's despicable treatment. She told her Michael had told her of Camay's sadness and needed to get away from where it happened. Perhaps she might like to live within such a large city as Pittsburgh.

Getting Delma Nolan's approval and finding Camay was delighted to accept, Joanne took Camay back with her and brought her to live and work for her mother, Alberta Van Buren. Camay settled in her new post very quickly, Alberta made her especially welcome, so that quickly Camay was glad to help and work for her. Now, also at last, had just a little money of her own to spend. Besides her wage as a servant, Joanne added a small amount each week to increase this. Gone was her feeling of isolation. Now she really would discover what it was like to live within a large city.

Very quickly Camay came to love Alberta, who would spend many hours talking with her about her past. Camay was amazed when Alberta told her how her father had found and met her mother, unashamedly telling her that her mother, before she married was Claire Collins. Then she amazed Camay by telling her Claire, was a prostitute in Bristol, England, before she came to America with a man who used her as his unmarried wife for many years before a Michael Casimir had befriended her an gave her the opportunity to meet Joanne's father, Philip Wycks. How they fell in love and married.

It seemed to Camay that in America a woman's past meant little. Claire Collins had discovered this, why should not she. Perhaps Devin – or some other man – would forgive her for her indiscretion. Even though he might know she was no longer a virgin. Camay felt she was beginning a new life and could forget her past. If only she could discover where Devin now lived for she had written to him at his old address to tell him where she now lived, but the letter had been returned labeled 'addressee not known'. It seemed he might have left New York, possibly even married, and gone elsewhere to live.

Poor Camay now really felt she had lost a possible life with Devin. Though still very sad, she now lived close to where so many lived. She even had a little money of her own. As soon as she had the opportunity she would go out into the city and begin to enjoy a life of her own. However she was determined she would never make the same mistake as she had with James. – If she met a man who seemed to like her, she would be very careful how far she would let it progress. Meantime she would enjoy working for this very kind lady who seemed to become another mother to her.

Actually Joanne had told her mother everything about Camay and Alberta now felt she too should try to provide a better life for Camay, realising that if James had acted differently she might have married become her granddaughter. An opportunity arose after only a few weeks. As Alberta suffered badly from arthritis she could not walk very far and so one of Camay's many duties was to escort her to her carriage, help her board it, then accompany her on her journeys into town. Then she would help her to go to whatever she wanted to see or even shop. So Camay got many chances of seeing at least a little of life there.

But this opened another promising association. Camay had to go to meet their head groomsman who supervised their black servants to look after the stables, Camay had to go to him and arrange for her mistresses carriage to be available. His name was Graham Stowe and was four years older than Camay. There was no doubt that Graham enjoyed talking with Camay ensuring she knew he was a little attracted to her.

Of course Camay quickly noticed this but after her previous experience was very careful, fearing to once again become too involved. However it did please Camay for it showed that men could still find her attractive. She would see if it might develop further, though she would take her time. At least she thought that life in Pittsburgh might offer greater opportunities than she had found in Annapolis.

11.

Kurt Sand's great interest in both Daniel Mason and Patrick Purcell was because of the way Collis Huntington had canvassed their help. But he, at that time, was not to know a great deal about either of them. Of course Patrick Purcell's expertise was in investment, originally as part of the Drew Company, and their recent involvement in railways. Although Patrick had fully supported Erin and Merle's efforts to help the impoverished Irish landing in America, this had been long before he had established the scheme to encourage these families to find a better life in the west.

Merle had born Patrick their second child, a daughter, Patricia O'Donnell, soon after the liaison with Tricia had become. She even came to the christening, knowing at that time Merle, was actually, Erin's sister and recognised by Patrick as his legal second wife. She admired him for this arrangement, and that she was not treated as a mistress.

It was soon after Merle bore her child that Patrick first met Collis Huntington, who had come to the east to try to obtain support for the new Central Pacific Railway Company. Inevitably Huntington had encouraged investment from the Drew Company with their knowledge of dealing in railway stocks.

Patrick was interested in the potential of a transcontinental railway line but, also, knew the enormous expense involved in such an enterprise. He had told Huntington he was interested, even suggesting the bankers in New York and Washington, who might wish to be involved. He had mentioned the Mason Bank in Washington, in which he had invested in some railway companies supported by Daniel Drew, though he only met the Managing Director, Daniel Mason occasionally, he was surprised that as a Virginian, Daniel was, so, opposed to slavery.

Patrick was, also, disturbed with his boss' growing relationship with Jay Gould and James Fisk.. Gould was dealing, somewhat illegally, with railway stocks and knew Daniel Drew was profiting in this way. Perhaps he might have made the decision in any case, however a letter arrived from another member of the Central Pacific Board, named Kurt Sand, living in Sacramento, offering his expertise as an engineer, and with sufficient resources to join with the Mason Bank in Washington to form a holding company, to invest in future railway expansion.

Patrick received from Sand a copy of the similar letter he had sent to Daniel Mason. Fortunately, involved in a different project they both met in New York and were able to discuss Sand's offer. Both thought it too early to proceed further. In any case they would want to meet Kurt Sand, before coming to a decision. This was impossible at this time, as the Civil War was looming, and California was thousands of miles away. This made any meeting very unlikely for some time However they both agreed to write to Sand explaining their future interest in his proposal

It was, probably, this letter which made Patrick come to the decision he had been considering for some time. He could not accept Sand's offer, even if he wanted, whilst he was still employed by Daniel Drew. He was now a very wealthy man. He decided to set up his own brokerage company in New York under the name of 'Purcell Enterprises'.

Patrick had several friends in the investment and stock brokering business who were glad to become junior members as directors, so he could quickly count on a competent staff. By now he had become to realise the wonderful ability Tricia had in stocks and shares. He could rely on her objectivity. With Erin and Merle's consent, making the others minor directors, he installed Tricia, as his personal assistant and a director in the company. She astounded his other colleagues, particularly as she was a woman, with her obvious experience and capabilities. She was to become an essential part of his future investments.

It was Tricia who convinced him that the Central Pacific proposal, especially with Kurt Sand's excellent and proven engineering qualifications, would more likely to progress further than the one which Gordon Taylor was proposing to form. A similar company to survey a possible route west from existing east coast railways, now being referred to as the Union Pacific railway. It seemed the Central Pacific had already made some progress whilst none had yet proceeded on the latter proposal.

Perhaps the salient reason, however, was that both Patrick and Tricia knew that both Daniel Drew and Jay Gould were considering Taylor's proposal. Well aware of the dubious dealings of these two gentlemen they believed they might only be interested to be able to milk it and derive the dividends for their own use, rather than the projected company.

Both of them now, when they met Daniel Mason on business matters, convinced him that the Central Pacific was a better bet if the government could become involved. These were the reasons why they told Collis Huntington of their interest, and why they were both pleased to receive these letters from Kurt Sand. Because of this, they ensured they met Daniel Mason far more frequently than in the past, establishing a good and trusted relationship.

Because of the need to encourage government investment and also with Collis Huntington staying there, most of these meetings occurred in Washington and not New York. Of course when they came to Washington it was Daniel Mason who received them and invited them to met his wife socially. However they were puzzled. If these meetings had been in New York they would have invited Daniel and his wife to stay with them on Long Island. Yet though the Mason were generous in entertaining there guests, both Patrick and Tricia.were never invited to their homes and had to stay in a Washington hotel during there stay.

Both of them felt that the Mason's had some secret and felt it was one they did not want them to discover. In fact this caused them to worry. They knew it was essential if two businesses needed to work very closely together on any project for any time, trust was essential Even in their private lives there must be an understanding. Of course with Patrick now virtually living with three wives, they were not anxious to confess this to the Mason's. However even if the Mason's came to stay with them on Long Island, they could appear to live separate lives, Tricia with her own large house and Erin and Merle living together as sisters.

Surely, they both thought, if the Mason's also had an unusual way of living like them, this did not mean he would need to disclose it to them, even if they stayed in his home. Temporary amendments could so easily be made during the duration of their visit. Tricia told Patrick it was essential that this matter was rectified, particularly if in future they should join with the Mason's and the Sand's in a consortium. Such secrets must eventually be discovered.

Patrick was not anxious to expose his family to such investigation but Tricia emphasised that in time this must be the case. Fortunately, at present there was no need for Patrick to expose his relationships and make them public, so they ignored Daniel's failure to invite them to his home and enjoyed the lavish provision both Daniel and his wife, Sally, gave them when in Washington.

Of course Patrick had written to his father asking him his advice on the formation of his new company. In the past he had told his father, in confidence, the relationship he had with Merle, adopting her baby. His father had approved even later telling him that Britain had commuted his crimes in the Young Ireland movement and it was safe for him to return to Ireland. However both he, Erin and Merle wished to remain in America. It did seem that his father disapproved of his new relationship with Tricia, who his father thought had seduced him, and that he was unfaithful to both Erin and Merle.

One interesting piece of information in the last letter was about his friend in the Young Ireland movement, Charles Doughty. Patrick knew much earlier that Charles and his family had like him escaped, going to live in France. Now his father told him that Charles had quickly established himself as a mineral surveyor for the French Government. It seemed that the Doughty family lived at Vendome, in the Loire valley near Tours. At that time Patrick was not to know that in future years he was to come know Charles Doughty's son, Paul, and along with Robert Sinclair and Otto Milliken would be involved with them building railways to export their oil findings in Texas.

The last six years in the United States had been years of discoveries. Following gold findings in California now gold had been discovered in Colorado and had created another influx of the population into these lands so recently received from Mexico. It was there that Robert Sinclair and Otto Milliken had discovered their growing fortune in gold, later to be used in finding oil in Texas. Even then, oil was been talked about as 'Black Gold'. Oil had recently been discovered in Pennsylvania. In future its value might be much greater than gold. But, also, the United States had expanded their trade with the outside world especially with Japan.

But to those families like the Nolan's and the Regan's, they had discovered love, though it seemed at this time it was unlikely it might lead to happiness, particularly for poor Camay Nolan. In different ways the Carroll Family Saga had been extended, now with them living in many parts of the United States. Yet to everyone there was a growing fear of conflict . Could it still be avoided. The next three or four years would tell if it could happen.

PART 6

PRELUDE

DISUNION PART 6 PRELUDE

PRELUDE

1.

There was no doubt but the greatest danger for peace came from the orations of Abraham Lincoln. He had shown himself as being a brilliant lawyer. Amongst other cases, his defence of William Armstrong, acquitting him of his offence by using the almanac to prove the key witness was lying due to the lack of moon-light to be able to identify Armstrong as the culprit. But this notoriety increased his already high political status. Illinois was his main political battleground and his chief opponent was Democrat Senator Stephen Douglas.

Senator Douglas was a very strong opponent as the senator even challenged President Buchanan for the control of the Democratic Party. He even swayed some eastern Republicans against Lincoln, but Lincolns oratory was winning him great support. Quoting once 'A house divided against itself cannot stand'. Strangely in spite of his entrenched anti-slavery, Lincoln was considered by many to be a moderate man. In a long speech he declared that Negroes and white men could never be equals nor was he in favour of mixed marriages, but Negroes had the right to live a life of their own.

Of course the Carroll Family descendents, still members of Congress feared him. Most of their wealth was in the area which would be destroyed if open conflict occurred, so they were some of his most vigorous opponents. They blamed him more than anyone for the terrible events in what was now being called 'Bloody Kansas' leading to John Brown's murder of white pro-slavers with local battles occurring all over the state. It was delaying the entry of Kansas as a state of the Union due to setting up of two alternative state governing legislates, including undoubted corrupted voting to obtain their majorities

The issue was equally disrupting the happy life of those families at San Marcos. The demand for slaves was considerable in eastern Texas, especially along the sides of the various rivers, where cotton growing was the chief occupation. Now new landowners often came with their own slaves and many others were easily obtained buying them in New Orleans. Slaves now numbered almost a third of the total population in these areas.

Those families at San Marcos were now certain that if a conflict occurred Texas would join any Confederacy fighting to uphold slavery. What then would be their position as they had long since freed their slaves. How could they continue to live here apparently opposed to slavery when neighbours in the south were fighting for its continuance. Which ever side won the they would be castigated and their rich possessions possibly taken from them. They knew only too well the terrible events in Kansas – supposed this state of affairs were to arise here.

In far away Colorado the question of Civil War was not an issue. They faced far more present dangers as together with their hired men they dynamited the rocks freeing the gold in the veins, then had the task of separating the nuggets from the surrounding granite. However now both the Sinclair's and the Milliken's had money to spend from their rapidly growing wealth

Robert Sinclair had been intrigued by what Nan Milliken had told him of her earlier life and knew he wanted to learn more. Nan had mentioned that Mormons believed in sin, an idea that had never entered his mind never being taught anything much about religions, only how a boy was expected to behave. Again he remembered that Sunday when she had told him she had sinned and came back, somewhat in pain, but said she was now atoned.

But there were other times. Now Robert knew what they did when they went into town, he begged his brother to let him come with them but being only just fourteen, he refused saying he was not old enough.

So the days and months past and the spring and summer of 1859 passed, just as the previous year, but each month they all grew richer. Several times Robert heard cries from the next room, as it seemed someone claimed aloud they were wicked, and asked Jack about them. Jack had laughed and then told him he was still too young to understand, indicating it was a private matter between the Milliken's. But Robert did notice that it was after these events that the following Sunday, if they were still at the shack, Nan would leave followed by Otto and return in some pain .

When Jack and Otto had gone in to town one night Robert decided to question Nan to try to find an explanation. He had already questioned her about the Mormon beliefs of sin, even daring to ask about intercourse. She had told him that intercourse between a woman and a man she was married to could never be sin. God had sanctioned this, for how else would they beget children. When he then asked what about Otto and time Jack visited the town. She had calmly replied that these women sinned, dreadfully, every time, but as neither Otto nor Jack had married their sin was very much less and could even be accepted, as it was the women they met who sinned.

That night after Vera had gone to bed Robert reintroduced the subject. "And what about it happening between a brother and his sister, and a mother and her children, and those of other wives and their children. When do they sin and if so what is the punishment?"

Nan had already guessed what was behind his questions so she answered carefully.

"Intercourse between step-sister and step brother are discouraged and usually both are punished for their sin when they ask for forgiveness. Intercourse by sister and brothers is a very bad sin and strongly condemned though I have to admit it does occur. Nan guessed what was coming but could not avoid it.

Robert continued. "And is intercourse of a mother and her son considered a sin."

Poor Nan blushed, then hid her face and started weeping. "You've guessed my terrible sins. They are all mine and not Otto's. His duty after his father's death to see to *all* of his mother's needs, whatever they may be. Please do not consider me too evil, though I often think I have lost my chance of going to heaven. Let me try to explain before you judge me."

She paused, obviously embarrassed. Robert waited wanting to know her answer. Then in some trepidation she continued. "I have always suffered great urges that is why I married Morton. He knew I had sinned before we married – it was with other men – but he forgave me. We had a wonderful life together. We truly loved each other. I did not mind that he had two other wives, we all loved him and he pleased all of us. Then he died, so suddenly. – But you must learn a woman's urges – particularly if she has lived such a long loving life with her husband - do not go away."

Again she paused then said, "I have been tortured by them ever since we came to Colorado – perhaps I should have stayed and found another husband – though I knew I would never find a man as good as Morton. Otto is very kind. He loves me as much as any son loves his mother. He knew all about a woman's needs long before we came here. He could see what I needed but knew it was a sin."

After a further pause she continued, "Before we got this shack there was little either of us could do, but I could not hide the torture I felt it inside me and it troubled him. Finally as I sobbed on my bed one night he came and comforted me. I shall always remember his kind words. 'Please, mother, let me end your agony, I understand. It is my duty to see to all your needs – I believe it includes this one'. Without saying more we lay together and I let him seduce me – I wanted it. He knew of ways which could help me. When it was done we both knew I'd sinned terribly but I absolved him of any sin. This must be between me and my God – no one else. You remember the first time I went outside with him."

Now she even smiled, "He took me outside and caned me. His cane strokes were agony but I honestly enjoyed every painful stroke. When I came in I felt he had absolved my sin. Yes! It has happened several times since then and I have paid the price each Sunday as you have guessed, as it did that week. Perhaps now you consider me a terribly evil woman – far worse than those who satisfy Otto and Jack in town. You are probably right – perhaps I am damned - but I cannot help it – it will happen again."

Having heard her confession she now broke down completely and bent over sobbing violently, her body shaking with emotion. Robert took pity on her. "I did not know of these things until tonight, but from what you have told me I can understand what and why you have done these things. Even if it is wrong, I shall never condemn you and I thank you for being so honest with me. I'm certain my brother has either guessed, or Otto has told him. That does not matter. I shall never speak to either of them about tonight. That will be our secret. Wrong or right I still believe you are a good woman to come here, with all it's hardships, to provide a home for all of us."

He then kissed her lightly on the cheek and helped her still sobbing into her bedroom and laid he on her bed before going back to his bed to lie and remember again what she had said.

Robert's education had been greatly improved. As an adolescent boy he had, already, discovered the elementary facts of life but before today he had never considered that a woman, also, suffered from similar urges.

2.

Meantime in New York Devin Regan had began his new employment. He had seen the premises set up to receive new Irish immigrants who were willing to travel west and start a new life there. The accommodation he was allocated, slightly above the place temporary given to these people, until they began their long journey to the new lands on which to work and derive a living. Though only two small rooms, it was far superior to where he had lived before in New York. However his first task was to meet these immigrants and persuade them to adopt this new life.

He was delighted for this meant he did this alongside Morna Lynch. The two good ladies would bring Morna with them and he joined them at Ellis Island. Both Morna and he would meet and mingle with the new arrivals whilst the Tammany Hall League tried to do the same. Their kind attitude to these poor people knowing they felt desperate just as the Nolan's and Regan's had done when he arrived, made it easy after they had been questioned by the port officials. They were able to persuade a number to come, together, to meet the good ladies.

Now it was left for them to explain what they could offer them. Telling them both the difficulties and the dangers of staying too long in New York City. Morna, unashamedly, told them of her own terrible experience and Devin was able to confirm this, admitting, though not actually involved in this, he could tell them what Morna had suffered was not unique and occurred very often. They were quite honest telling them what they were to offer them was not an easy life but it was much preferable than staying here, still living in poverty, and with the consequent dangers.

Soon they would be able to gather a sizeable group of families who were at least interested in listening to their offer. They were told that if they accepted, they would for a short period be taken into the city to live together, never parted, until arrangements were made to escort them on a very long journey. However when they arrived there, they would be given free of charge, good land which with their own efforts, they could develop into good agricultural land, on which they could both feed themselves and in time become more prosperous.

Never having known city life, and knowing how to farm, many considered this to be a better option than the others offered to them that day. Further more that land would be theirs, they would not have to pay any rents, everything they earned would be theirs to keep.. To their delight they were told once settled they would be given a horse and wagon both for transport in those isolated areas, as well as the means to plough their land.

All four of them were delighted at the many families who gladly accepted their offer. It seemed to them America might be a far better place to live, than as they had to exist in Ireland. Then it was Devin's duty to leave the ladies and Morna, help them to take the boat to the mainland, where there would be covered wagons to take them all to live temporary in the basic accommodation in that large building in the city.

Even before this had occurred, Devin, with the assistance of the city men who ran the scheme had appointed a number of good men and women, ones which Devin felt were very trustworthy, to staff the building and to provide the necessary transport, but more important provide eating facilities for the many people who stayed there. As even this accommodation, large as it was, was limited, it was essential that these families should begin their journey west as quickly as possible, leaving room for others to come and spend a little time there.

Again before any of this happened Devin had been informed that another of his duties from time to time, was to escort these families on their journey, and see them settled on their new land. Of course he would be assisted by one or two of their newly appointed staff, who in time would replace the need for him to be involved. In fact this thrilled Devin for it meant, at last, he would see far more of the United States than had been possible during his previous stay in New York.

All the arrangements for settling these immigrants on their land were done by the city men. It was the families like the Purcell's who had established these facilities. It was they who purchased the land and provided the means by which these could travel there. This was not Devin's task. His, until he trained others in this work, was to accompany them on their journey, ensuring they had the means to feed their families and be escorted there, as they were not used to such matters. So even before he, with Morna and the ladies, persuaded them it was what they wanted, Devin must make the journey himself, to understand what was required.

Taken by one of the city men he traced the now well known route out west, up the Hudson, along the Eire Canal then on to Pittsburgh and, finally, on the Carroll/Marshall boats to Independence and into the west. It was a completely new life for Devin. Since his arrival in America Devin had spent his entire life close to New York City. Now he was to experience, what he had known so many people did, leaving the east to settle on land in the wilderness. To Devin it seemed he had been given a holiday. However he was very intelligent and leaned quickly what he must do when he shepherded those families to their new land.

He realised one of the most difficult parts was that from Buffalo, where the canal finished, to Pittsburgh, were they set sailed on the Monongahela River to go to Independence. So on his first journey Devin was taken and introduced the many Holstein families living there, who also, were interested in helping new families to travel to the west, and which provided some of their wealth.

One of these were Joanne and Philip Holstein. Though time prevented him talking long with them, they did ask him when he made that journey to Pittsburgh again, he should find the time to call on them, giving him their address. Devin, very delighted to be invited knowing the high status of the Holsteins, so promised to do so.

Having been taken further along the river to Independence and then further to the lands already purchased for these immigrant families, he returned with the city men to New York. Devin knew he was now fully prepared to tackle this new work and knew he would enjoy it, though he had been told he must soon train others to do this as his presence in New York was more important. In spite of this Devin was now determined to retrace his steps once or twice more, longing now to see more of life outside the cities.

When he returned Devin was even more delighted to find that Morna, beside their task of meeting the immigrants, was now often working close to him in the building ensuring the families staying there were not in fear and that soon would begin their long journey to be given their free land. It was better a woman did this and it helped Devin to gain their confidence, explaining he would be accompanying them, so they need not fear the difficulties of their journey.

During the times Morna was with him she stayed the night, in her own small apartment allocated to her close, to where the immigrant families slept. However this meant that they were both near and together each evening, and inevitably, it strengthened their growing intimacy with each other. Of course Morna, knowing about this other girl Devin felt he loved, was doing everything to prove that she, now living close to him, seeing him each day, might prove a more attractive alternative than her rival for his affections.

Morna, after her raping and pregnancy, felt already she was a fallen woman. She liked Devin, and she knew, at least, he was attracted to her. So as a woman she was not adverse in using her feminine wiles to try to seduce him to even more intimate relations, ones she knew she now desired, however wrong her church would condemn her. Her condition was not her fault. At least she now knew how to protect herself, for following her abortion the kind doctors had ensued she knew how to prevent it happening again – until she wanted it.

She began her seduction soon after he arrived back to New York It was easy for her, for Devin denied for so long even the far less intimate pleasures Camay had been able to give him on the ship, now willingly responded to the pleasures Morna offered him. Very soon Morna when she stayed at the building left her own bed and gladly went to sleep with an equally pleased Devin. Soon it was fully consummated and there was no doubt each enjoyed the experience, Morna not suffering any adverse reactions from her life in the brothel.

Morna at last began to feel she might now might have a future with Devin. It was the same for Devin, who felt that now, separated for so long, it was likely that Camay may have found another man to interest her. Though he knew he still had strong feelings for Camay, his first girl friend, Morna was here living with him offering herself willing to him. At last he felt no conscience in indulging in the pleasures they could give to each other. Yet, even then, he could not decide who he liked most – the absent Camay – or the present Morna Lynch.

3.

Robert Sinclair never discussed what had happened that night.. He did not know if she had spoken to Otto but when his fifteenth birthday arrived in October, Otto and Jack told him he was, now old enough to have his knowledge of women expanded. That evening they took him into town to 'the House of Pleasure' as it was called to, further, increase his education.

Having paid for their pleasure they introduced him to a pretty, and buxom girl, of twenty two years of age, who traded under the name of Sally, who they obviously new very well, and had used before. "Sally will teach you how to enjoy life and make you into a man." They left Robert in her tender care. When he left her the next morning, tired and exhausted, he had, quickly, learned what a girl expected of a man. Robert returned many times after that, discovering the intimate charms of several other females of the establishment.

Otto had boasted that once their claim was sufficiently developed and approached exhaustion he would establish a business. He would open a special, high class version of this house of ill repute, for the benefit of the more important businessmen who were arriving and helping the town of Colorado Springs grow in size. In the meantime the three men prospected and found further, if small but profitable, veins to add to their growing fortune, as the weeks turned into months.

Now Robert often accompanied Otto and Jack when they went into town and availed himself of the pleasant times the 'House of Pleasure' could offer him. Not having any strong religious beliefs he could never understand why Nan felt these were a terrible sin. In any case what troubled him was why, even if Nan felt she had sinned, only she had sinned and must accept her painful punishment and not Otto. He knew that both Otto and Jack never considered they sinned when they took these prostitutes into their beds.

In fact, though he never felt any strong feelings for these poor girls who for money so willingly sacrificed their quite attractive bodies to him. In a way he did feel a little sorry for them. Though he was not foolish enough to believe what they told him as they often talked to each other after giving him his pleasure, he was not a cruel man, and felt a little concern for them. Whatever might be the true reason for their plight, he did feel it must be terribly humiliating for them to yield themselves to so many different men.

He knew they received only a smaller portion of what he paid for his pleasure. – the rest going into the coffers of the brothel owners and was why Otto was considering setting up a much more elegant establishment of own. Robert thought, 'What was the future of these poor women he so readily misused.' Once their youth and beauty deteriorated who would want them. How then could they live denied this chance of survival. Again the chances they took in conceiving, or worse a disease – for he knew they would abort their child if it happened. Young as they were, he felt their lives might be very short. Still this did not stop him enjoying his times in their beds.

He now enjoyed talking with Nan. At this time though he experienced the usual adolescent feelings, his times at the brothel cared for these, so he felt no wish to find a girl friend who might become his partner in future. In fact, though he knew he could never accept what he believed were Mormons foolish ideas on religion, he was intrigued with their practice of polygamy. He even fantasised with the idea that someday he might chose three women from a brothel and take them without any marriage ceremony to live with him, providing him with a harem. Certainly it seemed he may soon have the recourses sufficient to enable him to do this.

Though living so far to the west they could not avoid learning of the growing tensions of the southern states with the north. Neither he nor Jack had any strong feelings concerning slavery. Certainly where they lived in relative poverty so long near the Pecos, there was little, if any slavery. However they were Texans born and bred. If Texas voted to retain slavery, then they should be willing to fight to ensure their rights. Fortunately now living so far from these dangers in Colorado, at present there was no need to do this..

Now it seemed they might become even richer than they had dared to hope. Jacob's ability as a miner had achieved this for them. Far from fearing that their gold discovery might soon come to an end, Jacob had found near to their original find an even more richer gold bearing ores, yet still within the area they had claimed, which would take several years to exploit. It appeared incredible to all of them. This included Jacob and the men who worked for them, for they ensured that they too would benefit from their discoveries.

Just over two years ago Jack and Robert had left their ranch almost destitute. It was sheer desperation which had driven them to Colorado, feeling it was better to starve there rather than in Texas. At least, however improbable, they would be trying to better themselves. At that time they feared it would prove useless. It was more bravado and being young, a chance for adventure, which had brought them here. Now it seemed a miracle had happened and they might soon have so much money they would not know how to use it.

Jack and Robert knew little more than how to farm land and raise a few animals, but Otto, mainly due his contact with Harrison Anderson, had learned as a boy, money must be made to work. Otto knew they must invest their wealth in ways which might even increase their riches. Besides mining they must become business men in some way or another. He spoke to them and they agreed he understood more of this than they did.

They would go along with any ideas Otto may have of doing this. They could now afford to lose a little of their accumulating wealth and would give him their support, in any venture he might want to explore. One near to Otto's heart was to buy the brothel they so frequently used. Improve it – make it more desirable for frequenting by the richer business men now establishing themselves in Colorado Springs. Make it a much greater high class brothel catering for the sexual desires of these men, with private areas, even suites, where they could entertain their whores, with eating facilities, giving them pleasures which were quite impossible at home with their wives.

They did this – bought the 'House of Pleasure' – expanded and completely changed the layout – then reopened it under the new name as the 'Palace of Pleasure'. The few weeks when it had closed had built up a great demand to use what was now available. They knew very quickly it would be a 'new gold mine' but of a very different kind. Not only could they themselves enjoy its offerings it also proved they must soon find other means and attempt other means of increasing their wealth..

4.

Patrick Purcell quite apart from his attempts to help these Irish immigrants so dear to the hearts of both Erin and Merle, was involved heavily in ensuring the profitability of his new company. Now, even more than his sexual relationship with Tricia, he listened very carefully to her advice on investments. She had one advantage over him in these matters. As a woman, an unusual position in investment, she was able to use her feminine wiles to interest others even able to obtain somewhat confidential information denied to Patrick. The whole family now realised how much they now owed to Tricia's abilities.

When Tricia told him of her distrust of men such as Jay Gould and Daniel Drew, Patrick fully agreed with her. He distrusted Jay Gould, now a firm friend of Daniel Drew, and the way he had manipulated stocks to get control of many railway companies, becoming manager of the Saratoga railway, along with a James Fisk, including Drew's association with them, in resting control of the Erie Railway. Patrick, on Tricia's recommendation, had invested in the Santa Fe Railway which was producing rich dividends.

Later his decision, not to invest in the Union Pacific railway was proven when together these three men were indicted in the Credit Mobilier scandal, the finance company associated with the construction of the Union Pacific, which they corruptly milked from the railway, almost resulting in bankruptcy, until exposed by Granville Dodge, when he became chief engineer

During these years Patrick became friendly with Cornelius Vanderbilt, and a young Henry Harriman, who was to play an important part in his future prosperity. He now realised how import were his sexual relationship with Tricia. She was supporting him in his work, besides her love for him, which was as great as both Erin and Merle. Yet she was, already, rich. She need not concern herself with monetary matters.

By now he lived happily with three women who he regarded as his wives. It was fortunate that Tricia's admission to the family circle had not created any jealousy between them. They both loved her. They admitted she helped them, as Patrick was a very demanding man, often exhausting their bodies, during intimacy. They also appreciated Tricia's love for their own children, as well as Ranee. They also knew how it hurt her that she could not give Patrick the child they both wanted.

By now the whole family spent as much time at Tricia's home as their own. It was this fact which until now, Devin Regan had not known of Tricia's existence. In each they had constructed an unusual arrangement of rooms. A quartet of bedrooms. Each having their own private room into which Patrick was invited when they wanted to sleep with him. His own private bedroom was similar, but there was a fourth, much larger bedroom with an enormous bed, sufficient to sleep all four of them, together, at one time. To all there joy, it was this room which was used more frequently.

They had no secrets from each other and certainly not with Patrick. Without any embarrassment they always stated when at times this was not desirable, surprisingly, even Tricia suffered, occasionally this way. This hurt her even more, for she knew she could not conceive a child. The admission was to ensure Patrick did not, then, invite them to his bed. However, it was not really necessary for them to tell him, for in the house, at his request, they did not wear many clothes. Their children spent most of their time, naked. This was important as Ranee's black body was conspicuous but it ensured that, apart from this, she was no different to them.

Tricia could not help feeling inferior when either Erin or Merle had conceived Patrick's child. Erin and Merle would find her crying at her inability to conceive his child. She would tell them. "I don't know why dear Patrick bothers with me. I'm not a whole woman. He just wastes his seed on me."

At these times it was Erin, still a very religious Catholic who would comfort her. "Because he loves you just as much as he loves both of us. Of course he would love to give you a baby of your own, but this is not why he his intimate with you. He knows, and we know, his present success is because of the help you give him. Help we cannot give him. This is how you repay him. Believe me he has told me he feels he cannot ever repay you for the joy you have brought into his life. We both know this and owe you a great debt. That is why we both love you so much."

Tricia knew she meant this and it eased her pain. But she could also repay him in other ways. Used to suffering so terribly at her cruel husband's hands and learning even this could somehow increase her own satisfaction. She could enjoy at the cost of only a little pain as she had seduced him, partly against his will, to treat her in bed, far more violently than she knew he did with the others.

Jokingly she told him. "After all I rob you of watching me so painfully deliver your child – believe me I know what agony it was when I bore Ranee." It still did not remove the pain she endured in being barren. Yet in someway this increased further their love for each other and was even delighted when in his love making he occasionally squeezed her breasts before he placed his lips on them to kiss them.

By now a great deal of his income came from their investment in railway construction for which their was an ever growing demand. Here again he respected Tricia's advice on which they should invest. Yet both knew they lacked one vital component. Information concerning the engineering difficulties which would be engendered once construction commenced.

Now they knew how valuable would be Kurt Sand's abilities in these matters. Tricia and Patrick quickly brought this fact to the attention of Daniel Mason, who they now met frequently. It convinced all of them of the great advantages they would have if they were to accept Kurt Sand's suggestion in forming a consortium using their three special abilities to decide the best ventures into which they should invest.

But Kurt Sand's still live many miles from them, with even greater distances which any of them would have to travel, if they were to discuss such a venture. Again they both knew, from experience, such a business arrangement, not only depended on their abilities, but the complete trust they must have with each other. So until that was possible they dare not proceed further with the idea.

This did increase their interest in the possibilities in the far future of this Transcontinental Railway. If constructed they would then have the means of easy access to each other. In fact they knew of Cornelius Vanderbilt's interest in perhaps developing railway construction in the new state of California, schemes so similar to the many occurring in the east.

California was a huge vast area for exploiting, for they knew that so far there were few roads and certainly no railways to bring the results of the California fruit and vegetable farms, quantities now rising very quickly in that state. Commodities which would find an easy and welcome markets in the heavily populated east, and numbers which at present they knew was not available in California.

Apart from any other reason it did emphasise the need for this huge railway and how it would develop the prosperity of the entire United States. So they now met Collis Huntington more frequently, adding their own political pressure to his own on the federal government for essential investment if the idea could become a fact. They told him if it occurred they would readily invest more in the Central Pacific than the Union Pacific. Naturally this pleased Huntington very much and was excellent good news to Kurt Sand, David Reid and others in California who wished their project to reach acceptance

5.

Meantime, after Abraham Lincoln made his famous speech uttering 'A house divided against itself cannot stand' but not being the front man in the senatorial campaign, he decided to share in Senator Douglas fame, forcing him to let him debate with him on these issues. This ran into seven debates including the future of Kansas as a state of the Union. Lincoln stressed the gulf of principle between the Democrats and the Republicans on the principle of slavery. Particularly he opposed the idea of 'popular sovereignty' as being immoral. in the case of slavery. He claimed that Douglas, the Chief Justice Robert Taney and the last two presidents had conspired to ensure the continuance of slavery. .

By his vigorous oration Lincoln won all these debates and now was gaining considerable national fame. Though he failed to win the Senate seat in Illinois, which was dominated by the Democrats who re-elected Douglas, he had now become the most famous man fighting against slavery, which gave him the support of most residents in the northern states. His national popularity was enormous.

In February 1860 Lincoln made his first national political appearance in the northeast, addressing a rally in New York. It was obvious to those who opposed his views, such as the Carroll's, Chalmer's, Tencin's and others, fearing he was leading the country into civil war, which could mean the destruction of their way of life. Now Lincoln had been so well known that it was obvious he was becoming a candidate for the Presidency, and would stand for that position at the Republican national convention in Chicago. William H. Steward was the leading candidate but everyone knew Steward had qualities which might make him undesirable in the critical states the Republicans had failed to win in 1856.

It seemed to everyone living at Rockville, Racoonsville and Gordonsville that Abraham Lincoln might be chosen as the Republican candidate for the Presidency in the 1860 election, and they felt they could do little to avoid this happening. Still they had to make provision it were to occur, for they knew if he was elected President then the southern states would rebel if he tried to destroy slavery in the United States.

The major battles must take place close to Washington and so Virginia, even more than Maryland would be a center of conflict. It would be their own prosperous estates and their way of life which would be destroyed. This particularly effected those living in Virginia for they knew, although they would vigorously oppose a civil war, if it happened their beliefs would mean them siding with the northern states against slavery. How could they live there fighting against slavery whilst everyone around them, even those working farms and cotton fields on land still owned by them, would be fighting for the south.

Again it would be their men who would fight in these battles perhaps being killed. Afterwards, even if they survived, the basis for their wealth would have been destroyed. Furthermore it was imperative that their womenfolk must find salvation away from their estates and the question was where should they go. Once again they saw the same terrible divisions which had occurred during the American Revolutionary wars. However this time the division within families would become much greater – possibly fighting on opposite sides.

*   *   *   *   *   *   *   *   *   *   *   *   *   *   *

Camay Nolan was now happy living in Pittsburgh and helping as the personal servant of Alberta Van Buren, who treated her almost as if she was her daughter. However her own personal life had matured a little. There was no doubt that Head Groomsman, Graham Stowe, found her very attractive and was trying to interest Camay in his life.

Of course Camay quickly realised this and still very lonely, wished to reciprocate but was very mindful of what had happened to her when she allowed her affections to grow for James Holstein. She was determined not to make the same mistake again, so she allowed this relationship to develop more cautiously. If anything, this increased Graham's interest in her.

Whenever possible he found an opportunity to meet Camay. This was not difficult for Camay had often had to come to him to arrange transport for herself and her mistress, Alberta, to visit the shops in the city. Each time they met Graham took some liberties in engaging Camay in conversation. Of course Camay was very careful of how she replied but was willing to tell him of her families difficulties in Ireland, their coming to America and her work with her family acting as a servant for the Casmir/Holstein residence in Annapolis. She willing confessed the kindness of Joanne Holstein in bringing her to Pittsburgh as her life in Annapolis was so far from the town, and had brought her to work here so she could see more of what city life was like.

This fact provided Graham with an excuse to offer her, on her times off her duties, to come with him into the nearby city to see the sights. Though cautious, Camay agreed to him escorting her some evenings for this purpose. These visits were not the opulent and expensive excursions she had enjoyed with James, but never-the-less Camay did enjoy once again being with male company. This time it was not for eating in large restaurants, but stopping for a moment at the many snack bars which frequently the waterfront by the river. Soon, however she felt a little more relaxed in his company.

Sometimes they would merely walk, hand in hand, in the large park. Other times he might take and pay for her for a short excursion on the many pleasure boats which sailed the great river. Again this was something Camay had never previously had the opportunity to enjoy. It was a new and exciting life for her, without the intense sexual excitement which had been her downfall with James. She did relent a little and let Graham, occasionally peck the side of her face as he held her in his arms, even once or twice stealing a quick kiss on her lips. Never did he take unwanted liberties which she foolishly had allowed James to take.

By now Camay had decided that Devin would not be making any further approaches to her. It seemed Devin must have found another girl that interested him and so was lost to her. She knew she was sorry, for she knew she still felt a strong attachment towards Devin, but she also knew now that any kind of relationship with him was very unlikely.

Accordingly she let her new relationship with Graham develop, but purposely let it develop slowly, but as she wanted it to continue, she did at times let Graham take a few liberties with her, even demonstrating with him for this, but then quickly showing she was not adversed for it happening again. Slowly she was learning how to use her feminine wiles to encourage a more intimate relationship.

It seemed her mistress quickly saw what was happening and knowing her difficult past, Alberta would kindly assist her, warning her of how far she should let it develop but at the same time providing her with opportunities to meet and talk with Graham. At last Camay felt she might, sometime in the future have perhaps a more permanent and exciting life with this man, for their was no doubt that he was now very attracted to her.

6.

Now in France, Louis Napoleon had down graded the Parliament of France, which he was supposed to lead, and reduced most of its powers. Then in 1852 he established himself as King of France, as King Napoleon III. Certainly he was by decent the true descendent of Emperor Bonaparte, or Napoleon I. He married Eugenie de Montejo and established good relations with Britain with an alliance against Russia during the Crimean War from 1854 to 1856. He was determined to restore France as a feared military power once again with military excursions into Indo China and Italy, where he supported the Pope's maintenance of the Papal State, whilst still helping to unify Italy as a single country.

However he cleverly maintained a strong presence in Algeria which greatly added to the importance of Charles Doughty, for he was the man who provided his new king with rich mineral discoveries which helped the king's excessive expenditure. So each time Charles returned to France he was received by the king with dignity. However once again Charles resumed his illicit associations with Marie de Freycinet, though this greatly hurt is wife Matilda.

Nor had he ceased his efforts to seduce his own daughter Teressa, who by 1859 was now a young lady of sixteen years. Though Teressa had developed a pleasant relationship with Marie's son, Jules de Freycinet, she was intrigued by her father's obvious interest in her body. Foolishly when alone with him in the house one day she let his now frequent explorations of her young slim body continue and became excited.

Then it happened, as it lead that day to her first of what later was to become more often fully intimate liaisons with her own father. Afterwards she regretted what she had done – but though now she did her best to discourage her father, however he virtually blackmailed her into having to submit further to him. Now she felt ashamed of her behavior but though she no longer wanted this to occur with her father, she knew she had enjoyed their intimacy. Further more she at last realised that she had a body very desirable to any man and was disappointed that she could not persuade her very religious Roman Catholic, Jules, to more intimacy than what he asked of her.

After Charles returned from North Africa he had boosted of the number of French women he had enjoyed in Casablanca. Paul thought of his own escapes before, when at college, with quick affairs whilst there.. He knew he had inherited his father's addiction for women and remembering whilst at college, as he had laid naked and they both recovered from their recent exertion, Paul knew how much he would have liked the same opportunities now he had returned home.. Yet what actually did happen was by accident.

Foolishly, without knocking, he had blundered into his sister, Teressa's, bedroom. He found her completely naked. It was the first time he had seen his now eighteen year old naked body since he was very young. Now he was just fifteen with all the passions of a boy of that age. He could not take his eyes off her charms which were normally hidden from his view.

Teressa noted it and laughed. Slowly she turn her body completely round so he saw every inch of her mature body. Then facing him again she laughed again.   "Do you like what you see - Do you approve? " Paul was made speechless by her beauty   Then as if to break the spell she spoke again. "Now let me see if I like what you have. Come let me take off your clothes." Without waiting for a reply she came to him and took off every piece of his clothing until he was as naked as she whilst he stood helpless almost in a dream.

She looked approvingly at him saying, "Yes! I approve. You've developed in the parts that matter since I last saw you like this." Her words broke his trance. All he could see in front of him was a very beautiful girl so much more lovely than the few younger girls who had willingly, entertained him at college. It mattered nothing to him that this lovely girl was his sister, he thought nothing of the natural prohibitions to what they were doing. He could not help himself. He drew her naked body to his own, clasped her tightly, and kissed her passionately. Together, they began to explore their naked bodies. In spite of his age and remembering what his father had said, he realized this was not the first time she had been with a man, but this only made him more excited

After a long time she broke away, though seemingly, reluctant. The kiss appeared to break down her own barriers to what was happening. Not caring what she was doing she led him by the hand to her bed and gently pushed him on to it before climbing up on top of him. The inevitable happened. It took many wonderful minutes but at last they broke apart. He heard her say in a whisper. *"Dear Paul I would so love to give you a child".*

Seeing his reaction she realized that unintentionally she had spoken the words in her mind. Suddenly she was afraid and buried her head in the pillow before telling him to get out of her bedroom. He went somewhat embarrassed himself. Yet he knew he would never forget those wonderful moments.

It never happened again. It seemed that they tried to avoid each other. Then their mother died and soon afterwards Teressa married her boyfriend, Jules de Freycinet. Though at the wedding reception he saw her looking at him and saw tears come to her eyes, he had since wondered if it was her memory of their illicit liaison or simply because she was so happy to be married.

Whatever her glance had meant Paul knew he would never forget those stolen moments. Had she really meant those secret words which he was not meant to hear.. *"Dear Paul I would so love to give you a child."* It was their secret, one he remembered so vividly each day. However when the holidays were over and Paul returned to his studies trying to achieve as high as possible credentials in both geology and mining, he put this experience to work.

Now his girlfriend discovered he was now a far more competent lover, and this attracted even more girls to enjoy now, far greater intimacy with them. It did seem that he was destined to become a womanizer probably just as infamous as his father. In fact he felt little for these women who yielded their charms to him. Yet even this did not seem as wonderful as those illicit minutes with his sister.

Meantime their father returned many times to Algeria and Morocco finding even more useful miner deposits and his king rewarded him financially. He new Emperor Napoleon III wanted to achieve even greater military acquisitions and all knew he had his eyes were on possible possessions in America though they were likely to be in either Central or South America. However what would be the reaction of the United States as it would be a defiance of what they called the 'Munroe Doctrines' being very opposed to any interference in any part of America by any European or other powers.

However Charles now knew that if the opportunity arose he would gladly follow the troops and see if he could find and possess great riches to keep for himself in those wild areas. This was not possible where he worked in Africa but in those isolated areas it should be possible to find ores, yet not disclose them to the government.

He had read with interest the gold discoveries in both California and now Colorado. His expertise told him the Rocky mountains were formed in the same mountain building epoch as those mountains which lay in both the other Americas. However he had to admit it was unlikely that in those wild areas he would be able to enjoy the conquests he had enjoyed in both Morocco and Algeria. Still he knew that silver would exist in quantities in Central America and both gold and silver were available for discovery in South America. It was the death of his wife Matilda, who in spite of his other affairs, he still loved passionately, which made him hope he could soon leave France.

7.

Now having completed the very detailed survey along with Theodore Judah of a possible route through the Rockie Mountains, which their proposed Central Pacific railway would have to take. How it was to overcome the supreme difficulties and break out on to the plains, to meet any other railway driving east to meet it, to become a Transcontinental line. Now Kurt used his acquired knowledge in railway construction to fully cost it if it was to be undertaken. Even he was astonished at the level of money required.

He knew, even if they could win governmental monitory support for such a line there would be need for much more investment by many private persons. As Donald Reid was now quite an enthusiast for the project Kurt took him and Crocker on the long journey to Salt Lake City to meet again Harrison Anderson.

Harrison confirmed what they had already heard from Huntington, about his two sons involvement with government officials endeavouring to gain support for the entire scheme. The report was not very promising. As expected with the possibility of civil war looming, the Unionist were far more interested in expanding their military necessities. Never-the less they were all delighted to find Harrison Andersen was still very interested and would gladly, invest with others, if they got government support.

Gradually Kurt was helping to establish a consortium in California and the west, who would consider investing on the same terms. At least Harrison informed Kurt of the success his cousin, Otto Milliken, had achieved in gold discoveries in Colorado. He knew what Otto had done in refurnishing the local brothel, making it yet another source of money. Harrison felt sure, that if such a railway was to be started Otto might too wish to invest.

On the strength of this Kurt obtained his address and wrote to him explaining what he had in mind. Otto replied – but only promised to consider investing if the Anderson's did the same. But by now the Reid and Sand families had become frequent visitors to each others residences. No longer did the Reid's, the Backhouse's as well as Cherie and David Wilson concern themselves of Kurt's unusual relationships with both Agnes and Anita. In fact Cherie, due to her somewhat intimate life with Gordon Taylor before he re-discovered Sheila, had accidentally acquired a good knowledge of railway construction and was now a very strong supporter of the idea.

Anita had now born Kurt her second child, a daughter, Edwina Sand, after Conchita conceived by her raping, and soon Agnes wished to conceive their third, but actually her fourth, child, and Kurt was very willing to oblige. So with a laugh, when they stayed, they would ask which room he wanted for their night's stay. Actually their families were becoming very close and spent long periods enjoying the facilities California had to offer them.

One journey they expressly enjoyed was their visits to Yosemite when they often stayed with a Mexican family Kurt had helped to protect in those dangerous days of 1849 and 1850. Again the absence of decent roads further indicated the need California had of the new railway form of transportation. Now a frequent correspondent with Tricia Drake, Kurt had learned of Cornelius Vanderbilt's interest in railway building in California, even if at this time he was not enthusiastic in the 'Golden Egg'.

Now Kurt felt there was little more he could do to further a possible Transcontinental Railway and immersed himself in ensuring the profitability of his existing business, at present the only real source of his wealth. He did this with the added assistance he received from his two 'wives' not forgetting to ensure they also enjoyed their times with him.

* * * * * * * * * * * * * * *

By now Sophia Danton knew that Alan Mosley, whilst not committed in any way to a future life with her, never-the-less Sophia knew she was by far the most frequent woman to share their pleasures in bed. There was no doubt that by now her husband, Hugh, suspected her many infidelities. However what could he do. She had resources quite separate from any monies he gave her. Also her dominating father, Albert Sand could do him great damage if he made any objection, for Hugh was still employed by Albert in his company.

Also Hugh still loved Sophia, and when he was at home she willing offered her sensuous body to him. So he decided to accept his position, delighted that Sophia now wanted to conceive her fourth child by him. Sophia bore him a son, Stephen Danton in 1859. This fact did nothing to deter Alan Mosley enjoying her pregnant body whenever Hugh was away. Proud of her conquests, Sophia ensured in her letters that Kurt knew everything about them, even surprising him with her detailed and somewhat intimate accounts of these encounters. By now Kurt even showed these letters to both Agnes and Anita who equally found them amusing. However they warned him they thought Kurt should not consider making his sister his third wife.

* * * * * * * * * * * * * * *

As Gordonsville was somewhat to the west, it might avoid the worse part of the confrontation should a civil was ensue. At present they did not need to consider any action. However both the residents of Racoonsville and Gooshland knew only too well that if the war occurred – the important battles would occur in the land between the City of Washington and either Richmond or Petersburg. This then would be on the estates they owned possibly destroying them.

Neither wished to leave their homes at present but felt they should be prepared if the worse happened. It was Estelle Carroll who suggested a solution. Rockville was north of Washington, although along the River Potomac, it might be spared the worst of the fighting which would be to the south and fighting for the control of the seaboard and ports whereby they could transport their troops. Again Estelle was so very proud of Rockville and its long history. In some way all these residents of Gordonsville, Racoonsville and Gooshland were related to the original David and Amelia Carroll. Estelle knew whatever the dangers she would never leave Rockville whilst it still stood. She felt she owed it to her distinguished predecessors that she should try to offer a haven for these families within the vast Rockville mansion.

Very quickly she went to call on them and included the descendents of all living on the Racoonsville estate, who Daniel Carroll had at one time offered security. She came to beg them to leave their houses, even if someone in the family chose to remain, and come to find far great security at Rockville, until the war was over.

Estelle knew she would never leave Rockville whatever the dangers. She felt Amelia would never forgive her if she did this. – If later it was better for others to leave then there were opportunities with their many friends in both New York or even Canada, that decision must be theirs.

To Estelle's pleasure she discovered they were delighted to take her advice and so now all them began to plan, in earnest, deciding who should travel to Rockville but who should stay behind as long as possible. They all knew their support would be for the northern states but could any of them actually take up arms against the south, no matter whatever was their dislike of slavery. They knew and understood the entrenched views of their tenants. They had known their families for so long and helped them establish themselves, more as friends.

Could any of them actually join the army and go and fight these very persons who they had known for so long. Perhaps even more than the loss of the estates and mansions, this was a fact they feared. Like all civil wars it would be fought often by different members of the same family who felt they must fight each other, perhaps killing each other. But could this civil war still be obverted.

8.

In February 1860 Abraham Lincoln made his famous speech in New York City to the Cooper Union. It was brilliant and Lincoln appeared to be a moderate on the question of Slavery. Back in New York a possible civil war was not troubling Devin Ragan. It was his conscience which was troubling him. He knew now how much he was enjoying his intimate relationship with Morna Lynch. Now she stayed with him at least once each week and if so, after they both completed their days tasks, Morna rarely retired to her own little room but happily joined Devin in his bed. Devin knew now how much he enjoyed these times.

Could he possibly be actual falling in love with Morna. Had he, at last, lost his previous desire for Camay Nolan. He could not be sure but he did regret his failure to write to her. He knew by now she might easily have found another man to interest her. Even now Devin knew he should write to her – but his conscience told him this might be unfair on Morna.

After one of the many times they now enjoyed their new relationship. Though tired as Morna had willing yielded her body to him, she must have felt a little shamed to have so recently yielded herself to him. She asked, "Devin, please tell me truthfully, do you think that I am a wicked woman to let you do those things to me. – Perhaps now you think I am really only fitted for life in that brothel."

Devin took her lovingly in his arms and pressed his lips once more on hers but breaking and saying, "Don't talk nonsense. I really do think you are a wonderful girl and you are so kind to me. – Please do not think these things. – I like every thing about you ----Well my trouble is –er

-well – I do not still know if I love you – or anyone. Dearest –you must be willing to give me time. – But I do think you are a wonderful girl."

There was no doubt poor Morna was disappointed. "Then you still would like to be with Camay again?. She questioned. Quickly he responded "No! Dear! You are wrong. –I doubt I will ever meet Camay again. – In any case, by now, she may have found another man. – Frankly, I don't know what's wrong with me. I just don't feel I can make a commitment to any woman at present. – In any case I know I'm not rich enough to keep a wife – and the children she would give me."

Now he took hold of her hands. "Tell me, please, - after what I have said – do you still want us to continue as we have done." Poor Morna sighed, "Oh! Yes! Devin, please. I think I'm falling in love with you – but then you are the only man I've ever properly known. Perhaps I am not the woman for you – maybe your not the man for me – but please let it continue. Then we may discover what are our true feelings." There was no more to say. They kissed briefly each telling the other they would like that.

So it continued, but soon it was time for Devin to transport his first consignment of Irish families to the places designed for them in the west, and so now he had to spend most of the days in planning their journey. At least he now knew what was required of him. In fact he was relieved for, at least for a time, he would be many miles from Morna. He would have time to think.

He was allocated two other men to accompany him, so that in time they could take over this task, allowing him to plan other groups going west. The plan was to take about twenty families and their children, to settle around the new town of Junction City, Kansas. This lay alongside the Republican River, which was a tributary of both the Kansas and Missouri rivers. Land had been purchased for them there. Kansas was now considered safe after the dangerous disputes in that state the previous years,

The journey would be easy as far as Independence, though they would have to negotiate the short journey from Buffalo to Pittsburgh where they could board the Carroll/Marshall Steam boats to Independence. Then by wagons across the prairie lands of Kansas to arrive at their destination. They all knew it would be a long and tiring journey, particularly with young children, but after fully explaining the difficulties Devin was able to convince all of them it would be successful.

In any case these families were only too willing to leave their cramped accommodation with the promise of free land to work, as they knew how to work this, to establish a homestead, with a chance of a better living than any had enjoyed in the past. They all knew by now that the wagons which were waiting for them at Independence, and by which they would complete their journey, would be theirs with four horses, which they could keep and use for both transport and working the land.

The first part of the journey was not only easy but restful and they were delighted to see new parts of the United States which Devin had explained to them before they left. So they were reasonably refreshed by the time they arrived at Buffalo. All though it was more difficult from Buffalo to Pittsburgh, they all accomplished it and were temporary housed in small accommodation outside the city. Here they must rest for a time whilst arrangements were made to transfer them onto the boat to Independence.

Devin knew he could depend on his two colleagues to attend to this which left him free to once again renew his acquaintance made on his previous journey and went, to call on Joanne and Philip Holstein. He had written to them to tell them he was coming and a letter was waiting for him when he arrived at Pittsburgh asking him to call one afternoon, as soon as he arrived in the city.

Devin felt very proud to receive the invitation. He had enjoyed that day on his previous visit of meeting them. He knew of their high standing in the community and had been pleasantly surprised at his reception the last time. Dressing in his best clothes, which his salary now enabled him to purchases, he called a cab and was driven in style to their house. Once again he marveled at its size, even grandeur than that in which the Purcell's resided on Long Island. So it was in some trepidation he rang the bell on that large front door, to be opened by a maid and a fully dressed butler, who led him into the hall and towards the large reception room which he had not seen on his last visit.

It was obvious that their were several persons in that room as the level of conversation showed this to be a fact. The butler opened the door and stood back to let him enter, then announced his coming proudly announcing him as Master Devin Ragan, so he was received as if he was an important gentleman. However as he entered he received and even greater surprise. Joanne Holstein came forward to meet him smiling but she was bringing with her, holding by the hand a beautiful young woman who was also smiling.

Poor Devin could not believe his eyes for that beautiful young woman was none other than Camay Nolan, now dressed as a lady herself, the girl he had last kissed goodbye to on Ellis Island as they parted. Camay to go to Annapolis to work as a servant, he to go with the League to bring help for them with their work. Now all he could see was an extremely beautiful and smiling Camay who came with Joanne to meet him.

To Devin it appeared that a beautiful angel was there offering her hand to him but now almost laughing with pleasure at once again seeing the man she felt, months ago, she would never meet again

9.

In March Camay Nolan began to consider that, the approaches of Graham Stowe to her were completely honorable. Unlike James Holstein, Graham never made any intimate attempts on her except those she now so willingly allowed. Camay began to think Graham's approaches were, to her delight, leading to him possibly proposing marriage. Now she knew if it happened she would accept and be glad to become his wife.

After he had once again taken her on a short river cruise and they left the boat and both stood looking across the wide river on the landing stage. As Graham stood behind her hugging her body to his, his hands once again were covering and pressing on her covered breasts, a liberty she now willing allowed him. A delightful thrill passed through her body, yet at that moment as it happened she suddenly remembered that day so long ago on Ellis Island as Devin Ragan left her on another landing stage to make their separate journeys and to part, now she felt for ever.

Even now she remembered his promise to come to visit her when she got to Annapolis. How much, at that time, she had so desperately wanted it to happen. But he had never come to visit her, and after a short time she no longer believed he would keep his promise. She knew it was her despondency that had led to her terrible yielding of her body to James. Now it was another man who was giving her the thrills she so desperately needed. Reluctantly Camay knew she could never expect a life with Devin. In any case she realised even these memories were unfair to Graham who had now become so much a part of her life.

Yet the following day her mind was torn apart once again. Joanne Holstein had called to see her mother Alberta and Camay was sitting close to Alberta as Joanne was telling her mother of recent events. Suddenly Camay's heart almost stopped as Joanne spoke so quietly to her mother

"Mother, you know that very nice man who now works for the Purcell family and others bringing Irish immigrants who want to travel west, not to stay in New York, with all its dangers, but to settle on the free land to cultivate and have a future. The Carroll/Marshall line are happy to contribute by providing free passage on the steamers from Pittsburgh to Independence. Well he called on us the last time as he was pioneering the route they all must take. He is a lovely man and we begged him to call on us whenever he came with those families. His name is Devin Ragan, also a Irishman. Well he has written to me and will be calling on us in two days time before taking them further to Independence and beyond."

In spite of herself, Camay could not control herself, she whole body jerked and she sighed loudly. Devin who she though she would never see again would be visiting the Holstein household in two days time. It seemed Joanne had seen her reaction as did her mother. Now Joanne spoke to her for the first time "Of course, I should have remembered Camay what you told me when I first came to you to persuade you to have that abortion. You told me you meet Devin Ragan on that ship when your two families first sailed to New York. Look, Alberta you must bring Camay to my house on Thursday, so Camay can renew her acquaintance with Devin Ragan.".

Now Thursday had arrived and a very happy Joanne had taken Camay by the hand to lead her to meet Devin. In spite of herself, Camay was smiling happy as she now met Devin again. Almost in a dream as she heard Joanne say to him, "Devin Ragan let me introduce Camay Nolan once again to you. I believe you both travelled on the same ship when you first came to America. Please take Camay to the next room. I'm certain you both will have a lot to say to each other about what has happened in those years since you last meet."

Devin, who was as astonished as Camay, gladly took Camay's offered hands and led her to the room Joanne had indicated knowing they both would have lots to tell each other. Yet at that moment though they were so delighted, and even more surprised, to have this opportunity of meeting again. Both now could not but feel terribly ashamed for each knew that had by now found another who soon might become their partner for life. Though the moment was supreme, an event they had never expected now for some time, yet circumstances were very different from when they parted on Ellis Island.

Devin closed the door behind them, still holding one of her hands. Then Camay looked at him and said, "Devin dear, you promised to call on me. – You did write for a time – then it stopped. A little time ago, I wrote to you but the letter was returned telling me you no longer live there." She paused then continued, "have you married?"

Poor Devin did not know how to reply, "Oh! Camay! No! I'm not married - but it is very wicked of me not to contact you –But you must believe me. I've been very busy with my work for the league – well then there were some things I hated – the way they used young Irish girls – trapped them into their brothels – Please believe me I was not involved in this but I did need to carry messages to these places. Then I helped two dear ladies who were trying to warn new immigrants of what might happen and then Patrick Purcell gave me this chance to escape. He, with others provide the means for us to bring many Irish families to travel west, and rest a good living from new land there. That is why I'm now in Pittsburgh. – I shall accompany a number of these families tomorrow. I'm paid a salary and I like my knew work."

Camay somehow felt pleased he had not married and smiled approvingly. "Yes! Joanne has told me what you do. I think it is very kind of you, but really I am sorry you did not come to see me. – I went to work in Annapolis. It was hard work but quite pleasant." Again she paused wondering what else she should confess. Then thinking it better not to mention James Holstein she continued, "However in Annapolis – well the house was outside the town – I felt very lonely with only my family to see to me. – Then a miracle happened. – The house was used by both the Casimir's and the Holstein's. On one visit Joanne Holstein saw how unhappy I was. – She is really a very wonderful lady – she gave me this chance to leave Annapolis. She brought me to live here as a servant to her dear mother Alberta Van Buren. – Actually she has virtually made me her personal servant and I do love living and looking after her. It was there I heard two days ago that you were coming and why Joanne so kindly brought me today so I could meet you again."

At least that information pleased Devin, "Then you are not married?" Again Camay was not sure what to say,. But felt he might soon discover so she responded, "No! Devin like you – I am not married – though a dear man, Graham Stowe, seems to like me and we are courting."

Though disappointed, Devin was not surprised. At least it eased his own conscience so he replied, "Of course I would have expected this. It's been a long time since I last saw you. I too have a girl friend Morna Lynch, who with the help of those two lovely ladies, I rescued from a brothel. – Now she works with me in New York persuading these families to take our offer." He wondered what else to say but felt a few more words were necessary, "I like Morna and she likes me. After all she is grateful for me taking out of that hell. Fortunately she had only been trapped there for three months."

What he feared happened. He could see Camay was disappointed. Of course he had expected this and her question. Camay looked straight at him. "Devin do you think you may soon marry Morna."

He turned away but was still holding her hands then turned again to her. "Camay I really do not know. She is a fine woman. She was not to blame for what had happened --- Well – oh, what can I say – I'm not sure I really love her. – in any case let's not say anymore about our new partners. I am so very pleased to see and meet you again. – Look if you would allow me – whatever are our true feelings for each other – and you know at one time we were very great friends. Now I know you live here. – I shall be coming many times to Pittsburgh. Would you allow me to call on you. – I would really love to do so."

Devin was rewarded for a lovely smile appeared on Camay's face, "Oh! Devin that would be wonderful. I would so much like you to call. – Well now we can have the rest of today together. Joanne wants you to stay for lunch and dinner. Let us enjoy our surprise meeting today. You can tell me about the exciting life you seemed to have lead. – I'm afraid it was not the same for me. But - Please this time – after today – please do call on me whenever you come to Pittsburgh."

They returned to the others and both enjoyed those six hours together. Whatever might be the future for either of them – at least it seemed that at last they might meet again more frequently. In spite of the commitments both had made it was obvious they both still felt a strong attachments to each other. Perhaps during those future meetings they might, at last, decide who might be their long time partners for life.

10.

However once again events may happen which would prevent there being many future meetings of Camay and Devin. After Lincoln's brilliant speech in New York he easily carried the Republican Illinois Convention and was elected as their candidate at the main Republican Convention, in May 1860, fortunately held in Illinois in Chicago, within a brand new convention hall now christened the 'Wigwam' The Democrats had held their own convention but it was a very disunited party. The southern states even held a separate convention and though Senator Johnson eventually acquired the right to stand as the Democratic nominee, others would stand against him. The situation was placing the Republican Party nominee as the one which might yet become the next President.

The front runner for the Republicans was William Steward and it was thought he would be their choice. However they knew he was not popular in the several states the Republicans had failed to win in 1856. Also Lincoln now saw his chance. He ran a brilliant political campaign with his strong supporters, even forging convention passes ensuring these made the first persons in the queue into the hall, which limited the number of Steward supporters able to enter.

There were several contenders for election. Lincoln and his aides knew they could not have a chance of winning nomination for him on the first ballot. However he gained 102 votes to Steward's 173. However on the second vote due to the work of his supporters a number of states whose candidate had failed changed the allegiance to Lincoln.

On the second vote the result was very near with 184 for Steward and 181 to Lincoln. Now the surge of support came to Lincoln and on the third vote Lincoln polled 231 votes to Steward's 180. Still it was just short of the necessary total. However when Ohio changed 4 of its votes to Lincoln he was elected and now became the republican Candidate for the Presidential elections in November. So 'Honest Abe' became their cry.

The election occurred on November 6th. 1860 Lincoln gained 180 electoral votes, Johnson received 12 , Breckenridge polled 72 and finally Bell gained only 39. So Lincoln had an absolute majority of 57 over all the opposing candidates and so became President-elect to assume office in March 1861. Lincoln was still not president and there were many rebellions by people who strongly disliked him. Yet there was nothing he could do.

The southern states were appalled at the result and it seemed Jefferson Davis was the front runner in those states who were so violently opposed Lincoln's presidency. Johnson was still President. To his credit he did his best to withstand this vocal and demonstrative opposition. Meantime Lincoln was an astute politician and proceeded to try to unify the sections of the Republican Party who might still be against him. He did not feel victorious– in fact he could see very well the dangers ahead.

So he appointed as his future cabinet, Steward as Secretary of State, Chase as Secretary to the Treasury and Bates as Attorney general. Even finding places in the minor appointments for men who might want to contest him. He realised he must have men standing resolutely behind him if, as he now expected, a civil war might occur.

Of course because of their involvement in Congress the Carroll Family and their many relatives were quickly made aware to the dangers to their country. They had never supported Lincoln and always considered him a very dangerous man. Now it seemed he would soon become President and therefore Commander-in-Chief of the army. They had no doubt but as soon as he took office the southern states would never accept him and they would succeed from the Union. Therefore it now seemed a civil war was inevitable.

All they had tried to avoid had come to haunt them face-to-face. It seemed Estelle Carroll was the one who would take the lead. She knew in the circumstances dear Amelia would expect this of her. The Carroll family and all Amelia and her mother, Margaret's, descendents must be prepared for the eventuality, and Estelle, in spite of her age must plan for it happening. Whatever happened Rockville must survive. For over one hundred and seventy years Rockville had been the source of both their wealth and prosperity. War or not, Estelle was determined to stay there and meet whatever privations which might befall them.

She sat and wrote several letters to any persons who might be considered her relatives irrespective of how little she knew them. Naturally the residents of both Gordonsville and Racoonsville were the recipients of her first letters, again emphasising that if war should breakout near their estates it would be much safer for all of them to come and stay at Rockville. Then two letters to the Brookes part of the combined Chalmer's estate as well as one to the Chalmer's Then a letter to the Reid family in California, though she realised that they might not be too effected by the war. Finally a letter to those in Texas and Kentucky, though she felt they would want to stay near their homes.

So it seemed she had made all possible plans to limit the damage a civil war would create. She was rewarded by those at Gordonsville and particularly, Racoonsville, all promising if it should become necessary they would avail themselves of her offer. She was equally rewarded by the fact that, whilst not necessarily against slavery they all thought the continuance of the Union as a united county was paramount. So even civil war would not divided them.

In February 1861 Congress had stated that Abraham Lincoln had won sufficient electoral votes and so would become President for four years beginning March 4th, 1861. During the period from December to Lincoln's inauguration various slave supporting members of the present President Johnson were secretly moving ammunition from northern arsenals to those south of Washington. Almost every naval ship of any size had been sent to destinations far from where a future government could call on them for assistance. The south were preparing for war.

Meanwhile Lincoln had made his own preparations but kept them secret until he voiced all his plans and future actions during his inauguration address in Washington. As he toured the states around Washington due to the information obtained by Allan Pinkerton, a detective soon to establish the famous 'Pinkerton Men' Lincoln was able to avoid an attempt on his life in Baltimore.

So on March 4th 1861 Abraham Lincoln became the 16th. President of the United States. By then South Carolina had already seceded from the Union and in February Jefferson Davis had inaugurated the Confederation of Southern States. This was followed by the secession of Florida, Mississippi, Alabama, Louisiana, Georgia and Texas.

As Lincoln had increased the numbers defending Fort Sumner this action produced the Confederacy attack, the first of the war, and fall of the fort, shortly followed by the secession of Arkansas, North Carolina, Tennessee and finally Virginia. Though Missouri and Kentucky were divided with two factions supporting either side, and the new state of West Virginia announced they supported the Union. Whilst California and all the northern states pledged support for the Union.

However the attack and captured of Fort Sumner by the Confederacy had commenced hostilities. So what so many feared for over forty years, the Great Civil War of America had come to past. It was to be five long years of death, toil and destruction. Disunion had occurred to the Union.

———————————————

PART 7

REUNION

DISUNION PART 7 REUNION

REUNION

1.

So the American Civil War began which was to last four long bloody years resulting in the deaths of almost seven hundred thousand lives all fighting and dying for the Union or the Confederate forces, though many deaths were due to disease, especially to those supporting the Confederate cause, due to their poorer medical recourses. It involved many parts of what was then the United States, and the death rate was greater than in any previous wars for the past hundreds of years.

This book is not intended to be an account of this tragic affair and it will only dwell on that part which greatly involved the Carroll families and other relatives associated with them. It was a tragedy which should not have happened and though it was fought to maintain the principle that 'all men and women are created equally', its true basis was the simple fact, that in the industrialized north, slaves were not essential for their prosperity, whilst in those in the agricultural south, it was felt slaves were essential.

During that terrible time there were many episodes which are regretted by every one, and though for a time afterwards there is no doubt, but the defeated south were severely punished for it happening. Though it did eventually restore a united country still a Union of Federal States, as first envisaged in the Declaration of Independence, a single united country. Perhaps its true value is that all now truly believed that colour was not a reason for enslaving any human being.

It seemed to Estelle Carroll and all those living in Rockville that they were to be engaged very early in this civil war. It happened when Colonel Stone left Washington with three regiments and entered the nearby town of Rockville on June 10th. 1861, took possession of the town as a base, and sent others to occupy all towns along the River Potomac. Though they did not take possession of their estate, they were forced to billet soldiers there.

This action polarised the views of those for the Union and the others for the Confederacy, though fortunately, Stone received orders to take his force and advance on the Virginian town of Leesburg to which Confederate forces were going. Stone's forces halted that advance and were then ordered to reinforce General Robert Patterson's forces coming from Pennsylvania. The Rockville Expedition ended on July 7th. when they were withdrawn and proceeded to take possession of Martinsburg,

Though there had been no fighting on the estate it proved how vulnerable it was to invasion. Estelle was even more determined that Rockville should be a bastion against any attacks and a place of security for anyone who wished to reside there. Of course Estelle's eldest daughter, Audrey married to Jack Steward lived close by in one of the houses the original David Carroll had built near the river on his estate. With her children Audrey and Jack would be staying close by and would move into Rockville if necessary.

What Estelle feared was that her youngest child, Steven Carroll, now forty and Audrey's son, James Steward, being thirty five might yet join one of the northern armies as an officer and she feared, if so they might lose their lives. Her eldest son Peter and Amy were still living in New York. Neither he nor his son, Andrew, also married to Edwina Palatine, being so involved in their shipping empire, would do so and would remain there now offering their services to the Union in planning and building ships to fight the war.

They were all well informed as to what was happening, as Estelle's second son, Martin Carroll married to Heather Beverley, was the Representative from Maryland to Congress. They quickly learned of the constant defeats of the Union army against the better trained Confederate troops. One, the Battle of Bull Run had been fought nearby with the Union suffering a very heavy defeat. Now the invasion of the Shenandoah valley had begun which threatened the whole of

West Virginia. For the moment neither Martin, nor his sons were joining but might be called upon to do so in future.

Meanwhile the residents of Gordonsville, Racoonsville and Gooshland had to consider their positions very carefully. Gordonsville had quickly become an important base for the Confederate forces being at the junction of several railway lines. At present it was not an area likely to be attacked being so far west of the opening warfare. All the residents felt strong affinity for what the Union was striving, but their friends in the surrounding areas were supporting the Confederate cause. So they did not appear to take sides and the women, particularly helped to transform the local Exchange Hotel into a military hospital for tending to wounded soldiers now arriving from the eastern battles.

However the position in both Racoonsville and Gooshland was very different. Again they lived in an area which held strong Confederate views and Richmond, to the south, was the Confederate headquarters. They realised that soon all the land between Washington and Richmond must become an area of fierce fighting.. Probably the residents of Racoonsville were in the worst position. In 1856 Mark Carroll had stood down from the position of Senator for Virginia which he and his deceased father, Robert Carroll had held for many years. In his place his son Danton had become Senator and so was at present away in Washington attending Congress and many knew, though he was violently opposed to the election of Abraham Lincoln as President, had with him his son, Paul married to June Brookes, now a member of the House of Representatives. However everyone knew they had now, with reluctance, supported the Union in the struggle.

However this branch of the Carroll family had done so much for their area and were held in great esteem. Though no doubt in due course many of Mark's sons or grandsons might go and fight for the Union cause. It was better that as many persons as possible took Estelle Carroll's offer and went to live at Rockville or one of their nearby mansions. However Mark and his wife Estelle, a Tencin before she married and who both felt so strongly that Daniel and Michelle Carroll would never expect them to leave Racoonsville, decided they would remain with a minimum staff. So very quickly the others left by coach and made the journey to Rockville.

However due to marriages those living in Gooshland, possibly in even greater danger if hostilities occurred in that area, were equally involved.. It should be remembered that the present Gooshland estate was created when Sophia Brookes married Colin Chalmers uniting her Brookes estate with his. The inheritance had been continued as joint ownership by Kenneth Brookes, Sophia's grandson, who would be responsible for her old estate but working with Steven Chalmers, Sophia's grandson due to her second marriage to Colin Chalmers. It had been a very amicable arrangement with no disputes – but now what should they do.

Again it was the women who decided. Kenneth and his wife, and Stephen Chalmers and his wife, would stay to still attempt to run their combined estates but again all other members of their families should leave at once and travel to Rockville accepting their offer of accommodation.

So by June 1861 there had been a massed migration from these estate to come and live with Estelle Carroll at Rockville. In fact they arrived just before the serious Battle of Manassas occurred near the Maryland/ Virginia border on July !8th and the less important one of Ball's Bluff in October. In fact it seemed that for the present , though it might not be so in the future, all the residents of all four estates had found ways of limiting serious disruption just as the war was increasing in intensity.

Throughout the whole of 1861 and the beginning of 1862 nearly all the battles were in the east of Virginia especially along the coast on Chesapeake Bay to the north of Richmond, as the Confederate army tried to attack and possibly capture Washington with the Union forces attempting to prevent this, though most of the victories fell to those of Confederate President Jefferson Davis. However many other important battles were being fought many miles apart, in Missouri, Tennessee and many other places. Soon it seemed the whole of the lands to the east of the Rockies and as far south as Texas and Florida would be where thousands of American would fight and die for what they considered their rights. It seemed the next year might become far more decisive.

2.

So Mark Carroll and his wife, Estelle, stayed in charge of Racoonsville, just the same as did Kenneth Brookes and Janis looking after Sophia Chalmers old estate, whilst Steven Chalmers and Hattie remained in charge of the Chalmer part of their combined estates. Mark's son, Danton and his wife, Claudia, would be at Congress in Washington. However the rest of their families took temporary refuge at Rockville glad to accept Estelle Carroll's invitation.

Of course most of the male residents there would soon join the Union army to fight to retain the now very fragile union of the country. This was to bring great fear to their mothers, sisters and daughters, believing they might soon die in the bloody carnage, for it seemed that this war was going to be far worse than any before. Already the death rate on each side was growing alarmingly.

Everyone near Racoonsville knew that Mark Carroll, who had for so long been Senator for Virginia, and now that his son. Danton, occupied this post, had aligned themselves with the Union cause, whilst most around had joined the Confederacy. However the family was so well respected and for so many years had helped the community, little resentment was shown to them and their estates were not violated though they often had to give temporary residence to Confederate battalions as they passed through on their way to battle.

Fortunately the chief battles of 1862 at Beaver Dam, Hanover, Oak Grove, Glendale and Yorktown were to the east, nearer the coast, though the Battle of Cedar Mountain and worse, that of Rappahannock Station in August 1862 was fought only a few miles away. So it seemed for the time Racoonsville would remain still intact throughout 1862 and early 1863. But then, so far most of these battles were victories for the Confederate armies and the Union had few victories in other states such as Kentucky, Tennessee and Florida.

In Texas, apart from the coast near Galveston, conditions were quite tranquil. The Downey's and Eliot families, having proclaimed their allegiance to the Union in a very strong Confederate community, had absolved their 'crime' by being willing to join the border militia to guard the state from indian invasion with so many men now gone to fight the war elsewhere, leaving behind their older kindred's and women to see to their horse breeding establishment which, in turn, produced much needed horses for Confederate Calvary regiments.

The Union defeats had caused Lincoln to, already, make two changes in the Commander-in-chief of the Union armies, and there was no doubt but that it seemed that it would be the Confederacy which would be victorious. Never had the Union of the United States been in greater danger since 1783. To his credit at this moment in its history Abraham Lincoln made the most important decision to ensure its future. Lincoln knew it would be useless for the Union to win this war unless it had a prosperous economic future. The war, besides the appalling loss of life, was draining the resources of the country. Further more if victory was achieved it would be essential to unite together all the states in a truly Federal Country from the Pacific to the Atlantic. It must seem to every one that this was the case.

So in the midst of a bloody war, which they were not winning, Lincoln insisted Congress passed an act which might bring this about. It was an act which truly made the country united once again.

*　*　*　*　*　*　*　*　*　*　*　*　*　*　*

On July 1st. 1862 Congress passed the first of the two Pacific Railway Acts. This was the most important acts of the United States in the entire nineteenth century. It authorised the building of a railway and granted rights of way to two companies. The Union Pacific, to build westwards from Omaha, Nebraska, and the Central Pacific to build eastwards from Sacramento, California, until they met and produced a united railway. Each company's length, and therefore its wealth, depended on how far they travelled east and west until they joined.

The act granted alternate sections of public domain land per mile, on each side of the track, providing 'loan bonds' for each mile laid, in 'dollars per mile' escalated in accord with the difficult of terrain. These loans were to be repayable in thirty years. Now there was no reason why the Central Pacific should not start laying tracks on the land already surveyed. This provision won by Huntington, due his presence in Washington and the help given him by the Anderson family, was vital to the Central Pacific owing to its path through the Rocky Mountains, creating this provision in that Act might make this possible.

Kurt Sands took this opportunity to write to the banker in Washington and to the stockbroker in New York, clearly stating his engineering experience, naming his father's company in its achievements in Pennsylvania and the Erie Canal. He begged them to invest in the Central Pacific, even if they did not do so in the Union Pacific, even then suggesting, again, a joining of their three investments, including his own, in forming a holding company for, not just this project, but other future railway projects.

Kurt was gratified in receiving a reply from each, firstly agreeing to invest, but hoping in due course they might all meet together to consider his offer of a consortium. It seemed that, now, it was essential to both the Purcell's and the Mason families, already closely associated in their business ventures, that they should together form a closer association of their own. Not just for this railway, but for the future of the project Kurt had suggested to them.

Kurt's immediate task was to use his knowledge as an engineer and help Charles Crocker, with that man's ability of organisation. To start laying track from Sacramento. Now a Central Pacific part of this new Transcontinental Railway was a financial possibility. The investment would seriously strain their own resources and the problems ahead were enormous. However no longer was it a dream. The 'Golden Egg' was within their reach. No longer was it a plan to sell their survey to others. Government money was at last available. Now the future was in their own hands, but if it failed, they knew they all would face bankruptcy.

It had been proved exceedingly difficult, as soon as the reached the mountains. Crocker was right, labour was short. It became imperative to employ and train Chinese workers, many brought to this country by Donald Reid's shipping company, to do the job. For the next few months his family saw little of Kurt Sands. Everyone in the Central Pacific Company feared then the Union Pacific, with fewer obstacles would reach westwards many miles further that as the Central Pacific moved east. This could mean a bleak future for their part of the railway.

Fortunately for them the Civil War would effect the progress of the Union Pacific as much as their own structural problems. Kurt and his colleagues knew little could be done in the east until the war ended, whilst the war did not affect their own section. There was, also, so much corruption in the Union Pacific's management which must delayed track laying.

It was with vigour as well as trepidation that they set about their task. However Kurt, in spite of his fears, receiving the blessing of both Agnes and Anita, and was now a happy man. He was back doing the work for which he had been trained. He was not born to be a stock keeper. At last he could write to Gordon Taylor telling him his plans, hoping when the Central Pacific and the Union Pacific met, he would once again be able to come to meet him.

3.

Now that the Transcontinental Railway was a possibility and both the Purcell's and the Mason's had accepted Kurt Sands advice to invest in the Central Pacific instead of the Union Pacific. Tricia once again reminded Patrick about her concern at the secrecy of the Mason family. "If as Kurt Sand's suggests we form a consortium with the Mason's, for this and other railway projects, it will prove disastrous unless both families respect each other and have no secrets, however embarrassing it may be."

She smiled at Patrick threw her arms around him and kissed him. "They must know of our relationship and that Erin and Merle are also your wives. – Patrick we must confront them – force them to tell us their secrets – otherwise I must advise you that such a consortium must fail. I am not ashamed at my life with you, neither is either Erin nor

Merle. Let us pressurise them to come and stay with us. Then we can openly explain our own secrets and at the same time demand they are, equally, as frank with us."

Patrick still did not want to expose his way of living to others but he knew Tricia was right. In any case their secrets must eventually be discovered if they did work closely together. So somewhat reluctantly Patrick capitulated and left Tricia to plan for a confrontation. Tricia felt she had one trump card. It was her black daughter, Ranee. Daniel Mason had so often asserted that black and white people were equals. Ranee would test if his views were honest.

She took the initiative, when they met again in Washington, in 1863. Daniel had, long suspected, that Tricia was far more than a brilliant, and rich, business associate of Patrick. Being used to the social customs of the capital, he felt certain she was his mistress. So he was not surprised when she confirmed this.

Now she attacked. "Daniel, I know you are well aware of the life we all live in both Washington and New York. You must have guessed about my relationship with Patrick. It is true. I have had a long and loving relationship with Patrick for several years. I am his mistress but I am happy that he treats me, more, as his wife which you have not met. Erin approves of this. We are good friends. Unfortunately I am not able to give him the child we both want. Although we have had the pleasure of meeting your own wife, Sally, you know little about us – nor do we know little about yours. If we are to become more closely associated as business partners, I feel we should get to understand the type of people we are."

She paused noting the look of urgency in Daniel's face. "Though you have refused before, please accept our invitation to come to New York, an stay with us. So we can rectify this." It was what Daniel had feared, the life he felt they would disapprove. He was, desperately, trying to find an excuse in refusing. Realising his torment Tricia tried to disarm him.

Smilingly she continued, "I believe for some reason you are trying to hide something from us. We cannot afford to ignore our differences.

Let us try to break down these barriers – or both our business futures will be in jeopardy. Please come and see the way we live – I warn you, you find it shocking – though I suspect there are similarities to your own. Please bring your wife so she can see our secrets."

Daniel felt he could not refuse and reluctantly agreed to accept their hospitality in fortnight's time. They met on arrival at the station and driven to Long island, where they received their first shock. Not only were they met by Patrick's wife, Erin but another beautiful woman, Merle, who was, quite obviously, well advanced in pregnancy. Both Sally and he were surprised at the loving way they embraced both Tricia and Patrick, though they must know she was his mistress.

After being shown to their rooms they came down for refreshments. Now they were confronted with ten children. Since Tricia had told them she was infertile they felt certain that they were not all Erin's children., and a lovely completely black girl of eighteen was introduced as Ranee Drake. So this was Tricia's child.

"This is my secret", Tricia explained, "our first secret. Ranee is my child by my cruel husband Thomas Drake, who, thankfully for me, died fourteen years ago before I met Patrick, the man I love more than life and who loves Ranee as much as his own children. You see my father married a wonderful young coloured woman who was my mother. It was a marriage of true love and it destroyed my father when she died in childbirth bearing me. That is why Ranee is coloured. – It's in my genes. Thomas never forgave me believing it was not his child."

She smiled. "Come let us eat and let each of us tell you are secrets. Our children know all about us and love us, as we love them We want them to hear what we say. In view of your own views I believe you will not condemn, either my father nor me, for none us here today she anything wrong in a white man associating with a black woman, provided it is what both want. There are no barriers between Ranee and our other children."

Tricia knew she had struck a chord. Neither Daniel nor Sally disapproved. In fact they looked at each other and then at her, in appreciation, so she was pleased to enlighten them of her past history, the cruelty of her husband, the wealth she had acquired on his death due to her own investments. Finally she told them how fortunate she was to find a man like Patrick who could give her so much happiness. Then embracing both Erin and Merle. "—and to find two such wonderful women willing to share him with me "

As she ended their story, Patrick continued. "As you must have guessed Merle, like Tricia is my mistress, all but one of her children are mine, conceived with the full approval of my wife, Erin. You see that although Merle is known to our friends as Merle O'Donnell, the name I, purposely, entered when we became American citizens in 1850, Merle is Erin's younger sister. But I do not have any mistresses – I am fortunate, no honoured, to have three wives who I love equally and wish to conceive me children."

Now Patrick told an astounded Daniel and Sally his story, starting in Ireland and the raping pregnant of both Erin and Merle, their escape to America and detailing everything that had happened since that time.

As he finished he turned to them. "So now you know all our secrets and the life we live. None of us, including our children, are ashamed. We simple ask you to try to understand – perhaps may even approve, for if we are to accept Kurt Sand's proposal we shall have to live closely with each other. I beg you to tell me your own secrets. After what we have told you, you must realise, nothing you may tell us will surprise us or make us feel ill of you. Tricia feels you have very similar views to her own, as the child of a black woman, conceived in love with a white man."

Daniel looked at Sally, he was confused as to how he should reply. Then he spoke quietly to her for several minutes. They could all see and appreciate his difficulties and were willing to wait as long as was necessary. Then having got her approval Daniel decided to tell their own story. Before he began, Daniel took a firm hold of his wife's hands and looked lovingly at her. "It seems we have misjudge you, terribly – we have thought you would have misjudged us, as so many seem to do in Washington – disapproving of how we live. For sometime we thought you must have heard of the rumours about us. This was why we could not take you to our home – You see they say we are 'Nigger lovers' – and 'Nigger fornicators'. We are not ashamed of this but feared you would think the same."

Now once again he looked lovingly as Sally, smiled, and began to tell his own story.

4.

Devin Ragan kept his promise to Camay. Though by now others were trained and able to escort the Irish Families to their new lands out west, Devin made it a point to join them on one or two of these journeys. Then, with Joanne Holstein's assistance he was able to once again renew his acquaintance with Camay. However it was a platonic relationship with no intimacy given nor expected, though both enjoyed the occasions.

The truth was neither could be sure of their true feelings. Camay by now was enjoying her courtship by Graham Stowe, gladly submitting to his now more intimate explorations of her body – yet she still felt, after her terrible affair with James, she could not yield her body completely to him. She had no doubt but that by now Graham loved her dearly and might soon propose marriage to her.

Camay thought, 'If so should I accept – I like Graham – He is kind and generous. I know I could have a long happy life with him – I want a family Why should I not become his wife if he should ask me.' Yet, she knew meeting again Devin Regan had disturbed her. 'Oh! Why should I allow it to do this. Devin has already found another girl – however uncertain he feels about her.'

Meantime unknown to her Devin back in New York, was experiencing similar misgivings. He now knew he like Morna very much. Loved the way she so unashamedly yielded her body to him. He now felt sure Morna loved him. However like Camay their short times together had once again rekindled his previous feelings for her, developed on that terrible ship's journey. 'Surely', he thought, 'I could never expect Camay's attentions. She has already found another man and it seems he his kind to her. Morna is offering me a happy married life with her. – I respect her – Her past means nothing to me. - She was blameless. – She so willingly yields her body to me. – Why cannot I convince myself and ask her to marry me. – I know she would make me a good wife.'

So it continued in New York but events were to happen beyond their control. Lincoln was elected President and the Civil War had begun. Immediately, this stopped for a time either the arrival of new Irish Families from Ireland or the need to transport them west. Patrick Purcell informed him that, though he would continue, for a time, to continue paying him his salary, soon this must cease and he must find other employment.

Until this was obtainable, and Devin knew, with the coming war, his chances of obtaining a new job would be difficult, soon he would not have the resources to keep a wife, and any children she might bear him. Marriage to Morna, or any women, was impossible for the time being. So he spoke at length and with great kindness to a devastated Morna.

"Morna", he said, "I do like you very much. I think you are a wonderful woman. I know now you would make me a good wife – and I know I want that – but I have not the means to keep any wife. It would be so unfair to offer you such a life. ---- I have decided – I strongly support what the Union stands for. – I intend to join the army and fight for what I believe in. – I am not asking you to wait for me – for I do not know if I will survive. – However when this is over, I would hope there may a chance for us in the future. That is as much as I can offer you."

Morna, though she had been expecting this, was devastated. "But Devin you must know I love you. Of course I understand – I am willing to wait.--- But please! Please! You must survive. Please come back to me." He took her once again into his arms and kissed her passionately. They talked for a time and then said farewell. Devin Regan went and joined the New York 3rd. Division and was soon sent into Virginia to fight there, quickly establishing his self as a good soldier, rapidly raising first to lance-corporal then corporal and finally sergeant, as the terrible casualty lists increased, making promotion even easier. Though most of the battles were defeats for the Union.

It was the same for poor Camay. The war descended just as it seemed Graham was about to propose marriage to her. All Pittsburgh strongly supported the Union. The Holstein and Casimir families were violently opposed to slavery as were all connected with the Marshall families. Camay understood when Graham at last took hold of her hands telling her how much he wanted to make her his wife, but like Devin, so many miles away, he intended to join the Union Army and fight, so he would not have the resources to marry her.

Camay understood, and kissed Graham passionately, telling him she was willing to wait, but pleaded with him to survive and come back to her. By doing so she was committing herself to him, yet she was still unsure if her decision was right. She knew she would honour that promise – yet she strangely felt pleased – her final commitment to Graham was delayed through no fault of her own. It helped to ease her conscience, for she still wondered if she should accept Graham as her husband. – It seemed so unfair to her. She liked Graham – no felt certain she loved Graham – but Camay knew Devin was her first boy-friend and their recent meetings had once again awakened her interest in him.

She thought, 'Oh! What is wrong with me. Graham is a good and kind man. I have never given Devin any commitment. – He never kept his promise to come and see me in Annapolis. I owe nothing to him. Graham offers me a very happy married life and the many babies I crave for. Graham will make me a good husband. – I really must, somehow, forget Devin and try to make Graham happy. – Oh! Please God let Graham survive this fighting. I need him.'

So both Devin and Graham went off to war. Graham joining the Pittsburgh Volunteers and was quickly sent to the new fighting in Tennessee in both 1861 and 1862. Sailing down the Oho River to where fierce battles were already in progress. It was fast becoming a national conflagration, occurring so widely in many states, and the terrible death rate was to devastate so many families who lost their love ones. Both Devin and Graham knew their chance of survival were very few, but they would do their best to survive.

It seemed in Texas, so far from the main areas of conflict, these families too feared the loss of their love ones as so many men had joined the Confederate forces and were fighting well away from Texas. Many in those disastrous battles in Virginia trying to force an entry into Washington which would probable end the conflagration. Yet Texan's were dying the same as everyone.

Amazingly it was not the case for wither the Eliot's nor the Downey's. Two families who previously had felt sure they must support the Texas beliefs in their right to democratically decide by the vote whether to continue the practice of slavery. Now all the younger members of these families having committed their support for the Union – though ostracised for their support – they had joined the Border militia and now had the far less dangerous task of fighting the indians, now intent on regaining the lands lost to them during the last fifty years.

They were in fact in less danger than the relatives on that Camargo Ranch in Kentucky, as Kentucky was a divided state with the state split in two – half supporting the Union – the other half committed to the Confederacy. All eligible males of those families joined the Union army but fortunately were not sent away and were committed to fight against those other Kentuckians who fought for the Confederacy.

So like Devin and Graham, many descendents of Amelia Carroll and her mother, Margaret, – were now placing their lives in danger fighting for the continuance of the Union. The fighting was intensifying as it entered 1863 and already there had been casualties with several sons, of those descendents, all dying as they fought for a cause they supported so strongly.

5.

The State of California had immediately committed the state to the Union cause, but being so far from the site of hostilities, it was impossible to believe a Civil War existed in California. In fact, now with its ever growing population after the California Gold Rush, it was becoming a thriving state. Though in some ways trade with the east was curtailed, in many cases it had increased the trading position of this new state. This especially added to the wealth of the Reid family and its associates, still easily trading with the orient and managing to send goods, not easily obtainable in the east, even up the east coast of America as the Union Navy was so much larger than the Confederate Navy.

Donald Reid was becoming wealthier each day. Now he had heard of the passing of the Pacific railway Act. At last government money was available to start building the Central Pacific Railway – until now only a dream. However Donald had heavily invested in its project and may eventually profit from it. He now meet Kurt Sand whenever he was available, however he knew that both Kurt and Crocker were heavily involved in trying to begin building the actual railway. In a way Reid helped in this by importing ever more Chinese workers which were willing to work on the line, but required much training before they cold be usefully employed. Also importing from the Far East the materials necessary to construct the line.

This was what both Sand and Crocker were doing. Their families saw little of them. In fact Kurt was not able to help with the one business which at present represented his income. Knowing this both Agnes and Anita had taken his place in the offices helping his colleagues, even surprising them with their efficiency. The two women knew that until the line became a reality, and that would take years, they must somehow ensure their families had sufficient means to keep themselves from starvation, and Kurt was a very amorous man. Even though often away, when he returned he made sure both Agnes and Anita were rewarded for their own efforts in the Warehouses. Perhaps a little too often, for it seemed both Agnes and Anita wanted, in turn, to add to their existing families.

Still the construction of the Railway was their first priority. It proved exceedingly difficult, as soon as the reached the mountains. Crocker was right, labour was short, it became imperative to employ and train Chinese workers to do the job. For the next few months his family saw little of Kurt Sands. Everyone in the Central Pacific Company feared that the Union Pacific with fewer obstacles would reach westwards many miles further that the Central Pacific move east. This could mean a bleak future for their part of the railway.

Building a railway was often a dangerous job and the Rocky Mountains were a formidable obstacle. Kurt well knew the maximum gradient a steam train could climb, so the route, previously surveyed, needed to be checked and changed if necessary, to keep within that limit. This meant many more miles needed to be laid to avoid some obstacles and failing that there was the need to use dynamite to either construct a cutting or even build a series of tunnels. It was a very dangerous task.

The Chinese's workers, at first, were very inexperienced if willing. Many times the explosion went wrong. The whole tunnel collapses or the side of a mountain, made unstable by the explosion, collapsed on top of the working men killing many. However Crocker was a very ruthless master and drove them on caring little for their deaths. It seemed that in Charles Crocker the consortium had found a man ruthless but equally determined to drive men to do tasks often thought impossible. Yet he obtained results. He had the ability to organise and plan work, and there was no doubt but that he enjoyed his work.

Though Kurt Sands, if he thought necessary, would also support Crocker and assist him in any way, Kurt's task was the one he enjoyed. He was a brilliant surveyor and would quickly find some way of avoiding an obstacle, planning it, and then leaving Charles to ensure the workmen carried out the task. In spite of everything, often to their own amazement, they were progressing but the progress was very slow. Yet they knew every mile laid was essential if they were to compete with the Union Pacific as it drove west towards them. Yet most of their allocated land in the east were of responsible gradients so progress there would be much quicker to the serious detriment of the Central Pacific Railway.

It was fortunate that Collis Huntington had won that one concession which allocated government money with respect to the difficulties of the terrain over which it was laid. Fortunately for them the Civil War effected the progress of the Union Pacific as much as their own structural problems. Little was done until the war ended, whilst the war did not affect their own section. There was, also, so much corruption in the Union Pacific's management which also delayed track laying.

Gordon Taylor in Pittsburgh was furious at this and it seemed to him that Daniel Drew and his colleagues were secretly channelling large portion of the investments made in the Union Pacific into their own hands. So for a time the rail line west did not progress, with little if any work done.

Perhaps the civil war might yet prove a boon to the future of the Central Pacific. Yet even with the federal financial help, it soon became clear that, the Central Pacific would have insufficient funds to continue. Huntington, again attempted to come to the rescue, for he knew the President wanted this railway. The President wanted it built. He knew not only would it be essential for the future financial prosperity of the United States after the war, but more important, it might be the means by which a disunited country could become one again when the warfare ceased.

Still both Crocker and Sand were away from their families for many months and the progress was very slow. However, no matter how difficult everything seemed, it seemed to galvanise the two men, now becoming life-long friends. Each problem brought them ever loser together, and the partnership ensure its success.

Whenever it was possible they both arranged a little respite to allow each other, in turn, to return to their homes and enjoy a short break in the monotony. When Kurt returned he was quickly assured of a very loving welcome from both his wives. Kurt knew now that without their kindness, no enthusiasm, he would not have been able to continue. He remembered, only too well, just how fortunate he had been to meet both of them and knew that without their continuing love he would have long since capitulated and given up his task.

He now realised if he had not decided to leave his fathers company and for adventure. Make that wagon journey to the gold fields, he would never have met either of them.. More than ever Kurt now was determined that both the women he loved so passionately, would for always be the only important factor in his future life. He was pleased that the Anderson brothers were helping Huntington so greatly in seeking further government finance, for they reported to him by letter what they were doing. Both Crocker and he knew they must somehow get further government monetarily support or soon they would all be bankrupt.

Yet the ferocity of the war was increasing, and 1863 was one of the bloodiest years of the war. Battles were occurring everywhere. Though at last the Union was making some good gains, there was no certainty that it would be victorious. New generals had arrived with the will and ruthlessness to ensure success, though not always given the right opportunities. Two were General Grant and General Sherman, though each suffered defeats, if it was not always their fault.

In California Donald Reid could not but feel his conscience when he learned of the deaths of Carroll sons on the battlefields whilst he sat in security and wealth doing little to help the outcome of the war. Even Charles Crocker and Kurt Sand were doing their bit. Now, at last, everyone knew the importance of that Transcontinental Railway.

6.

So far neither Racoonsville nor the combined Chalmers estate had been damaged by shellfire or bombs, and Mark and Estelle Carroll as had both Kenneth Brookes and Steven Chalmers and their wives, stayed valiantly guarding their possessions. Many times soldiers of either side passed by but though the officers usually called, they were not molested. However they all learned with great sadness the deaths in battle of some of their grandsons and the husbands of several of their granddaughters.

It was the same at Rockville where so many still sort refuge. However there was sadness for both Estelle Carroll and her now infirm husband, Adrian. Like the others their were deaths of several of their grandsons and those married to their granddaughters. However it seemed that Rockville was still a little distance from the fighting and those that stayed were still quite safe. So most of 1863 passed, though the battle of Brandy Station was close to the Virginian estates. So far Gordonsville had been far away from the conflict and though they supported the Union, the residents who stayed guarding their estate willingly helped in the hospital the wounded Confederate soldiers. So it seemed they were spared any real bitterness as the lists of the dead grew ever longer.

Meanwhile in Colorado the Sinclair's and the Milliken's continued to grow richer as gold was extracted from their mines and now Otto had established his 'Palace of Pleasure' which was perhaps another type of goldmine. By now both Jack and Robert frequently used its facilities. Then in 1861 the American Civil War began. Although, at that time, it effected only the land far to the east and left Colorado Springs untouched, everyone learned of its progress. Jack, though he did not hold any strong views on slavery, felt strongly for the state of Texas and considered that the Southern States had every right to dissociate themselves from those to the North.

Although Otto did his best to dissuade him, Jack decided to travel east and support the cause of the Confederates. He was twenty five years old. Robert, now eighteen, he reluctantly felt he should support his brother, and in early 1862 went off to join the war. Robert did this simply because Jack had acted like their father ever since he died and they came to Colorado.

Otto promised to look after their claim and make sure they were, both, rich men when they returned. The next two and a half years were the worse years of Robert's life, even worse that the desperate years of his childhood. The end came, ironically, near the city of Vicksburg. It occurred months after the Battle for Vicksburg in May and June 1863 and months after it had been captured by the Union Army. Ironic, for the association with Vicksburg was to have another dramatic effect on his future life. The unit in which Jack and he were serving had been surrounded by Union forces. They had been deputed to find a way through Union Lines for their battalion. In the melee Jack was killed and Robert and only two others managed to escape.

Robert was devastated,. Jack had been more than brother to him ever since their parents died. Now he was left alone for the first time in his life, to look after himself. But Robert was a realist who lived one day at a time. Though he felt strongly for the future of Texas he knew the Confederate cause was lost by the autumn of 1864. There was no sense in him remaining in the army simply to follow Jack and die. He deserted and never returned to his battalion, presumed dead. Slowly he retraced his steps back to Colorado Springs, arriving in December.1864 and receiving an enthusiastic welcome from Otto glad that he was still alive but sad that Jack had died.

* * * * * * * * * * * * * * *

Unknown to anyone in Colorado a family which in future years was to bring to the Sinclair's and Milliken's enormous wealth, in association with others connected with the Carroll families. Others were now also living and working in America but this was in the country of Mexico. It was here that both Charles and Paul Doughty had come to extract rich minerals for the benefit of France in 1863. The French Government had invaded Mexico on the pretext of unpaid debts and deposed the Radical Mexican Government of Mexico headed by President Benito Juarez.

Benito Juarez had in turn deposed the aristocratic dictatorship which for so many years had controlled Mexico making most of its inhabitants virtual slaves as they profited by their control. It had been this which had lead to the war with Texas and later the United States-Mexican War. However in doing so they had virtually bankrupted the country and Juarez had been unable to pay the long standing debts to France.

Emperor Napoleon III had seen his chance to extend the boundaries of his country and used this excuse to invade and so depose Juarez and in doing so placed on the throne the puppet Emperor Maximillian from Austria. So the country was now ruled indirectly from France. Due to the Civil War the United States were not in a position to object or claim the 'Munroe Doctrine', which forbid any attempt of European powers to meddle in the affairs of any country in America. It involved both Britain and Spain as well as France.

To recover these debts in May 1863, the three countries landed a combined force at Vera Cruz but both Spain and Britain, realizing Frances' ambition to control the whole country quickly withdrew their support, but Napoleon III saw his chance and with the support of the aristocracy persuaded Archduke Ferdinand Maximilian of Austria to support Napoleon's ambitions and come to Mexico. In June 1863 a month after Charles and Paul arrived Maximilian was crowned Emperor of Mexico in Mexico City as soon as the capital was conquered.

Charles Doughty was a brilliant mining engineer with much experience He had already proved his expertise to the French Government work in North Africa. His son had followed him and had recently passed his examinations and now acted as an apprentice to his father. As already explained they both came from Ireland and both wanted an Ireland free of Great Britain. There presence in Mexico was much appreciated by the French occupying forces.

His family enjoyed a comfortable life style in France ever since he fled from Ireland to avoid imprisonment. Then in 1862 Charles' wife, Matilda, died suddenly and the next month Teressa married her boyfriend, the eldest son of the Freycinet's, Jules de Freycinet. The truth was though Charles Doughty was a womaniser and had enjoyed many illicit affairs with other women, including his affair with Madam Freycinet which had so much hurt his wife, but Charles had still deeply loved his wife.

Her death was unexpected and greatly troubled both Charles and Paul. Charles felt he must leave France and its memories. Perhaps in Mexico, there may be many more attractive women and in time, he might find another woman, this time, he hoped for a more permanent association, as he was growing old. Likewise his son Paul, now that his sister had married and never forgetting those wonderful illicit moments when Teressa had been so willing to yield her body to him, felt now he too should get away.

So the two of them left France and sailed to Vera Cruise going to Monterey, where the French Commandant allocated an area for prospecting, and began work in the neighbouring Sierra Madre Mountains. The major had allocated a poor dilapidated hacienda in the mountains to use as their base. During the summer of 1863 they had successfully discover silver ore and gem stones in the mountains to the north west of the town of Cuidad Victoria. Although they had managed to keep a reasonable supply of gem stones for their own property, they had no means of separating the metal from the silver ore and so, under military supervision, they had hired local labour to mine the ore and transport it to the town for processing.

However the previous day they had discovered a cache with seemed to be pure metallic silver. Now in spite of the weather they were determined to discover whether their find was a valuable to them as they now hoped. If so they knew that they would have no intention of informing the French authorities. They would keep that silver find for themselves making them potentially very rich.

7.

It was April 1864. The still bright rays of the later afternoon sun shone on a small cleft in the mountains and was reflected back with brilliance onto the eyes of the two onlookers. It had been a warm day for April in Mexico in these high mountains of the Sierra Madre, but now the evening was approaching, porting a very cold night with cloudless skies. Charles Doughty and his son Paul looked happily at each other.

Now he said, "Well son we were right. This could make our fortunes. At least we can return to France richer than we left. It looks as if the vein is almost silver metal and not just ore. We shall see. Tomorrow we must begin early. We must widen the cleft. It's going to be hard work and we need to act quickly if we are to avoid suspicions. Come let us return to our tent and get some warm food inside us before it's too cold."

The next morning they started their task, dynamiting the cleft to give them access to the vein. Then until the end of May they removed all of the silver, working every hour of daylight. Then they transported it on their wagon to the hacienda and buried their precious find in two strong boxes under the floorboards. With this find and the gem stones, they had, also acquired, they were now rich enough to see to their needs for several years.

In early June they returned to Monterey and reported their other finds to the Commandant, Major Pierre Mentor, and arranged for a work force with military support to mine this ore. Now they had returned again to Monterey, accompanying the several wagons filled with rock ore and defended by soldiers. They had explained to the Major how to separate the silver ore from the rock and left him to have this transported elsewhere for refining. From now on the major was a good friend of them.

Now they were both resting in adjacent rooms in the best Bordello, Monterey had to offer. Although they had used a little of their horde of silver to pay for their pleasures this would not create any suspicions. Because of the poor state of the country the Mexican currency was rarely used and silver and sometimes gold was used. In fact their own salaries was always paid in silver.

Neither did they have any language problems. After living so long in France they were masters of both languages. Charles, during his work in North Africa, had developed a good grasp of Spanish. During the voyage over from France to Mexico he had had tutored his son in the language, sufficient to make themselves understood when they arrived. Now after a year and a half they both could converse fluently in all three languages

As he lay with Conchita, the girl Paul had purchased for the night, he wondered if his recent pleasures would result in Conchita conceiving his child. He thought not. Conchita was twenty years old and no doubt had been involved in her profession for a long time. He was certain she knew how to look after herself, in any case he did not care.

From being a young boy he had known his father was an inveterate womaniser. He well remembered his father's short affair with Madame Freycinet, the mother of the son to whom his sister, Teressa, was now married. He had been old enough to know how much this had hurt his mother, Matilda. He knew he had inherited his father's addiction for women and as Conchita lay, naked, beside him as they both recovered from their recent exertion Paul remembered again that wonderful moment in early 1862, though it had all happened by accident.

It never happened again. It seemed that they tried to avoid each other. Then their mother died and soon afterwards Teressa married her boyfriend, Jules de Freycinet. Though at the wedding reception he saw her looking at him and saw tears come to her eyes, he had since wondered if it was her memory of their illicit liaison or simply because she was so happy to be married.

Whatever her glance had meant Paul knew he would never forget those stolen moments. Had she really meant those secret words which he was not meant to hear.. *"Dear Paul I would so love to give you a child."* It was their secret, one he remembered so vividly today. Today they had received a letter from Teressa, written many weeks, before telling them of what was happening in France. Teressa had only embraced the Catholic faith in order to marry Jules but the family were strong Catholics. She had told them that, although they supported Napoleon, they were very disappointment at him withdrawing his troops from Rome, leaving the Vatican and the Pope in danger.

She also written, " I know you both will be happy *and particularly Paul.* as I gave birth to a daughter, Cherie, last January. *I know Paul will understand when I say Cherie is already the image of him."* Now after reprising his wonderful day with his sister he knew, that in her letter she was reminding him, again, of those secret words she had not intended him to hear. Those few lines in her letter were a special message to him.

The rest of the year of the year and throughout the next, to the middle of summer 1865 Charles and Paul had continued to explore the Sierra Madras mountains looking for minerals. They found a few gem stones which went into the strong box under the floor boards in their hacienda, they also found several small veins of silver ore. But they had no means of separating the silver metal from it so they reported it and supervised, under a guard of soldiers, the mining of their find, returning it to Monterey for separation of the rock from the ore before sending on to be turned into silver

It was, now, October and in August they had learned of a great scandal. Involving the important Arista family at their estate near Montemorelos, twenty mikes south east of Monterrey. It seems that the husband, Alonso Arista, had been killed when he resisted arrest on a charge of embezzling money given him by the French to help him defend the area against insurgents.

Even worse, it seemed there was a struggle during which the arresting officer, Colonel Albert Berthole, was shot dead by Alonso's wife, Irene, whilst her daughter, Anne also shot dead a French soldier and were now being held awaiting execution in the garrison in Monterey. It seemed the scandal was made worse by the fact the wife, Irene, had been a daughter of an equally important family of Nicolas.

It is doubtful if either Charles or Paul would have taken any further notice of the affair which was to, dramatically, change both their lives, except that they brought with them a newspaper from Monterey when they had returned that afternoon. Since it was now late October and the killing had occurred in August they had both assumed that both Irene Arista and her daughter, Anne, would long since been executed Everyone knew that any attack of any kind on the French military, meant instant execution. Yet in the paper they had clearly stated that they were still alive and the sentence of death pronounced on them had not been performed.

The news intrigued Charles. He was silent for a while, thinking and planning. He guessed that the importance of the two involved families was causing a political problem for their friend the French Commandant, Major Pierre Mentor, and this gave Charles a brilliant, if risky idea.

They had been offered help from the Mexican peasants, But because Charles doubted if they could be trusted and might be followers of Juarez who would murder them, and in any case this would prevent them hiding any treasure they might discover, so they had refused. "Paul," he said, "it's high time we both had feminine company in the hacienda. In any case I'm tired of looking after ourselves and cooking our own meals. At least we gain some servants to make things easier. You and I are returning the Monterey tomorrow morning. I have a plan which may help our major with his delicate problem."

8.

But these happenings in Mexico were well into the future and the savage civil war continued to the north and now embraced most of the central and eastern United States though the vital battles in 1863 and 1864 were for that area between Washington and Richmond, the provinces of the two contesting governments. Though the Battle of Gettysburg, in Pennsylvania, was probably more important because of the famous speech Abraham Lincoln made after the battle, 'Of three scores years and ten....' – a speech to be remembered later for centuries as he set out the very reason for the conflict.

The Battle of Shiloh in June 1862 is remembered for the terrible loss of life on both sides and ensured everybody now knew the high price which must be paid before any result could be obtained. In spite of the tragic deaths of many of the more youthful descendents of the Carroll families, so far the mansions in Virginia and Maryland still stood unharmed still guarded by the elder members of the Carroll and Chalmer families. So ended 1863 and now the battles in 1864 became even more intensive. But now the Union armies were gaining more victories.

The truth was it was a question of numbers. The Union could call on an enormous population to replace those who died so vainly in battle. This was not the case for Confederacy. President Jefferson Davies had far fewer men to take the place of those that died, and its resources in armaments were dwindling. It was a question of attrition. Further more they had not as many trained medical persons as the north and too many wounded soldiers were dying due to neglect, after receiving wounds from which they could be saved.

The Union now virtually controlled the Mississippi River, preventing easy transfer of Confederate soldiers from one place to another. The capture of Vicksburg along with Gettysburg are considered the turning point of the war, as this established Union control of the river. General Grant had perused Confederate General Pemberton, already suffering from deleted soldiers. Pemberton retreated into Vicksburg and tried to hold the city and so safeguard their access to the river. He expected General Johnson, in command of the West to help free him but their were conflicts in command and after a siege Vicksburg fell to the Union army in June 1863.

This was followed by the Battle of Chattanooga in November 1863 now known as the 'Gateway to the South'. By now Grant was made Commander-in-chief of the Union armies and he promoted Sherman to be General and given control of the Georgia campaign. Sherman was an aggressive general but rarely wasted the lives of his soldiers. He pressed Confederate General Hood, though each attempted to turn the others flank. Eventually after several minor battles Sherman entered Atlanta on September 1st. 1864 with the city alight due to Hood burning his armaments before giving control of the city to Sherman. Though it was a great victory, Sherman failed to capture Hood or the Army of the Tennessee. However it did much for Union morale in the north an ensured Lincoln's re-election as President in November.

This opened what has been called Sherman's 'March to the Sea'. Leaving burning Atlantic Sherman ignored all military logic. Without any chance of receiving supplies he marched southwest adopting a 'scorched earth' policy destroying everything in sight after ensuring supplies for his attacking troops. Tearing up the railway lines and twisting them beyond recognition. He pressed on the enemy not sure which direction he would take until he captured Savannah . Even holding a mock assembly proclaiming Georgia as a State of the Union. It was a brutal campaign. It freed thousand of slaves who hurried to support Sherman's armies but many dying of starvation but eventually he reached and took Augustus, when he reached he sea.

General Grant saw an even greater effect of Sherman's victories. His armies were hard pressed on the Potomac and he was making little progress with large casualties. Now the Confederate territory had been split in two and President Davies knew he may soon be attacked from the south. He knew he had insufficient men to fight on two fronts. By 1865 the end was in sight for the Confederacy,

But in 1864 the number of battles in Virginia multiplied enormously throughout the state, with over thirty two battles everywhere. Nowhere was safe. At last both the Racoonsville and Chalmer mansions were shelled leading to the deaths, first of Mark Carroll and his wife, Estelle, as part of Racoonsville was hit. Then later Steven Chalmer's and his wife

Hattie died, when part of what had been the mansion of Colin Chalmer's before he married Sophia Brookes, was completely destroyed.

It had been a very sad day for Estelle Carroll still living, though now eighty four years old, and still defiant in maintaining the ancient base of the entire Carroll family. She had liked and loved both Mark and Estelle, who she had come to know soon after she assumed her position as Mistress of Rockville. Also the love of her life, her husband, Adrian, who had died after a long illness in 1863. So she was left alone though her daughter-in-law, Amy, came to live with and console her, leaving her husband in building naval ships for the Union. Yet Estelle in spite of her sadness and loneliness felt she had only done what Amelia Carroll would have expected of her After all was not both she and Adrian very directly descended from Sir David and Amelia Carroll, though through two different sons of Amelia. Rockville still stood defiant as it had always done. At least Estelle had ensured this.

Estelle thought of the past life. Born in England, within a family which, though it was no fault of their own, had little money. Her father in danger of landing in a debtors prison. Engaged to man she disliked, even fearing for her life, but knowing by marrying him she might save her own family. The terrible journey across the Atlantic – the attack by a French privateer – her own mother struck down and killed as she held her mother's hand.

Her landing at Annapolis and befriended by the very person who with another was responsible for her parlous position. Their kindness.- her confrontation with Daniel Carroll, the man she blamed for her families bankruptcy. Yet, to her amazement he provided the means by which she could avoid her fate. Her love for Adrian. His proposal of marriage, and the very long and happy years she had enjoyed with him. Her becoming Mistress of Rockville, their ancestral home, and why in this war she had to ensure its continuance as she knew dear Amelia would expect it of her. Now she felt she had kept faith with Amelia. Her work was done. Perhaps now she could go and re-join her dear Adrian, for she knew her work was over.

So 1865 began and each day it was obvious that the Union was now winning the war. The Confederacy knew it was only time before it must capitulate, with his army surrounded, his men weak and exhausted, Robert E. Lee realized there was little choice but to consider the surrender of his Army to General Grant. After a series of notes between the two leaders, they agreed to meet on April 9, 1865, at the house of Wilmer McLean in the village of Appomattox Courthouse. The meeting lasted approximately two and one-half hours and at its conclusion the bloodiest conflict in the nation's history neared its end.

At four o'clock in the afternoon the two generals faced each other. They spoke to each other telling each other of the previous times they had met. Then General Robert E. Lee pulled out his long jewelled sword and handed it to General Grant. Then he signed the necessary papers, saluted as did Grant. Lee had surrendered the Confederate Forces, their entire remaining Army, to the Union Army.

After five long bloodiest years of travail with hundred of thousands of people both soldiers and civilians dead, the great American Civil War ended at Appomattox. The Civil War had ended. The Union army had been victorious. The country had been once again enjoined. It was a Reunion of the entire United States – now one country once again. The war may have ended but the recriminations, the lust for revenge, ensured new atrocities were to occur. It would be the southern states which were to pay a very heavy price for their rebellion.

PART 8

FIDELITY

Disunion Part 8 Fidelity

FIDELITY

1.

The Civil War had caused great sadness throughout the entire Carroll Family and their many descendents, even with different surnames. Many young men of all these families had lost their lives during the five years of conflict. This included the important pillars of the past, Mark Carroll, the grandson of Daniel Carroll who had helped George Washington win its independence and create the United States. His loss with his wife, Estelle, a descendent of Anton Tencin,, illegitimate son of Claudine Tencin and King Louis XIV, caused great sadness Also, Steve Chalmers and his wife Hattie, descended from Daniel Carroll's wife, Michelle, and Sophie.

The original home of Colin Chalmers had been completely destroyed and part of Racoonsville had been destroyed. Still the ancestral home of the Carroll family, Rockville, still stood unharmed and still guarded by the descendents of Sir David and Amelia Carroll. Yet, in spite of this, there was relief and even joy. The terrible five years of warfare had finally ended. However it now remained to truly reunite this devastated country and make it one again. This must be their first necessity.

There was great rejoicing in the northern states. It had been fought to ensure the colour of a person did not make him different from another, but a very hard price had had to be paid to ensure this fact. There had been too much hate engendered by the struggle, the terrible death rate and the chaos which the war had ensured. Now unfortunately the northern states, the victors, would make the southern states pay for it happening. Pure revenge was the motive, and it did not end with wars end.

This was certainly not thought of by Abraham Lincoln, now elected for a second term. He was determined that it should not happen and immediately started to attempt a complete reconciliation. But on April 14th. whilst attending the Ford Theatre which was presenting 'Our American Cousin', John Wilkes Booth, a strong Confederate supporter shot Lincoln in the head, as he sat in his box. He died immediately. Senator Steward was also injured but recovered. Now there was no one to stop the malice, and the death of the President ensured it would intensify, not reduce it. So began the program of revenge on the south, which was to continue for many years.

Gordonsville had been spared most of the fighting, though for a long time it was a Confederate base. However the residents, in spite of their views, were well respected, and they worked tirelessly in the hospital. So with the war finished they resumed their previous lives. Danton and Claudia Carroll came as soon as they knew his father and mother had been killed. Now temporarily released from his duties in Congress they both set about rebuilding the damaged Racoonsville, just as it was in Daniel Carroll's day.

Claudia found that her brother, living in her mother and father's mansion in the hills, in Tennessee, had survived though their town house, in Nashville had been destroyed. Although in Florida for a time her brother and sister's houses had been occupied but being Union supporters, once the Union occupied Florida, they had no further problems.

Now it was left for Kenneth and Janis Brookes to restore their mansions and rebuild the old Chalmer's residence, after Steve and Hattie had died as it was destroyed. Rockville had not been touched and Estelle still lived as Mistress assisted by her daughter-in-law, Amy. Soon Amy's husband Peter Carroll would come from New York, and Amy felt sure that he would now come to stay, if only to help his mother. As soon as possible all branches wanted to return to the peaceful and happy lives they had enjoyed before the war.

But Estelle was more practical. "Amy," she said, "The Carroll family for over one hundred and fifty years has always led the way. Our predecessors pioneered the expansion of this country. We must continue to do so. What was that project Donald Reid told us about in California. Wasn't it building a railway – a special one – right across the United States. Daniel Carroll with others invested in many ideas which enabled expansion west. Now we must bring the west and east together. We must write to Donald. Now the war is over we must invest in this same railway he was supporting. We must contact Mr. Purcell – we have always found 'Purcell Enterprises" most reliable where investment is concerned."

Of course Amy, through her husband, knew well Donald Reid and had joined in a company before the war. So now it was easy to get more information about this mysterious Central Pacific Railway which was being constructed under the most terrible circumstances. For Estelle like many others knew now a Transcontinental Railway must be built, if only to re-unite this seriously fragmented country, and now with the war over it was possible.

* * * * * * * * * * * * * * *

By the spring of 1864 both Kurt and Crocker and all investors in their line knew that they had not sufficient resources to complete the railway. If they continued they would be made bankrupt. Even with the present Federal financial help, it soon became clear that, The Central Pacific would have insufficient funds to continue. It seemed that the 'Golden Egg' would never be delivered. All now depended on what aid could be obtained in Washington, just at the most critical time in the Civil War. In desperation they pleaded with Huntington to inform the government of the position. At least Huntington and the Anderson's knew Abraham Lincoln supported its building.

Huntington, again came to the rescue. The President wanted this railway. He knew its economic necessity. A second Pacific Railway Act was passed on July 2nd. 1864, doubling the size of the land grants, granting both railways the right to sell their own bonds. Work continued from both ends, the Union Railway making rapid progress after the end of the Civil war in 1866. However Charles Crocker, now that funds were available, was determined to press ahead irrespective of the dangers.

Every mile laid made their own investment more worthwhile. They had to beat the Union Pacific now that it had commenced construction after the war.

Though Kurt Sand resolutely support Charles Crocker being as determined as him to make the Central Pacific Railway profitable they continued to allow themselves brief periods of recovery, returning, in turn to their own homes. On the previous visit Kurt had received a communication from his mother that his father had died, two years before, aged sixty five, and she thanked him for the income she received from him as payment for the original investment his father had given him when he left for the gold fields. He also learned that his sister's husband had died soon afterwards and she had moved in with her mother, in Pittsburgh, with the four children she had born her husband.

Now another letter was waiting for him from Sophia. It was very informative and exciting. It said. "Though mother misses father very much she still has the intimate friendship of several male friends, even though she is now fifty eight – she will never change – why should she. Neither do I lack male company even before my husband died. Incidentally, at thirty nine, after baring four children, my body could be as enticing as I seemed to you, twenty years ago – and now I have no husband – Please come to see us as soon as you can." This promise for the future made Kurt smile.

Nor had his long absences reduced his sexual pleasures so willingly offered to him by his two 'wives'. Anita was delighted to, at last deliver him a son, which they both agreed to name Karl Sand after his uncle who had been the reason for his father fleeing to America so long ago. Furthermore both knew they would both want more children.

By now the family included ten children all registered as 'Sand' though only eight of them had been fathered by him. Fiona, was a beautiful girl, nearly seventeen. Her indian parentage added to her beauty. Similarly, Conchita, now twelve, had inherited her mother, Anita's Mexican features and would soon show her Spanish inheritance. Both knew, by now, they were not Kurt's daughters but still considered him their father, who they loved, deeply.

Kurt would have liked Fiona to become involved with the sons of his many friends. Though she enjoyed flirting with them she told Kurt she had no wish to settle down and marry. To his surprise she told him, whilst he was away, she had seduced at least two of them and that she was no longer a virgin, but she had learned how to protect herself. Kurt did not mind, even welcoming it. His only fear was this might be because of who had fathered her. Never the less he gave her his blessing..

So with great difficulty the Central Pacific Railway pressed ever eastward as the Union Pacific, now the war was over pressed even more quickly westward to meet them.

2.

Whilst this was occurring and the Purcell's and the Mason's were becoming ever closer after their confessions, unknown to them events in Mexico were occurring which in a few years would involve the Sand's as much as themselves, in future business ventures which was to eventually ensure they all became multi-dollar millionaires. But much was to happen before this happened.

Both Charles and Paul Doughty had come to visit the French Commandant, Major Pierre Mentor. Charles began by placing three bags of silver, part of their own holdings, on the table before him. "Open these. I believe you have a problem which we may solve. If so and we succeed you can keep them. This silver will be yours. You need not fear it will be discovered. It has never been registered. Now tell us the problem you have with the Arista woman and her daughter. Don't try to prevaricate I know you have a political crisis, dangerous to your own future."

With this encouragement the major explained that the two important families had persuaded Emperor Maximilian to intercede on their behalf. However the French authorities in Mexico City were being swamped by the continuous corruption of these high born families. They felt they must make an example of them. Yet at the same time they did not wish to alienate the few friends they had in this country.

Maximilian, with his liberal ides, his refusal to restore the Catholic Church with the land, Juarez, had taken from them during his own Presidency, had seriously affected their position. So the poor Major had been told to find some way of eliminating the two women without a formal execution. He admitted he had, already, tried two methods, but they had not worked.

He had deliberately reduced the supervision hoping they would see this as a chance to escape. He had placed two trusted soldiers in a position so that when they attempted it they would be shot whilst attempting to escape. Either, because they were suspicious or because they did not know how to do this, nothing had happened.

It seemed that Irene Arista had three other younger daughters than Anne who were at present being cared for by friends in Monterey. He had told them that unless they agreed to commit suicide he would ensure her daughters were removed. Irene had accepted the threat but said that as devoted Roman Catholics they could never take their own lives. In any case the major admitted that had he attempted to kill her daughters the news would have caused an even greater scandal. Yet every day he received letters demanding to know what he was doing.

He really was at his wits end. He feared each day that he would be removed from his post and sent back to France in disgrace – his career ended. So he was willing to listen to Charles offer. "I want you to turn over these two women to me, on parole, as servants. In doing so you will help me in my discovery of minerals. But you will, also, give me a document stating they are sentenced to death. Should they disobey my orders or try to escape then they will be, immediately, returned to Monterey and the sentence will be carried out. I admit that this may place you in some danger but then you are, already, in this. Your superiors may even like the idea."

Charles waited for his answer but the major merely emptied the silver from the bags in his desk and looked at it, thinking. 'In French currency, this represented the largest sum of money he had ever possessed.' Even if he escaped the wrath of his superiors, Pierre knew the military situation in Mexico was serious. The occupation must soon end and then he would be transferred to some other area according to the ambition of Napoleon. Finally he smiled and looked at Charles.

Then he said, "And what other duties have you in mind for my prisoners. After all it will be two women and two men in one house?" Now Charles laughed. "That will be my responsibility, not yours. I can promise you that if they obey my orders you will not be troubled with them any more." Pierre nodded and understood before adding he accepted their proposal.

Charles explained what he had in mind. "It seems that your previous attempts means that they will be very suspicious and will probably not accept. We both must realize that only if they agree to my proposal of their own free will the scheme work. Any attempt to force them would soon be learned by their friends and reported to Mexico City. I suggest you give me a chance to interview both of them in private. I am an Irishman and apparently have no connection with you or the French authorities. I'm, simply, a mining engineer." It was then the major's turn to laugh. He stood up and shook hands with Charles. The proposal was agreed.

Charles, Paul and the two women met in one of the officers houses the major had placed at their disposal. They met alone except for two soldiers standing outside, preventing any escape. The two women had been allowed to bathe and change their clothes and then four of them sat down to a meal accompanied by fine French wine which the prisoners had not enjoyed for some time. Afterwards Charles explained why they were here, to offer them a parole under his jurisdiction explaining their duties and explaining he and his son were Irish.

He spoke to them in Spanish. "I know this offer must be demeaning to you, to work as servants for the first time in your lives. I must warn you the hacienda is isolated and is not the luxury accommodation of which you are used. I must also warn you, again, that you will be responsible to me and any attempt to escape would result in your return to Monterey – this time to be executed. However, basic as this life would be for both of you, it will be superior to what you have endured these past months. But the decision must be yours – and yours alone"

To his surprise Irene gave a cynical laugh and replied to him in perfect English. "Mr. Doughty, as you are Irish I reply in your own language. I am a married woman of thirty two years. I am not a young innocent girl. Only too well do I know the desires of men. You ask my daughter and I to come to live, alone, with two men in a house miles from other people to act as your servants. Tell me what other services would you expect us to perform?"

Charles had never expected that a woman of such lineage would hint of such things. He was astounded, further more he knew his plan had been exposed. She was, evidently, an astute woman. If he lied it was unlikely she would believe him and so refuse his offer. Yet, if he told the truth, then she had even more reason for refusing. It seemed, that whatever he said there was little chance of her accepting but he took this chance. "Yes! I confess it will mean you suffering even more indignity. Surely you realize you have committed a terrible crime and deserve some punishment. My offer is an alternative to both being executed in the near future. In any case is it not possible you may suffer this here before they dispose of you?"

Irene did not answer immediately and was thinking deeply. Eventually she turned and faced him. "At least you are honest. We now know what to expect if we came with you. As a devote Roman Catholic you have no need to remind me of the punishment I deserve. I have committed the most heinous sin of taking a life. For that I must be prepared for a far greater punishment from my God. Yet now you expect us to commit another terrible sin which must jeopardize our souls no matter what may be the excuse. You do not offer us a chance of freedom but you expect us to let you dishonor us and become your whores. Why should we accept?" Charles had already decided they had lost.

So he said, "Only a chance to live. You should know Paul and I are already reasonably rich men and whilst we stay in Mexico we expect to get richer. If you accept we will promise that when we return to France we will provide, adequately, for your trouble. If you do not wish to face life in Mexico, we promise to take you both back to France and see you are both well provided for a new life there. Neither of us are heavy drinkers. We can promise you will not be subjected to any brutal attacks. But I ask, again, what sort of future awaits you here, if you refuse.

Again Irene was silent. Then she said. "You are right about dangers here. I have been raped, twice, by soldiers and have only just been able to save Anne from a similar fate. Yet the authorities dismissed my complaint as imagination. If we stay, no doubt it will occur again to both of us." She turned and conversed in private with her daughter for some time exploring her views. They waited. Charles felt that there might be a chance of success. Eventually the both turned to them.

Even smiling she replied, "We can only hope you will honor your promise and not discard us after you have had your fun. We would accept but only on certain conditions. Anne is only fifteen years old, and is still a virgin, far too young to bear children of her own. I must ask you to promise, on your honor as gentleman, that you will not place her in any such danger for a least a year." Charles knew he was willing and was ready to compromise. "I will, only give you a solemn promise that Anne will not be subjected to intercourse for one year after we reach the haciendas. That is all,"

Irene guessed what he inferred. "Secondly, you may not know but I have three more daughters, at present in the care of my friends in the town. Eve, is twelve years old, Carlota, is nine and my youngest, Raquel is not yet six. If we come with you then you must take them with you. If so I must again ask for a solemn promise that you will make any such demands on them. At least you will gain more servants."

Charles gave these assurances. "Neither of us have any perversions concerning young girls. We will, willingly, agree to your terms." She replied, "Then we both agree. We will surrender ourselves to you on these terms and will go with you to your hacienda as soon as you can arrange for our parole."

They were returned to their prison whilst Charles and Paul went to report their success to a very relieved and now, potentially richer, Major Mentor. It took longer than they had expected to get the parole accepted. It seemed Major Mentor thought he should let his superiors in

Mexico City know what he was intending to do. Communications took several weeks but to his surprise they not only agreed but seemed pleased with the idea. So, eventually, Pierre Mentor, passed all the documents to Charles giving him the family to become his responsibility under parole.

In early December 1865 Charles, Paul and the Arista family left Monterrey and travelled in a large wagon with a few belongings to the hacienda. Here they all, quickly, became accustomed to a new life.

3.

For three weeks Charles and Paul were busy supervising the mining in the mountains under the guard of the French soldiers, often away for the entire day before returning at night. They were too tired to make any demands on their women but did enjoy returning to a clean and tidy house and prepared hot meals. They all celebrated together Christmas and New Year and the young children enjoyed being with their mother again. Then at the end of New Years Day 1866 Charles came to Irene and told her to join his bed that might. Irene knew the time had come and knew what to expect. She was resigned to her fate and had expected to suffer this earlier.

Charles and Paul had occupied separate bedrooms since the family had arrived. Irene and Anne had been given separate rooms with the other three girls in a single room As she followed Charles into his bedroom Anne watched them knowing what was going to happen to her mother. She turned to Paul. "Oh! Why must you men do these things to us."

Paul, pleased that his father had, at last decided to begin the pleasures both had anticipated since they evolved their plan in October, turned to Anne in anger as she was touching his conscience. "Because we are men and meant like to do this. I can assure you many women like it. Sometime you will find you will enjoy it too – as much as we do." Anne did not continue and commenced her duties as a servant before sending her three sisters to their own bedrooms. Though tonight was different, possibly only Eve had any idea of what was expected of her mother.

The next night it was his turn and Irene joined him in bed after he had enjoyed watching her undress and display her still very attractive naked body to him. As they lay together Paul tried to speak to her but she merely placed a finger on his mouth before submitting to his attack on her body.

The process was repeated many times though the men were often out in the cold weather still prospecting for more finds as they both hoped to discover another pure vein. However, except for find a few gem stones which went into their own strong boxes they only found a few lodes of poorer silver ore. Sometimes they were both too tired to indulge their passions. It was the beginning of March and Paul was sleeping alone in his bedroom, being, like his father, too tired for pleasure.

Suddenly he was awakened and knew someone was in his room. To his amazement even in the dark he could see Irene undressing at the side of his bed. She said, "Please do not think this alters my opinion of what you all do to me, but I come to you in desperation, begging you to help me. Last night your father told me he wanted to give me a child. I need your assistance, and only you can help.."

Paul was mystified, "Irene what can I do. I cannot stop father doing this to you – even if I wanted to. I'm surprised it hasn't already happened?" Desperately Irene replied, "I Know! I know! I wouldn't expect you to but there is a way you help – if you are willing. Remember I was married to Alonso for sixteen years. He was a very passionate man. Yet in those years I only conceived four children. There are ways, not always successful, by which we women can avoid this happening. I know your father has known for some time, I have trying to avoid conceiving. Last night he told me this must stop and let nature take it's course.

Sighing she continued, "I have come to you tonight without any protection. You are much younger than your father and I am frightened at what will happen to any child I bear him. In, the life I must now endure means I cannot expect to live a long time. I don't mind that. It would be a happy release from my misery. Somehow, -- I may be wrong, - but somehow I believe that if the child was yours – your first child, you would look after it. Please, Paul, I want you to take me – now – tonight and give me that child. I give myself to you, willingly, you need never have any conscience about what you do tonight. Enjoy me in any way that gives you satisfaction. I do not mind – but please do it for me. - Help me – please help me."

She turned and buried her face in the pillow sobbing violently. Paul suddenly felt differently about her. He genuinely felt sorry for her for the first time. He tried to comfort her and gently turned her over. "Irene, dear, - if this what you want – and I mean, if you really want me to do this to you - I will. But how could we be sure the baby was mine. Charles will take you tomorrow night. You may then conceive by him."

Irene corrected him, "Now you are wrong that its why I have come to you tonight. Charles has told me he has to go into Monterey tomorrow and will be away three days. He wants you to stay here. His excuse is that you need to supervise the work in mines. Actually, I believe he does not trust me. You have never been away before for so long. I think he believes you must stay to prevent this. If I yield my body to you, tonight without constraint. You are a very virile young man. With three days to use me as often as you want I'm certain that in that time I shall conceive your child. In any case, you must believe me – as a woman I know these things – it will be too late for him." He took hold of her seeing the pleading in her eyes. He pressed his lips to hers gently and reassuringly only slowly, ensuring she was ready for him. That night it happened more than once.

The next day his father left for Monterey warning Paul to watch Irene closely in his absence. After he had left Paul carried out part of his father's wishes. Both knew they could not repeat last nights affair during the day, in front of every one. So he took Irene into the nearby country. The weather was kind. Here they repeated their escaped. He knew Irene did not mind. At last she relaxed and gave herself, willingly, to him. She wanted this.

It did not matter that when Charles returned, after proving she was not protected in any way, he used her. By April Irene was pregnant and she knew she was carrying Paul's child. She told him how grateful she was to him. "Whatever happens to me in the future I shall remember your kindness in my time of need. You need never worry about the way you use me in future. I shall understand."

Paul, also received respect from Anne, who, up to now had regarded him with utter contempt.. She said to him when they were alone. "I know what you did for mother. She has told me in confidence. I do not blame you in any way. Whatever you do to me in future I shall remember this kindness to my mother and understand."

As her pregnancy progressed both Charles and Paul still continued to use her but now Paul knew his demands on her were not disliked. Their times together were happy ones. No longer was it passive submission to his embrace and they often spent time exchanging their past lives. As he had suspected from her earliest remarks her marriage to Alonso was not always a happy one. Her marriage had been arranged by both their parents keen on combining the two aristocratic families together but Irene had not minded. She was a happy girl of sixteen and Alonso was a very handsome man. She probably conceived Anne during her honeymoon and lived an almost idyllic life on their large estate. He was a very virile man but she did mind his demands on her.

However by the time Eve was born in June 1852 things began to change. She knew from the start that Alonso was a inveterate gambler and often lost. She now discovered that after four years of married life her husband had taken several mistresses. She accepted this for her mother had told her that men behaved in this way and needed variety in their love making. However before she conceived her third child, Carlota. In June 1955. Alonso's gambling was severely threatening their fortunes.

His father had left him a rich man but with his losses and the deteriorating state of the economy, their wealth was evaporating. Alonso started to drink heavily and would sometimes beat her with a cane simply to alleviate his worries. Then he began to bring his mistresses, no longer women of his own statue, home, and flaunt them before Irene humiliating her before her children. It was in this way that she conceived Raquel who was born in January 1859.

As they lay together in each others arms she kissed him lightly and said, "You see I have suffered more than, either, you or Charles have treated me. This is why I could accept your offer even though I knew what I must expect. These last few months with you brought back the memory of those wonderful days when I first married Alonso. I can, also, tell you that the joy you have given me – yes, for I will admit, I have enjoyed it as much as any embrace in the past."

All these confessions occurred over several nights. Her tale continued with the fact that she found out that her husband was virtually bankrupt. She felt certain this was why he embezzled government money. Then she stopped. She refused to tell him what happened on that night in August. However much Paul tried she refused to explain. "Dear Paul that night I committed a sin which I am sure will result in me falling into hell fire. Since then I have never had the opportunity to confess my sin to a priest or directly to my Maker in church. Until I have done this my religious devotion forbids me to discuss this with anyone."

By now Paul's true feeling for Irene were very different from how it had begun. He knew she now meant a great deal to him. He could see just how unhappy she was. He was determined to somehow persuade her to tell him about that terrible night, and would with time get her to confess to him.

4.

In Colorado Robert Sinclair, destined with the Doughty's, Purcell's and Mason's to become rich men by eventually meeting and working together. Though in doing so, they were to add further riches to many members of the Carroll family. Robert was enjoying life once again in Colorado Springs. Knowing he was now a very rich man, he stayed to enjoy life, at any cost to his future soul. Otto, kindly, put the renovated shack at his disposal, as well as all the facilities his new 'Palace of Pleasure' could bring – all the women in it were at his disposal, but he also enjoyed visiting Nan and relieving her of loneliness when Otto stayed long with in his own mansion, with his mistresses.

He had long discussions with Vera, now twelve years old, and rapidly becoming a beautiful young woman. Of course she was well aware of her mother's relationship with her brother and did not condemn her in any way. Vera told him she loved her brother very much for all he had done for them. When she saw an unspoken look in her eyes she guessed what he was thinking.

She gave a little laugh. "The answer is – yes! – I would love him to do that to me – but he doesn't – I shall have to find my own man – It's a shame he has to take other women whilst I am here." She even hinted that she would not be adverse to a relationship with him but Robert drew back from this, though he admitted – he was tempted.

As a Texan, he was sorry when he heard of General Lee's surrender in April 1865, though it took a month before the news reached them. But Robert had, long since, known that their cause was hopeless. He also learned of the treatment metered out to the southern states after the surrender, but he decided to stay in Colorado Springs and live his own life.

Instead he came to know the women of the Palace intimately. Gradually he came to like one girl more than the others. She was Joyce Close and was the same age as him.. He found that in her twenty years she had needed great strength to even survive. Her parents had died and left her destitute. Her uncle, a bachelor, had taken her in. Though only fourteen he had misused her cruelly and raped her several times. Innocent as she had been she admitted she did not know why she had not conceived.

Beaten frequently with a cane on every part of her body, she had run away, eventually coming to Colorado Springs in 1860. She had learned that the only way to survive was to sell her, already, misused body, and join the other girls in the old palace. It had been a hard life. Although the other girls showed her how to protect and look after herself, accidents still happened and the four yours she had been here she had suffered either, two miscarriages or abortions. Robert never found out which.. Things had improved since Otto had taken over and she had entertained a higher class of men.

Although Robert was her most frequent client he was not her only one. One night when he came to her after enjoying other girls in the palace, he had a surprise. When she undressed he saw she had several small wealds on parts of her body, now healing but still visible, Several were across her ample but firm breasts. Naturally he wanted to know how this had occurred. She just laughed; "Many of our men friends like to do this to us, and if so we are well paid. My horrid uncle introduced me to the cane. Most of my men friends want to concentrate on my bust – I can tell you it hurts like hell, there – so they pay double for each stroke on that area "

He thought of Nan and her suffering this agony, voluntarily – to absolve her sin. He is thought, cynically, this was a way their men folk could get their pleasures for free. Now he knew the reason for his excitement that night four years before. Perhaps this was the reason he usually chose woman with large breasts. He remember how he had enjoyed, Sally, his first girl, so long ago.. But Robert knew he could never treat any woman that way.

That night completely altered his relationship with Joyce. In spite of this cruel treatment of her, Robert knew his liking for Joyce was different to that of the other girls in the establishment. Marriage never entered his head but he knew he wanted to make her as his mistress. He no longer wanted her to go with other men. He carefully considered matters and came to a decision. He would offer her a contract to live with him. He did not love her but he needed her. He wanted a woman for himself, but he wanted Joyce in a different way to other mistresses Otto kept and for a longer period, and he knew he wanted a family.

As they lay together, one night, after he had enjoyed her body he made her a proposition. "Joyce I want to take you out of this place and make you my mistress. I will treat you as my wife for six years and ask you to come with me to my shack, which I will extend and furnish to you taste – but in those six years I will expect you to live me as a true wife, with no other lovers – though I might, still, visit other women. As a wife I shall expect you to bare me two children in that time. You know I am, exceptionally rich, I will provide sufficient money, deposited in advance, in trust under Otto's supervision, to ensure that you and your children, who will of their own free choice, decide with whom they wish to live. They will be able to live in comfort, like you, for the rest of your lives. I shall not marry you and may decide to leave you or take another woman for the same purpose when the six years have ended."

Joyce was surprised and confused at his offer. Up to then what she did and endured was, simply, to give her a chance to retire in comfort free from any attachments provided she lived long enough to enjoy it. Now Robert offered her a secure future, far more than she could have hoped for, but at the cost of tying herself to him for six years and worse, being willing to conceive two of his children, without any promise of a future life with him.

She did not attempt to answer, nor had he expected to do' "Dearest Joyce, I do think of you in a different way to any other woman I have known. I enjoy being with you not, just, for what you let me do to you. I like you as a person, but the war has changed me, particularly the loss of my brother. I'm not prepared to make any permanent attachments – not yet – not until I'm sure. I feel I need more than one woman. As you know I'm not a Mormon – I'll never be one but I can see some sense in their ways. . Please, Joyce, think about this carefully. I will give you a week to consider it. Please talk with Otto, he is a good man, let him advise you. I will not come to you or any others in this place during that time. The decision must be yours, and I will await your answer."

Robert left her alone to decide. It seemed a long time but at the end of the week Joyce told him she was willing to accept his proposition – with all its commitments. It was late October 1865 Joyce came to live with Robert in the enlarged shack, now a beautiful house His mistress but not his wife, contracted to serve him for six more years..

After she came to live with him she admitted it was his condition to bare him children which had been the deciding reason for her acceptance. "For so long I have been used by men for their pleasure. I've longed for children, I have already lost two babies, but it seemed it would never be possible. I realized few men would ever want me after my past life. Whatever you may have use for me in the future you have given me the chance to have a family. For that I will always be grateful." Joyce was pregnant by December. It was her choice.

There was no doubt about the tenderness in which they cemented their liaison. It was a coming together of two people who cared for each other and as the weeks passed, as her pregnancy advanced, they grew, ever, closely to each other. Their was mutual respect. Joyce felt Robert treated her more as a wife than a mistress. In return she did not mind his occasional absences when he felt the need for other women and went back to the palace., particularly as she grew in size. They happily discussed his experiences without embarrassment. Happily Robert and Joyce though not married, now awaited the arrival of their baby

5.

With the beginning of the war it was impossible to keep trying to find a future home for any Irish Families arriving in America. So the installation in New York was shut down. Now Morna, as Devin Regan had already left to join the army, returned again to the Purcell mansion on Long Island, again to help both Erin and Merle, and now was soon to learn that these two good ladies, with a third lady, Tricia Drake, were really three women who Patrick Purcell considered really his wives. It did not shock Morna to discover this and in fact only proved how fortunate she was to find sanctuary in such a loving household.

Of course she hoped that soon she would hear from Devin and where he had been posted and that he would continue to write to her whenever he was able. She was sad and missed him very much but just hoped that some how he would survive the conflict and some day come back to her. However as the years passed and Devin never wrote she began to feel he might have been killed, for everyone knew how great were the casualties.

Gradually Morna felt she must give up any hope of enjoying a happily married life with Devin. Her sorrow was lessened by the considerate way both Erin and Merle and now Tricia Drake treated her. Though Morna had never received much training, her parents had at least taught her to both read and write. Also, she had learned elementary arithmetic and her time at the New York temporary residence had forced her to develop theses latter skills quite considerately, for Morna was a very intelligent woman.

Tricia quickly discovered this and knew how lonely she felt, now without Devin and virtually locked away from other men in this large mansion. Tricia spoke to Erin and Merle and got their consent to take Morna into their offices in New York and personally help her to do minor things for her, which widened Morna's horizon considerably.

She now frequently met other men, some of a quite higher status than her, as she worked there. As the years passed, now certain that Devin was dead, she began to think of her future life – a life without Devin. She was an attractive woman and soon, encouraged by Tricia, who took a motherly interest in her, help her to develop these associations further. Soon to Morna's delight she discovered that two young gentlemen showed obvious interest in her, one she was determined to cultivate. Morna was no different than many women, she wanted babies and be part of a loving family. With Devin gone she was anxious that she might be more fortunate with the new men who interested her.

*   *   *   *   *   *   *   *   *   *   *   *   *   *   *

In Pittsburgh now Graham Stowe had left to join the forces Camay continued her duties to Alberta, who understood Camay's sadness now derived of Graham's company, but now losing contact once again with Devin Regan. Unlike Morna, Camay had no wish to develop any fresh male associations. She felt herself committed to Graham even though he had not actually proposed marriage to her. She knew it was only the uncertainty of the war which had prevented this. She was willing to wait. At least she did receive an occasional letter from him, now in fierce fighting in Tennessee. Never-the-less Camay was disappointed that Devin Regan never wrote to her.

The reason Devin had not written either to Morna nor Camay was because he did not know his own mind. He liked Morna very much and until he once again met Camay he had virtually decided he would ask Morna to marry him. Now he could not be sure who he loved the most yet Camay had told him she considered she soon would marry Graham

Stowe. In the past his lack of letters had caused this to happen, now he was committing the same faults again, and the years were passing though he now fought more in West Virginia than as previously north of Richmond.

*   *   *   *   *   *   *   *   *   *   *   *   *   *   *

With her husband dead, Sophie in Pittsburgh had moved in with her mother and ensured she was not short of male attention. As explained to Kurt both she and her mother were not short of male attentions. In fact Sophia was enjoying her new freedom. Nor was her association with Alan Moseley reduced. Sophie knew now that her relations with him were growing stronger since Hugh Danton had died. She felt it was only because he felt a reluctance to tie himself to one woman that he had not asked her to come and live with him.

Sophia now knew her desires were so intense she would gladly have been willing to become his mistress, but unfortunately to her, he did not offer this to her. So instead she tried hard to cultivate his attentions and meanwhile enjoy writing to her brother, Kurt, describing somewhat intimately her sexual conquests.

*   *   *   *   *   *   *   *   *   *   *   *   *   *   *

During their visit to the Purcell's, Daniel Mason now explained once again to the Purcell family how came to know, learn to love Sally, and after her terrible raping by Nat Torman and knew she had conceived, he demanded she married him, not caring that she might deliver a black child . He had informed her of the degree of her father's debts. She was penniless. The Bank owned her plantation. If she married him his father would sell her property but place the proceeds in trust for her to use as she wanted and not become his property.

He then asked her a favour – he never demanded it – he merely felt he must right a wrong. He wanted to take both Harriet and Janet Torman into their home – not his father's but his own home, which he would purchase for all of them. I would help to right the terrible thing her father had done to them and what had resulted in her own desperate position. If so Sally must be willing to bring up their children as part of their family, and not as servants, accepting their children as if they were his.

Sally had been delighted to accept, especially has he had not made any attempt to force her into agreeing. It was the least she could do after what her father had done. Now both Daniel and his father were realistic. By then they knew Sally was pregnant. There was no way she could live here in Virginia after what everyone knew had happened, as the sympathy of the local owners was for her father and they considered Sally should have aborted her child.

His family were rich. The bank was prosperous but there was a growing hatred against them and their ideals. They were Quakers not god loving Anglicans. The growing tensions between north and south must soon reach a climax. If secession from the Union occurred, they could not stay there in Petersburg with their anti-slavery views, with Virginia fighting to maintain slavery.

Daniel would take his new wife and the two pregnant Negress to Washington and open a bank there using their expertise and their support against slavery to attract customers from the rich industrial northern states. It worked and before any babies were born the Washington branch of the Mason Bank had been successfully established. It quickly grew in size. By then Sally, Harriet and Janet had become close friends, each pregnant by a man they disliked but united in their grief.

Harriet was the first and bore a nearly white son she called Desmond Torman and the next week Janet bore a colored daughter she called Natalie Torman after her father. Then just two weeks later Sally bore a completely black daughter, Sharon, which Daniel demanded was registered as his child. Sally told them this act, even more than his willingness to marry him after what had happened, not only proved how sincere his beliefs were but showed just how much he loved her. She knew then she would love him for the rest of his life – no matter how many other women he might find.

By then she knew that Daniel was not looking on either Harriet and Janet as servants. She knew he would never force himself on them but she knew he was already in love with him. Just as they had desperately fallen in love with him. Further intercourse between them was inevitable, as to him they were as beautiful and as equal as any white woman. She knew she would accept that arrangement. It was the summer of 1853.

Sally explained that everyone knew very soon that Daniel had taken two black mistresses. This was acceptable but not that he kept their children and seemed to treat them as his wives. Soon they were not accepted into Washington society especially when Sally did not have her black child adopted. This did not affect their banking prosperity and the Civil War, eventually, made life easier for all of them. After all this was what the Union was supposed to be fighting for.

The war had ensured that they must close their bank in Virginia and his family had bought their own estate in the capital and fully approved their son's life style. It seemed that Daniel was not too demanding in expecting them to conceive too regularly. In fact it was always planned and done with everyone's agreement. First Sally bore his child in 1856 and then Harriet and Janet conceived at two year intervals

Now Daniel concluded the important part of his history. "So you see why we have not invited you to our house. Everyone calls us 'nigger lovers', we thought you must have known of this. Now you may wish us to leave, for we are proud of how we live."

It was not necessary but all of them came to shake hands with Daniel and hug Sally to them. Finally Patrick Purcell said, "Now we all know how we wish to live, I hope that all of us can continue to enjoy each others company and ensure our friendship is increased. Now I also feel we can become business partners and establish together a consortium for both our future prosperity." This was unanimously agreed by everyone.

6.

In Colorado, Joyce Close soon realized he had found another favorite in Audrey Bowen, a dark haired girl of nineteen, who had come with her sixteen year old sister, Sarah Bowen, only six months before Joyce left. Joyce had known both girls. Neither were virgins when they joined, escaping from a terrible whorehouse in Central City to which they had, virtually, been sold by their drunken father who had beat them frequently. They were fortunate that Otto had discovered them as willing, and of course, very pretty converts to his high class establishment. Joyce told Robert she approved of his choice.

It was after Joyce, to both their delight, was delivered of a son, christened, John Close, at the end of August 1866, after a long and painful labor. Although there had been little danger he knew Joyce had suffered, greatly, in baring his son. "Well my dear Robert. How soon do you want me to start another child. We both know, the way you have continued to enjoy my body since the birth –" then she laughed, "—not to mention your considerable – and - er – *appreciation of my breasts* – I do believe you enjoy their present condition even more than John."

She continued, "I also, know you are really a very kind man and do not want to place my life in danger. I saw the fear in your face when it took so long to deliver John. I believe you might have been more frightened than I was. You know that is one of the reasons why Mormon men and women agree to taking more wives. Would you consider taking more mistresses on the same basis, on a similar contract to mine. You are rich enough to enjoy several women in this way. If so you could space out our pregnancies – If you like take us in turn - I would willingly extend my six years with you and not expect more payment."

The ice was broken. Joyce had approached the subject with trepidation. She knew she had no right to suggest this to him. They both laughed then Joyce continued in the same vain. "As far as I can remember Audrey Bowen had similar generous breasts as mine. I believe you like her and she is a woman who can satisfy you. You have told me she is your favorite choice at the palace."

Robert liked the idea and suggested to Audrey as he lay with her the next night, that she joined him at the shack to spend a night, there, in his bed. Audrey knew of his arrangement with Joyce. When she accepted, she guessed that Joyce knew about this and thought she might receive a similar offer. Audrey knew she would be willing to conceive his child, so long as she was well paid. She was a realist. She knew she had been fortunate not to conceive so far with so many different men enjoying her body as well and her younger sister, Sarah. Robert had enjoyed Sarah's body several times, as an alternative to Audrey.

From the start Audrey made it clear that she had guessed the reason for her invitation. "I will accept your proposition, only, on condition you will take my sister Sarah, as your third mistress. If so I would try to conceive your first child this December and Sarah, who then, will be seventeen and easily old enough to bare a child, would begin her pregnancy next December. After that it would be Joyce's turn again. So we could all complete contract in the eight years. After that we will all be old enough to look after ourselves "

Robert liked the idea of a third mistress particularly one as young. as Sarah to start her family. Audrey stayed and Sarah was invited to share his bed the next night. She too was glad to be invited. After that all three women shared his house and alternated with each other in his bed and offered him the additions, they were, now, used to. A week later all three contracts had been, agreed, and signed, in front of Otto's lawyer.

In December 1866 Audrey offered her body to Robert without protection and was confirmed pregnant immediately after New Year 1867. Sarah appeared to be the most enthusiastic member of the trio and made no secret of her desire to conceive the child she had wanted for so long, now it was possible. However Robert continued to enjoy the pleasures all three women, freely, gave him. So much so, that he began to think of what he would do when their eighth years of servitude ended. For the first time he considered if he should offer to marry them.

So Robert went away to think. Suppose they all left Colorado Springs. In another place he could say they were Mormons without joining and claim they were his three wives. However is this what they wanted. It was the beginning of April 1867 and Spring had arrived and the snow was melting. Audrey was now. five months pregnant and he knew Sarah was counting the days until she could conceive a child. One night he called them all together and told them he wanted to change their contracts. It made them afraid

But he smiled and said, "Would you be willing to extend your contracts - say – for the rest of your lives and still alternate in giving me babies." They looked at each other not understanding what he meant. It was Joyce who answered "You mean you want us to marry you" To their disappointment he said, "No!"

Then he went on to explain the difficulties – the impossibility. He told them he would never choose just one of them as a wife and he could not marry all three. However he saw an alternative if they were willing to come with him a long distance where he could pretend they were Mormons and had married.

Robert had given thought to the problem. For sometime he had wondered what had become of his young sister, Molly. She would now be about thirteen years old, only two years younger than Vera. He had decided to return to Texas, collect Molly from Sheffield on the way, and go to the old ranch which was now his property. He would modernize it and make it their new home.

"It's going to be a long journey – particularly for you, Audrey – but we will use the best equipment – we'll all get there, eventually. – We are all going to Texas. Now the decision had been made there was much work to be done. The purchase of their transport, two of the finest wagons available at that time, with a selection of good horses. Provisions for the journey, though they would many opportunities to buy more on their trek. Joyce had been brought up on a farm and knew how to drive wagons and Sarah was willing to learn so they would drive one wagon and both practiced near the shack. Robert would drive the main wagon, assisted by Audrey, as much as her pregnancy would allow.

It was necessary for Otto's lawyer to amend and extend the women's original contracts. Robert insisted the three girls attended and satisfied themselves that they approved of its contents. They all knew the provision was far greater than any of them would have received as his wife and they showed their gratitude. They were not bad women – unfortunately, it was the men who were evil. .

Robert had discussed with Otto and the traders, who came from all parts of the country the best route to Texas. He found there were better ways than one he and Jack had traveled and planned it accordingly. He also learned of the parlous state Texas had become. Poverty was rampant. Many ranches had become bankrupt and sold to the land grabbers from the north who came to profit from their victory. There was much unemployment

The only problem was that the bank in Cagtry, near his ranch, was too small to cover such large credits, so it was deposited in a bank in San Antonio nearly two hundred miles to the east. It was essential, therefore, that Robert took a considerable amount of gold to see to his needs after he arrived, particularly, if he was to modernize and improve his property.

They left on the 21st. April 1867 and their journey was expected to take over thirty five days. The first twenty miles to Pueblo was easy, the road was well used. From there they had to skirt the edge of the Sanges del Cristo mountains to travel to Trinidad. Here they found a good trail to the south east to Tucumcari and after another one hundred and seventy miles arrived at the growing township of Lubbock, where they rested having, already, traveled nearly four hundred miles and still had to cover more than two hundred miles.

They decide to stay overnight and sleep in an hotel after enjoying a good meal served to them. Little did they know this stay would alter the lives of all of them.

7.

Meanwhile in Mexico, Paul Doherty was determined to discover what happened that night Irene committed her crime. He knew he had to shock her. Paul then began to tell her of the day he possessed his own sister, Teressa, watching the horror on Irene's face as he described in detail how it had happened. When he had finished he took her hands in his.

He said, "Irene, my dear, I know to you, I have committed a terrible sin. I don't regret it now, nor I believe does my sister, though at the time we were shocked afterwards at what we had done. The little things she has said in her letters is written in a way that only I can understand. I remember at the reception after her marriage how she looked at me across he room and saw tears run done her face. I don't believe it was tears of joy about her marriage. She was trying to tell me she wished her husband was me." He knew Irene was shocked but still Irene refused to tell him. But an event was to alter this.

The Yaqui Indians to the North had never been completely controlled though, in the past, the Mexican government had confined them to isolated areas of the country. Now, however, since the French occupation, their troops had been fully stretched dealing with so many local uprisings. Though Benito Juarez had left the country, his supporters acted as insurgents used guerilla tactics to monopolize the soldiers attention. This had given the Yaqui's the opportunity to roam further in search of loot..

In late September 1866, a band of Yaqui's had attacked some mine workings only fifteen miles from the hacienda. The guard of soldiers quickly dealt with the situation killing all of them but this alerted the residents to the serious dangers. Charles and Paul quickly obtained and distributed riffles to everyone. They all knew if the Yaqui's had attacked the hacienda, instead of the mines, they would all be dead. Irene was, particularly, concerned for her unborn baby.

That night, it was Paul's turn and as she lay in bed with him, Paul tried to comfort her. Irene turned over and kissed him. "You are a good man. My times with you have been happy times. It is wrong but I will admit that I have enjoyed them, but I am worried about *our* baby, for you know it is yours. - I may die in labour. These are primitive surroundings, please promise me you will look after our child. It will be your first. Be proud of your child." Paul kissed her, with passion, but with love. "Dearest, I promise. I could not do otherwise. But don't talk of death. I want you to live. I want us to be together for a long time, if

317

that is what you want. She smiled and simply replied, "I do for as long as you wish" Then she became silent and Paul could see her mind was in turmoil. He did not interrupt.

At last she spoke. "I fear what I am about to do will destroy my soul. I cannot accept your views on religion, but I know you are a good man. Since I feel I may soon die even though I have not tried to absolve my sin with a priest, I cannot die not confessed, so I confess it to you. I will tell you of that terrible night. ------ I knew Alonso had embezzled the money the French had given him. Then when the French Colonel arrived I knew Alonso was in serious trouble. I heard them arguing. Their voices carried. I knew it concerned me but I could not make out what that was. Along with Anne we entered the room and faced the two of them."

"Seeing me the French Colonel virtually spat at me saying, 'I will take your wife upstairs and she can absolve you from your crime against France. She can pay your debts. I may, unintentionally, give her a parting gift' To his credit, Alonso, in spite of his past treatment of me in the past, took a revolver he kept in his desk drawer shouting 'Never! She will never be yours'. But the Colonel had been watching and quickly drew his own and fatally shot Alamos. As he fell Alonso pushed his own revolver across the desk between us."

Poor Irene sobbed, "Seeing my husband die, and knowing what that evil man intended to do to me I completely forgot my years of tuition at the convent 'Jesus forbids us to hate our enemies' I was angry. I simply did not think. In my anger I committed the terrible sin. I grasped the revolver and shot the colonel through the heart.

"Disgusted at what I had just done I threw the revolver on the floor behind me. This was my second terrible sin that night, I showed no remorse for what I had done. The door opened and a French soldier entered the room, saw what had happened and leveled his rifle at me. I awaited him to fire - I knew I deserve to die. A shot rang out but I felt no pain. Instead I saw the soldier fall wounded and dying. My daughter, Anne, had seen everything that had happened, understood everything the colonel had said. As the soldier entered she had picked up my revolver, seeing he was going to kill me she fired that shot which condemned her to eternity by committing this sin."

Now exhausted she collapsed on top of him sobbing violently almost screaming. Paul held her close to him and gently stroked her long hair which streamed downwards over her shoulders. Letting her continue her sobbing on his bare chest. Every so often he would part her hair and kiss her lovingly on the side of her tear wet face. He knew she must release her emotions. Then after a long time her sobbing eased. Only then did he lift her face to him before gently kissing her lips and speaking.

Then he said, "But you are wrong, - so very wrong, - I believe, neither, you nor Anne have committed a crime. Any unbiased court of law in a civilized country would never condemn you. What you did was in self defense Your daughter is completely blameless. The soldier entered and was on the point of killing you yet at that point, neither of you, were holding a revolver. There was no proof that you had shot the colonel, it could have been your husband. She had every right to shoot to prevent your death. When I have the opportunity, and now you have confined your secret in me, I shall do my best to console her."

She did not attempt to counter his statements, though it is doubtful, at this point that she accepted them. But she did seem relieved, as though a heavy burden had been lifted from her shoulders. A slight smile spread all over her tears wet face. Then looking into his eyes she merely said. "Thank you Paul. You are a kind and good man."

It was early December when Irene went into labour exactly a year and three days since she had arrived at the hacienda. Both Anne and Eve helped her and it went well It was over in five hours and Irene delivered a seven pound boy she named Martin, to the joy of everyone. His father was, obviously, very pleased believing it was his child but Paul looked at Irene as she held the child to her in her bed and they both knew it was his son.

Up to a point Charles had kept his promise to Irene concerning Anne – but he had many times humiliated her by forcing her to undress for him, even massaging her naked body, whilst Paul had never done this. This had pleased Anne and Irene had told Paul Anne was grateful for his consideration. Irene laughed, "You know I think now she actually likes you." – However the year was up and now poor Anne expected the worse.

However events were occurring in Mexico which would decide that their stay in the country she now hated, for what it had done to her, would be a short one. The American Civil War had ended in April 1865 with General Lee's surrender. Unfortunately many Confederate soldiers refused to follow suit. The invasion of Land grabbers and 'Carpet Baggers' stealing the remaining assets of the south, ruining the local economy, caused a number to swear they would never submit to the Union and the hated northern 'blue bellies' preferred to enter Mexico and offer themselves, as mercenaries to both Maximilian forces, or alternatively those supporting Benito Juarez.

It did not effect the Sierra Madre mountains. But there were several incursions towards Monterey from the east. The strain on the French Command-in-chief, Bazaine, was considerable, as well as consuming considerable amount of money. Major Mentor in Monterey in late January 1867, said he was very concerned, and he strongly advised Charles to travel with his enlarged family to Vera Cruz and to France. He reminded Charles of Juarez threat to execute any persons who had assisted the French in any way.

Two things prevented them doing this. Firstly, Irene, pointed out that Anne and her were still sentenced to death and only under parole to Charles. Should they go to Vera Cruz it seemed certain they would be executed.

The second reason was that early in March, Charles and Paul had found another extremely rich vein of nearly metallic silver. It was too large for them to repeat what they had done in 1864 without the authorities discovering their theft. Reluctantly they turned this over to the authorities to mine their find. However seeing the French were, already, leaving Charles proposed to his son a dangerous scheme, which if it were successful would make them rich for the rest of their lives. So they stayed at the hacienda.

In early April they discovered the French had left to return to France. Now their recent horde of silver now rested in three large strong boxes in the new Mexican administrative buildings, awaiting safe transport to Mexico City, Charles explained his plan to all of them, emphasizing the dangers, but promising, if successful, he would then set Irene and her family free after giving them a sufficient share of their spoils to enable them to live comfortably in the United States where her sentence could not be carried out.

It was for them to steal this treasure, which was not adequately guarded So with this and the other boxes hidden under floorboards, to cross the border and enter Texas and the United States. If successful they would, all, be very rich. Charles left the final decision to Irene. "Irene, if this should happen I will be responsible for your death, and the rest of your family. Whatever way we have misused you in the last two years. Whatever you may think of us we still have a sense of duty. The choice must be yours for neither Paul nor I would desert you. "

Irene was amazed. "I now have no doubt that if we are successful but that you would honor your promise and set us free with sufficient funds to see to our needs. Your plan would have a greater chance of success if not encumbered by my family. There is no future here in Mexico for either Anne or myself and without us my other four daughters would be destitute. We will, willingly, travel with you northwards. For all of us it is either death or salvation."

Paul felt that at last they were all one family. His only fear was what would happen if they arrived in Texas. Irene could then utilize her freedom. He would have no hold over her.

8.

All branches of the Carroll Family had always been proud of their ability to improvise whilst extending the boundaries of their country. Now it was time for them to do this again. In California, Donald Read had been unaffected by the war. In fact he had profited greatly from it and felt conscience stricken but absolved it by investing most of the profits in the building the Central Pacific Railway which he felt might unify the country.

In Texas the Eliot's, Downey's and others were castigated for their support of the Union, yet their ranches had supplied many horses for use by Texans and others serving in the Confederate forces. Now they returned to the ranches and tried to win back public opinion by fighting any injustice mounted on the defeated state, managing to do this because of their contacts in Congress. Fortunate that their relatives in Kentucky, in spite of the battles in that state, had not suffered any damage and known throughout as strong Union supporters.

By the end of 1866, Racoonsville and later the Chalmer's mansion had been rebuilt. Kenneth Brookes now began restoring the profitability of the combined estate. At Racoonsville, Paul Carroll had survived the war and now with wife, Janis, a Brooke before she married, had taken control now his father, Danton, had left to return to work in Congress.

At Rockville at last Estelle, had died peacefully, being nearly ninety years of age, very contented that she had played her part.. Now Peter and Amy had kept their promise left New York and become Master and Mistress of Rockville. Peter, as he knew it was his mother's wish had used the facilities of Purcell Enterprises to invest heavily in railways, particularly in the Central Pacific Railway which he knew Donald Reid strongly supported. So very quickly and by 1867 the Carroll Families throughout the United States were once again assuming their rightful place.

*   *   *   *   *   *   *   *   *   *   *   *   *   *   *

In New York, Morna Leach had by now been convinced, as Devin Regan had not attempted to write to her, that he must have been killed. It made her sad for knew her now happy life was entirely due to that day when he took her from hell in the brothel and brought her to live with Erin and Merle, giving her a new life. She knew she would have been happy to spend her entire life with him and together raise a family. Now she feared it was impossible. In any case she had often thought his first choice would have been this Camay Nolan he met on the ship coming to America.

Now she knew she must try to interest another man sufficiently for him to eventually propose marriage to her. At least she now had two men who courted her, and interested her. She knew she wanted babies and so decided she must respond to both these men, to see if it might provide a happy future for her.

They were Leo Ramsay and Ian Verity, and she knew both men had greater wealth than she knew Devin Regan possessed. Assisted strongly by Tricia, who acted more as a substitute mother than her employer, but assisted by both Erin and Merle, she cultivated both their attentions. Both knew they had rivals for her attention and demonstrated their interest by frequently taking her out for dinner and bestowing gifts on her.

Having been willing to offer Devin even greater intimacies, Morna allowed them pleasant but less intense offers of her attractive body. Soon she knew she liked Ian Verity even more than Leo Ramsay, and quickly, Ian realised this was the case. By 1865 even before the end of the war Morna felt sure that soon Ian would propose marriage to her and if so Tricia told her she should accept and marry him promising to fund a special wedding for her is so. Eventually, but very carefully, she let it become fully intimate, careful that he did not consider her wicked by doing so.

Meanwhile in Pittsburgh Camay was to learn in 1863 from Joanne that her son James had lost his life fighting. In spite of his treatment of her, Camay felt very sorry, remembering the many happy hours he had given her before he took such liberties with its terrible results. She still received occasional loving letters from Graham Stowe and both now knew that as soon as the war ended it would lead to marriage.

Then to her horror in January 1865 with the promise of a soon ending of the conflict, Camay learned that Graham had been killed. So once again a chance of happiness had alluded her. As she had not heard from Devin she felt sure he too had succumbed, though he had never promised her more than what he had said on that ship. Now it seemed she had lost the two men in her life. Still she was fortunate in the kindness she received from both Joanne and her mother and now felt she should devote her life in caring for Alberta who was growing very old and needed her assistance.

Joanne had told her that her mother was equally devoted to her and was so sorry that Graham had died. Joanne said, "Please don't let mother know I've told you this, but she is so grateful for the care you take of her, she wants to make sure you have a happy future after she dies. I know that in her will she intends to settle a reasonable amount of money on you. It is meant to become a dowry whenever you meet another man you want to marry."

Far away in the Shenandoah Valley, Devin Regan had distinguished himself fighting. His promotion through the ranks had been rapid with so many casualities. Finally he became a hero when at the imminent risk to his life he had saved an entire battalion and as the Lieutenent in charge had been killed, Devin Regan, to his amazement, was promoted to that position and finished the war as a Union officer. However he still could not overcome his reluctance to write to either Morna and Camay.

He now knew he liked Camay more than Morna, but he could not forget the wonderful way Morna had so readily offered her young body to him. He had occasionally written to Joanne Holstein who he respected, and she had sometimes replied having been informed where he fought.

Joanne had told him that Camay now felt he was committed to Graham Stowe and would married once the war ended. So he felt very sad – yet in a strange way relieved. He felt sorry, but at the same time pleased for Camay, knowing how much she liked Graham. At least he decided that once the war ended he might first go to Pittsburgh and congratulate Camay before he returned to Morna in New York. Then he decided against this as it would be so unfair on Morna. Now he was faced with this decision with the end of hostilities. Yet he was still unsure what he should do.

So the great Civil War had ended. For the Carroll family and all its descendents both of the Roman Catholics and Protestants and those related to the original Margaret Eliot, it was merely an terrible episode which had claimed the loss of many of their children, as well as the thousand others who gave their life in the struggle.

For others, it had brought sadness and to some indecision concerning their future. However unknown to all of these events, in Colorado, though now these persons were traveling to Texas, as well as those still in peril in Mexico. Yet it would be those people along with the Sand's, Purcell's and Mason's who would provide a very wealthy future for all the descendents of the two original Carroll families. Soon they were all to meet and by doing so would lead to great riches.

———————

PART 9

ANTICIPATION

DISUNION PART 9
ANTICIPATION

ANTICITPATION

1.

Donald Reid had told everyone about the Central Pacific railroad and why they should invest in this and not the Union Pacific in which Gordon Taylor, was investing. Of course they took his advice. However he had told them a lot about this Kurt Sand and his engineering capabilities. They discovered that he had been in correspondence with their investment firm, 'Purcell Enterprises' and their banks, 'The Mason Bank' about a possible consortium specialising in Railways. They had already told Patrick Purcell if formed they would support it.

However through Daniel Mason they had heard of another interesting development. He had heard of this from the Andersen brothers, now openly living with his step-sisters as their two mistresses. They all knew how the House of Anderson in Washington had helped Collis Huntington to persuade the government to pass the second Railways Bill which prevented bankruptcy in the Transcontinental Railway.

Of course they knew the Anderson's were Mormons. This provided no difficulties as they did not have very strong religious presumptions. However it seemed that a cousin of the Anderson's, Otto Milliken, had written to them telling them that his partner had decided to leave Colorado and travel to Texas where he had previously owned a very derelict ranch on the banks of the River Pecos. His name was Robert Sinclair. It seemed like Otto he had come prospecting during the Colorado Gold Rush and together, they had been successful and now owned a very rich and profitable Gold Mine near Colorado Springs

Now he was returning to re-claim his ranch – not to work it – but to make it his home. Also Otto told the Anderson's that this Robert Sinclair was undoubtedly a very rich man and would probably, like Otto, be considering investing his wealth in worthwhile projects. To everyone it seemed this was a man who should be cultivated. Perhaps they might interest him in Railway construction, though it seemed his present interests were in more mineral discoveries, perhaps in the mountains in western Texas. It seemed this was a matter for both the Purcell's and Mason's to pursue.

After Lincoln's assassination his Vice-President, Andrew Johnson, took the oak of allegiance on 15th. April 1865. Johnson had been a southern Democrat from Tennessee but quickly aligned himself with the Union cause. His war record ensured he became Vice-president in 1864 when Lincoln won his second term of office but Johnson had stood as a Nation Union Candidate and not either a Democrat not a Republican. This was to bring him much opposition from both parties.

He tried hard to introduce Lincoln's views on reconstruction and allowed ex-Confederates to stand and win seats in the southern states but the Republican Party refused to let them sit in the new Congress. There was a great feeling for revenge after Lincoln's death and many now demanded revenge to fall on the southern states and the Republicans supported the appointment of Southern Senators in place of the duly elected ones. This was so they could use their power to make these states pay for causing the war.

Yet there was a strange dichotomy. Johnson whilst desperately trying to unify the country with moderation, he still could not accept that coloured freedmen were given equal rights as United States citizens. On the other hand the Republicans, whilst seeking revenge introduced a Civil Rights Act which would make them all equals. Though Johnson vetoed the bill, it was passed and became law giving all freedmen equal rights yet at the same time denying the southern states the right to vote. Because of this the Republicans won a landslide election in 1866 and now virtually controlled the country, removing most of the powers from President Johnson.

This resulted in an outright war between the Republican party, who now controlled Congress, and the Democratic party which supported Johnson's moderate views on reconciliation Johnson was virtually powerless. Because of this Johnson was impeached but the vote failed and he remained in office but without any powers. There was no chance he would be even chosen as a candidate for the Presidential elections in 1868.

The Carroll members of Congress and other family representatives did their best to move forward with compromise but now the entire southern states were left for the opportunists to make their fortunes with the 'Carpet Baggers' and Land grabber's forcing previously prosperous estates and ranches into bankruptcy. Then the 'incommers', as these northern invaders were called, were able to buy them for themselves, becoming rich.

This was particularly felt in Texas. The effect was more serious for women. Now the wives of many Confederate soldiers whose husband had died in the conflict were left starving with their children. Left no real alternative but to die, many accepted the only other alternative and become prostitutes. It was this that the Texan families of Eliot's, Downey's and others, tried the best to improve. Even Robert Sinclair had heard of this before he made that long journey from Colorado to Texas. Also the three women who gladly now followed him willing, to begin a life as near his wives as possible, knew of this, and knew they were fortunate to find a man like Robert to give them a far more superior life.

As they made that long journey and at last deciding to rest for a little while at that hotel in Lubbock, they now knew they loved him deeply. He had taken them from a life of prostitution and now was giving them a life as close to marriage, which at the time was impossible, so they would be glad to give him the privileges any wife would willing give a man. They were delighted to yield their bodies to him and, when he asked them, conceive his children, for they too wanted the babies he would give them, anxious to form one large happy family.

At least Robert Sinclair had discovered before he left that that ranch was still his own, though he had been told there had been many inquiries as to its ownerships and if he wanted, there would be many willing purchases. But Robert had only, at that moment, two concerns. One to find sister, Molloy, who he had left at Sheffield so many years before, then take her with them to the ranch, renovate it, and make it a very happy and suitable place to bring up that family his 'wives' were so willing to give him.

Furthermore, his 'wives' for so long denied a home to live in were just as determined as Robert to ensure this would be what happened. Audrey, now six months pregnant with Robert's child was anxious to get to Texas as quickly as possible, just like her sister, Sarah, who could hardly wait until her sister gave birth, as her longing for a baby of her own, had been her greatest desire during the horrible years she had to yield her body in the 'Palace of Pleasure'. All three of them would give their beloved Robert their fullest support. The man who had made this possible.

So it was four very tired but still very happy persons who entered the town and registered at the hotel, little knowing that all their lives would change for the better that same evening.

2.

In New York Morna Leach was happy again, delighted at the way Ian Verity courted her. It was fortunate that Ian, like Leo, had not been required to volunteer for the Union Army. Both Leo and Ian with their own financial expertise had, from the start, been playing their part in trying to restore the failing financial resources of the government. They were as valuable to the war effort as if they had been out there fighting and Tricia Drake had persuaded Patrick through Daniel Mason's contacts with the Senators to make sure their knowledge was useful to the government. That is how Morna had come to know them.

Now Morna readily yielded herself to Ian who quickly realised what a very desirable woman she was. Then, to her delight, at the beginning of 1865 Ian proposed marriage to her. She was delighted to accept and they married in May just after General Lee's surrender to General Grant. By

June Morna was delighted to know she had conceived Ian's child and was a very happy pregnant woman.

Then suddenly out of the blue Devin Regan appeared again. He had travelled to New York. Found the old offices had been closed soon after the war had started. Not knowing where Morna had gone he had gone to Long Island to meet again Erin and Merle and to his disappointment discovered that not only had Morna married but was already pregnant with her husband's child. He was devastated for he had decided he would now ask Morna to marry him.

He told them he would leave immediately and not return but as it happened Tricia was there. He knew little about her but knew both Erin and Merle liked Tricia very much. Of course Tricia could see his reaction so took hold of his hands as she smiling said, "You must not blame Morna – You never wrote to her – she felt sure you were dead many months ago. Then she met Ian Verity. – He is a very nice and kind man – they fell in love and Morna was so pleased to be given a secure future after what she had to suffer in the past. You cannot blame her and must not"

Now she smiled again "But before you leave you must go and see her. Congratulate her. You owe that much to her, for I know, for a time, she did love you very much. Surely you cannot blame her when you failed to even write to her. However I do believe you owe this to her. Please try not to feel ill of her and I know, if you could do this, it would set her mind at rest, for I know she still thinks a lot about you. – If you are willing I will prepare the way, for she has helped me in our work. I shall ensure you meet her when alone without Ian being there."

Suddenly Devin realised that once again his failure to write had caused this. He was far more to blame than Morna. He had always wanted her to be happy since that first day when he discovered her, He knew now if he had proposed to her before he went to fight Morna would have accepted. She was completely blameless. Sad as he was he knew he must do as Tricia requested and told her so, asking her to set up this meeting.

As he waited Devin realised that his failure to write, first to Camay, and now to Morna, was the reason that Morna had sort another to take his place and why Camay had found Graham Stowe was the man she could love. Now he believed he had thrown away two excellent opportunities for a future happy life. Neither Morna nor Camay were to blame – the fault was entirely his own.

So, now prepared, he came to met Morna again. Tricia had prepared the way and Morna knew he had reappeared. She felt ashamed she had not waited for him but now she had found happiness, and at last achieved what she had wanted for years. Soon she would be a very happy mother and raise a family with a man she loved. Yet but for Devin finding her and bringing her to meet Erin and Merle, this could not have happened So it was with great trepidation she met Devin alone.

She need not have feared. The moment they met Devin came smiling to her took her hands, as he had done so often before, and kissed them. More he was smiling as he addressed her. "Morna, I am so delighted you have found the man you could love, and wish to congratulate you. – Please – I know you must feel strange meeting me again. – I understand. Whatever were our relationships in the past, I never gave you any idea I might mean any more to you than what I then offered. It was simply that we had met in rather strange circumstances, and for a time were attracted to each other. Now you have found the man who can make you happy. Really I am pleased it is so."

In spite of his kind words Morna still felt unsure. So Devin continued, "I am entirely to blame for you finding another. I never wrote to you. You must have thought me dead. – Now you must try to forget the past and try to make Ian happy. You are not to blame in anyway. – I really do hope you have a happy marriage for you deserve it. - I am leaving New York immediately. I doubt if we shall ever meet again but perhaps, through Tricia, you may sometime write to me if only to tell me the names of your children – for I do hope you have many – for I know you want them."

Then having kissed those hands he turned and left her without giving her a chance to reply. There was no doubt that Morna felt sad but at least pleased that he did not seem to feel ill of her. On the other hand, Devin now felt the bottom had dropped out of his world. His own foolishness had meant he had lost a chance of happiness with the two women he had loved.

In spite of this. Now realising the terrible results of his failing to write to either Morna or Camay for four long years, he decide he must go to Pittsburgh and at least congratulate Camay on her marriage to Graham Stowe for he was certain that, by now, it would have happened. It would be a penance. He owed this to Camay. Further more, though he would have never dreamed telling Morna, he now knew at last that his love for Camay was much stronger than he had for Morna. To late for it to be realised, he still felt bound to go to Pittsburgh, somehow find Camay, and congratulate her as she too found happiness. These two women in the past had made him such a happy man but he had squandered their affections. He knew he deserved his present position and deserved to suffer.

The question was how could he find where Camay now lived. She had told him she was a personal maid to a relative of Joanne Holstein, but never knew who she was or where she lived. The was only one solution. At least he knew where Joanne lived he would go to Pittsburgh and ask Joanne to give him her address.

During that journey he remembered again the many happy times in the past. He cursed himself for not only his foolishness but also, now, his unfairness to the two women who perhaps had loved him. He was pleased, now, he had parted with Morna in a kind way. He knew he must behave the same when he, once again, met Camay. She deserved her happiness and he would make sure she knew this when he left her.

So at last he went to Joanne's house lucky to find she was in and she was delighted to meet him again and was happy to entertain him, for Joanne had always thought a lot about him. She told him how glad she was he had survived the war but had to tell him the loss of her son James. Only then did he have the courage to tell her the reason for his visit.

"Mrs. Holstein I would like you to give me Camay Nolan's present address. Since, as you know, I knew Camay quite well in the past. I feel it is my duty to call on her if only to let her know I am still alive and not died in the war. – I presume by now Camay has married Graham Stowe. The last time we met she told me she was happy as Graham was courting her and she felt he might soon propose marriage to her. If so I do want to congratulate her, for I believe she is a fine woman.

To his amazement Joanne threw up her hands and said, "Then you have not heard. Graham Stowe was killed a little time after James died. – Now dear Camay is so sad, as Graham meant so much to her. Devin could hardly believe his ears. Even if they had married she was now a widow. Camay was now a free woman.

3.

It was 16rh. May, and it was a tribute to their endurance and the capabilities of Joyce Close and Robert Sinclair as wagon masters, which had enabled them to travel so far in just twenty five days although the new sprung axles had helped. They decided to stay overnight and sleep in an hotel after enjoying a good meal served to them. Robert wanted to book four rooms but only two were available. At the desk the three women told him to book just one room. They wanted to share the night with him and did not want to sleep alone. Robert grinned and then agreed.

The male receptionist was evidently used to such behavior and guessed they were his mistresses. "Are they all your wives?" Robert told him they were not. Again he was not embarrassed but demanded they all sign as 'Mrs. Joyce, Audrey and Sarah Sinclair in the company of husband, Mr. Robert Sinclair, and his three wives.'. The man explained, "This is necessary to prove we do not run a brothel at this hotel", and smiled.

All four raced up the stairs laughing. "Well at least for tonight you do have three wives, one a most obviously, well used wife." It was Audrey who made this remark. Her six months term of pregnancy must have been seen by the man at the desk. The girls were anxious to have proper warm baths after washing for so long in ice cold streams.

Robert arranged this for them and waited at the bar until it was to be his turn.

The receptionist, who also turned out to be the owner of the hotel, served him with drinks and questioned him. Robert had asked him previously whether he wanted paying in dollars or gold and without hesitation the man told him he preferred gold.

Now he continued, "I'm sorry about that charade. The town marshal demands it, but we live a very understanding life here. It is obvious from the bags you have deposited in my safe, you are a very rich man. If I may be excused for my rudeness. I must say you have three very pretty wenches as your companions. It seems we are a very hypocritical people. You are strangers but where ever you stay in this state you will have to sign up in this way. Multiple marriage is accepted. In fact the local preacher is quite happy to marry and legally register more than one woman as the wife of a single man".

Robert could not believe his ears and questioned him further to ensure he was telling the truth. Then he asked how long would it take to make the arrangements and the man said he could set up a meeting with the preacher this evening and they could all marry tomorrow.

He had been certain for so long that such a dream was impossible. Now, if the information was correct perhaps that dream might become a reality. When the three girls emerged from their toilet he sent them upstairs to dress in the very fashionable gowns they had brought with them from Colorado, without informing them, and took time to enjoy his own bath. When he returned to their room he, merely, proceeded to dress in a frock suit and coat for dinner, as they continued with their cosmetics.

When all was finished he said, "My dears, it seems I have three extremely beautiful mistresses but after tonight I am sorry to say I hope I shall have none. I no longer want or require three mistresses. I'm sure you will understand." The poor girls were shaken. He had told them he was discarding them. They could not believe it. They were so unhappy they broke down sobbing on each others shoulders.

Still tormenting them he continued. "I do not understand why you are so upset. I did not say I did not want all of you to live with me. It is simply that I do not want three mistresses. What I yearn for and beg you to accept, is a joint proposal. If you want I will go on bended knee. What I, really want, ---- is *three wives*. -- If you will all agree to marry me and make me an honest man we can marry tomorrow and spend the rest of our lives together. It can be done. But it all depends on you accepting a man who has, so, misused you, for so long and though married will still continue to misuse you for the rest of yours lives. It will be a life sentence. I beg you to accept me as I am."

Now it was the girls turn to not believe what they had heard. When, he told them he could make the arrangements that evening and be married in church by a preacher the following day. They would all become his legal wives and have certificates to prove it. Their answer was not in words they simply crowded around and hugged him knocking him to the floor.

Still tormenting them, Robert managed to raise his head saying, "Girls! Girls! Please behave yourselves - As my wives I shall expect you to obey me - we shall not indulge in anyway tonight after we return from dinner. I must retain my strength for after the wedding ceremony and a sumptuous reception. Tomorrow we shall retire upstairs and take off all our clothes, then we will have *a single night of a honeymoon* where all three of you will do your duty to me as wives and poor me, will attempt to reciprocate and ensure we each enjoy that night."

They still could not believe he really meant it. In spite of what he had ordered they all lay with him for sometime kissing him passionately but without going further. Then they got up, repaired the ravages of their exchanges, and prepared for dinner. First, however, all four of them would have to walk over to the church and ask the preacher to marry them the next day.

The preacher put on his spectacles and looked questing at all of them. He saw Joyce carrying her eight month old baby, John. Then he saw the swelling below Audrey's waist not to mention he way Sarah was lovingly holding Robert's arm and he sighed. "Yes! Yes! I am certain I should marry you –er – that is all of you to this man. It would be a greater sin not to do so. Can you all swear on he bible that none of you are at present married." They, all, told him they could and did. The wedding was arranged for the following afternoon.

The day dawned. It was a beautiful sunny spring day, a good omen for their future lives. May 17th 1867 was going to be a day that would change the life of all four of them - for ever. It was more than just their wedding day, and they knew it. There were arrangements to be made. Robert went out and ordered the bouquets. The hotel owner, gladly, agreed to be their witness and, also, agreed to arrange a magnificent reception for after the ceremony in the restrained way they had dinned in the night before. As his wife was helping Robert invited her to dine with them. She was pleased and offered her son to he his 'best man' and two daughters to be his 'wives' bridesmaids. Robert was pleased.

Robert, even, managed to purchase three wedding veils from an astonished store man and returned with them – and of course three wedding rings. The girls were delighted. They were behaving as three blushing brides who had never know a man but now waited, in anticipation, for what was to come. Fortunately they all had three white dresses, though not the elaborate type usually worn but their headdresses would help. Then he left them to bathe and dress in another room the owner had supplied for him, before fortifying himself with several whiskies. He did not return to his room until it was time to escort them to the church.

It was an unusual service. There were few guests in the church though it seemed the locals were, by mow, used to these occasions. It was short. Robert willingly promised to 'take and honor all three of them as his wives for as long as they live' but he was amused when they in turn, accented the part where they 'promised to *obey*' He could see their happiness as he slipped the ring on each of their third fingers. Then it was over and they walked down the aisle each walking a little in front of him as they could not do it at his side, to walk the short distance to the reception.

It was as happy occasion as any bride and groom had enjoyed before. There were few speeches but Robert pleased them with a few carefully chosen words which in no way did it refer to their past life. Though not drunk they were all a little worse for wear when they retired to their room in the hotel and hurriedly undressed. Robert kept his promise, making sure each one, in turn enjoyed that night with him.

They left before noon the next morning after saying farewell to the hotel, owner and his wife. Robert thanked them, profusely, adding a substantial amount to his bill and promising to return again someday. As he shook the owner's hand he said, "You will never know how this chance coming to your hotel – and the information you gave me, has altered , all our lives, for the better – You know money isn't everything ------ but it does help." They all laughed appreciatively. Now Robert had three legal wives and all four of them were exceedingly happy.

4.

Far away in Mexico the Doughty's and Arista's were planning their raid and escape to the United States. As previously agreed. They would load all the essential belongings and the two treasure boxes in one wagon. Then Irene and her entire family would drive to a point on the map, five miles north west of Monterey still in the foothills of the mountains and wait for them

Meanwhile Charles and Paul would drive the other wagon in the middle of the night, go into Monterey to military quarters in which their treasure rested, and which they knew was inadequately guarded, to gain those other two strong boxes.. Having gained them, they would travel to the meeting place after which the two wagons would attempt to drive along the lower slopes of the Sierra Madre mountain and attempt to cross the border into Texas near Laredo, a journey of approximately one hundred and twenty miles. This route should avoid any of Juarez's forces on the plain and still be sufficiently east to avoid attack be marauding Indians.

The plan should have worked perfectly. Charles and Paul had no difficulty in overpowering the small guard and a small charge of dynamite opened the large safe. It seemed to be a perfect theft. Even the small noise of the muffled explosion had not alerted anyone. They loaded the precious boxes in the wagon and had just set off when a small group of Mexican soldiers returning from a time in the Bordello saw them. They had no idea what they had done, but quite drunk even they were suspicious of a wagon leaving their headquarters at that time of night. They took their riffles from the shoulders and fired, at random, at the retreating vehicle but made no attempt to follow them.

Paul was elated they had won, a veritable fortune was in those boxes. He knew with those in the other wagon they need never work again providing they all reached Texas.

Paul was driving, anxious to get away fearing, wrongly, that they would be pursued, making sure they kept to the road in the dark. Suddenly his father sitting next to him on the board fell backwards into the wagon. Paul then knew a bullet from the soldiers must have hit his father. Knowing he could not do anything at the moment he drove the wagon the remaining three miles to where Irene was waiting. There, he shouted her to come and help.

They both looked at Charles who was now unconscious. He knew Irene knew more about wounds that he did. Part of her training in the convent had been in nursing to fit her for her future life when she married. He turned to her and saw the look on her face. "Your father is seriously wounded He needs medical treatment and may die if he does not receive it. We must turn back." As she was speaking Charles had regained consciousness and had heard what she said.

Charles managed to speak. "No! We won't. I'm still in control of this party. I do not want to live penniless. In any case both Paul and I would be executed for what we have done. Alive or dead I want to get to Texas. That is an order Paul – and you will obey me." There was nothing more to be said. The two wagons set off northwards. Paul led the way in his wagon whilst Irene tried to see to Charles' wounds. At least she stopped the bleeding. It was left to Anne to drive the other wagon assisted by Eve. Paul was surprised at the way she drove but Anne had laughed telling him she had learned to drive when only ten years of age, though it was the first time she had driven a wagon as large as this.

When it was light they stopped for food which Ann and Eve prepared, whilst Irene attended to Charles. He was conscious but in great pain. She feared there was internal bleeding and the bullet was still inside him but he managed to speak. "How much you must hate me for what I have caused you yet , now, you try to help."

Irene smiled and there was no anger in her face. "My religion has taught me not to hate anyone. In any case if you had left me in the prison, I know now, I would not be alive. Let us believe that my affair with you is payment for saving me from that. At least I am still with the family I love. At least you have done that for me." Then he went on. "Yes! But please ask Paul to see to Martin's future."

She knew he still thought that Martin was his child. For a moment she wanted to disillusion him but then she knew it was very wrong instead she replied. "I have no doubts but Paul will look after him. Your son is a very special man who I admire very much." Charles must have guessed what had happened between them for he went on "Admire him. Is that true -.do you not love him? I've been jealous for months at the way you look at him. – Come you can tell me – now – I know I am dying"

Irene was taken aback. "Love Paul – what is love - I have forgotten what that word means – Men are only interested in a woman's body." Charles responded, "After the way I've treated you – I can understand this but listen to me - Paul is not like that. What is important - Does Paul love you."

She thought for a moment. "I am a woman of thirty five whose body has already born five children, your son is only twenty-one. I know it not merely lust, with which he comes to me, but I'm a realist. It won't be long before he tires of me and finds a younger woman, perhaps, even my own daughters." A shot of pain raked Charles's body. Irene knew his end was not far away.

At last he managed to reply. "You may be right. I doubt if any man only loves one woman. Yet in all my philandering days, I still loved my wife very much. It was her death that made me come to Mexico to try to find another to love. It was my foolishness and my lust which made me use you. Only too late did I discover my mistake, for you are a truly wonderful woman. I'm dying – You know that – in my last few hours

I hope I can persuade my son, how wrong I was, and hope he will not make my mistake. Someday you may even forgive me for you are a good woman." Irene was overcome. Suddenly her hatred of this man vanished. "Thank you, Charles --- I have, already, forgiven you."

Whilst they have been talking Paul had been reading the papers they had taken from the safe as they collected the two boxes. The information they contained made their future, even more, dangerous. Now he came to his father to explain his discoveries. Irene was about to leave but he asked her to stay.

It seems the Mexicans in Monterey were well informed of the military situation. "We dare not try to cross the border at Laredo It's become Juarez main base in the east, while his western and central forces have joined and besieged Maximilian's remaining army in Mexico City and must soon make him surrender. In the east they have captured the town of China, only twenty miles east of Monterey, which soon must fall. We must push much further north towards Conpasso and Sabinos."

Charles sighed. "The decision must be yours. I know I shall never make Texas. Keep traveling north, and away from the coast. It's your only chance." Once they found Irene was in full agreement Charles asked her to leave. He carried out his promise to talk to Paul. Paul always remembered his father's words. "Do not loose Irene, I believe she loves you. Try to make her happy if only to repay her for what I have done to her. Believe, me son, I know you can be in love with more than one woman at a time and age is no barrier to real love."

They did travel north and Charles died before they reached Compasso. They buried him, there, in the mountains. It was his wish. For he had always loved the isolation mountains gave him.. They pressed on slowly passed Compasso to Sabinos intending to go down to Piedras Negras and cross into Texas at the Eagle Pass but when they arrived Paul went to investigate the situation. It was impossible, Juarez forces already held the town.

They must find an alternative route. But they knew the dangers they faced once they entered the mountains.

5.

Meanwhile with the war over the Union Pacific Railway recommenced building from Council Bluffs, Omaha westward towards the Rockies and to join up with the Central Pacific Railroad. However the project was beset with difficulties far worse than the terrain on which it was to be laid, and even indian attacks which were frequent. There was considerable corruption between the directors of the company and many eminent politicians illegally benefited financially from its construction. The Credit Mobilier Company had been set up just to limit the directors liability

The directors gave substantial numbers of cheap shares in the company to many members of Congress in order to ensure the second Railway Act. This greatly reduced the money available for the railway's construction. At one time this nearly resulted in bankruptcy, and certainly delayed its progress for many months. Though many knew about this, no action was taken to bring the people to justice until 1872, when it ruined the careers of many politicians. Of course this delay was to the benefit of the Central Pacific Railway with its formidable mountain obstacles.

Gordon Taylor who had invested in the Union Pacific, through his companies lawyers investigated the rumour, though not substantiated at that time, it did result in the appointment of a man well used to railway construction during the last war. He was Grenville Dodge, a Union brigadier general in the war, who became chief engineer, overcoming, not just the site difficulties, indian attacks, and more so, the terrible corruption of its directors and now work began again in earnest.

Though this delay was welcomed by those in California, it still did not make their own construction any less difficult. In fact Donald Reid, who was well informed of the railway's progress and would suffer a great financial loss if it did not succeed. He wrote to all the Carroll's in the east explaining the situation, for it seemed for a little time the actual construction ceased.

I happened when Kurt was away on a short visit to his family, and as their Chinese labourers thrust forward through the rocks, driven without mercy by both Crocker and Sand, through appalling weather, with rocks falls and several deaths. Kurt had been away with his family for many weeks. Finally their pressure was too heavy, the Chinese went on strike.

But Crocker was merciless. Trapped in the mountains he decided to starve them into submission. Finally he broke the strike and work continued. At last they were through and ahead of them were the great plains. The going, though still difficult, was easier.. Now the rate of track laying was quicker and every mile laid meant a great deal of money coming into the Central Pacific coffers. Though it was a near thing, they were still solvent, and there was the great prize within their grasp.

With this solution of the problem, the Carroll, Purcell and Mason investors in this along with many others, were now delighted they had chosen to invest only in the Central Pacific, for it seemed that Graham Taylor's advice had proven wrong. This had convinced Patrick, Tricia and Daniel that Kurt Sand's idea of a consortium expressly to construct railways would be very profitable. Now they knew how much they needed Kurt Sand's engineering capabilities.

Though this must wait until Sand's was able to come and meet them they began to explore the possibilities of the rich Carroll family members forming part of that new company, and received encouraging responses. Again the Anderson's had told them of this Robert Sinclair rich in gold holdings was going to Texas. He would have the wealth to also invest in such a consortium. At present there was no way they could contact him but told the Anderson brothers they would like to meet him in the future.

Even during this altercation in the mountains, Kurt was enjoying a short vacation away from the stress of railway building. Kurt had received a very warm welcome from both Agnes and Anita. The latter was particularly delighted for she was now eight months pregnant, with Kurt's fourth child. having born her third, another daughter, Deborah Sand in 1862 and Agnes had given him second son, Albert Sand, called after his father. Both their pregnancies had started during his short visits.

Anita had told him how much she wanted him to be present at the birth. His wives had not been idle during his long absences continuing to work in the offices of his Sacramento partnership ensuring it was still profitable in his absence. For the salary he receive there was still the mainstay of their comfortable family life.

Now Anita was delighted to, at last deliver him a son, which they both agreed to name Karl Sand after his uncle who had been the reason for his father fleeing to America so long ago. Furthermore both knew though worried at the length of her painful birth, he was even more delighted that she had born him a son.

Then he returned to the railway. However now with the part of the line already constructed it was much easier to travel back and forth. Accompany the material laden trains going west and returning in one of the coaches attached to the empty train, so he could enjoy more short vacations with his family Although when at home he was immersed again in his firm, he did enjoy making these trips on their extending railway and see how quickly it was extending. This continued to 1869, by which time Agnes had born him another daughter, Margaret Sand, bearing her mother's name. Then they learned the two railways were only two miles apart.

General Grant had stood as the Republican candidate in the 1868 elections and had heavily beaten his opponents because of his distinctive military achievements. Poor Andrew Johnson, the retiring president did not even receive a nomination. Grant assumed office in March 1869. A massive celebration was arranged for the actual joining of their tracks, to be attended by many of President Grant's ministers and members of Congress . Of course the families of all the directors of each company were invited to attend and Kurt took his entire family including baby, Margaret.

Naturally Danton Carroll, still a Senator in Congress was invited and delighted to accept once he knew that Kurt Sand was coming. Danton had been deputed by all the Carroll family to, if possible, make contact with Kurt Sand and explain they were interested in investing in any company he considered joining but especially if this was, also, in association with both the Purcell's and Mason's.

Special trains had been gathered to take all the directors of each company to where ever they wanted – Sacramento and California or New York and onto Washington. Kurt had promised to take his entire family to New York. Firstly to see again his mother and sister, who told him they would wait his arrival, but he had another, even more important, reason. That was to meet for the first time both Patrick Purcell and Daniel Mason who had written to him telling him they would be waiting for him when in arrived at New York.

So Kurt was delighted when he now met Danton Carroll who was part of the Congress delegation. The meeting of these two lines was so important for the future of this country, everyone ensured they would mark this auspicious occasion appropriately. It would be the first Transcontinental Railway crossing the whole of America from the Pacific to the Atlantic. Perhaps this momentous engineering achievement might truly unite the United States as one single country again.

6.

Unaware that several important persons in the east were making inquiries about him, Robert Sinclair, now a very happily married man accompanied by his new wives had only two ideas in his mind. Certainly it was not that of possible investments. That could wait. The first was to find and collect sister, Molly, at Sheffield and then take her with them to the old ranch. Then renovate it and make it their home. Then to ask his wives to continue to add to their family. He was tired if very happy and the sooner he reached the River Pecos the better for all of them.

The weather was still kind and Robert had told them he wanted to press on and get to Sheffield to find his young sister, so they would be sleeping, rough, until they got there. Their journey took them south through Midland, but it was high plains, and much easier than what they had needed to accept before. They made good progress reaching the Rio Pecos, east of Sheffield crossing the river there, proceeding through the town to the small ranch house where the McDonald's lived. It was deserted.

They were all heartbroken. When they made inquiries in Sheffield they found the McDonald's had left five years before to go east, beaten by the hard conditions, hoping to set up a store now the Civil War was in full flow. No one knew where they intended to go, except it would be much further east, perhaps San Antonio or beyond.

So Molly was lost to him. There was nothing they could do in Sheffield so they continued their journey to Robert's old ranch arriving in the evening of May 29th. It was still standing but in poor condition, but it was habitable, and they were thankful to sleep again on bare beds with a roof over their heads. They were too tired for any lovemaking content to have arrived. They had traveled almost six hundred miles in thirty eight days. This, in itself, was quite an achievement.

The next morning after breakfast, leaving the three women to try to improve their living conditions, he went into Cagtry. It was important to get the five boxes containing their considerable store of gold into the bank for safe keeping. Keeping a reasonable amount in a smaller box under the floorboards Robert took the others to the bank.

Having received a favorable, even enthusiastic, welcome from the bank manager, especially finding Robert was a Texan and the owner of the ranch now that the John Sinclair he knew was dead. He was delighted to find that Robert was not one of the rich northerners who used his bank but who he detested. The man happily informed him of where he might find people to help him restore the ranch but warned him they were already in demand and contracted to the 'incommers' as he called the northerners.

To his sorrow Robert found this to be a fact and it would be nearly a month before they would be free to help him. Still he did deposit a sum of money with them ordering them to obtain the necessary materials to renovate the ranch when they were free. Meantime he loaded a stock of timber, mails, and necessary tools into the wagon to make temporary repairs. Especially to the roof, which needed urgent attention.

He also replenished their food supplies and bought, both, bedding and fabrics which he knew the girls could make into curtains. He did buy a few luxuries to make life more pleasant returning to the ranch before dark. He found a very much more pleasant place than when he left.. The girls had worked hard and, like him, were tired. At least they had bedclothes when they went to sleep that night.

There was no hiding everyone's disappointment in not finding Molly but at least the heavy demands on their time to improve living conditions prevented them dwelling on the subject. For the next two days Robert worked on the roof and made simple improvements inside whilst the girls used their talents to make curtains and covers. They would have to exist in these poor conditions for sometime until the builders were able to start.

On June 2nd. Robert had to return to Cagtry to get further supplies and other materials to improve their accommodation. Poor Audrey was feeling the effects of her six month's pregnant body. The journey, the disappointment over Molly, and the intense tabor of the last two days had place a strain on her body. So to her delight Robert invited her to go with him into Cagtry. Working as a team, they quickly, completed their purchases and loaded them into the wagon. Then after a quick meal they returned to the bank for Robert to change more of his gold into dollars.

They entered, just in front, of a man about his own age and an attractive, but more mature woman. In spite of the stains on their clothes which told him they had traveled far, they seemed people of good breeding, very different from the locals in Cagtry. Robert went to a teller whilst the young gentleman went to the next man. Robert emptied his bags of gold on the counter at the same moment the gentleman by his side emptied his bags of silver. Robert was amused and surprised because gold was the normal metal exchanged for notes. He turned to greet them.

* * * * * * * * * * * * * * *

In Mexico, Paul and his party continued their terrible journey. They had already travelled a hundred and ten grueling miles and it had taken them seventeen days. They had left Monterey on April 30th. And it was now May 17th. They must move north west to Nueva Rosita and then enter the Serreanias del Burro mountains so that they could then press north again towards Texas. But this now placed them in danger of attack from the Yaqui indians and progress would be even slower.

Paul discussed the situation with all of them. He could not see them pulling two wagons through the inhospitable territory. Frankly they had not the muscle power to at times, push both wagons over obstacles, and their food supply were critical They must abandon one and crowd all their goods, treasure boxes and six persons into one wagon Irene had no doubt and pleaded with him to take the risk. The others agreed, and they set off.

It was nightmare journey. Their hands became raw with coaxing and pushing the heavy wagon over many rocks. At least they had retained the horses from the other wagon, which at times gave them additional power. It also enabled them the rest each set in turn saving them from utter exhaustion.

This was not their only worry for they often saw smoke signals in the mountains to the west and feared imminent attack, but it never came. Then on June 1st. thirty one days since they left Monterey they came to flatter ground and beneath them they could see the Rio Grande the border with Texas and happily descended to the river. Even more fortunate the found the river low and were able to find a ford some two miles to the west of where the Rio Pecos joined the Rio Grande.

Having crossed, they rested for a whole day and Paul shot some game for their food. They had crossed the border. They has left Mexico and were now in Texas. Throughout the journey Paul had made no demands on either Irene or Anne. They had all been too tired. He still would not have made a move but that night as he slept on the ground Irene and Anne came and laid on each side of him. They both loosened their clothing indicating they were giving him access to their bodies. "We both love you. We know we owe our lives to you. This is just a little reward to you for what you have achieved. For we know, but for you none of us would be alive."

Paul was moved with emotion. He lent over and kissed each of them in turn on the lips. "I know I love you both. It was father, before he died, who told me I could love both of you – equally – I love you both, at this moment – Irene – and Anne – both equally. You must believe me. There may be other times – that is if you want it - Remember we are now in Texas and by our promise to you – you are both free women." Eventually they all fell asleep in his arms.

Rested, the next day they set out along the Rio Pecos knowing they must soon come across a town. They found the border town of Cagtry, small, but to Paul's delight he saw a bank. They stopped at the very edge of town and Paul alighted and helped Irene to descend.

Paul said, "Anne you stay with the wagon and guard our treasure – for now it belongs to all of us, for as long as we stay together – or divided if you feel you should leave me. Irene please come with me we must change a little of our silver for American Dollars then we can find a place to stay and take away our hunger."

A young man and a woman entered to bank just before they went in. They did not know it then but this meeting was to change the life of all four of them. In the bank they each went to adjacent Tellers. As Paul placed a couple of bags of silver on the counter asking for American currency, the other man placed similar bags before his bank clerk. When he emptied them Paul saw it was gold nuggets. Both looked at other then the other man's face broke into a smile.

The man said, "Touché! It seems were are both in a similar business. I am Robert Sinclair. Let me introduce you to my second wife, Audrey." Paul shook hands and introduced Irene, inferring but not stating that she was his wife. It again was a meeting which would change the lives of all four of them.

Paul Doughty misunderstand his phrase 'second wife' and replied, "I'm sorry, Robert, that you lost your first wife but I am more than delighted to meet your very beautiful new partner" It was impossible, not, to notice that Audrey was probably six months pregnant so Paul believed Robert's first wife must have died sometime ago.

It was Audrey who laughed as he once more shook hands with her, "I'm afraid you misunderstand my husbands introduction. You are evidently strangers to Texas. Robert dear, has two other wives waiting for him at the ranch – we are all legally married to him and I take the second place in our family."

Both Paul Doughty and Irene Arista were speechless.

It was June 2nd. 1867. This meeting was not only to alter the lives of these families, but in future years was to improve the fortunes of the many descendents of the Carroll Families.

7.

Devin Regan could not believe what Joanne Holstein had told him. He had to ask her to repeat it again. Now it was time for Joanne to smile but asked, "Devin have you married ?" of course Devin explain he was still a bachelor. Then again smiling Joanne asked. "I know you once had strong feelings for Camay. – Do these still continue ? I understood you had discovered another woman you liked in New York. I am surprised you have not yet married her."

It was left for Devin to tell her of his own stupidity in not writing to either Camay nor Morna. How he had found that Morna, believing him to be dead had found another man to love and marry him. Devin confessed he had felt sure by now Camay would, also, have married Graham Stowe. Now he explained he had come to Pittsburgh to endeavour to meet Camay again, and prove he was still alive – and to congratulate her on her marriage.

Joanne could not help herself she saw and heard the sad way he had spoken, so she threw her arms around him, to comfort him. Then she asked, "Do you still have strong feelings for Camay ?" He looked up at her then replied, "Mrs Holstein I believe I still love Camay – perhaps I have always loved her. – well – it was my meeting and rescuing Morna – and – er – the way she was so kind to me. You see I felt I ought to ask Morna to marry me."

Now Joanne laughed, "Please tell me, were you intimate with her. Was that your reason for believing you should marry her. ?" Poor Devin was even more ashamed when he replied. "You see I felt she had fallen in love with me – I knew I liked her – and she was so kind ---- Oh! The truth was I did not know my own mind - was it Morna I loved or Camay. – That is why I could not write to either of them during the war. – I can see now how cruel that was and why I deserved my punishment. – I've been to Morna and told her she must never consider she did wrong in finding and marrying Ian Verity. – It was the least I could do and I do believe she now understands. I only hope that Ian makes her very happy."

Now Joanne released him but asked, "Would you like to begin again with Camay were you left off years ago ?" He smiled and told her it would be his greatest wish. He knew now, at last, he loved Camay and always loved her. It was just the discovery of Morna and the terrible life she had to endure which complicated matters, as he did not want to hurt either of them. Until he came today he had thought his foolishness had lost him the two women he might have married. Now she had told him Camay was not married or was a widow. Joanne quickly explained that Camay had never married Graham.

Again Joanne smiled at him. "Devin, Camay means a lot to me – Her happiness is paramount in my mind. I cannot explain, but I owe it to Camay to ensure she has a happy life and I believe if she had married Graham it would be possible. With my mother we have ensured that Camay will inherit a lot of money when my mother dies. I owe this to Camay. Perhaps someday she may tell you why. I cannot say what, now, are her feelings about you. I know, like Morna, she had thought you dead. Her feelings for Graham were very strong."

She continued, "Now I know you still have strong feelings for Camay, I will arrange for you to meet her. Then it will be up to both of you to see if your feelings are mutual. However I warn you, Devin, - should you ever again treat poor Camay as you have done in the past. Not only would I not forgive you but I could see that you paid a heavy price for it."

Though sheepishly Devin replied, "If so then I would deserve it. – Of course I cannot believe after how I have treated her she still will have any strong feelings for me. But I promise you, whatever happens, I will do everything possible to make her happy, even if she cannot find she could love me. I promise I will not make her any sadder than she must be at this time, for I know she loved Graham."

It took a few says and Devin stayed at the Holstein's house. Then Joanne came to tell him she would take him to see Camay. It was in great distress he road with Joanne to her mother's address, led him into the house then left them to speak to each other, whilst she went to talk to her mother. At last they were face to face. Then Camay smiled.

"Devin," she said, "I'm so delighted to meet you again. Honestly, as you never wrote I thought you dead – but then you have rarely written to me." Devin felt even more ashamed for he knew she was right. However he had to reply, "Yes! Camay. You are right, I've never kept my promise. I feel so ashamed. I cannot never apologise enough for this. However I felt I must come to visit you, for I thought by now you would have married Graham."

He looked straight into her face, "Dear Camay I'm really so very sorry that Graham died like so many in the conflict. I knew you loved him. I think he was a very good man and I have no doubt but that he would have made you very happy – and after my unacceptable treatment of you for so long you really did deserve that happiness. In fact as I explained to Mrs. Holstein – I felt I had to come – first to let you know I was still alive – but really to congratulate you on your new found happiness. "

He saw Camay was pleased with his words. She said, "Joanne tells me you did not marry Morna Lynch – When we last met I thought you would propose marriage to her before you went off to fight in the war."

Even more ashamed he relied, "No – You see I treated Morna the same as you. I assume Mrs. Holstein has told you, since she thought me dead – I never wrote to her just as I failed to write to you – well she has found another man she could love– a fine man – Ian Verity – and is now married to him. I have already called on her and wished her a very happy future. It was the least I could do after treating her so badly."

Now in some fear he continued, "After my past treatment of you I fear you could never trust me again – but if you could find some pity for me - I would like so very much to begin again as we did so long ago on that ship I now know I love you – perhaps I have always loved you – and may be why I could not appreciate what a wonderful woman Morna was. – Camay – my dear Camay –is there any chance you might allow me to court you again. I don't suppose after my past you could ever love me. – However I would like to stay in Pittsburgh and try, in some small way try to remove the sadness of Graham's death and give you just a little happiness. Please give me the chance – I feel I owe it to you to try to make you happy once again."

Of course Joanne had been talking with Camay and had already told her how strong now were Devin's feeling for her. Frankly, as much as she wanted this, she could not believe it. Now he had come and she had listened. Now, in spite of the past, she felt he was sincere and did believe he loved her, but her experience with James Holstein made here careful So she merely took hold of Devin's hand, kissed it then said, "I think I would like that."

Devin's heart soared, took the hand by which she held his and kissed it. I was a small beginning but Devin now believed he might have a chance of a happy future. Not only did he talk at length with her telling her a little about the war, even encouraging her to tell him a little of her life during that time. Joanne Holstein desperately wanted Camay to achieve a happy life after the way her son, James, had dishonoured her. She invited Devin to stay at her house so his courtship of Camay could continue. In fact she found him a position of responsibility in their shipping company now expanding again after the war, so he was not short of money.

Over the months Devin went out of his way to make Camay happy now he had the means to entertain her even better than Graham had done. However each night he took her back to her house. Gradually Camay let him take liberties with him. Now she trusted him. They always kissed passionately before they parted. Then one evening as he was about to leave she pulled him to her, kissed him again and said, "Devin now I know I do love you and know you love me. I would be very happy to spend he rest of my life with you." Devin stayed longer and they went to speak to Alberta who had by now made her a ward of her family.

After that it only took a very few weeks before both Devin and Camay stood before a preacher, neither had difficulties with a best-man or bridesmaids. Her mother and family and his family had come to the wedding. Devin Regan married Camay Nolan and was to begin a very long and happy life together and quite quickly, together, they raised a family.

The romance begun on that terrible ship so many years before had eventually produced a very happy ending. So, though their connections with Carroll's were quite distinct the Holstein's and the Casimir's had always had a close relationship with them. Now it was the turn of others to again enable the Carroll families to increase their wealth but, as in the past, by doing so, help to ensure the prosperity of the United States when such measures were vitally needed.

8.

Patrick Purcell, and Daniel Mason were waiting at the New York station when the special training bringing so many important persons from Promontory arrived. However it would be the first opportunity they had of meeting this man Kurt Sand, who had fought so hard to make this Transcontinental railway a reality. They knew now how much they needed his expertise if they were to invest in any further railway construction, delighted that he had written to them to tell hem he was coming and wanted to discuss a possible business relationship. Of course they knew this first meeting would be very brief

A golden spike was inserted as the final act at Promontory, Utah, on May 10th. 1869. It was a magnificent occasion. Kurt now knew, that although his shares in Central Pacific were much less than the others, even without the special bonus, generously granted to the instigators, the new transcontinental line would prove a goldmine. He would soon be an exceptionally rich man, of which his original firm played only a small part. Railways, not gold mining would be his future. Along with other future profitable investments of his, newly, acquired capital

He had written frequently in the last two years establishing excellent relationships with both Daniel Mason and Patrick Purcell. This had resulted in both of them agreeing to meet him in New York as soon as the railway was joined. Now with the profits which would soon be theirs, due to their accepting his invitation to invest. Now they were anxious to discuss further his original proposition, many years before. They were interested in considering the formation of an investment company, mainly, involved in acquiring further wealth from railway investment. They knew their meeting this time would be brief.

His family was met at the station when this special train arrived in New York. It was just forty nine years since his father, Albert, had landed, penniless after his hurried escape from Germany. Now Kurt was returning as a very rich man with a large loving family. His mother and sister were there, as promised. He had reserved, several large suites, for them to occupy and so they could get to know each other.

However Sophia had with her, her newly acquired husband, Alan Mosley, to introduce to her brother. Sophia had been astounded as she lay in bed with Alan after enjoying their mutual pleasures, when he turned towards her and said, "Sophia will you marry me." Though it was so unexpected Sophia responded quickly, "Oh! Yes! Please! I would love to marry you. – I need you." Alan kissed her passionate then continued. "Sophia I know you will want others the same as me. But I feel, now, our relationship is strong enough to overcome these affairs. – It seems there are more pleasant ways than being a bachelor." Sophia felt he was right. In any case she had known for some time – her maternal instincts made her want more children. However she had wanted these to be born legitimate.

Of course they all knew of Kurt's two 'wives' and approved as soon as they met them. It was a fortnight of sheer pleasure, seeing all New York had to offer, and sailing up the Hudson River, enjoying the theatre life. Only then did Kurt leave them to explore further.

So in June 1869 Kurt went to the meeting he had arranged with the two men who were soon to become his partners in a very successful new venture. Soon to become his special friends. Of course he had met them both, briefly, at the station, the day he arrived. Now he walked into the offices of Patrick Purcell, a New York Stockbroker, where awaited him the third part of his future partnership, Daniel Mason of the Mason Bank of Washington

They all agreed that there was a growing market in railway construction in which a joint company could profit. That day they agreed to invest equal shares in the holding company, agreeing an initial investment to establish it with joint offices in both New York and Washington. The first to be the center for market speculation and the other to have easy access to politicians. All agreed that Central Pacific would never have started without Huntington's lobbying of Congress.

So money was to be set aside for this purpose. It was impossible in such a short time to go into more serious details but that day they decided to set in motion the formation of a joint company calling it the MPS Brokerage and Investment Company using the initials of each of their surname.

The business finished Patrick entertained all of them to a late lunch at his favourite restaurant. They decided to not discuss their business any further that day and each told the other a little of their immediate work in the Sacramento, New York and Washington. They then invited Kurt to a social dinner in this same restaurant the following evening with their wives. Unknown to them Kurt would have preferred to include Anita in the invitation but wisely considered they might not like to find so soon he had a mistress who he regarded as his wife. He little knew they also may have liked to include other women. So it was arranged.

Patrick had placed his own carriage at Kurt and Agnes disposal to bring them from their hotel and was waiting there was Patrick and Erin,

Daniel and Sally to welcome them. It was a very pleasant occasion. The three women got on famously, each dressed in glamorous gowns. After cocktails they enjoyed an excellent meal in a large private room waited upon by the owner, who they explained was the essence of discretion, and would never divulge anything they might say. During the dinner their conversation was devoted to pleasantries and amusing episodes in their past. Then Patrick looked at Daniel. They had agreed before hand that they should now divulge a little of their life style. It had to be done.

Kurt had felt since their meeting in the office and the subsequent lunch that both men were hiding something, which they wanting him to know, but were afraid to broach. Now he saw the way they looked at each other and nodded, before Patrick began to speak. Agnes over cocktails had told him that Erin and Sally had, inadvertently, indicated that things were not so clear, not such a normal wife and husband relationship. She believed both men had mistresses. Now Kurt was certain and decided to disarm them.

As Patrick, quite obviously embarrassed commenced. "Er- both Daniel and I – that is we both agree – if we are to form such a close relationship – which our company demands – we should not keep secret from you – that is – details of our private lives – it could compromise all our futures – You – see we both have ----"

At this point Kurt interrupted him, placed his hand on Agnes' arm and completed Patrick's next sentence "--- mistresses. I guessed this some time ago. I'm told it's usual in both New York and Washington society. Also that in most cases your wives accept it – even approving it, as it limits the number of babies they must bear you."

Both Patrick, Daniel and their two wives were both shocked. Before they could continue Kurt was speaking again. "Can I say, that if this is the case, and I hope it is, - it will save both Agnes and me from embarrassment. You see I too have a mistress, though I refuse to think of her as such. I am fortunate in having a wife like Agnes, who is willing to accept my dear Anita, not as my mistress but as much a wife, as if I had married her. We live together in a loving arrangement. I can never repay both my wives for their understanding of my sensual desires and for giving me the support and happiness without which, I would not have achieved the success I have enjoyed."

He leaned over and kissed Agnes on her lips, Then continued. "In due course I shall inform you of the dangerous circumstance and terrible sufferings both my wonderful wives had to endure, which were to bring us so closely together as one family. You must have noticed my large family when we arrived – I will tell you these two wonderful women have given them to me, completely of their own free will. For I would never demand pregnancy from any woman unless it was her wish –"

Now Erin looked at Sally. "It seems your secrets are not that different to ours. In due course you will find, as wives, again because of terrible experiences in the past our husband both have loving women who we adore and who our husbands treats like yours as his wives – with our approval."

She stopped but prevented Patrick interrupting by looking critically at him. "As you've guessed this was our own fear tonight – that you might be shocked at discovering the life we lead – Patrick, I suggest we say no more tonight. We have enjoyed a lovely evening. Please Agnes bring Anita and all your family over to our large estate on Long Island to meet our combined families. There we can each confess our sins and see it we can all understand the reasons why it has happened. Neither Sally nor I are ashamed. We both, deeply, love our husbands – as it seems you and Anita do."

They all readily agreed, arose and left the table, going downstairs to their carriages, – three very happy couples who had enjoyed a wonderful evening. Now with the promise of a more wonderful future. It seemed it might become even more than a business relationship.

9.

All three families met the following Friday on Patrick Purcell's large estate on Long Island. Daniel Mason had gathered the whole of his family there before they arrived and Patrick had sent coaches to the hotel to bring all Kurt Sand's family, including his mother and sister, though they had considered they should not have come.

They were all introduced as they arrived to everyone including the Purcell and Mason children. Sally saw their surprise when they were introduced to Harriet and Janet and she proudly presented her sixteen year old daughter, Sharon, not caring that she was black. Sally smiled at them. "The colours of our children do not matter here. Harriet and Janet are also my husband's wives, as is their children. You will find there is a terrible reason why this happened. None of us need be ashamed."

Now it was Erin's turn. "Merle here is my sister though in this country she is registered as Merle O'Donnell. We too have suffered – possibly the same as you but now we are Patrick's wives, who loves us equally." Although there had been no explanation, Agnes and Anita seemed sure they would learn they have suffered the same as they had. Whatever the reason everyone felt relaxed as if there was no need to confess. It was an auspicious beginning, boding well for their future relationships.

Finally Erin brought Tricia forward along with her nineteen year old black daughter, Ranee Drake. Tricia explained, " Ranee is my daughter by my late husband, Thomas Drake. He was a very cruel man who beat me refusing to accept Ranee was his child. I had not been unfaithful, you see he did not know that my mother, Emily Backhurst, before she married my white father, Stephen Hawthorne, was a very beautiful coloured woman, who he loved deeply. Father never recovered when Emily died bearing me. Unfortunately Ranee's birth was a bad one and since then I have been barren."

Agnes saw Sally was trying to explain, hoping they would be accepted. Agnes threw her arms round Sally and hugged her. Then motioned Anita, Conchita and Fiona too come forward. "I do understand, you see we too have suffered terribly – just like you. You too will understand in a little while." Now it was time during the remainder of their stay for everyone to explain the terrible circumstance, the raping of Agnes, Anita, Erin, Merle, Harriet, Janet and Sally resulting in them bearing children.

It was left to Sophia, who had listened with interest to their stories, to sum up. "It seems to me that if a woman truly loves a man, she can understand his needs. No man can be satisfied with one woman, he needs more. Provided he loves each of them, equally, and provided it is real love and not male lust for their bodies, she can be willing to share him with others. I confess, now, I feel the same. Perhaps the Mormons who we castigate have the right way of living. Polygamous marriages may be the solution."

Now all their secrets had been exposed there was no reason against the formation of the MPS Brokerage and Investment Company. Though it was essentially a social occasion, the men did take the opportunity, before they parted, to cement further their basis of their new business, confident it would produce rich rewards.

There was the question of finding a suitable house for Kurt and his family in the north east. Its location was discussed with them and finally decided it should be in New York and not Washington. Daniel offered his mansion in Washington whenever it was necessary for them to come to the capital, probably for political reasons. Fortunately a smaller estate than Patrick's, adjacent to his, had become vacant, and felt sure he could. quickly, obtain its purchase. When completed Kurt decided he would change its name to 'Sandiways', invoking his own surname.

However it was now imperative that the knew MPS Company obtained as many investors as contributors to their financial stability. At the first meeting of the new board at which Tricia, now a fellow director, was able to inform Kurt of their fortunate contact with the extensive Carroll family and their friendship with the House of Anderson in Washington. They were both amused and delighted when Kurt told them first, of the financial help the Central Pacific had received from Donald Reid and his previous association with the two Anderson brothers.

This lead to their knowledge of Robert Sinclair now resident again in Texas. Knowing he was already a very rich man they all felt he should be approached, through the Anderson's to see if he might become an investor. It was agreed. However none of them knew then, nor did the Anderson's of his meeting of Robert Sinclair with Paul Doughty and his family. Neither were they to know that in years to come these latter families, whilst being willing to invest in railway contraction, were to discover an even more profitable, if risky, investment in 'Black Oil'. The mineral which in the coming years was to outstrip all our types of mineral acquisitions. These developments were in the future. Yet, it was in future years to lead to wealth hardly thought possible, but especially so, after the motor car was invented.

These last twenty years had completely altered the lives of everyone. At the beginning, it had only been a reoccurring fear. Yet in those years a number of new families had come into existence. Yet, - who, inevitably, were to become known to others. This had occurred in Texas, Colorado and even Mexico. At the moment only a little of these people were known to those living in the east. This was still an unknown quantity. However it would become a reality in the future.

Then the secession of the southern states had occurred and the great Civil War had begun. It had torn the United States in two for four bloody years. The death rate had been enormous, and this had caused chaos and great sadness. Many members of the Carroll family had died in battle, their mansions had been destroyed or at least damaged. Those living in the west had been spared much of this, but at last the conflict had ended.

It was a time for everyone to begin again. Heal their wounds and start rebuilding a new United States, once again a united country. The war had destroyed the economy. Now it must be restored again. It was left for the Purcell's, Mason's and the surviving Carroll's whatever were their surnames, but all descendents of those two Carroll families who had come to America – to Maryland - in the Seventeenth Century, though who were now spread widely across the growing United States.

The Carroll Family Saga would continue indefinitely – and there was still much for it to do. However, as in the past, when its future and the future of the country had depended on the new immigrants who sort refuge from persecution, the future of all the descendents of the Carroll family would need the assistance of many other families if it was to be successful.

In the last twenty years it had been the coming of the Sand's, Purcell's, Mason's and others which had enriched the expanding United States. These additions had helped the Carroll family to continue to play a major part in this expansion. Perhaps in a few more years it would be the existence of the Sinclair's and Doughty's who would play a vital part in this scenario . Perhaps this would happen. However all the descendents of Edgar Carroll, David and Amelia Carroll and those of Margaret Eliot from Ireland, would continue in the same way, and keep faith with their forebears.

It seemed as Estelle Carroll had so wisely said in 1850 – the **Carroll Family Saga** would continue - **ad infinitum.**

THE   END

OTHER BOOKS BY ROYSTON MOORE

ALL PRINTED AND PUBLISHED BY TRAFFORD PUBLISHING

MAKERE – THE FEMALE PHARAOH – QUEEN OF SHEBA

Makere Hatshepsut was the only Female Pharaoh of Egypt who wore the Double Crown , destined to be worn by a man, for 25 Years – the last 10 Years as Sole Pharaoh

This book is her life written as fiction but it is her true story. It is her own love story with the two men in her life.- Web Priest Senmut – who she raised to high office – and King Solomon, the King of All Israel. Although she bore each of them a child, she was never allowed to marry them. – Enjoy lovers living for each other three thousand years ago.

The Carroll family sagas
Five books concerning Love life in America covering the period 1687 to 1850

MARYLAND – A Rags to Riches Story – Amelia Eliot sent as an indentured servant, already raped pregnant, and to conceive and bear three more children within five years by men chosen for her. Amelia became his Cinderella when she met aristocratic David Carroll on the small ship sailing to America. How he became her Prince Charming by later marrying her and giving her a title.

OHIO – five couples both French and English meet during the Seven Years War. Enemies who became friends. – Extending the Carroll Family Saga with now, Daniel Carroll, the grandson of Amelia and David Carroll. Introducing many new persons who fell in love as Britain fights France in America

LIBERTY - Daniel Carroll helping his friend George Washington during the American War of Independence. – Introducing other Carroll descendents and many others fleeing from persecution in Europe – Yet it is a series of Romantic tales still possible in spite of the war with Britain, Civil and Indian Wars

GENESIS - The United States a new country, ruled by an elected President not a King. Struggling to stay neutral whilst Europe descends into chaos during the French Revolution. Carroll descendents and many new persons finding refuge and love in this new country – Then in a day the Louisiana Purchase doubles it.

LEBENSTRAUM - Further Carroll descendents along with others continue the expansion West. Mexico, and Texas and California are acquired. The growing industrial might and both River and Sea Transport. Now Railways to take new immigrants to new lands to the West and to the Pacific which is now reached.

MAKERE – THE FEMALE PHAROAH – QUEEN OF SHEBA

The passionate love story of Makere Hatshepsut – the only Female Pharaoh of Egypt – with lowly peasant Web-Priest Senmut – and Solomon, King of all Israel

Makere was a very beautiful, intelligent and courageous woman in a man's world. Yet who established herself and was to wear the Double Crown of Egypt for 25 Years, ruling as Sole Pharaoh, The Living God, for the last 10 Years.

Although Fiction, it definitely portrays her true life story 3,000 Years ago.

Made Joint Pharaoh by her beloved father, forced after his death to marry her perverted and evil step-brother, meeting and receiving the love of this Web Priest Senmut who gave her the desire to live. Raising him to positions of supreme importance but, though she tried, was never allow to marry him.

After enduring years of hell she eventually becomes Sole Female Pharaoh of Egypt. Then invited by King Solomon, as his 'Queen Shwa – or Sheba', -now because of the proven 500 Years error in the chronology of Egypt – Makere is therefore the legendary 'Queen of Sheba" who travels to Israel.

A story of love and intrigue, though written as fiction, but accurately portrays life and events, in Ancient Egypt over three thousand years ago. Today her two Obelisks stand in the Temple at Karnak, her Magnificent Mortuary Temple now called Deir el Bahri, and is available for all to see and visit on the banks of the Nile near Luxor, as is the engravings on the cliff walls at Syene, placed there by her lover Senmut over three thousand years ago

ROYSTON MOORE

SEE – *www.shebamakere.com*

MARYLAND

This is the story of how the aristocrat David Carroll met and came to love, peasant girl and indentured servant, Amelia Eliot, condemned by an Irish Court to a life of virtually sexual slavery in Maryland, the British colony of Charles Calvert, Lord Baltimore, at the end of the 17th. Century.

It is set in the time when first King James II and then King William III and Queen Mary ruled Britain. It is a Rags to Riches story.

There is no doubt but that Amelia Eliot, was indeed 'Cinderella' and that David Carroll was to become her 'Prince Charming' turning her into his own 'Princess', though it took some time before the fairy tale took shape.

It is the first of five books which form the family sagas of the two Carroll families and their descendents. David Carroll is a young member of the Protestant Carroll family from Somerset going to America for the first time, where the Roman Catholic Carroll family from Yorkshire, have lived for sometime.

Every attempt has been made to ensure the historical accuracy of events at that time introducing into it the lives of several well known historical personages. John Washington was the grandfather of George Washington,. Sir Winston Churchill, was the forerunner of the World

War II Prime Minister, and his son, John, was to become the Duke of Marlborough. Charles Calvert was the third Lord Baltimore, and did own not only Maryland but lands in Ireland granted to his predecessor by King Charles I, when he once again became a Roman Catholic and had to retire as a Privy Counsellor.

However enjoy this love story whilst Britain and France continue their wars which have lasted centuries.

ROYSTON MOORE

OHIO

This book is the second book continuing the family sagas of the Roman Catholic and Protestant Carroll's began in book one – '*Maryland*'

The story of five couples, five men and women, born in England and France, who find love for each other. Who in spite of the war between their countries, which forces them apart, finding solace with others, go to America, to eventually find each other again.

Set in Maryland and Ohio in the 18th. Century at the time of the 'Seven Years War'. Introducing Daniel Carroll, grandson of Sir David and Amelia Carroll, with his boyhood friend George Washington exploring the region of Ohio, where France and Britain go to war to decide who owns it.

It may shock you but it is a fact. It accurately describes the true lives of several white woman sentenced for a crime in England, to endure both domestic and sexual slavery, to men without marriage, for several years. Desperately trying to limit the number of children they may bear them.

It accurately describes the licentious life at the court of Versailles and the salons where titled ladies bestowed their favours on men for benefit.

The love stories of men and women, torn apart, though of different nationalities, virtual enemies, meet, come to know and understand each other, becoming friends. Overcoming their differences helping them to meet again the women they love.

Made possible, only, because of this region called 'Ohio'.

Though a fiction story, and including many families introduced in the previous book, every event is historically accurate, including the lives of George Washington, as are the many actual governors of the colonies and military persons. Enjoy the love stories and enjoy living in those far off days.

ROYSTON MOORE

LIBERTY

It is the third book written as part of five books, following my books, 'Maryland' and 'Ohio', before Books "Genesis" and "Lebenstraum"

It continues the saga of the Carroll family. Daniel Carroll, the grandson of Sir David and Amelia Carroll, now happily married to his French wife, Michelle. Daniel now helps the friend of his youth, George Washington, married to Martha, living on his estate of Mount Vernon. Daniel having promised to stand 'side by side' with George, when war breaks out, having previously been trying to keep peace in Maryland, Virginia and West Virginia, now with help of his friends, ensures they all support the rebellion.

The main characters are fictitious and includes many families from the previous books. Yet it is' essentially. a love story based on the lives of people living in America, just before and during, the American Revolution However it introduces many new persons fleeing from Europe. Some quite rich like the Casimir's from Poland, and the Holsteins from Sweden, buying estates near the Potomac and land in the Wilderness, but others such as the Scott's, Reeves' and Collins escaping from England, devastated, that the land they were given is covered in Hardwood trees and not suitable for farming, until helped by Michael Casimir for personal reasons, concerning his first love, Carla who committed suicide when Michael was forbidden to marry her, her likeness to Claire Collins.

However there are other couples brought together due to the war, and who discover love. This was not only a war with Britain, but a Civil war, and an Indian war. How France, Spain and people from Europe helped, in achieving, eventual, victory.

It is a romantic story. How the war with Britain brought together many people, who learned to love each other, leading to the creation of land of West Virginia, with exiles coming from England, France and other parts of Europe. How they lost their nationalities, and became Americans, creating the United States of America, when victory was assured in the Treaty of Paris.

ROYSTON MOORE

GENESIS

A romantic story of love triumphing during the Genesis of the birth of a new United States, as it fights to survive, as Europe goes mad with wars and revolutions. This the fourth book in the five book saga of continuing the lives of the two Carroll families descendents of protestant David Carroll and Roman Catholic Edgar Carroll. Following the previous three books, 'Maryland', 'Ohio', and 'Liberty'.

The first country with a democratically elected President, instead of a King. Having won its independence, trying to survive and prosper, attempting neutrality as the world lapses into chaos.

The saviour for many men and women escaping from war torn Europe to settle and expand this new country. Including the aristocratic Hapsburg Prince and Princesses whose scandal threatens them with death, to those exiles escaping death by the guillotine in France, and the many settlers beset and in danger from indian attacks.

Yet it is essentially a story of romantic love and lovers, new emigrants and those resident here for many years. How, in their own way they endeavoured to establish this new country, providing a refuge from many new families coming from England, Ireland, France and Austria, forgetting their previous nationalities and becoming Americans.

All events are all historically correctly described, including the despicable treatment of many women. How the descendents of Edgar Carroll help establish the industrial revolution and steam river boats, whilst Daniel Carroll continues to help the Irish descendent of his grandmother.

Then on a single day in October 1803 the United States doubled its size by the 'Louisiana Purchase'.

Enjoy this story of love of many men and women in America at the end of the 18th. Century.

ROYSTON MOORE

LEBENSTRAUM

(Living Dreams)

LEBENSTRAUM

THE UNITED STATES CONTINUES TO
EXPAND

HELPED BY FAMILIES LONG ESTABLISHED
AS WELL AS MANY NEW FAMILIES
COMING TO AMERICA FROM OVERSEAS

A CARROLL FAMILY SAGA

ROYSTON MOORE

A story of Romantic Love triumphing over all problems, as the new United States continues to expand westward towards the Pacific Ocean. Opening new lands beyond the Mississippi and Missouri Rivers, and into Mexico in Texas and California. Also *continuing the Carroll Family Saga* as descendents of Margaret Eliot of Ireland, but particularly those of Sir David and Amelia Carroll, who, still, continue to play a vital part in ensuring the rapid development of this expanding country.

Though both Michelle and Daniel Carroll are now deceased, their protégée, Mark and Estelle Carroll of Rockville, and their son Danton, now married to Claudia Albrecht, become part of the Diplomatic Legation in Mexico City. But, also, of the Downey, Eliot, and Reid families who were so greatly helped in the past by Daniel Carroll and Michelle to establish themselves. These were, also, aided by the other branch of the Carroll family, previously Roman Catholics, but who became Protestants when Edgar Carroll married into the rich New York, Dutch families. All fully described in the previous books covering the Carroll Family Saga.

This book "Lebenstraum" is the fifth in the series following the previous books "Maryland", "Ohio", "Liberty" and "Genesis". Though events in those books contributed to everything which happens in this current book, it contains sufficient information, necessary, to explain how important this was in deciding and contributing to their present lives.

Introducing Gordon Taylor from Manchester, Sheila McLean from Northern Ireland, and Rachael Gilbert forced to marry an evil Elder of the Mormon Sect. The escape of Otto Fallon from Austria bringing to this country his knowledge of banking and the investments made by the Ibsen family, coming from Scandinavia, and Otto's growing love for Freda Ibsen. Yet, how, the present long established residents of the United States, were to eventually, after many tribulations, find love and a very happy future.

All historical references are accurately described, when required, in this book. How the expansion west was to add the Mexican lands of Texas and California to the map of the United States, until it became a country stretching from the Atlantic to the Pacific Oceans.

In spite of this, enjoy the many romantic love stories of life in this country from 1828 until after the U.S.A./Mexican War until 1850. Love stories, but which enabled the countries development in river, shipping and the advent of railways, adding to the agricultural wealth, the growing industrial, and economic richness. This, only possible because of the influx of so many new emigrants from Europe. Romance made all their troubles worthwhile, as they established themselves and added greatly to the future prosperity of the United States

ROYSTON MOORE